Common Threads

Common Threads

L. A. Champagne

iUniverse, Inc.
Bloomington

Common Threads

iUniverse books may be ordered through booksellers or by contacting:

iUniverse
1663 Liberty Drive
Bloomington, IN 47403
www.iuniverse.com
1-800-Authors (1-800-288-4677)

ISBN: 978-1-4759-6884-2 (sc)
ISBN: 978-1-4759-6885-9 (hc)
ISBN: 978-1-4759-6886-6 (ebk)

Library of Congress Control Number: 2012924186

Printed in the United States of America

iUniverse rev. date: 01/03/2013

Dedicated to Granny

Acknowledgments

FIRST AND FOREMOST, I WANT to thank my wonderful family and friends. Without them all constantly saying, over the last six years, "Are you done yet?" And, "How's the novel coming?" . . . this book would never have been finished! Their constant love and support, is what kept me going!

Although my daughter and my 'fella of 20 years' never read one word, they were constantly there for me to bounce ideas off of, and get opinions, for which I thank them! They were both always there for me.

The day my second granddaughter was born, was my inspiration. I went home from the hospital after seeing, and holding her, after she was born, and after I fell asleep...this entire novel popped into my head, and I got up and started making notes. Thank you sweetie!

I thank iUniverse, my publishing company who had the foresight to make me see that this book was so long, that I turned it into a trilogy!

The biggest thank you has to go to Dr. Joseph A. Zadra, BSC, MD, CM, FRCS(C) Urologist. Without his help, this novel would not be written with the medical and golf knowledge, it contains. This man was a wealth of knowledge, when it came to all the medical facts, and I credit him for writing the famous 'Honeymoon Golf Game, with The Bet', at St. Andrews Ancient Golf Course, in Scotland, 1850's, which appears in Book 1.

Without Joe's help, this would be a mundane, average novel, but with his infinite energy, dedication, enthusiasm, and great encouragement, it is a novel filled with intriguing medical and golf information, as well as an incredible story. Thank you, my dear friend . . . Dr. Zadra!

The other writing assistance I received, came from Reverend Donald French (Ret.). I wasn't much on writing funerals, so Rev. Don came to my rescue. He wrote a very dignified funeral for a major, beloved character in Book 2. Thank you Rev. Don.

To Rita Quinn, BA., - My great proofreader, who took on this massive project. It was her wonderful reviews, after she read each section that also kept me going. She encouraged me to keep writing, and helped keep me positive. After the first section, she told me I was her new 'favorite author' and couldn't wait to get the next section. Thank you Rita, for your belief in me!

I also wish to acknowledge the following people, who helped in their areas of expertise. Their knowledge was invaluable. Thank you.

Esther Ofori, BSc N, RN, Toronto Western Hospital - Toronto, ON (Twi Translation) - As I was a patient, on the Neuro-Surgery Ward, in this hospital, Esther was one of my nurses. I learned that she came from the Ashanti Tribe, and when she walked into my room, she was my character, Afua (Mary). She is a beautiful lady, who brought my character to life. Thank you, and your family, Esther.

Rev. Bruce Musgrave, M. Div., Certified Chaplain, CAPPE, RVH - Barrie, ON

Susan J. Booth, Funeral Director - Steckley-Gooderham Funeral Home - Barrie, ON

Dr. Russell Price, MD FRCP (C) FCAP - Medical Director Dept. Laboratory Medicine, RVH - Barrie, ON

Dr. J.J. Scheeres, MD FRCS (C) Obstetrics & Gynecology, RVH - Barrie, ON

Sergeant Sandra Gregory, Toronto Police Services

James Sweeney, RgN RMN RN - Patient Representative, RVH - Barrie, On (My wonderful Scottish connection)

Carolyn Moran, M.R.C.S.L.T. Speech-Language Pathologist, RVH - Barrie, ON

Caite Harvie-Conway, BSc IBCLC Certified Lactation Consultant, RVH - Barrie, ON

Patricia McAllister, Seed Potato Specialist, Alberta Agriculture and Rural Development, Crop Diversification Centre North

Liz Taylor - St. Andrews History

Terry Reimer, Dir. of Research, National Museum of Civil War Medicine
Frances McLay, PA to Deirdre A. Kinloch Anderson, Director - Kinloch
    Anderson Ltd. (Marriage Kerchief)

Last, but certainly not least I thank all my fellow RVH Auxiliary
Volunteers and staff at the Royal Victoria Hospital (Now called Royal
Victoria Regional Health Centre) in Barrie. I wrote a very large portion of
this book, while sitting in the Café Royale, and everyone stopping by and
give their support and encouragement. For this, I am very grateful to all
of you. Thank you!

Chapter 1

African Beginning

I N 1854, AS JED STOOD beside Jacob at the Port Royal harbor, his mind drifted about eighteen months back to a frightening time—the first time he was on this same Jamaican dock.

Jamaica, a beautiful but small island in the Caribbean Sea, south of Cuba, during the eighteenth and nineteenth century was the world's largest sugar exporter, and Jacob Marcus saw that this was the place to make his riches. Jacob's brother and sister tried to persuade him not to move all that way from their comfortable home and lifestyle in the United States, because they'd heard it was dangerous.

They heard and read things about Jamaica being a historically cursed island at times. For example, a devastating earthquake hit in the 1600s, crumbling part of the island into the sea. Since that time, there had been other earthquakes, hurricanes, tidal waves, fires, and more; but Jacob still wanted to go. He wasn't afraid, for he saw sweet opportunity knocking and was determined to leave his ancestral home in Mississippi right away.

In the 1650s the English took over the island from the Spanish, and within a decade its city of Port Royal was known as the wickedest place in the world, due to the slave trade, piracy, and the unruliness of the inhabitants with their looting, prostitution, and constant drunken behavior. It was well-known that there was one drinking or public house for every ten people!

This was also the era of some of the best-known pirates who ruled the seas. Buccaneers found Port Royal to be ripe for the picking, seeing as Jamaica was right on the shipping route between Spain and Panama.

Standing on that dock, Jed knew this time was different. This time he was on land; he was not sailing aboard the *Destino*. He was waiting for it and its unlawful cargo. He watched unknowingly as his future wife arrived in this harbor, as he once had.

Jed was a young, handsome black teenage boy of small stature, but not determination. His smile was ever present, and you couldn't help but like him.

His memory went back to a rainy day in May, or was it June? He wasn't sure. He only guessed maybe a year and a half had passed since his arrival but had no real concept of time. He lost himself in thoughts of the coast, but not this coast: The coast of his homeland. That's where he belonged, not in this new land, thousands of miles away from his family.

He looked at Jacob and then looked to the *Destino* again and wondered who would it be that was herded down the plank this time. What had *their* trip been like? He wanted to know, but he knew his place, so Jed did not speak out. After the ship docked, Jacob turned to Jed and said, "They're almost here, Jed." Jed just grinned and nodded his head excitedly.

His mind drifted again as they waited. Africa. That's what Jed was dreaming of: his home and family. Jed, whose birth name was Berko Yaba, was born in 1840 and a member of the Ashanti tribe in Ghana, West Africa. Ashanti people spoke Twi or Akan. In the Twi language, Berko meant firstborn. He had three sisters and one brother, all younger.

Berko's people lived near Africa's beautiful west coast, which was rich in gold and minerals.

He lived with his extended family in a village near the capital city of Kumasi. His family was not just his parents and siblings. Ashanti families traditionally were very large. Extended families were common, even expected. Some families could consist of thirty people or more. They all lived very close to each other and supported each other. What wealth one had, they all shared equally. Families were strong in their values and community, concentrating on caring for their elders. It was one of the most ancient cultures in Africa. The tribe was known for their expert crafts. Through the ages, they produced beautiful wood carvings, metals, and jewelry (mostly working with their ample supply of gold mined there) and their prized Kente cloth.

This was *his* coast. It was where he belonged. Ghana had changed over the centuries. What used to be thick forests was cleared to use the land for farming. Not a task easily done by themselves. The Ashantis were the first tribe to actively kidnap and force other Africans to be their slave laborers. Little did they know that this custom would be the downfall for millions of Africans, including many from their own tribe.

When the Europeans arrived and saw this system, they knew they could profit from it. If they rounded up Africans and sold them into slavery around the world, they could become very wealthy. The white men recruited African men, even kings and dignitaries from many tribes, to go into other parts of the continent and kidnap other blacks. This curried favors and saved their own lives. Africans sold them or traded goods with the white men. Some parents were even forced to sell their children in order to provide for the rest of their family.

In the Ashanti tribe, the women alone raised the children. Ashanti girls were as important as boys. The men and boys did the hunting when needed, but they all worked together as a community to complete the remainder of the chores.

Family lines had always been determined by females. But men came before women, and the elderly before juniors. An Ashanti man's priority was to build a house and have a family. Polygamy was practiced by some of the tribesmen. Men who married more than one woman and started more than one family showed they were wealthy and generous. The more wives a man had, the more wealth he had, for everything a wife inherited became the property of her husband.

Women and children participated in most craft making, but traditionally it was the Ashanti men who made the Kente cloth, which was known and admired for its beauty in many regions of Africa and around the world.

The Ashanti people became skilled farmers over the centuries. They planted and harvested much food. Their main crops were plantain, gourds, yams, kola nut, and rice. They also grew cotton, which was spun into yarn by women and then used by the men for Kente cloth. When the white men arrived from Europe and the Americas, they brought corn and cassava to add to their diets and traded for the Kente cloth to take around the world.

Everyone was expected to do the daily work of the village and participate in every domestic and social event. Huts were many sizes, depending on how large a family was. Most children, boys and girls, would sleep together in an area on one mat; parents slept on another.

Due to the hot climate of the country, there was no need for elaborate clothing. Men and boys wore a type of loin cloth (unless they owned a Kente robe), while women and girls only wore a wrap around their waist that was tied at the hip. Instead of shoes they sometimes wore a piece of leather tied to the foot and leg by laces, but most of the time they preferred to be barefooted.

Berko was almost thirteen years old when a strange black man came and took him while he was playing in the rain, something most children did during the wet season, which always preceded the yearly drought. They were playing a game where one person closed his or her eyes and counted to ten and the other children were to hide. On this day, when the counting stopped, the other children could not find Berko, and never would.

When the large man tried to capture Berko, he bolted. He was so terrified he could not scream. He had always thought of himself as a brave, strong warrior. He was usually confident and cocky.

One time while hunting with his father and the other men of the village, they killed a father lion for food and his hide. A lone cub was with the male lion. Berko quickly asked if he could kill the cub to take home for the children to feast on. He thought that if he hunted and killed it, he should be allowed to keep the hide for himself.

He was trying to show how brave he was by sneaking up behind the cub, when all at once the cub reared up, turned around toward Berko, and let out a fierce growl. Berko fainted. The men in the hunting party could not stop laughing.

Now running for his life while being chased by this big man, he began getting chest pains but kept running. The pain became so strong he had shortness of breath. Maybe there was somewhere he could hide. There was nowhere. He was caught and was struck on the head, which knocked him unconscious, and he was carried away.

While unconscious, he dreamt about that hunting trip again and how he had wanted to show his bravery by running from the man but was caught nevertheless. He dreamt about their Bible classes and the lesson from the book of Amos 2:14. "Fast runners will find no place to hide, strong men will have no strength left, and warriors will not be able to save their lives!"

When Berko woke up, he found himself in a dark smelly room. He was naked, along with all the others. Why were they left here, and what were they waiting for? Their death? Their life? No one with Berko knew.

They were all imprisoned in the famed Elmina Castle, built by the Portuguese in 1482. This castle was built close to the rich gold mines of Ghana, West Africa. *Mina* is the Portuguese word for "mine," and enslaved mine workers were housed in the dungeons below.

About two weeks later, Berko and all the men, women, and children were forced to run along the beach. There was a small boat that would take them to a ship, anchored in the harbor. Many screamed as they ran, and those who tried to run away were shot by the white men and left to die on the beach. The others were ordered to board the ship, the *Destino*.

This bold wooden Portuguese brig had been at sea for over fifty years, the last twenty-six under the command of Captain Reginald Sebastian. The *Destino*, an old but sturdy ship was a two-mast square sail ship that could carry a large payload of cargo. Brigs were fast and easy to maneuver. They could almost be turned 360 degrees on the spot. But in order to do this, she needed a large crew. Although crew took up valuable space, they were necessary for the smooth running of the ship. The rigging, which was backbreaking work, took most of their time. In its history, this brig was a carrier of many large guns for wartime use. Afterward, the guns were removed, and plenty of space was available for the cargo it would carry back and forth across the Atlantic. There was much to transport both ways. Cargo trading was very common between Africa and Europe, the Caribbean Islands, and the Americas. The *Destino* would carry coffee, tobacco, ironware, cotton, guns, gunpowder, ammunition, alcohol, sugar, cloth, jewelry, horses, livestock, and . . . *slaves!*

Although slavery had been outlawed officially on the island of Jamaica where Jacob and Jed were waiting, there were still a few slave ships that slipped by the law and made it into Port Royal. If a ship made it to the docks, the slave auctions went on. Unsuccessful ships were boarded by authorities and the captain arrested, heavily fined, and jailed for a time for the illegal purchase and selling of slaves. These lucky slaves were released to a free life in Jamaica.

The most successful slave ship was the *Destino*. Captain Sebastian had never been caught. The *Destino*, originally from Portugal, was later purchased by Englishmen for the Atlantic trade, when they discovered the lucrative slave trade and started working directly off the coast of Africa. This ship was actively working the Atlantic slave trade for a quarter century, completing at least two trips per year between Europe and Jamaica, carrying many tens of thousands of African slaves to their tragic fate.

At sea Berko was chained between what he thought were two men. In fact they were only a couple years older than him. The boys were chained at their necks and legs, and all slaves were chained to the deck.

The boys were able to communicate with each other. Even though they each came from different tribes, a sort of kinship ensued. Berko felt safe with these boys chained to him. They saw terrible atrocities on their trip, such as one slave, desperate for much needed air, strangling the man next to him to enlarge his space, to breathe better.

Many men, women, and children died of dysentery and other diseases on this voyage. Slaves were customarily branded by hot irons, on the arms for men and under the breasts for women. This branding mark belonged to the person selling and shipping them overseas. Sometimes these wounds would stay open and become badly infected. Some died because of the infection. When slaves were dead or dying, they were unceremoniously tossed into the sea for the sharks.

The captives were let up on the top deck only once a week. This was so they could get water thrown on them and the human waste could be shoveled off the ship. The saltwater on their open wounds was like torture. This was also their only chance to breathe clean air, drink fresh water, and stretch. This was also the opportunity to commit suicide by jumping to their deaths. These slaves felt this was a much kinder death; their suffering would be over.

Captain Sebastian was accountable for everyone. The slaves were owned by businessmen from England, working out of Africa. These men ordered the capture of the blacks and had them brought to Elmina Castle, where the captors held their cargo. The cargo was heavily insured as incentive to the captain to deliver as many live slaves as possible, or he would not get paid in full. It was in his best interest to keep his cargo alive and healthy.

After many weeks, the *Destino* arrived in Jamaica. Berko's trip was a very poor one for the captain. Out of the 323 slaves on board, he only delivered 238. They lost eighteen men, twenty-one women, and forty-six children. There was influenza and tuberculosis traveling through both the male and female cargo holds, and he also lost three good crew members to illness.

The lung infection tuberculosis was killing millions of people worldwide. In only a few years it was easily transported by ships to other countries. Of the slaves dead, there were also three men chained together that jumped in the sea to their deaths. It was a pact made between them while suffering the cruelties below and from fear of getting the disease.

Before descending onto the dock in Port Royal, the slaves were "showered" on the deck of the ship in front of what Berko thought was the whole town. He got used to the nakedness on the ship, but now he felt embarrassed. He had no way to hide himself as they were led down the gangway through the large crowd who was sneering, laughing, and shouting obscenities at them. They shouted one thing frequently, Berko remembered—"dirty niggers"—and he thought to himself, *What were they saying? What was a nigger? Is it their way of saying hello?* He then smiled at the crowd. They laughed. He would later learn from Jacob what a nigger was, and all he could feel was shame. This became the most despised word to Berko! That and the word "slave." He'd never known this degradation in Africa.

The slaves were led to a large area near the center of the town. They were placed in a small shack, and one at a time, each was dragged out by his or her neck chain and shown to the crowd. It was now Berko's turn. He had to step onto a large wooden block. He was spun slowly around for the crowd to see every part of him. While being shown, he was even made to open his mouth to show his healthy white teeth.

Then came his genitals; the man showing him put his hand around Berko's penis first and then lifted his scrotum. Berko didn't like someone touching his penis, or *foto*, an African name for it. The man held each testicle individually to show how large each one was, saying, "This one could father many children, which could be brought up to be slaves, and you would never have to buy another one." His penis was large for a boy of twelve. He could not control his prepubescent erection. Women giggled and tried not to look, but they were secretly noticing how well-endowed this young circumcised boy was. He was ashamed that everyone could see his hardness.

The men in the crowd were more interested in seeing his physical features. They wanted to know how much work they could get out of this "young buck," as he was referred to. Was the spine aligned correctly? Was there good muscle tone in the legs and arms? Sometimes, depending on how long the voyage took, it was difficult to judge. If the voyage took a couple of months, no physical activity made the slaves' muscles atrophy and sometimes useless.

While they were being shown, men and boys were expected to lift a heavy weight to prove their strength. If they could not lift it, they would not get a good price from the owners or not even sold at all . . . and that was just as bad as, or worse than, being sold!

Berko lifted the weighted block with no problem. While in the ship, he and the other two boys he was chained to decided to keep their minds and bodies busy. They exercised together at night when no one could see, and they talked often to keep their brains active and pass the time.

As the crowd in the square looked on, this boy astonished them when he lifted the heavy block, for he was slight in appearance. The white man beside Berko now started to talk fast and call things out to the crowd, and they were calling back. First one man, and then another, and it went on for some time. There was one kind-looking white man standing apart from the crowd who kept calling things out too. Every time someone else called out, this man responded again and again! Berko did not understand what an auction was, but at the end of the shouting, Berko was led to the kind-looking white man.

Jacob took Berko by the hand and led him to his horse and wagon. He now belonged to Jacob Marcus. Berko was his first chattel slave. Jacob reached into his wagon and pulled out a pair of Negro cloth pants, which he let Berko put on. He was then chained to a seat in the wagon and given a drink and corn bread, while Jacob went back to the auction area. This routine was repeated four more times.

Each time Jacob came back to the wagon, another slave was with him. To Berko's delight, Jacob had also bought the two boys he was chained to on the ship! He was surprised, since they had all been auctioned off separately throughout the day. But Jacob had good instincts. He felt the boys were friends and wanted to keep them together.

Each boy would be given a pair of thick coarse trousers and then chained to the wagon along with Berko. Jacob had a pail of clean water in the wagon, and each slave would also get a drink and a large slice of corn bread. You would think that it was pure gold that the slaves were given, but Berko, being born and raised on the Gold Coast of Africa, knew the water and bread were much more valuable. When Jacob had acquired the other four boys, he was ready to go back to the farm.

Jed's boss, Jacob Marcus, was a good man—a much better boss than most and a shrewd businessman. He was handsome and tall with salt-and-pepper hair and moustache and very pale skin. His blue eyes matched the sky, and many women were interested, but Jacob was married to his plantation. Some islanders referred to him as Whitey, which he was amused at, but his staff or slaves never dared to use it. They respected him too much.

He did not like terms like "slave," "master," or "overseer." He was to be called Jacob-Sir. The white staff on his farm was to be called by their Christian name, followed by "sir" or "ma'am." He cared for his workers, but there was discipline under his rule. You did not cross Jacob, but then there was no need to. He was not only fair but also kind and a gentleman of his word. His rules were abided by, or punishment was meted out, which he would see to as well but would be a very rare occurrence at his place.

Jacob hadn't always lived in Jamaica. He was originally from the United States. His family lived in Mississippi, on the banks of the Grand Ole Mississippi River. Cotton country! But it was the 1840s, and there was money to be made in sugar! Lots of money! People thought he was crazy for leaving the comfort of the Deep South and cotton for the Caribbean Island of Jamaica and sugarcane. He bought a fledgling sugarcane farm and said good-bye to family and friends and was gone. Over the span of a decade, he would develop this farm into one of the finest sugar plantations on the island, which made him a very wealthy man.

Jacob purchased this medium-sized sugarcane farm and became one of the most successful sugar exporters on the island. Within only a few years, he turned it into the successful Maisy-Lee Plantation, named after his beloved mother, Maisy-Lee Marcus. Every businessman and *most* farmers on the island knew Jacob and had great respect for him.

Although he first gave jobs on the plantation to the locals, he found over time that they were becoming too informal and lazy and he needed better workers to keep the plantation running at a good profit. Jacob was slowing down and his health was deteriorating. For a man of thirty-nine, he had reason to be concerned.

He had been experiencing different ailments and wasn't sure what was happening to him.

There were many medicine men on the island, but at the same time Jacob arrived in Jamaica there were other people emigrating as well. He was fortunate one of these men was a British doctor, Alexander Brookes. Jacob and Alex became good friends over the years, and Jacob trusted him with every medical need in his life and the lives of his workers.

One morning before his boys arrived, Jacob awoke with severe tingling in his arms and feet. He'd experienced it before, but never quite this bad. His mind was not as clear as it should be, and he felt dizzy. He had a hard time focusing his eyes on things.

Most times, through the nights, he suffered muscle spasms and had some trouble moving. The symptoms had been starting to show up through his waking hours too, but he tried to hide it from others. This night, like others, he didn't have time to make it on the chamber pot. He urinated and soiled himself. Although no one was around, he was so humiliated.

Jacob didn't feel sick in the way of cold, island fever, or influenza, so he thought it was just part of aging. Although fit, he was often winded when he climbed the stairs, or when he walked out to the fields, his chest would start to hurt. When he felt like this, he would have to sit or lie down, and it would seem to get better. He still didn't think much was seriously wrong.

Although no one thought of it as a contributing symptom, the heat was getting to him in a bad way. Living in the islands was hot. Customarily, a distinguished plantation owner always wore a hat. It was partly for the look and partly for protection from the sun and heat. Dr. Brookes didn't realize it at the time, but the hat was holding the heat in, causing Jacob's condition to become more unbearable. Jacob was very fatigued from his symptoms but didn't want to admit it . . . to anyone.

The ride from the auction to the plantation took about one hour over very bumpy roads.

The five boys were so happy to be breathing fresh air again. They filled their lungs, until they thought they would burst. The slaves didn't know what was in store for them, and right now they didn't care. They had crude clothing to cover themselves, food, water and fresh air—something they hadn't had since they were in their villages in Africa.

When they got to the plantation, Andrew was there. He was Jacob's white hired hand. Andrew lived in a little cottage on the plantation with his wife, Laura. They were a young couple in their twenties who worked hard for Jacob and looked after him, without him realizing it.

They had just been married for six months when Jacob hired them to help out. Andrew was actually what would be considered an overseer on other plantations, but Jacob preferred to call Andrew his field manager.

Laura was a sweet girl who had lived in Jamaica all her life, the daughter of the apothecary store owners, one of the few white families to have been on the island for several generations. Her father was very protective of her, due to the many rapscallions on the island, and wanted to make sure anyone who would ask for her hand in marriage was worthy and true. She was, after all, their only daughter, and a beautiful one at that.

She had black hair and silky tanned skin, with eyes as green as the seawaters around the beaches of the island. She was educated and brought up properly, as a young lady should.

Andrew was from England, a refined, educated young man of quality and ethics. He was handsome to the ladies, but he was serious about his schooling. His uncle Dr. Brookes asked him to come and live on the island. He came and helped his uncle in his medical office. One day Andrew's uncle asked him to go to the apothecary store to pick up supplies and prescriptions for him. Laura worked in her parents' store, and it was love at first sight for both of them. They were inseparable, and it seemed so natural for them to wed.

But they needed her father's approval. It took many Sunday outings and dinners with the family and several private talks in her father's library, which one even included Andrew's uncle, but Laura's father finally consented to their marriage.

When Jacob needed more reliable help on the plantation than what the locals could give him, his doctor and good friend suggested his nephew Andrew and his wife could move in right away and help run things with him. Jacob was very pleased . . . and he was thinking about bringing in his first bunch of slaves to work at the same time. Andrew started learning from other plantation owners on the island how to introduce the slaves to their new lives.

Laura knew a little of Jacob's health troubles. She had seen his sweaty pale skin as he tried to get a breath after coming in from the fields. She heard his irregular breathing as he washed up for lunch at times. She saw the way he would silently put one arm across his chest as he picked away at his meal sometimes, but he never complained. She came to look upon Jacob as a sort of uncle and felt great respect and admiration for him. She and Andrew enjoyed living and working there. They both knew Jacob needed them.

The first order of business when Jacob returned to the plantation with the boys was to change the slaves' African names to English ones. This was customary on most plantations. Usually the owners would give them their own surname, which symbolized property and ownership of the slave. Jacob didn't want to do this. He wanted them to have an identity of their own. When he decided to buy slaves he wanted to give them a new last name as well. The boys' surname was given by using Jacob's brother's first name, Allen, who had died during the Mississippi River cholera outbreak of 1849.

He named Berko "Jedediah." He would forever be called Jed Allen. The other four slaves with Jed that day would be named Isaac, Thomas, Timothy, and Caleb. The five slaves were now a family of five brothers by the surname of Allen.

The boys were introduced to Andrew. Jacob and Andrew both knew the ways of traditional masters and overseers on plantations and abhorred the slaves' treatment. Jacob thought the best way to run a profitable farm was to keep workers healthy and content.

Jacob also didn't want the other plantation owners to know how his farm was run. The other owners would likely ostracize Jacob, or even worse, they may sabotage his farm, or the slaves could be hurt or even killed. When he was having a visit from another plantation owner, he would tell Andrew and the slaves that they were going to get rough treatment, shouting, and possibly a light snap of his horsewhip. This was just to hide the fact that Jacob was treating his workers humanely. If others found out, there could be trouble. The average life span of a sugar plantation slave was seven years. Most were worked to death. Not at the Maisy-Lee. Jacob would never do this to "his boys."

Andrew saw to their living arrangements. There were three slave cabins. One was for all the boys to bunk together. There were three cots and one with a bed on the bottom, and it had bedposts at each corner holding a second bed on top. Jed and the other boys had never seen anything like this before. He and the others laughed, but no one wanted to try sitting up on the top bed. It was decided to draw lots.

They took five thin sticks, four long and one short. Whoever pulled the short one would be using the top bunk. Timothy held the sticks. Jed drew the first and it was the short one. He climbed up, and as everyone held their breath, they realized it was going to hold his weight. In their cabin, they had a wood stove for heat and cooking. Lighting was by coal oil lamp. Jed wondered what the other two cabins were for. He would learn that answer some day.

Since it was late in the day when they arrived at the plantation, the wood stove was already burning, and there was food already cooked and left warming on the stove. They were told that starting the next day, they would be responsible for making their own meals, except for lunch. After they gratefully ate their wonderful meal of fish, potatoes, and corn bread and drank the milk provided, they all fell fast asleep. Today had been a very important day. It was the first day of their lives . . . again. Tomorrow would be their first day at work. They would arise at 5:00 a.m. to start their day.

As Jed and Jacob watched the *Destino* dock and unload a year and a half after *he* had arrived, he caught a glimpse of the most beautiful girl in the world. And to his surprise, she was wearing an Ashanti Kente cloth robe! He grinned from ear to ear as he kept his eyes on her. Jacob was watching Jed and his reaction. He saw what he was sure was a young boy losing his heart that day! Jacob was determined to do something about it.

Afua Kakira was considered a very beautiful Ashanti girl of twelve. She was small and demure. She had the darkest eyes and had almost black hair down to her shoulders, which her grandmother braided every day while she braided her siblings' hair back in her home.

She came from a very large family and had many friends in her village. She would learn Jed was from the same tribe and that they lived in the same region of Kumasi, though separated by many miles.

Afua's father was an expert at making Kente cloth. Strips of cloth were sewn together to make a long flowing robe, which was usually worn by kings, noblemen, and dignitaries. Over time, these robes were worn by ordinary tribespeople, including women. Males made their own robes, but a female would usually have to buy or trade for it.

One day Afua asked her father, "May I make a robe for myself, Father? Could you teach me the way? I want to make one and our laws forbid it. May I learn from you, my father? May I have your blessing and your guidance? I want to so much . . . please." She pleaded with him, her big brown eyes cast down and irresistibly begging.

He smiled at her but took his time to answer her questions. "It is not our way for women to learn the skill," he said as he dragged out his answer, "but . . . it is acceptable sometimes. Since you do so well in your studies and chores, my little one, I will teach you the skill. You make your father very proud with your great ambition." Afua was ecstatic! Her father agreed to pass on to his daughter the skill, values, and dignity of making her very own Kente robe. From that day on, whenever her chores and lessons were completed, she worked alongside her father.

After the Ashanti women spun the cotton into yarn, they added color to it. Color was produced by cooking different tree barks, plants, berries, and seeds. Each one would make a different color of dye for the yarn. The different colors made beautiful cloths, and each pattern had a different meaning. Afua created her own design for her robe, which her father was very impressed with. Her pattern symbolized what the Ashanti teachings conveyed as antiquity and heirloom. She chose her favorite colors of light blue, mixed with both green and red threads, and then used black thread to define the pattern.

Afua decided that she would make her robe larger than she needed because she wanted it to last for all time and to also pass it down to all her future generations. In the beginning it was quite loose on her, so she made a sort of matching belt. Her father taught her how to tuck the robe and wear it so she could let it out as she grew. She wore it often, and when the villagers saw her wearing it, they too were proud of her for her newfound skill and confidence.

One bright sunny day, Afua had been with other youngsters of the village in a nearby forested area, gathering nuts, berries, barks, and plants. She went behind a very large tree where she knew a good berry patch existed. She never noticed the man! He was a large black man. He took one step toward her, scooped her up in his arms, put a piece of cloth into her mouth, and held it there so she could not scream. She was never to see her home again.

She believed, somehow, he had made her sleep. She awoke and found herself in a wagon with many other women, children, and men and didn't know any of them. A short time later they arrived at their destination. It was a large building, a sort of castle, Afua thought. She didn't know it, but she was right. It was Elmina Castle!

As she got closer to the building, she heard dreadful moaning and yelling from people. She heard their cries of "Let me go, let me live." And the horrible smell in the air, she didn't want to know what that was. The people in the wagon all stared at her in her robe, and she felt uncomfortable because many of them were naked. The man stopped the wagon and he ordered everyone out. The men and boys were separated from the women and girls—men into one large room, overflowing with many others. Some were yelling, some crying, and many were dying.

The women and children were sent into a similar room as the men and older boys. They were all stripped and inspected. Stripping the people was a measure of control for their owners. It also stripped them of their dignity. As the women and children were forced in to a room, Afua, who was at the end of the line, was stopped from entering. The man took the prized robe she had made and pushed it off her, and it dropped to the floor. After she was inspected for deformities or disease, she was allowed to put her robe back on, and the man said, "You will come with me." She obeyed and he took her up a set of stairs. She wouldn't see this room again or these people for some time.

Afua was taken to the upper chambers of "her castle." There she discovered a kitchen, a living room, a parlor, bedrooms, a dining room, even a room with a type of toilet . . . in the house! She never would have believed it if she hadn't seen it for herself. This room also had a large tub to wash in—all things she had never seen or heard of before. She was scared and didn't know what she was expected to do. For the brief time Afua was in the upper chambers, she would find out what slavery meant, for she was to work in this place for eighteen hours a day. There were several men living there. For the first time in her life she saw white men. There were black men living there too.

She was picked from the crowd of women and children to look after her captors. She prepared food, laundered, and mended all of their clothes and kept things clean in the castle. These men had no interest in anything else from her; they only had interest in each other.

At night while she tried to sleep, she heard a lot of noises and drunken talk between the men. One night she gathered the nerve to go to the bedrooms and see what the noise was. She was surprised to see three of the men in one bed. This reminded her of her home and family. She and two brothers and her little sister slept together on one mat but never before had she seen anything like what the men were doing to each other on the bed.

There were two white men and a black man together on this bed. What she saw she would never forget, for it puzzled her so. The black man in the middle was eating one man's *foto*, while the other one was behind him, on his knees, rocking back and forth. She didn't understand this at all, so she thought the man moaning was being hurt, but he was smiling. He seemed to be happy. When they all collapsed on the bed, they all smiled and hugged each other. She went back to her room and was glad they didn't touch her while she lived there.

During her time in the upper chambers, she learned some English and also discovered one of her captors was Ashanti. She could scarcely believe that an Ashanti man could be part of her horrible nightmare. Sometimes when she cried at night, he comforted her by telling Ashanti tales and singing Ashanti songs to get her to sleep.

One day she was told to get ready and go to the lower chambers. She was allowed to keep her robe on. Most in the rooms below were still naked, except for a few she had not seen when she was there last. There were fewer children than when she was there before, and there were also fewer women from the wagon that she arrived in. She wondered where they went. Little did she know that they were not simply gone—they were dead.

Many of the new naked captives disapproved of her body covering. This time her Kente robe was nothing to be proud of, she thought. All of a sudden the door was opened, and they were pushed underground through a tunnel that would bring them out onto a beach and a small boat that would row them to a large ship anchored many yards out on the ocean. It was the Portuguese slave ship *Destino*, the word for "destiny" in Spanish. For all who sailed on her now, it was their destiny, as horrifying as it was.

After they were underway, she heard talking from the deck above her. What were they saying? She recognized some English but still did not understand much. What she did understand was that there was to be a long sea voyage, and they were going far away. That, she unmistakably understood. She became very frightened and sad. She knew she would never see home again.

The captives were all let out to the top deck twice a week so their feces could be shoveled off the ship. They could breathe fresh air and drink water that was not contaminated. They were allowed to walk around the deck in a strictly supervised circle. Some were crippling from being below in very cramped quarters—and what quarters they were. Each person, large or small, had a space the width of a coffin and a height of three feet to "live" in. At night, when there were not as many crew about on the upper deck, those below would all whisper in their tongue to learn things.

They somehow each knew what was to become of them.

Many slaves in the hold of the ship Afua was in were getting sick. The crew talked about something called smallpox. The smallpox started to show on a couple of children a few days into the voyage. Some women fell ill with it too. They had sores in their mouths, which was overlooked during inspection in Africa, and they developed more on their hands and arms within a day or two.

The sick were moved to a small area of the ship, where they all eventually died and were thrown into the sea. The rest of the women and children remained uncontaminated. There was now only common seasickness to contend with in the hold until they landed.

Since the men were separated from them, in another cargo hold, none of the men had contracted the pox. However, they had dysentery, which was taking men's lives in their part of the ship. They were not getting enough to eat or drink, but vomiting and diarrhea persisted. It did not take long to die under these conditions, even for the strongest man. Each morning when the crew threw their food to them, they checked for dead slaves and threw them overboard. This included men, women, and children. If a sick person had a weak pulse and the crew felt that they were going to die that day, they were thrown into the sea that morning, alive. This would save them from checking their statuses later in the day.

After the first week on board, Afua was awakened by one of the crew at night, when everyone was asleep. It was one of the white men who gave them food each day. She seemed to trust him and she smiled at him. He took her up on the top deck to an area not seen by her or the other slaves and seldom used by the crew. He had a bucket of water and some soap. He took her robe off her and he washed her. After he was done, he washed her robe too, and he hung it up on some rigging to dry. She felt strange all of a sudden. Why was he nice to her?

Her twelve-year-old body was developing well. She had small breasts and was thin with hunger. There was no talking during this encounter, but she now started to fear him. As the white crewman lowered his trousers to show her his already-hard *foto*, Afua thought to herself, even after seeing the three men together on the bed in the castle, she had never seen one like this before, or this large. She thought it looked strange, much like a large plantain or a long thin gourd that they grow in their village garden. She was terrified when he put his hand over her mouth to stop her from crying out loud. He made her lie down on the deck and he was quickly on top of her. He struggled to get inside her. It was her first time.

She suffered so much pain that night. She did not understand why he was doing this to her.

What had she done to deserve this punishment? This encounter was to be repeated several times before they would reach land.

By the time they arrived at Port Royal, forty men, women, and children had died of smallpox, dysentery, suicide, and murder. Some slaves murdered each other to get a larger space to exist in. A few captives got hold of nails and other lethal implements and drove them into their neighbor's brain to kill them for their precious space and air.

As Jed and Jacob watched, the *Destino* docked in Port Royal with the live cargo, including Afua. She felt uneasy. Jed kept his eyes on her and wished he could speak with her. He remembered that she must forget everyone and everything she knew of her previous life. It no longer existed. He knew she would be frightened and wanted to be able, somehow, to let her know it's all right. He wished he could help her through it but kept silent beside Jacob.

Afua was trembling as she prepared to disembark. Her "punisher" was there. What did he have in mind for her this day? She could not look at him. She feared him now. All the times he brought her up on the deck and assaulted her, she will never forget. Was she doomed to stay with this man?

As on the other trips, all the slaves were made ready for auction by stripping them and giving them a shower on deck. This consisted of the crew throwing pails of cold, salty seawater on them.

Again, if there were open sores on their bodies, which almost everyone had, the agony they felt showed on their faces. As Afua was being showered, her eyes scanned the dock. She was very shocked at what she saw. She found a handsome young black man standing with an older white man. He was looking at her.

Captain Sebastian was now the owner of the *Destino*, and by this time, things were done differently. He let a few white men board his ship. They were going over some papers and started counting people and calling out numbers. If the captain delivered the amount promised, he would get the full and much higher pay. Unlike all his previous trips, he now personally owned the slaves on this trip. On his previous trips he was only paid a very small amount per head to transport them for the British owners.

Now he was the one who ordered the kidnap of Africans to be brought here to Jamaica and sold. He was one of the men that Afua looked after in her castle. The payment for his shipment was to come from a slave broker in Port Royal. They were the ones to take the slaves off his hands and auction them off.

Afua's voyage left the Gold Coast with 281 slaves aboard. Due to illness, suicide, and murder, eleven men, three women, and twenty-six children had died and been thrown overboard. Captain Sebastian was now delivering 241 live slaves to be auctioned off in the town square that afternoon. That was good, compared to a trip he remembered eighteen months earlier when many men, women, and children had died. He lost a lot of money on that trip. That was the voyage that had brought Berko across the Atlantic.

Jacob and Jed watched as the cargo was brought down the gangway, chained together on one long chain. First were the men and then the women and children. Afua was near the end of the chain. As she walked clumsily down toward the dock, she was looking for the boy she saw earlier. For a minute she lost sight of him but found him again. He was certainly watching her, and he was smiling the biggest smile since that day he was playing with the other children in his village . . . the day he was captured. She smiled a little shy smile. She did not want her punisher to see her, for if he should like her smile, he might keep her for himself. During her times with him, she never smiled after that first night.

They all were off the ship now, and it felt strange to be on the ground again. Her trip only took seventeen days. The weather was good and it was a smooth sailing. They were led away to the same building that Berko was led to almost two years earlier. The procedure for the slaves had not changed in that time. The men were auctioned off first, and then the women and the children.

Afua was eventually brought out in her Kente robe and put on the same block that Berko had stood on long ago. The auctioneer pulled off her robe and it fell to the ground. Tears started welling up in her eyes. She didn't want to cry, but the tears would not stop. She felt stripped of her heritage.

The women and children were shown much in the same way the men and boys were, with attention being paid to their breasts, hips, and pelvis. This was to show that they were able to bear and nurse many children. The man was talking so fast, and she did not understand what he was saying. The men in the crowd were showing interest in her, but not for working. They were interested for sexual reasons. She would not understand this for some time yet.

The auctioneer was telling everyone about Afua and her skills, looking after the men before her trip. The women liked hearing this. They wanted her for a house slave. She was young enough to train the way they wanted, and they were able to keep a closer eye on her in the house, away from their husbands, sons, and other male slaves. The crowd was told that this child was extra special because she came with her own world famous Kente robe, which African kings wore.

Although not said, maybe they thought of her as royalty. This made the bidding start higher. The spectators also had no idea that it was quite possible she may be with child by now . . . since her horrendous voyage!

The bidding started and it was going very fast. Jacob was right there calling out his bids.

After every bid, he was placing higher ones. The auctioneer called, "Five guineas, do I hear ten . . . ten, thank you, sir, do I hear fifteen . . . fifteen guineas . . . thank you." He pointed to Jacob. It continued and she was up to forty-five guineas now. "And to you, sir," he said, pointing at Jacob and the other men bidding on her too. "Fifty, fifty-five, sixty, sixty-five, seventy . . . thank you, gentlemen. This is one very prized slave girl. What are my bids now?"

Jacob called out, "One hundred guineas!" No one had ever bid so high on a child before. Especially a girl! He was going to take this girl home, no matter what the cost. The bidding seemed to go on a bit long for Afua. She was chilled and trembling . . . or was it fear? She wanted to pick up her robe and put it back on. She didn't dare, until she was told to.

Jacob spent money that day. When he finally won Afua, he paid out 125 guineas, a price never heard of for a child, let alone a girl! Even when he bought Jed, who was a rare find because of such strength and obedience, he only paid sixty-five guineas for him. Jacob also bought two other young girls that day.

The other girls and Afua were taken to Jacob's wagon. Afua was allowed to put her robe back on as soon as Jacob bought her. She still trembled. Not from cold or fear, but because Jed was right there, so close to her. He was still smiling. Jacob repeated what he had done to the male slaves to the newly purchased slaves. Each girl was given a sort of a sack dress made of Negro cloth and given a drink of fresh water and a large portion of corn bread. They were nervous but elated and hungrily devoured the food and drink.

Jacob was indeed a shrewd man. He was not simply buying female slaves; he was buying a modicum of what he hoped was happiness for his boys.

As the girls rode to the plantation that day, they were happy to be out of the ship's hold and breathing fresh air again. When they arrived, as was Jacob's custom, he renamed his slaves. They were renamed Esther, Amelia, and Afua was given the name Mary. Jacob gave the girls the surname Belle, in memory of his sister who had also died of cholera in the Mississippi outbreak in 1949, like their brother, Allen.

Jacob Marcus was the sole and legal owner of eight chattel slaves now. With the arrival of the girls, life on the Maisy-Lee Plantation was going to be much happier, or so Jed thought.

Chapter 2

Scottish Beginning

B Y THE MID-1850S IN CUPAR, Scotland, Johnny McDonald was a strapping lad, like most teenage boys in his farming community. They worked hard on their farms and were strong, healthy boys, their family's pride. Johnny was no different; and just down the way, near the banks of the River Eden, lived his bonnie lass Diana McGee.

Cupar, Scotland, in Fife County, is one of the oldest burghs in Scotland, said to date back to 1382. It is commonly known as the Kingdom of Fife, due to its link with royalty and the Scottish monarchy. Fife County boasts beautiful cathedrals, castles (including Lordscairnie Castle, complete with ghosts and inexplicable happenings), and royal palaces and has the distinguished honor of having the most famous golf course in the world. St. Andrews has one of the oldest golf courses in history. The Scottish people have a great passion for golf. Following close behind is a love for the Highland games and tennis. The word "fife" is an Old Danish word meaning "wooded country," which was so abundantly true. It holds the richest soil and minerals, its main being coal. The most successful crops are corn, potato, flax, cotton, and barley. There are great pasture lands for cattle, sheep, horses, and ponies.

The River Eden provides the water power to run their mills and breweries. There were two corn mills, breweries, two barley mills, flour mills, and flax, which, after spinning, was woven into linen. By 1845 there were six hundred home weavers of linen in the area. Both Johnny's and Diana's families were registered as linen weavers. It generated a small income, but it helped out during the winter months.

The Industrial Revolution was on. During this time, there was demand for textiles, chemicals, and materials, which, in turn, brought an increase in industry. There was also high demand for their world-famous whiskey.

Rail lines were great for business. In the early years, the four lines were primarily for transporting coal and other materials used in factories and farms. Most towns, villages, and cities were connected during this era. By 1842 the Edinburgh and Northern Railway line came to Cupar. Farmworkers were beginning to be replaced by machines and tools. The Agricultural Revolution was also on. The farming communities were introduced to better drainage methods so that the marsh lands could be utilized for more crops. Tree and hedge planting broke the high winds and protected the fields. Crop rotations started to be used, and many farms rented out space to other smaller farmers or crofters.

Johnny's and Diana's families and ancestors had been living in the same area in Fife County for many generations. Diana's family raised Angus beef cattle, Shetland ponies and Clydesdale horses. They also grew cotton, flax, and barley, which they rotated each year or two. Angus cows were bred for meat. They were considered the best beef cattle rose, since their yield of marbled meat was high due to their immense size.

Shetland ponies were used on both farms just as much as Clydesdale horses. Shetlands were known for their durability, power, good temperament, and adaptability to harsh conditions. They are the strongest breed of all ponies and can pull twice their weight.

Clydesdale draft horses originated in Clydesdale, Scotland. They are meant to work hard. The average size of these horses was eighteen hands, and they averaged one ton in weight and twice the width of a thoroughbred race horse.

The McGees were never without their Clydesdales and sold them on a regular basis throughout the British Isles but later sold to other countries. These horses worked hard plowing, pulling farm equipment, and eventually they were used in many communities as delivery horses, delivering milk, coal, liquor, beer, and any number of things.

The McDonald farm grew potatoes in very large quantities and also grew cotton and flax. Potatoes had been grown on this prime piece of land for hundreds of years. Then along came the Irish and Highland potato famines. Eighteen forty-six ushered in a devastating few years for potato farmers in both countries.

Scotland, like most countries, was dependent on potatoes for food, since it is the largest crop per field, and the yield is high. Potato crops were blighted by a fungal disease, which destroyed their crops. Scotland had a famine relief program, but people were expected to work for their rations.

As crops failed year after year, people died, and many packed up their belongings and emigrated to the Americas.

Like most families in Fife, the Scottish had their family tartan. Diana's mother was very diligent at keeping the tradition of having their own registered family tartan. Diana's father and farm hands constantly wore and wore out their shirts made from the family tartan. Diana, her mother, and her sisters wore tunics and dresses made from the same family cloth. The pattern that Diana's mother wove used light-blue threads, mixed with both green and red threads, and she used black as the main thread that helped define the pattern. The colored cotton and wool used was dyed by using simple homemade recipes, which involved cooking flowers, berries, and barks of trees to make many different colors. Diana loved the colors in her family's pattern and made a promise to her mother that she would see to it that the family tartan would be passed down through generations.

In summertime, the tartan was made from cotton that was spun from the McGees' crops. In winter, tartan was made from wool that was spun and sold by a sheep farmer down the road.

The McDonald tartan was made by Johnny's mother. Their colors were primarily red, with yellow and green, and had not been changed over the centuries. His mother made the clothes for the family and also prepared the kilt and sash for Johnny's wedding someday.

When it was not planting or harvesting time, the children attended a small school in Cupar, one of many one-room schoolhouses throughout Fife County. Their school was a half-mile walk from the farms where Diana, Johnny, and their brothers and sisters lived.

Johnny finished elementary school and afterward worked very hard on the farm. Not that he did not want more education—he would have continued if his father could spare him from working on the farm. His dream had always been to become a doctor. He studied animals, plants, and their diseases on the farm and wanted to study and heal people. The medical schools around were the finest in the land. By that time, they had finally recovered from the Burke and Hare days.

Johnny, as did most people, disapproved of the past in the medical teaching facilities. In the early 1800s Dr. Knox's School of Anatomy near Surgeons' Hall in Edinburgh was paying men to bring dead bodies to him for dissection. Two men, Burke and Hare, murdered people to bring to Dr. Knox. It was a horrendous tale when all was brought into the open.

Johnny promised himself that any children he and Diana had would be sent as far as education could take them. Not that there was anything wrong with farming; he would teach their children that too. He also knew there was a whole world to be explored.

Diana wholeheartedly agreed with him. Her goal was always to be a schoolteacher. Since she was the best student in the school, she would have no problem passing the exams to get her teaching certificate. She was allowed the privilege of going through only one year of high school, but that was it. Her parents were wealthier than most in the region and were going to be able to send all four of their daughters to high school, but Diana, being the eldest, had to quit school to look after her mother who had fallen ill. Her dream of teaching would have to wait.

The McGee sisters were loved dearly by their father, but what father doesn't want sons? So as his daughters grew up, he gave them boy nicknames, all in fun of course. Diana was named Pete; Carole was George; Penelope, Sam; and Lorraine, Joe! Their father was so proud of his girls, who were tough as nails and strong from working around the farm. They could also be feminine young ladies that both parents were proud of. The sisters loved both their parents dearly, and the family was a close one.

Diana now had to do all her regular chores and take her mother's place while caring for her too. She would not only prepare the meals for the farmhands, her father, three sisters, herself, and her mother but also had to get the girls off to school in the mornings and keep constant watch over her mother. When Diana found a few spare minutes each day, she would read from the Bible, which gave her mother much comfort. As her mother got sicker, thoughts of going home to be with the Lord was on her mind. Later, after supper and when her sisters finished their homework, Diana would read them a few chapters from the Good Book. She would also get her sisters to take turns reading so she could make sure they were keeping up with their studies. She liked to test them in arithmetic and other subjects too. She did not want their schoolwork to suffer. It was evident that Diana longed to be a teacher.

Their father enjoyed listening to his daughters read in the evening. He would close his eyes in his favorite chair and just listen. Sometimes the hard day proved to be tiring, and he would nod off. Diana gently would wake him long enough that he could make his way to the couch. Mother was in the bedroom, and they felt that he should not sleep with her, in case she was contagious.

The doctor in the village could not be certain right away but felt that Mrs. McGee had a severe form of influenza. After a short time, the signs changed the diagnosis—smallpox! She had developed sores in her mouth and then her arms and hands. She had to be moved to a house that was set up in the burgh as a temporary hospital, away from the family so they would not contract the disease. But it was a too late. Diana's youngest sister contracted it and was moved too. Within a few days, Mrs. McGee passed away and her youngest daughter, Lorraine, a few days later.

Cupar had many cases of smallpox but not all died. Johnny's family escaped the disease altogether. He and Diana were advised by the doctor not to see each other for about five or six weeks, and the town was also advised to do as little visiting as possible. The school was shut down, as were the churches. All the families worshiped at home for over a month, until the dangerous period was over.

After it was safe, both families needed and deserved a break. After spring planting on a beautiful sunny Saturday, it was decided that they would all go to St. Andrews Old Golf Course, just a few miles down the road. They all loved to golf, and although they could not play often, it was a real treat. The adults and older children played eighteen holes, and the younger children, who were not allowed on the course, spent their day helping Old Sam.

Old Sam was the caretaker of The Royal and Ancient Golf Club of St. Andrews. Sam was really not old; that was just a name given to him because he had been severely shocked by what he believed to be a ghost of a dead earl and Satan. At the age of nineteen, his hair turned completely white, and his face forever changed into that of an old man's, so the name stuck.

The McGees and the McDonalds had been friends with Sam for years. Both families never took stock in the ghost stories and legends around the area, but Old Sam believed. He believed he saw Laird Beardie, the Earl of Crawford, and the devil himself. After he recovered, he could no longer work on that farm, but he was able to take over the job as caretaker at St. Andrews. He loved to see his friends come to "his" course to visit him. Old Sam lived on the course, in a flat designed for him in the large clubhouse that had been built on the grounds. Sometimes on Sundays, when St. Andrews was closed for the day, he would drive down the road in his buggy to have dinner with either or both families.

On this Saturday, in the late afternoon after golfing, the families had a picnic nearby with Old Sam. It was there that Johnny got down on one knee and asked Diana for her hand in marriage. She had no idea he had discussed it with her parents and so was very surprised. As she took his hands, they stood up, hugged, and, with tears in her eyes, Diana said, "Oh my dear sweet Johnny, aye, aye! I'll be yer wife for as long as we live and love ye until the Lord sees fit to part us, and even longer!" Everyone around them who had heard the proposal cheered.

The couple decided on a date. Their wedding would take place on Saturday, October 10. The church where they were to be wed was Cupar's old parish church. The original church was built in 1415. Only the tower and spire were left from the old church when it was rebuilt in 1785. The old parish church was beautiful, and most couples in Cupar got married there.

The parish vicar was a very good friend to all his parishioners. He had christened most of the children in the area, including all of the McGee and McDonald children. He had also married both sets of parents.

Diana only had two sisters now to help her plan the wedding. Johnny's mother and Jacqueline, her maid of honor and lifelong friend, were a great help too. Johnny's mom, who became a great substitute mother for Diana and all the McGee children, helped with their family and the wedding plans whenever she could. The wedding party would include all of the McDonald brothers, Philip, Arthur, Jason, and Charles, and McGee sisters, Carol and Penelope.

For three consecutive weeks before the wedding, the banns of marriage were proclaimed. It was announced in the old parish church that John McDonald and Diana McGee would be wed on October 10, 1855.

One week before the wedding, there was the "showing of the gifts." This is traditionally done by the mother of the bride. Since Diana's mom had passed away, Johnny's mother held the showing in her home. The vicar of the parish gave a most beautiful, large white, gold-embossed, boxed Holy Bible, which he had blessed for them. Diana and Johnny made a vow that each night they would read Scriptures to each other. Eventually they would include their children. They wanted to bring up strong Christian children.

Most of the other gifts were for a new home, which Diana and Johnny hoped to have someday. For now, they were invited to live in the McGee house. Everyone who gave a gift received a personal invitation to the wedding. The same day that Diana opened her gifts, her groom was taken for a stag night, where the drinks flowed heartily.

As a wedding present, or the "secret project" as the two families liked to refer to it, Diana's and Johnny's parents bought the couple a small parcel of land not too far down the road. It was sold by a couple who had lost everything in the previous famine and could not recover from their loss. They had decided to sell it all and moved to the city to work in the industrial area of Edinburgh.

The property had a small, cozy two-bedroom house and a barn with several stalls for animals, which the families were going to provide too.

This farm was to be their very own. The couple was so busy with their chores they had no idea that the land was bought. The McDonalds were supplying them with a potato crop, and the McGees gave the kids their own horses, ponies, and cows. There were two of each, one male and one female, so they would be assured they would always have work animals and beef cattle. Their brothers and sisters put some money together and purchased some laying chickens for them too. What more could a new young couple in Cupar, Scotland, ever want?

Throughout the summer, farmwork took over most everyone's lives. While Diana and Johnny were working on their wedding plans, everyone else was busy with the secret project, getting Diana and Johnny's house and farm ready.

October 10 arrived. Waiting at the door of the McGee farmhouse for the bride and her father was a beautiful white carriage with gold trim, led by the most graceful pair of gray horses she had ever seen, gray being considered by the Scots to be good luck for a bride and groom.

Diana had long brown hair, which Jacqueline put up for her, and her brown eyes shone brightly. Her skin was tanned from a summer of hard work and golfing, and she was a tall girl, just shy of Johnny's height of six feet two inches. She was shapely, and the village boys were sad that they never had the chance to woo her.

She wore a long ivory gown with two layers: underneath, a cotton layer, while over top was a beautiful handmade layer of lace. The hat her mother and grandmother wore was damaged, so she had a replica made at a milliner in Edinburgh. The gloves were new and the boots high with laces. The dress belonged to her grandmother, who handed it down to Diana's mother when she married Diana's father almost eighteen years earlier. He was as proud then to see his beautiful bride approach the altar wearing it as he was now, walking their daughter down the aisle in it. She was just as beautiful as her mother.

But it was different this time. Diana had an addition to the dress. Before they left for the church, her father presented a gift . . . from her late mother. Before she got sick, her mother made a tartan sash that she hoped to see Diana wear over the wedding dress, in keeping with an old Scottish custom. Her father knew about the tartan sash that her mother had made and, as she got sicker, had told her not to worry and promised his wife he'd give it to Diana just before her ceremony. After the promise, he'd kissed his sweet wife without knowing that she would leave them all behind to meet her Lord shortly. There were a few tears between Diana and her father that day, but no words were spoken; they each understood.

Her bridesmaids were beautiful in pale blue. The bridal bouquet was all white roses with both families' tartan bands and lace throughout. The other girls carried baskets of flower petals to throw on their way down the aisle before the bride approached, and more tossed afterward.

John's square jaw and dimpled cheeks when he smiled were two of his most endearing features. All the girls in the village loved him for it too. But Diana McGee had won his heart in elementary school. His blue eyes were always watching her whenever they were together. He didn't care for beards, like so many Scottish men, so he was always clean shaven.

He wore classic Scottish groom's wedding attire: a kilt, made from his family tartan with a kilt pin, a Prince Charlie jacket, and a wing-collar shirt and black bow tie. He wore a white hose, ghillie brogues, and a piece of heather in his lapel for luck. The family tartan sash would top off the outfit.

The bride and groom decided together about the ceremony and the vows and chose to have the vicar recite a traditional wedding blessing:

> Miile faailte dhuit le d'bhreeid,
> Fad do ree gun robh thu slaan.
> Mooran laaithean dhuit is siith,
> Le d'mhaitheas is le d'nii bhi faas.

Translated into English, the blessing means:

> A thousand welcomes to you with your marriage kerchief
> May you be healthy all your days.
> May you be blessed with long life and peace
> May you grow old with goodness and with riches.

They wed with many traditions throughout the ceremony. The marriage kerchief was made by Johnny's mother. It was a square linen cloth with a cross embroidered on it. The four corners are folded over, so just the cross shows. Before the altar, the wedding couple each hold a side during the blessing. When the blessing is over, Johnny will then hang the kerchief in his belt as a sign of fertility.

Later, the kerchief is hung in the couple's home to symbolize their union. When one dies, the kerchief is torn in half, and half is placed in the coffin of the deceased partner. When the widowed one passes on, the remaining half of the kerchief would be placed in their coffin. This is done so the husband and wife recognize each other in their afterlife.

Then there was the tying of the knot. The bride and groom each tore a strip of tartan off their sash and tied them together, symbolizing the uniting of the two families.

Every bride knows the custom of having something old, something new, something borrowed, and something blue. Diana used her mom's wedding dress as something old, the sash her mother made was something new, and for something borrowed and blue, Johnny's mom loaned Diana her luckenbooth brooch. Diana would receive this brooch as a gift years later.

A luckenbooth brooch was customarily made of silver in those days. It had two hearts entwined, and in this case there was a beautifully set royal blue agate stone in the middle.

The vicar addressed the crowd, started the ceremony, and the groom recited the vows.

"Tha mise John a-nis 'gad ghabhail-sa Diana gu bhith 'nam cheeile phoosda. Ann am fianais Dhee na tha seo d fhinaisean tha mise a' gealltainn a bhith 'nam fhear poosda diileas graadhach agus tairis dhuitsa, cho fad's a bhios an diithis againn beoo."

Translated, it means, "I, John, now take you, Diana, to be my wife. In the presence of God and before these witnesses, I promise to be a loving, faithful, and loyal husband to you, for as long as we both shall live."

Diana then repeated the same vows to John, after which she received a wedding ring. Just looking at the couple, everyone could see their happiness and the love they had for each other.

Some of the smaller but just as important traditions were also observed. Diana carried a horseshoe somewhere on herself for luck. It protects her from Satan harming her. After the wedding the horseshoe is to be placed in the couple's home. Satan will never enter a home that has a horseshoe in it. It's used for good luck and is a symbol of fertility.

When the ceremony was over, Johnny and Diana were piped down the aisle and out of the church. At this time the ringing of the church bells started and lasted for a short period to let the town know a wedding was solemnized, and it also was said that the bells drive away evil spirits.

Relatives had agreed to hold the evening's festivities for the bridal couple. There was a great feast and drink of every kind, although Scottish whiskey prevailed. The lead piper piped the couple to the dinner table, and after the wedding was over, it was his duty to play the pipes and then hand a dirk or sharp Highland dagger to the bride. As the bride makes the first cut of the wedding cake, her groom guides her hand.

After the cake cutting, the pipers and band played a tune that Diana and Johnny picked out to dance to. They chose a song, originally a Robbie Burns poem, "My Love is Like a Red, Red Rose." After their wedding dance, the rest of the guests joined in and danced too.

When the bridal couple was ready to go to their new home, they would be piped all the way. Everyone followed and watched Johnny carry Diana across the threshold. Scottish superstition holds that evil spirits inhabit the threshold of house, so the bride is carried over it and is placed on the wedding bed. The revelers went back to the celebration and continued to drink, dance, and have a good time far into the night.

Chapter 3

Teaching a New Way of Life

A<small>S DAYBREAK CAME TO THE</small> Maisy-Lee Plantation, the boys awoke from a most glorious night, sleeping on real beds with mattresses, a quilt, and pillows that they didn't have to share. Most plantations gave each slave only one single blanket made of Negro cloth. In places where climates were colder in winter, there were no exceptions. Jacob would provide each of *his* slaves a quilt that was made with double thickness. It was much warmer than the other kind. Jamaica did not get very cold during the winter, but the quilt was appreciated just the same. Andrew came around and knocked on the cabin door to see if they were ready to work. They were!

It felt good to have pants on, even though Negro cloth was very coarse next to the skin.

It was a very inexpensive cloth, made from rough-milled, usually brown or blue cotton, sold primarily to plantations and prisons. The idea was to not spend more than they had to on slaves and prisoners. Jacob provided each boy with two pairs of these pants. They were also given an undergarment that they've never seen before. This was good to keep the roughness of the cloth away from their groin. They each received two working shirts and one pair of stockings. They did not have shoes yet. Jacob waited to get them home so Andrew could measure their feet to see what size of working shoes to buy them. When this was done, Andrew gave the measurements to Laura, and she and Jacob went to the mercantile to purchase them.

In the meantime, while they awaited their shoes, Andrew began to try to teach them English.

The best method that seemed to work was point and say. He pointed to himself and said, "Andrew-Sir." Then he did the same to each boy and repeated their names and pointed to them. This seemed to go well, so he pointed to and said everything they came across in their day. He took them first to the barn. They were shown the horses, cows, chickens and the small corn, vegetables and potato fields, along with some uncultivated areas nearby.

After their shoes arrived and they were taught how to put them on, Andrew took all the boys to the sugar field to show what was to be done. They included Jed for the first lesson. It was hard for Jed to do some of this work. Although he was strong enough, he was not very skilled with a machete. The older boys were. Jacob thought it was a bit too dangerous to have him in the fields. He decided that Jed would become the plantation gofer and farmhand. Jed reported to Jacob for his new duties. It was here he was introduced to Laura-Ma'am. She was the first white woman he had ever been this close to! She was beautiful.

Jacob seemed to really like Jed Allen. You could even say that he took him under his wing and was almost fatherly toward him. Over the next few weeks he planned to teach Jed how to drive the horses and buggy and how to work in the barn, feeding, cleaning, and caring for the horses and chickens, milking the cows, and working the vegetable crops. Jed was skilled in gardening, since he learned this in Africa. He also was to do heavier chores in the house.

Andrew showed the boys a mature sugarcane crop. Sugarcane fields need to be completely burned before they can be ready to work. Andrew started a match and lit the stalks on fire. The blaze grew quickly, and the boys were scared of this large fire at first. He tried to keep them calm. Sugar burns with great speed, and it took less than twelve minutes to burn the field. The fire burns off the dead leaves that may interfere with the harvest.

Jamaica's main export is sugar in refined and raw forms and rum. Harvesting was done by hand and machetes. It was hard work but the boys quickly caught on. Andrew helped load the stalks into the wagon and bring them to a designated spot. They continued until lunchtime.

At noon, Andrew let them in the wagon, and he drove them back to their cabin. Waiting there for them were milk and sandwiches. Jacob and Andrew ate at the house where Laura had prepared a good hearty lunch for them. One of Jed's new jobs was to take the sandwiches to the slaves. Each slave would be provided two sandwiches each of meat or fish, made in the house by Laura. They had fresh water in the cabin at all times. Jacob had Jed see to this. The milk was provided by Jacob's two cows, which Jed had to milk each morning and evening.

Jacob provided food for their breakfast and supper, but they had to prepare these meals by themselves. Each day, Jed would take the food to the cabin. Little did they know, this was *not* how a traditional plantation was run. They began to feel that this life was not so bad after all. They had no idea what was being done to slaves on other plantations.

Other plantations worked on a ration system. Each slave was allotted a certain amount of food for the week or month, and it was up to them to consume it with care. On other island plantations, and in the Americas, all slaves were traditionally only given two meals a day. The first would be around 9:00 or 10:00 a.m., after they had already worked a few hours of hard labor, and the other meal at the end of the workday. Jacob made sure his workers had three meals a day.

Starving workers did not produce adequate work.

Jed had cleared an acre of uncultivated area that Jacob had set aside as a vegetable garden for the slaves to use for their own food. They could plant whatever they wanted, and once they were harvested and successfully growing from season to season, Jacob would only be providing their meat and fish and the occasional chicken, as well as their milk. The boys planted potatoes, corn (lots of it to make cornmeal), squash, carrots, beans, peas, and cabbage.

At 1:00 p.m. the work started over. They worked until 6:00 p.m. During the mornings and afternoons, they always had fresh water to drink in the field. Jacob could not expect dehydrated workers to produce much work either. Jed carried the water to the others in the morning and afternoon.

Andrew transported the cane to the mill a few miles away each day. At the end of the week, on Saturday, Jacob would go with him to collect his money for the week's produce from the mill owners. They were always happy with Jacob's harvest. It was full of liquid and healthy. For this, he was given a slightly higher rate of pay than the other plantation owners whose harvest was not cut and cared for properly.

Sundays, Jacob observed the Sabbath as a day of worship and rest. Being a Christian, Jacob tried to instill in the boys a belief in God and his goodness. Little did he know that many Africans also had Christian beliefs. The sugar field was at rest for one day out of seven, but the barn work and tending to the animals was needed on Sunday, just as it was during the week. The other boys would help Jed. It was a change for them, and they could all work at a slower pace.

The five boys enjoyed each other's company and worked well together. The cows still had to be milked and a chicken would be beheaded and ready for Sunday supper at the plantation house. On special occasions, Jacob let the boys have a chicken for their supper too. This was on birthdays (if the boys even knew when they were born). Only the two oldest boys knew when they were born, since their parents had told them. The three younger ones had no idea when they were born, so Jacob gave them each a birthday. Jacob gave Jed his own birthday, May 24. Laura also made birthday cakes on these days.

Dr. Brookes always joined them for Sunday dinner and a weekly chess game with Jacob.

The first Sunday that the doctor was there after the boys arrived, they were all given physical examinations and all passed, with the exception of Timothy. His throat was very sore, and he had inflamed tonsils that needed removing after the swelling went down. He was still able to work, and Alex removed the tonsils a few weeks later. Jed told the doctor about the occasional chest pains he suffered, but Jacob still never told him about his own symptoms.

Every Sunday the doctor brought the news from town. Jacob was always interested in business, farming, and whatever Alex heard about the States. These were difficult times there, and the south and north states were having a difference of opinion over slavery. Someday, it was feared that this may lead to trouble in the form of a civil war, but no one wanted to be the first to step over the line and start military action.

Alexander enjoyed his visits to Jacob's plantation. He was happy to see his nephew and his wife so content to be helping Jacob. Alex was beginning to notice that Jacob was twitching and seemed to be dizzy when rising from the table. Jacob said to him on several occasions, "Don't worry so much about me, Alex. I'll be around to challenge you to chess for a long time to come yet!"

But then Laura spoke up and said to the doctor, "Sometimes I see Jacob stumble when he walks. He's having trouble with his vision too, and he holds his chest sometimes." Jacob gave a disapproving look but knew she said it through concern for him. Alex was indeed happy that Jacob had someone living with him who cared for him. He was in good hands with Andrew and Laura.

Alex was not overly worried about these symptoms at first but asked Laura to write down Everything, and he would go over it carefully to see the progression of what Jacob was experiencing, but so far, it was undiagnosed. Jacob didn't want to take the time off to go to a hospital and have tests done. That meant he would be away from the plantation, and he did not believe there was anything seriously wrong. Alexander tried every week to get Jacob to come for the tests, but the answer was always the same: "No, Alex, I don't have time!"

On Sundays the boys would all get together after the barn chores, and they would go for a walk around the plantation. The second day they were there, they discovered Jacob had a small pond on the grounds. It was freshwater, and the boys asked if they might get in to wash themselves and their clothes. It was okay with Jacob, and they were provided with two large cakes of lye soap per month.

After the first week at the plantation the boys decided that Jed would be their cook. Jed said he would be happy to do it. He was allowed to go into the house to watch Laura prepare food, and she taught him much. He also got to spend some time with her. She came to look upon him as a sort of son.

Word got around the island that Jacob had good workers at his place. A couple of plantation owners took it upon themselves to invite themselves to tea one afternoon. The visitor's "drill" was put into action. Andrew was out in the field yelling at the slaves; they were told to remove their shoes and shirts and prepare for rough treatment. While in the hold of the *Destino*, each boy got whipped on the back once or twice, just for good measure. They had really done nothing to deserve it. The other plantation owners saw the scars and knew they had clearly been punished properly. They automatically thought Jacob had done it. The visit went well, and the other owners never suspected that Jacob was treating them with kindness, instead of terrifying, brutal cruelty.

The boys were doing an incredibly wonderful job in the sugarcane field. Production increased over time, and Jacob was doing very well financially because of their hard work. After they had been with him well over a year, Jacob was starting to see that the boys were growing in shoe size, stature, and loneliness; and Laura started needing more help around the large house.

Jed did quite a lot now in the house for her so she could rest once in a while. He was indispensable in the house, in the barn, tending to the animals and vegetable garden, and driving Jacob or Laura to town sometimes.

One day, Jacob thought that the boys needed female companionship. This was when he decided to buy more slaves. Along came Afua (Mary), Esther, and Amelia. The day they were brought to the plantation was one of Jed's happiest days since leaving home.

During the last year and a half, there was an unnatural relationship between Timothy and Isaac. The other boys never said a word to Andrew or Jacob. They all knew with Jacob's strong religious beliefs, this could mean they would be punished or sold. No one in the main house ever knew the two boys were homosexual.

The three girls brought home from the slave auction were welcomed by the boys. The boys were so excited to see the girls that first day their excitement was actually showing, and not only by smiles. They were embarrassed, but the girls were too overwhelmed by everything to notice.

The girls would have their own cabin. They had their own cots, pillows, quilts, and mattresses. They felt like queens. Laura was to take measurements of the girls and would make proper working dresses out of Negro cloth for each girl, and they also had an undergarment. Mary was allowed to keep her Kente cloth robe, and she was allowed to wear it on Sundays.

They were shown around the plantation by Andrew and Jed. Jacob wanted everyone that worked there to see all aspects of a well-run plantation. The girls would eventually be taught English by the boys.

They found it much easier than when the boys learned; the boys used the African word first, and then the English word.

Mary was purchased for Jed in a way. When Jacob saw him lose his heart on the dock that day, he *had* to buy her. Mary was just as happy to be with Jed. She was to be the main girl servant in the house. She mostly helped Laura in the kitchen. The other girls were taught how to make beds, dust, sweep, cook, and look after the slave cabins. As Jed was getting busier and had more duties to perform, the girls eventually made the meals for all the slaves, and they would eat together. The girls would be given their noon sandwiches and milk in the outer kitchen in the house. Jed ate lunch with them and was always trying to get close to Mary, but Laura kept an eye on them.

A couple of months after the girls arrived, Mary was sick. She was vomiting all the time, and she was getting fat. Laura was shocked! She believed that Mary was pregnant. Mary had no idea what was happening to her. Laura asked Jed if he ever touched Mary or saw her without any clothes on, and he said, "No, ma'am!" He almost felt offended that Laura would ask this of him. Laura asked Mary if another man ever lay on top of her an right then, Mary started to cry. She told Laura about the voyage and her "punisher" and what he did to her. Laura talked to Jacob.

Sunday came and Dr. Brookes visited as usual. After talking to Jacob, he took Mary into another room. He did an examination, and he confirmed Mary was pregnant. Everyone was shocked to find out. Mary was so ashamed. Jed was hurt by it, but he still loved her and wanted to protect her forever.

One day Jed asked Jacob if it would be all right if he asked Mary to "jump the broom." Since Jacob did not understand this, he and Laura listened while Jed told him about this old African Ashanti custom of getting married. It was very common for young teenagers to marry and move to a private hut, away from their parents' hut.

The Ashanti tribe created this ceremony to solemnize a marriage. As they make promises to each other in front of their guests, a broom is waved over their heads. This was to ward off spirits.

The broom had two major symbols. One was the wife's commitment to cleaning their house and the courtyard in front of it. Second was to determine who would run the household. Whoever jumped higher over the broom, and it was almost always the man, was the decision maker in the home and head of the household. It represented the coming together of two families, their commitment to each other, and their strength, love, loyalty, and, most of all, respect for each other. Jacob agreed to let them have a little bit of Africa there on the island of Jamaica.

Jacob gave his permission, and he and Andrew picked the date of October 10 since it was the beginning of the harvest, and they could afford to take a Saturday afternoon off. With having Sunday off, this was considered enough time off for the slaves to enjoy the weekend and celebrate with the wedding couple.

Now Jed would understand what the third cabin was for. This cabin was to be used by a married couple. It was made ready for Jed and Mary to share after their wedding.

Chapter 4

A Bonnie Honeymoon at St. Andrews

AFTER SAYING GOOD-BYE TO THEIR families, Diana and John left for their honeymoon at St. Andrews Golf Course. Even though there were no bedrooms at that time in the clubhouse, Old Sam decided that he wanted to give them the use of his flat for their honeymoon. This was to be his gift to them.

He stayed that week at the McDonalds' farm. He was still afraid to stay overnight at the McGees and vowed never to set foot in their barn since the apparitions there changed him. He drove back and forth to work each day that week.

They stayed for the week, enjoying days of golfing, tennis, walking, and talking. In the evenings they read from their Bible and, through the nights, spent their time in each other's arms, enjoying the romance of a newly wedded couple.

On Monday, Tuesday, and Wednesday they played at least eighteen holes of golf each day.

They had an enjoyable time playing and meeting new people. Most people were accompanied by caddies, but John and Diana chose to keep to themselves and not use any. To make things interesting they challenged each other to a bet for the final game of their week.

While playing all week, there were a few times they let the more serious people play through, so as to not be in their way. They were just there to have fun . . . at least at the start. John was keeping score all week. He was slightly ahead, and he was secretly pleased with himself. Diana was allowed to start closer to the holes due to golfing rules for the more gentile sex, but they always stayed together for each other's shots. Walking hand in hand, they discussed their play, and John, being more experienced, was able to help Diana with some of the small errors he found her making. He was very patient and Diana was a quick study.

A couple of times in the afternoons, they both were allowed to play on the smaller caddies' course. Diana found this one easier, and it gave her practice to keep up with John on the old course. She would need the practice for their important game on Friday.

When they awoke on Thursday it seemed darker than usual. After pulling the curtains open what they saw was a great disappointment—*rain*! What a horrible start to their day, for they wanted to get out and practice. This was the last day before the "big game." They spent a lazy morning in the flat. After Diana had made some lunch, which Sam joined them for since he couldn't work outside with the rain teeming down, they all took a stroll through the clubhouse.

There was a billiard room. Ladies were not allowed to play, for it was undignified, but since there was hardly anyone around, Diana tried her hand at it. John had played a few times and was no expert by any means, but they still had fun. There were a few people playing cards in another room. They went in there and had a drink while watching the game and enjoying this relaxing time together.

Then came Friday, the day of the big game!

They both had breakfast, although Diana was nervous and didn't eat much. At 10:00 a.m., John and Diana picked up their rental clubs at the shop. They were lucky enough to reserve the same set of clubs every day. Since she had the same clubs all week, Diana felt confident. It made no difference to John since he was more experienced, no matter what clubs he used. Diana got eight strokes on their match-play minitournament.

They strolled arm in arm to the first tee, a 370-yard par 4. Diana liked this first hole. It was challenging due to the winds off the North Sea. John was able to make it in three shots, Diana in five. Her first drive was her first chunk shot of the day, and she was so embarrassed;

it wasn't a good start. Since it rained so much on Thursday, there were puddles everywhere. People who knew about their bet started to watch them play. As they both walked to their balls, they held hands, and folks could obviously see the love between them.

The second hole, a par 4, 411 yards with four bunkers, had a narrow fairway. Both drives were good; Diana did not chunk this one. Each knew their second shot should be to the right. Both second shots were average. As Diana did a great chip shot to get on the green, John did the same, and their balls now lay within ten feet of each other and only seven feet from the pin. Their putts were great, and they both finished the hole in four. They came upon their first large puddle of the day. John picked up his wife and gallantly carried her to the other side, and she tousled his hair affectionately when he set her down. This was the first of many times he carried her that day, as there were many puddles. It seemed to Diana that she spent a lot of time in her husband's arms that day, and she happily smiled each time he picked her up. He was her knight in shining armor.

One of Diana's strengths was chipping. She was really comfortable with her pitching niblick and had been constantly applauded all week even by the men, for she showed such form and promise. John's strength was driving.

When they reached the fifth hole, which they both regarded, as most players did, to be difficult, they both double-bogeyed this long right dogleg par 5. Here there were seven bunkers to avoid. They had trouble with this hole all week and learned that they would need to drive to the left. All of a sudden, John noticed that on Diana's drive she broke her club at the hosel. Since they were not accompanied by a caddie, John said, "To make this a fair game, I guess we'll have to forfeit and start over again. There should be someone to keep watch on the balls where they lie, so you can go back to the shop and get a new club." Diana was very disappointed.

All at once they saw two caddies walking toward them who had been closely watching their game. One of them said, "Please don't forfeit the game. It would be such a shame. I'll stay with your husband, ma'am, while Jimmy here escorts ya to the shop to get a new club, if ya don't mind. Would this be a help to ya both?"

She smiled and said, "Yes, thank you. That would be a great help!"

When Diana got back to John, she saw a crowd gathering. Everyone now was interested in this husband and wife's game and who would win the bet. On the next hole, Diana, using her new club, did her second and final chunk shot of the day. This was more humiliating than the first, since more people were now watching. John came up to her, hugged her, and tenderly kissed her on her cheek. As he did, she felt a special warmth that made her remember why she loved him so.

One of the easiest holes was number eleven, a par 3, which they both birdied. The longest hole at 523 yards was a par 5. This was the fourteenth hole. They had to avoid the famous "hell bunker." Diana parred the hole while John got another birdie.

As they walked toward the seventeenth tee, John said, "I am one up with two holes to go in our match play, and you get your last stroke on this tough hole."

"I have a good feeling about this hole," she replied. John placed his ball on the tee box, took out his cleek, and smacked the ball in the fairway, where it rolled into a puddle of water. Without saying a word, Diana walked to her tee box, selected her spoon, and swung with all her might, almost losing her balance. The ball sailed to the left of the fairway and landed on dry grass, past the wall of the hotel on the right.

As they walked up the fairway, John mumbled something about his lousy wet lie. He took out his trusted 160-yard club and hit the ball slightly fat, creating a big splash and spraying mud on his pants. The ball only went about one hundred yards. Diana tried hard to suppress a giggle as she got ready for her second shot. She took out her Mashie 7 iron, hit the ball on the sweet spot, and it landed on the green, fifteen feet from the pin.

"Great shot!" John called out as he finished wiping off his pants. He walked the short distance to his ball, and with his sand wedge, he hit the ball a few feet closer to the pin than Diana's ball.

As they got to the green, Diana carefully studied her line to the cup and putted the ball within two feet. John shook his head and said, "With your stroke here, I cannot win the hole. It all comes down to the eighteenth, winner takes all."

"You know," she replied coyly and confidently, "the eighteenth is my favorite hole." They both drove the ball well off the tee in the fairway. John's second shot landed on the far end of the green, quite far from the front pin. Diana's second shot landed short in a depression in front of the green called the Valley of Sin. They walked up the fairway quietly together, with the cool breeze in their face and their hearts racing with excitement. John wished her luck and kissed her as they separated and strolled toward their balls.

Diana was first up. She had a tough chip up the big swale to the front pin. She breathed in deeply, trying to ignore the people watching around them and, from the clubhouse, chipped the ball beautifully over the mound. It stopped two feet past the hole. This brought a nice round of applause from the gallery.

John had a long downhill putt, and he hit the ball too softly for the wet grass, and the ball stopped fifteen feet short of the hole. It was his turn again, and he knew this was do or die . . . sink the putt or lose to Diana. He looked at the putt from all angles, and after what seemed like an eternity to her, he hit the ball smoothly, but it just lipped out. Diana confidently putted the two-footer in the cup and raised her hands in victory! John gracefully embraced her and humbly declared that he wanted a rematch. He took her clubs as a gentleman, and they happily walked to the ancient clubhouse for a well-deserved drink.

During this week they spent a lot of time planning their long lives ahead of them. They loved their life in Cupar and never imagined ever leaving it.

On Saturday after they got home, Diana and John, while glad to be in their new home, were sad that the honeymoon had to end. It was now time to pay the piper. The bet was now to take effect. It did, and they would keep the details of it between themselves, until the end of their days!

Old Sam moved from the McDonalds' farm back to his flat. The McGees had always looked after Sam since his traumatic experience in their barn too. One day he and Mr. McGee had been working in the barn during a severe thunderstorm, blowing up gale-force winds. The animals were inside for their protection. Everyone was uneasy for some reason. Mr. McGee went to the house to make sure everything was okay there.

While he was in the house, an apparition showed itself to Sam. Legend had it that Laird Beardie, 4th Earl of Crawford, was away from his own castle, not far from where the McGees lived.

He was visiting Glamis Castle. While drinking, he demanded to play cards. The Lord of Glamis refused due to the fact it was the Sabbath. Laird Beardie insisted, "I'll play with the devil himself!"

A knock came to the door, and an unknown visitor came and played cards with the earl. The earl lost and the devil took his soul.

There was much noise and lightning to be seen and heard by the servants through the closed door. When one peeked into the keyhole, they were blinded. It is believed that the earl and the devil are still in that room, but Old Sam believed they had moved back to the earl's castle nearby to gather more souls. He saw them in the McGees' barn, where the devil wanted to play cards with him. He fled in terror, knowing he would lose his soul. He ran until he collapsed. When he came to, he had a hard time getting up. Mr. McGee was standing over him and waiting to see him move.

Sam eventually moved; he wasn't dead or paralyzed, praise God! But Mr. McGee could not believe his eyes. Before him, the tall, lanky brown-haired nineteen-year-old boy had transformed into a wrinkled white-haired man showing an elderly stature. He helped Sam get to his feet, but he could barely walk. After struggling to get Sam up, Mr. McGee decided to take him into the house instead of the hired-hand cabin where he lived. He laid him on the bed and directed his daughters not to go around and bother him.

He set out right away to fetch the town doctor, regardless of the storm. When they returned, Sam was in great emotional pain. The doctor was certain that he had a nervous collapse. The doctor said he was not to be moved for a few days to let him rest and regain his faculties. The doctor gave him sedatives.

Sam was in the McGee home for several days. When he finally was able to talk about his experience, he said he'd have to leave his job and that farm. He could never return to that barn again. He would never do farmwork again. The McGee family would always care for Sam in some way for the rest of his life.

Diana and John started their life together, both tending to the animals and the potato crop and dreaming of the success they would make of their farm. Their first year together, the crop was fine. Then came their second year, which brought them as much happiness as their first.

Unfortunately the next crop of potatoes was bad. There was a cool damp summer, and they started to fear that there could possibly be a bad year for their potatoes, just like what brought on the Irish Potato Famine several years earlier. Their crop was harvested, and they had a cold room full of potatoes that would last over the long cold winter. During the winter though, their stored potatoes, along with most farms in the Highlands and parts of Ireland, started to become infected with zoospores.

The zoospore, a rapid-growing fungus, spreads through the crops faster than cholera through the human population! Stored potatoes were rotting at a tremendous rate. People were eating the infected tubers and the death toll was high. In previous famines, the McDonald farm was spared death because they knew the early signs and destroyed their crop, but this time they were not so lucky. Many families in the area suffered, but not nearly as bad as in the past. This time it cost the McGees and McDonalds terribly. Diana's father died and so did John's mother and two farmhands. Diana and John feared for their lives too, but they remained healthy by importing other foods for the winter. The potato crop was a complete financial disaster for many in the Isles and Europe, so some decided to try for a new life in a new land.

Johnny and Diana heard Canada was a good place to start over. There were vast farming lands, good climate, and they could be happy there, planning a family and starting a new potato farm.

John and Diana thought about their future in Scotland and felt that there were better opportunities in the New World. The families had given them what money they could spare for the move. John sought out a ship to carry them, their possessions, and some livestock to Canada.

Since the slave era was over and there were no wars to fight, there were a great many ships that were not being used. Many ships were refitted to have passengers and had stalls built in the holds to carry animals that were being transported too. John came home one day from town and told Diana the good news. He had booked passage on an older wooden brig ship that had a successful career in the transporting business. John met with the captain. He was a gentleman, and John could tell that he loved his business. Captain Montgomery had been captain of his own ship for just under two years.

Captain Montgomery was married and came from a well-to-do family in England who helped him set up his transport business. The previous captain of this ship had died in prison, and the ship was sold for very little money. He did all the renovations to the ship himself. Being British, he still had to follow the Act to Regulate the Carrying of Passengers in Merchant Vessels. It limited the number of passengers he could carry. It also regulated the amount of space they would have and that there be enough food and drink for all. He decided to build several stalls in the lower part of the ship. This would allow people to move lock, stock, and barrel! Animals were welcome, but people had to book their passage and pay for them too. There was a nominal fee per animal.

After they were finished working on the ship and he got all his proper papers in order for the business and sailing licenses, he and his wife decided that they would rechristen the ship by its original name. They felt that they were helping people start new lives and that where he took them to was their destiny. He renamed this ship the *Destino*!

By the time John met Captain Montgomery, he had already completed several crossings of the Atlantic. Some were enjoyable trips, and some were lengthy due to bad weather. He never lost a person or animal on any of his crossings. There were illnesses once in a while and a few babies came into the world on his ship, but he carried a nurse with him. Mrs. Montgomery sailed with him always, and she looked after everyone's medical well-being. She was an army nurse before she met and married Captain Montgomery. He was also fortunate enough to find crewmen who were acquainted with the ship. At one time or another, a few of the sailors he hired, he discovered, were members of the crew that served on this very ship before he bought it.

John and Diana had left the farm to their families. While packing, Diana remembered to bring the horseshoe for luck in their new home and a new country and also took down the marriage kerchief from their wedding ceremony.

The day came for John and Diana to head for port to set sail. They had their families with them for their good-byes, which was a mixture of happiness, sadness, and excitement. They had a wagon of personal belongings and small furnishings to get them started setting up house. There was a locked area in the ship's hold to store your belongings, which John arranged and paid for. He let the family keep his wagon. He would purchase one when they landed in Canada. They took two of each of the Angus cows, Clydesdales, and Shetlands with them. Due to the refitting of the ship the stalls that were built were a decent size.

Each family that traveled with animals was strictly enforced to look after their own livestock.

They must go to the holds frequently and see to their care. They were to shovel their waste off the ship twice a day for the comfort of all passengers and animals. John and Diana didn't mind this at all. They both were feeling homesick and apprehensive about their move already but trusted their faith in God to see them through. As they met people on the ship like themselves, starting new lives too, they relaxed and enjoyed most of the voyage.

These people were sailing to what was considered by past generations of Scots as New Scotland. These first immigrants arrived from Scotland in Nova Scotia, Canada, in 1622.

John and Diana had heard good things about a place in Ontario. This was in the middle of Canada and meant that there would first be a ferry ride from Nova Scotia to New Brunswick, and then the land ride would be many weeks, about 1,500 miles inland from the east coast of Canada.

During their crossing, there was one storm that was a menace. It was bad enough to cause much seasickness, and the ship was blown off its course. This storm made the trip about one week later than expected. If Captain Montgomery had not been able to correct their course, they were sure to get to Greenland!

It was common for ships to be plagued by storms and even hurricanes during their crossings. Hurricane season on the Atlantic was from May to November. There were several captains that refused to travel during this half of the year. But some, like Captain Montgomery, felt that if he were careful and trusted in the Lord, he would make all his crossings a success. There were, however, many ships that took people, animals, and valuable cargo to a watery grave, never to be heard from again, and families were left to wonder their fate.

Partway through the trip, there was a crew member, who was quiet most of the time . . . until he got into the Scotch whiskey. The drink loosened his tongue, and he started to regale tales about his previous experiences on this ship. Late one night, he was bragging to the men who were drinking with him. He told them of the days when slaves were brought from Africa to Jamaica. The more he drank, the lewder he got with his stories. He stood up to make his speech, but the rolling of the waves below knocked him to his seat again. "Gentlemen, I had the greatest pleasure of my life on one trip on this ship. There was this girl and men. I tell you, she was beautiful . . . for a darkie. I took her one night and she was sweet!" The men laughed, not sure of whether to believe him or not. He told them of her special robe she had made and how he washed it for her on the nights he would use her. He made it sound like she was willing, but the undertones of his tale told a different story. John and Diana were still awake reading their Bible and could not help but overhear this yarn being spun, since the drunken crewman was getting louder. Diana felt such pain for the girl. It was a tragedy that she was kidnaped for slavery. That was bad enough, but the constant rapes must have been torture for her. She wondered how old the girl was and whatever became of her.

As they neared the Canadian coastline, everyone was excited. It had been a good trip across the Atlantic, with the exception of Mother Nature's detour. But Captain Montgomery delivered all his passengers and the livestock to their new home in twenty-four days. They had finally docked in Nova Scotia.

Canada had a land mass of over three million square miles. The McDonalds were going to be very proud to be owners of many acres of it someday. During the 1850s there had been an economic boom with Canada's railways expanding. Eighteen fifty-eight was a good time to be moving to Canada.

The passengers of the *Destino* were glad to be reaching the port of Annapolis Royal. It was a coastal town on the Bay of Fundy. It served as the capital city of the province from 1710 to 1749. When Halifax was founded, it was declared Nova Scotia's new capital.

Across from the docks was the town livery stable and blacksmith shop. John left Diana to stay with their belongings and animals and walked across the road. He introduced himself to the owner of the stable and then said, "My wife and I just arrived here from Scotland. We need to purchase a covered wagon that will take us inland to Ontario."

The proprietor looked at John with understanding and compassion. He too was a Scottish immigrant some twenty years earlier. He sold them a covered wagon that held all their belongings, with room for more. John was also given a booklet by the man. You might say this book would become the second bible of the McDonald homestead, the *Farmer's Almanac*. John and Diana would trust in this book too. They were to find it most useful every day of their lives. During the days of their long journey, Diana would be reading from the almanac by day and their Bible by evening.

In Canada a male farmer could buy 160 acres from the Canadian government for only a $10 registration fee and a promise to cultivate forty acres and build a permanent dwelling within three years. For another $10 registration fee you could also buy the neighboring lot of another 160 acres, if it were available. They were hoping for a 320-acre farm if there was an area this size available.

While John was purchasing a wagon, Diana talked with people around the docks. She was always interested in history, and since this was their newly adopted homeland, she was going to start learning about it. Diana discovered among other things that this quaint port town was originally called Port Royal before Annapolis Royal.

The trip John planned, he estimated, would probably take about three to four weeks. Not only would they use their Clydes to pull the wagon, but the cows and the ponies also had to trail along. This could slow them down immensely. They would travel as far as they thought the animals could go during the day, and at night they'd set up camp. The weather was cold at night this time of year, but the covered wagon would provide a warm shelter and keep them dry during the rainy days and nights. The animals needed to remain healthy too. He thought they could graze during the day at several stops, and there would always be water for them in their travels since the route John laid out included traveling along, or near, the St. Lawrence River, Lake Ontario, Credit River in Ontario, and a small part of Lake Erie.

After wiring the family in Scotland to let them know they survived the ocean crossing, they boarded a ferry that would take them to St. John, New Brunswick.

After St. John, they went through Westfield, Fredericton, Woodstock, Grand Falls, and Edmunston. Here, and at all the towns, villages, and cities they went through, they could easily buy what food they needed for themselves and the animals. It was also the opportunity to talk with people to get to know their new country.

People were friendly and helpful during this first leg of their journey. When they came to pass through Quebec, however, they felt like they were lost and had crossed into a new country.

Some of the Quebec communities they traveled through included Rivier-du-Loup, Montmagny, Quebec City, Trois Rivieres, Joliette, and Montreal. Neither of them spoke French, so it was difficult to make people understand what they wanted when they stopped for food, water, etc. When they finally made it through Quebec, they were relieved. It was good to be talking to people who understood them again. Their journey seemed to pass slowly due to the rest stops they had to make for the animals, but there was also so much to see in this beautiful land, and they met so many kind people.

Finally they had reached Ontario. They were getting closer to their new home. As they followed Lake Ontario, and then Erie, they loved the land. It was so vast and fresh looking—ready to be worked. Diana was keeping a diary of their trip as they went along. She was very diligent at it because she wanted to be able to tell their children and grandchildren about their grand trip. In Ontario, some of the places they forged through were Cornwall, Smith's Falls, Brockville, Kingston, Belleville, Coburg, Bowmanville, Oshawa, and the large city of Toronto (or York as it used to be called), which scared them a little since it was bigger than any other place they had been through. After Toronto, they carried on to Oakville, Milton, and Woodstock. This was the second Woodstock they had traveled through, and they thought this funny. Next, they came to London and St. Thomas.

The area they were going to was considered southwestern Ontario. The area's climate, they would find out, was moderate humid continental. The region could have hot, humid summers and cold winters. It is considered to be milder than the rest of the provinces and could allow for longer growing seasons. They could expect severe thunderstorms from March to November. Ontario had always been considered dominant in the agriculture industry. This part of their education they received from the almanac. They were becoming knowledgeable about the land before they arrived.

By reading the almanac, they were both to learn much. They learned what the best crops were to plant by regions and when to plant by weather forecasts. It let you know where you could buy farm machinery, where the seed and feed stores were, and it also covered astronomical data. For the women there were fashion trends, home decor, the care and preserving of food, and gardening articles. Albeit it was an American publication, because they were planning to settle just over the border in Canada, they were able to stick close to the planting and weather charts for Michigan State since it was less than a two-hour ride to the border of the United States of America. The almanac even had printed the story of how President Abraham Lincoln used the publication in court, defending a man who was charged with murder. An eyewitness claimed he saw the crime committed by the light of the moon. Lincoln had the almanac for reference, and it was discovered that the witness lied, because the moon was in the first quarter and lying low . . . near complete darkness, making things very difficult to see at night. This gave them all a chuckle in the courtroom. Diana and Johnny had even enjoyed the story Before leaving Scotland, they were given advice to go to an area in the southwest of Ontario, where the land was very fertile and ready to work with and be planted in. Since they were traveling in spring, there was some urgency to find a spread and plant their crops. This would have to be done while also building a house and a barn at the same time. With some luck they might be able to purchase a ready-built farm, with a barn and house already built and land ready to be planted in. This was not a likely possibility, and they knew that, but it was nice to dream about. They still were aiming to own a 320-acre farm where they were going to plant potatoes. It would be just like their Scotland farm. The difference here was the climate, and the potato blights were nonexistent for the most part.

Finally they arrived in Chatham, Ontario, on a Monday. As they drove down the main street of the town, they noticed black people, and lots of them. They were, however, outnumbered by the white folks. They had never seen any black people before. There certainly weren't any in Cupar, Scotland!

"We're all God's children, John," Diana said with a smile. But nonetheless, it was different to actually see them walking and talking with white people, just like they were friends. John and Diana read in some newspapers on their journey that Americans were viciously arguing about the blacks and their position in the country. The Northern states opposed slavery while the Southern states were in favor of keeping the old traditions going. This included slavery. The opposition was so strong that there was talk of a civil war over it. John and Diana were shortly to learn that the blacks in this area had come by way of something called the Underground Railroad and that most "passengers" were runaway slaves from the Southern states.

There were many abolitionists in the Northern states and Canada who wanted slavery to end. But if you lived in the Southern states and agreed with abolitionism, you ran the risk of being killed for going against the Confederacy ideals. Many Canadians disagreed with slavery, and they supported and welcomed Africans. Many Canadians, in particular, Ontarians, were helpful in the Underground Railroad . . . whose last major stop was coincidentally in Chatham, Ontario. This system really piqued their interest for some reason.

John and Diana went to the land registry office in the town hall. There they met Jeffrey White, and he indeed had property for them to work on and *own*! John asked if there were any farms already built and for sale in the area. There were a couple. Little did they know it their dreams were about to become a reality.

Mr. White told them, "There are two different farms for sale, 160 acres each. One is to the north, just out of town about a half-hour away. It was abandoned a year ago due to lack of a good well and the distance from a river, lake, or other water source. Water for irrigation and personal use was not enough to sustain a farm and family. I really shouldn't be telling you this, since it is my job to sell the land, but I don't feel good trying to rook you into a bad deal. The crops all failed on this stretch of land. The family moved westward. The barn's almost falling down, and the house is overcome with rats . . . big ones. I'm not supposed to tell you this either, but to be honest, I like you both, and I really don't want to see you go there."

He continued, "The second 160-acre spread is to the south, about ten minutes out of Chatham. It has just been put up for sale this very week. The people fulfilled the three-year deal with the government regarding building the barn and house, and as a matter of fact, just last year they added a large driving shed. Instead of just clearing the forty acres required, they cleared all the land. In fact, these farmers were quite serious about the deal they made. Not only did they clear the land but they planted some hay and straw right away. This will be the third year for both crops. I believe they told me that there was another fifty acres that were ready to plow and plant whatever you see fit to." Was this too good to believe? John and Diana were both interested and enthusiastic.

Mr. White told them, "It's right on the Thames River." John and Diana grinned from ear to Ear . . . a little piece of home, they thought. First, the Thames River in the British Isles, and now another Thames River. They were starting to giggle and think this was all meant to be. Mr. White thought he had said something wrong.

John said, "Oh no, sir. I think we'll love this area fer sure."

Mr. White told them, "Since the land is already developed and ready to plant, we have to charge $100 for it. I know it's a lot, but it's ready to work. The other thing I can tell you is that there are also 160 acres on both sides of this property available and undeveloped and also along the river. If you choose to purchase it for the $10 fee since there is already a house on the other property, you will not have to fulfill the clause of buildings on the land, just clearing forty acres in three years on each property. So you could expand from the original 160 acres and have 320 acres if you like, or 480 acres, if you think you can handle it. And you can have it all for the price of $120."

They were excited for sure!

The government property agent suggested that they leave their wagon and animals at the livery, and he would drive them out to take a look. John asked, "If it be all right with you, sir, can m'wife and I take a bit o' time and discuss it over lunch now. I see a hotel and restaurant down the street. Would ye be recommendin' that it be a good place to fill the weary stomachs of travelers who left home sixty-seven days ago?" To look at them, you could tell they were tired.

The agent said to them, "Certainly I don't mind. The land is not going to be sold while you have your lunch. It will be still there after you are done. I'll promise ya that. Catherine's Eatery and Hotel is the best restaurant in the town, a bit pricey, but food's mighty good! As a matter of fact I'm meeting my wife there after her doctor's appointment. Would you mind if I introduced her to you after lunch is done? She doesn't get out much and is very shy, and I have an idea. Mrs. McDonald, you may be about the same age and will get on. Is that okay?"

Diana thought it would be a nice idea to meet her and said, "Please bring her by. Remember, we're new here and have no one else around. We could use friends too. As a matter of fact, why don't we get together for dessert and coffee after our meals? Would that be all right with you, Johnny?" John agreed. They really could use friends right now, someone to talk to after their long journey across half of the world. Real people to talk with. They looked forward to dessert.

John and Diana left the office and took the animals and wagon to the livery and talked with the proprietor, Adam, who happened to be the brother of Jeffrey White. He was happy to feed and water the animals as a favor to his brother and the newcomers. Right now, the McDonalds wanted to sit on a proper chair and have someone serve them a meal that they didn't have to make over a campfire. They also needed some privacy to talk about the farm deal.

Chapter 5

An African Wedding and Dangerous Escape

As time passed on the plantation, the boys were picking up the language but preferred to use shorter slang words. Jacob and Andrew often tried to correct them of their slang, but sometimes to no avail. The females, who were in the main house with Laura, were taught to use as much proper English as they could. Laura sometimes felt like their teacher and confidant, and she loved it. She loved her "girls." Some of the good habits and the language the girls were learning rubbed off on the boys a little.

Mary and the other girls looked up to Laura. They seemed closer than any other house wenches on most plantations. It was blossoming into quite a friendship, almost bordering on a maternal relation on Laura's part where Mary was concerned. Mary spent most of her time with her.

One day Mary saw something peeking out of Laura's sleeve. When she asked what it was, Laura pulled it out to show her and told her it was a handkerchief. It was beautiful linen with lace trim. Mary thought it was the most beautiful cloth she had ever seen. Laura told her Andrew gave it to her as a gift when they were courting. Mary could listen to Laura for hours about anything. She particularly loved hearing stories about their courtship and their wedding.

Mary was worried because her tummy was getting larger, and all she could feel was shame.

She was worried that Jed was marrying her for the wrong reason. She wanted to marry for love! One night as they stood together staring at the bright autumn moon, Mary finally got the nerve to ask Jed, "Does you really love me, Berko?" Sometimes they used their African names when no one else was around. It was their way of showing their young love and keeping their past African lives and memories alive. She was plagued by the question because her parents loved one another, but she always remembered her father saying to her mother, "The woman I love is the mother of my children." Mama would always turn to him, smile, and nod.

She wanted Jed to love her, just her! The baby was not his and she worried about this. She wanted to know that he was not just being noble and wanting to take care of her. She loved him and hoped his love for her was real.

He tried to reassure her, "Afua, I falled in love wit' you dat very minute I seed you on dat ol' dock in da town. When Jacob-Sir buyed you, I be da happiess I ever been. I knowed you was da one I be wit' till da end o' time. The chile inside youse not mine, but I'se gonna treat him like he be. I'se gonna be his papa juss da same." She knew Jed was special, but not until that moment did she realize how much. They held each other for a while and just stared again into the moonlight.

October 10 finally came. Plans were completed, and at 11:00 a.m. they all gathered in front of the slave cabins. The courtyard had been swept and tidied and decorated with some African paper decorations, which Jacob let them make and hang. All the decorations had to be made at night on their own time. He supplied the paper and other supplies they needed to make them. They all pitched in together to make them, even Mary and Jed.

Laura was preparing the wedding feast with Andrew's help. During their time at the plantation, the slaves often told Laura about a few African foods and dishes that they longed for. Jacob gave his permission for Laura to prepare some for the occasion. To everyone's delight, they were delicious. The ceremony was normally presided over by a village elder. Since there were no Ashanti elders there, they decided to ask Jacob to preside. His workers had come to see him as a father figure, and that was station enough to perform the ceremony.

Esther and Amelia helped to get Mary ready and dressed for the ceremony. Even though it was not Sunday, Jacob gave Mary permission to wear her Kente robe. The girls were allowed to pick flowers from Jacob's beautiful gardens to make a headdress for Mary and as decoration for around her wrists and ankles. They also made a beautiful bouquet for her to hold. They found some wild red roses and white lilies that looked beautiful together. When Mary was ready for the ceremony, Jacob looked at her and remembered a passage from the Bible. "She is clothed with strength and honor, and she can laugh at the time to come" (Proverbs 31:25). Mary would soon show the strength she drew from Jed, her new life, her robe, and her faith.

Jed was dressed in plantation pants. Jacob had provided a new pair, along with new shoes and undergarment for the occasion, but he wore no shirt. Jacob told him that would be inappropriate. Jed told him, "But, Jacob-Sir, in Africa, boys marry up wearin' only a cloth, coverin' . . . well . . . ya know . . . an' nuttin' else, 'less dey has deys own Kente robe." Jacob tried not to strip them of too much of their African heritage while living there, but there were some customs that Jacob could not accept and found barbaric, but despite his feelings, he let Jed marry with no shirt on.

Jed picked Timothy and Isaac to be the ones to hold the broom. They were pleased.

Everyone took their places and got ready for the ceremony. Dr. Brookes was invited to join in as well. He too was pleased to be witnessing this with his friends. Jacob allowed them to have the ceremony in Twi language and in English. The older boys knew some of the things that were said during the ceremony from the few they had been to at home in Africa. They taught Jacob a sort of blessing in Twi/Akan and a crude translation in English for the others to understand during the ceremony.

As the ceremony got underway, Timothy and Isaac handed Jacob the broom, and he waved it over the heads of the bride and groom to ward off evil spirits. At the same time they made their promises to each other. Jacob announced that the couple was going to recite their vows first in English and then in the Twi/Akan dialect. Jed started and was very nervous. He wanted to get it right. He began, "I, Jed, promises ta loves an' care fer ya, Mary, an' I'se will try in ever'way ta be worty of you'se love. I'se will always be hones' wit' y'all, kind, patient an' fergivin. But mose of all, I'se promises ta be a true an' loyal frien' ta ya. I do loves ya!"

Laura and the girls made a quiet giggle while Andrew and Jacob gave a caring smile of approval. Not to embarrass or hurt him, but because he tried so hard to remember the words, and he sped right through it all in one short breath. Next was Mary's turn. Laura had carefully rehearsed the vows with her many times, teaching her how to speak them in proper English. She spoke them slowly and clearly, and everyone was very proud of the way she spoke and for the sincerity in her voice and in her heart.

"I, Mary, promise to love and care for you, Jed, and I will try in every way to be worthy of your love. I will always be honest with you, kind, patient, and forgiving. But most of all I promise to be a true and loyal friend to you. I love you."

Next, she spoke the Twi translation to Jed:

"Me, Mary, merehy wo b s mm d wo, na mahw wo, Jed. Mm b mm den w kwan biara so ay de mm tumi, s de b y a wob d me. Mm di wo nokware; mm nya boaset ama wo; merenni wo ho yaw biara da. Ne titiriw no, merehy wo b s mm y w'adamfo pa a merenyaw wo da. Med wo."

The broom was given back to Timothy and Isaac, and it was time for the bride and groom to jump over it. Since Mary was pregnant, they all felt she could not be expected to jump very high.

Jed thought about letting her jump higher to win her place as head of the house. He also thought that it may hurt her someday if she were to find this out. So he jumped higher, and he became the head of the house according to Ashanti tradition. Berko Yaba was now wed to Afua Kakira.

Laura had prepared a large lunch for everyone. Instead of going up to the house, Andrew and Laura helped set up tables in the courtyard around the cabins, and the food was brought out and served here. They all ate together, with one exception. The whites sat at one table and blacks at the other. Thomas and Caleb had a surprise for the couple. They had made some primitive African musical instruments of drums and stringed gourds, which they played.

Jacob and Andrew decided to leave after eating and take their Saturday trip into town to collect the week's pay for the harvest. They all worked harder on Friday to make the crop quota for Jacob so they could have all of Saturday off. They had harvested a day and a half's work all on Friday. After lunch Laura cleaned up with the help of Amelia and Esther. The rest of the day was for celebration. Jacob's generosity was shown by even giving the slaves a large bottle of rum.

As dinnertime came, they did not have to retrieve any food from the main house since there were leftovers. As night fell, Jed and Mary retired to their new home . . . the marriage cabin.

There was an Ashanti tradition of carrying the bride over the threshold for good luck and prosperity. So Jed picked up Mary and took her inside. Nobody was to see them until they emerged from their home on Sunday. The rest of the boys already arranged it with Jed that they would take care of his Sunday chores in the barn and with the animals. He did not need to get out of bed early.

The six others carried on into the night, singing and drinking, with the boys getting drunk. They were so inexperienced with alcohol, it didn't take much.

Caleb had a notion for a long time to run off. He had a decent life here, but he craved freedom. The drunker he got, the stronger this feeling got. He told the others, "I'se gonna run tonight. Who comin' wit' me?" You could've heard a pin drop . . . even on the soft ground. No one answered.

Esther said, "You hush now. Don't you talk so stupid. You know Jacob-Sir will tarnish yo' hide when he catch up wit' you! What you gonna do fer food? Where you gonna sleep?"

Caleb continued, "I'se gonna leave when it be real dark. I'se gonna take food from da feas'."

Since Laura had made so much for the wedding feast, there was a lot. Caleb would take it with him.

He went on with his plan. "'Den I'se getting me a job someplace. Dey's niggers on da islan' dat's free. I finds me one ta he'p." He dressed up in all the clothes he had so he would not have to carry much. He wrapped up the food he was taking and said his good-byes. Off he went into the dark, dangerous night. Would they ever see him again? They all wondered.

As Saturday turned into Sunday, no one from the house came down to the cabins. Instead of Jed going up to the house to get their food for the day, Timothy went and got it. Laura had left it in the outer kitchen, including their lunch sandwiches. He didn't see anyone. He was relieved! This bought Caleb some more time to get farther away from the plantation. When Timothy got back to the cabins, Amelia took the food and started their breakfast.

Nobody talked much. They just thought and worried. Morning dragged into afternoon and then suppertime. Jed and Mary came out of their cabin around noon, and they had to be told. They were shocked. They had no idea that Caleb wanted to leave. Jed started, "Y'all knows Jacob-Sir punish us too. We knowed Caleb gone an' not tell him. Wha's he gonna do ta us?" The others hadn't thought about this.

Evening came and nothing was heard from Caleb . . . or the main house. They decided that when Andrew came to get them in the morning, they were all going to pretend to be shocked and that Caleb was there when they all went to sleep. He must have left through the night without anyone hearing. When Jed arose Monday morning, he had very quietly retrieved their daily food from the outer kitchen without anyone hearing him. He was glad he did not run into Laura.

Andrew came to collect the boys at 5:00 a.m. and was alarmed when Caleb wasn't there. He told the other three not to go to the field, and the girls would wait too. They were not to work until he told them they could go. For the second time since the boys were living there, their cabin doors were all locked from the outside. When Andrew reached the house, he ran in and found Laura and Jacob sitting down, talking over their coffee. Andrew said, "Jacob, Caleb's run off!"

Jacob choked, not believing his ears. "Why, Andrew? I've never treated them bad. They've all become my children!" He became more worried and continued, "We have to keep this as quiet as we can, or he could be shot down if the other slave owners or police knew a slave ran away." Jacob arose from the table and his legs started to shake. He lost his balance and fell, but Andrew and Laura caught him before he hit the floor. He was obviously shaken and needed to sit again. He said to Andrew, "You drive towards town, and I'll go down to the cabins to talk to the others."

"No, you're not, Jacob." Laura raised her voice. "The only way you are going down there is if I go with you!" Jacob gave in and said she could go with him. He was glad she was going; he was still shaky, and now his chest was hurting.

Andrew drove slowly toward town so he could scan the road, ditches, and what he could see of the fields he was passing. He knew it was more likely that Caleb had gone into the forested area to hide but continued along as Jacob asked. He passed many on the road this morning but was careful not to let them know a slave escaped. He saw slaves in fields along the way and wondered if he could trust them not to say anything if he inquired if they'd seen a runaway male slave. He took a chance. As he passed one plantation there were a few slaves close to the road.

He stopped his horse and asked if they had seen Caleb. The workers just kept their heads down and whispered to him, "'Scuse me, sir, we cain't talk. We see'd no one. If we does, who his name and massa?" Andrew quickly gave the information and rode off toward town. He looked around town and then doubled back to the Maisy-Lee.

When he got there, Jacob and Laura were not at the house, so he went to the cabins. Jacob was in the boys' cabin. He wanted to believe they didn't know about the escape, but there was no way Caleb could have gotten away without someone hearing. Laura questioned the girls and had the same feeling. They knew!

Jacob had no leads of where to look for Caleb. He felt that they should just leave it alone, and Caleb would have to take the punishment out there in the savage world of slaves and masters.

Jacob hoped by not raising the alarm for a runaway slave, Caleb had a chance to survive. He would gladly take him back, if the opportunity presented itself. Now he had to come up with a suitable punishment for the rest of his slaves. He couldn't let them know it was all right to disobey him.

From now on, the cabin doors would be locked at night and during lunchtime, while they ate. At night, to use the outdoor toilet near their cabins was not allowed. There would now be a pail inside of each cabin for their use.

When the boys first arrived at the plantation, Jacob had Andrew lock the cabin doors so they would not run away. Jacob was so much kinder than any other plantation owner could ever be, but they were not to know this for some time. After a while he started trusting them since there was no interest in running, even from the field when only Andrew was out there to supervise. They stayed, and they worked.

About two months after the boys arrived, their door would be left unlocked. The door was unlocked, and Jacob was convinced that there was going to be no disobedience on their part, and they would stay with him.

During their punishment, when the boys were in the field, they could not speak to one another at all. They could speak at lunchtime and at night while in bed, but that was it. The three boys would be going to and working in the field chained together at the ankle with no shoes on. Andrew now had to get the leg chains out of the barn. Jacob was given the chains when he bought the five boys.

Andrew chained Thomas, Timothy, and Isaac together without shoes on. Jacob let the boys decide who would be chained in the middle each day. That person would be shackled at both ankles, and the other two boys on each side were only shackled at one ankle. The chain between them was less than four feet long. They now had to figure another way to work since the rows of cane were farther apart than the chain. The work could not be done with each boy in a row by themselves. It was not possible to do three rows at a time. All three had to work in the same row.

The work was very slow. They had to spread out in the same row as far as the chains would let them and try to work the best they could. It was going to take a lot of practice to get it right, and without their shoes, their feet would be bloodied and sore in no time from the previous seasons' small, hardened burned stalks on the ground. Sadly, this would reassure Jacob they wouldn't run off while in the field. To compensate for the slower paced work, Jacob decided they would start one hour earlier and end one hour later each day. He expected the same amount as usual harvested each day. They were not in the field Sundays but were still working during their punishment.

Jed's punishment would be cleaning out the whole barn from one end to the other daily.

Even if the stall was not in use, it was cleaned every day. That included fresh straw and both the feeding and watering troughs kept clean and ready. Jacob would inspect them each day, which is something he didn't usually do.

Jed also had to keep the gardens looking their very best. Jacob must not see even one weed, or he would make Jed stand in the garden for an hour per weed, doing nothing but just standing in the hot sun one hour for every weed he found. After two weeds on the first day and one on each of the next two days, he would never leave another weed behind.

Jacob also split Mary and Jed up too. They could not sleep together during their punishment. All the girls were in one cabin and the boys in the other. The marriage cabin was locked.

They were still able to use their own vegetables for their meals, but there would be no meats, Fish, or chickens from the house during this period. They did receive their meat sandwiches at lunch. Jacob could not expect to get work done with undernourished workers.

Mary, Amelia, and Esther's punishments were extra work too. Mary stayed in the kitchen and outer kitchen mostly. She had to scrub the kitchens from side to side, top to bottom. She also had to wash the curtains in the kitchens daily instead of weekly. She had to help the other girls beat the carpets. After all the linens were dried, Mary had to iron them all. Mary was told she could not speak to Laura and only speak when spoken to. Laura felt awkward but had abided by Jacob's rule during their punishment.

The other girls still cleaned the rest of the house. They were now to take *all* draperies down, which they had only done once before, and now had to clean them weekly. *All* bedding and linens were to be washed daily, instead of weekly. *All* carpets were to be taken outside each day and beat until they were as clean as could be. The girls, like the boys, were not supposed to talk to each other while working all day. They could only talk in the cabins.

Jacob had been talking to Andrew about painting the total interior of the house and decided that on Sundays, the four boys and three girls would paint every room in Jacob's house. Jacob, Andrew, and Laura would be taking their turns on Sundays to supervise the painting to make sure it was done properly. Even Alex helped supervise when he came over.

The punishments were supposed to last a month and then things could go back to normal, with the exception of the locks. They would remain locked overnight but not at lunch. They would be able to eat their meals together, talk to each other, go back to their regular hours, and at that time, he would allow Mary and Jed to live together in the marriage cabin again.

Jacob was giving them the best life that they could probably ever expect to have in the slave world. They just had no idea how most plantations were really run. His punishments were really nothing compared to other masters! They knew nothing of the real horrors to slaves that went on at other plantations until neighboring plantation owner Ethan Jordan arrived for a visit one day.

Wednesday, the tenth day into their collective punishments, Jacob received a visit from a neighboring plantation owner. The word was given by Jacob, and Andrew told the boys, "Go into the slave act we taught you, until we tell you it's all right." They knew they could be given a light whipping for something serious or chastised for disobedience. They had to show fear at all times while Mr. Jordan was there. Having the chains on their ankles too would make it a more believable act they were putting on.

Ethan Jordan was a sugar plantation owner only a mile and a half away from Jacob's. He was a very tall, thin man in his fifties. He wore typical garb for a plantation owner. A white suit and hat, a black-string bow tie, and the meanest face you ever saw. He sported a narrow Spanish beard that included a type of handlebar mustache, which he was always touching or pulling on.

He came to Jamaica from Alabama about five years before Jacob arrived. Mr. Jordan was a man to be feared, and Jacob did not like him at all. He was a more typical plantation owner and treated his slaves with a hard fist and cruelty, mentally and physically. Jacob was not sure why he was being visited but tragically was about to understand.

The weather was beautiful that day, and Jacob hosted his company on the large veranda of his house. Mary brought them lemonade. Ethan took a sip and was offended. He threw it at her.

"Where is your rum, man?" Jacob was shocked with his rudeness and the early hour but said nothing about it to him. Mary looked to Jacob with a tear in her eye, and he nodded for her to bring out the rum. She came back immediately with it and set it down, along with a fresh glass. Mary also brought out the broom to sweep up the broken glass and ran back to the kitchen as fast as she could. She was scared of this man.

Ethan poured a large glass of rum while Jacob sipped his lemonade. "I heard a few disturbin' things about you and your farm, Jacob. People are starting to talk about some big troubles you're having here. In particular, yer niggers. On Saturday a week past," Ethan had begun, "my niggers told me of music and song they heard on the wind."

Jacob took a slow noncaring puff of his cigar, which was only one of two he had each day, against his doctor's advice, of course. He said, "Is that right?" He puffed slowly again and continued, "They hear music on the wind often, do they?"

Ethan cleared his throat, not sure if he was being mocked. "Yes," he continued, "they heard one of them Africa songs that tells a message. That's how they communicate between farms, you know. They tell each other news." Jacob became a little uncomfortable and twitched in his chair.

"Yeah, Jacob, one of my darkies told me the song they heard on the wind told of a wedding or that jumpin' the broom crap they talk about, taking place here between two of your niggers. Is this true?"

"Why, yes." Jacob told him, "I gave my permission for a couple to marry. What's it to me if they hitch together?"

Ethan's voice rose as he spoke. "Remember this, Jacob. The more you give in to their requests, the more trouble you'll have. Happened to me, you know. I let two of my niggers marry, and then they got the notion to run . . . they was captured, of course, and punished."

"Just how did you punish them, Jordan?" Jacob asked him as he started to become angry and nervous at the same time. Did he really want to know what this hardened, cruel master did to his slave couple when he hunted them down and caught them?

Mr. Jordan continued, "Well, seeing as I don't need any little nigger brats running around my place, I've seen to it that they're never going to be able to have any young 'uns . . . neither one of 'em." He had an evil smile on his face that Jacob became very afraid of. "You also might say they ain't going to run no more. It's hard to run with half of your foot missin' now, ain't it?"

Ethan thought about the marriage between Jacob's slaves for a moment and continued to smile as he said, 'Well, sir, after looking at your serving wench, I suppose it's her that married. I understand now . . . he had to marry her, eh?" He was now laughing boisterously.

Jacob was very offended and jumped up with an annoyed shout. "They married because they said they loved each other!"

Ethan laughed again, louder than the last time. "Oh, I see. The young 'un is yours, Jacob. That *is* a smart move. Make everyone think they are having the baby together, but what will everyone think when two niggers have a half-white, half-nigger baby?"

Jacob could stand it no more. He pounded his fist on the table, and it knocked him off balance a bit, but he stayed on his feet. He angrily said with a stutter, "I, sir, am n-n-not the child's father and am appalled that y-y-you or anyone would dare think so. Sh-she was tampered with on the way here on the slave ship and not by J-Jed. He was already living here when she arrived!' Jacob could not control the stuttering and was alarmed. He started to have bad chest pain and began to tremble all over as he flopped uncontrollably down in his chair again.

At that moment, Mary stepped back on the veranda with some cake for the gentlemen, and all at once Ethan Jordan leapt to his feet, grabbed Mary by the back of her neck and the back of her dress, and threw her down the seven steps to the ground onto her stomach, cake and plate flying through the air. "There," he said, "you have no more problem. No bastard's a comin' from this little whore! It's for the best, Jacob, I know." He very nonchalantly gulped down another full glass of rum.

Laura came running from the house, and Jacob rose to his feet again. Ethan took out his gun, pointing it at them and said, "Now . . . Jacob, there's no need to tend her. She's dead fer sure . . . maybe you can bury the two of 'em together!" He was smiling his most evil smile now while he spoke.

Laura and Jacob were confused and scared for Mary. "Are you insane?" Laura screamed.

The man furiously snarled, and the most fearful angry look came over him. It was frightening. They both thought Ethan would have shot them if aggravated more.

He was talking like a wild man now. "If you wasn't a white bitch, so high and mighty with your folks ownin' a store and your husband's uncle being a doctor in town, I swear you'd have my bullet in you so fast! No whore talks to me that way, white or black! You'd be fine to remember that. I hear the good doctor treats niggers too. Maybe you should tell him he would be good to watch hisself going out at night . . . to treat niggers! Something bad could happen to him. You never know what goes on after dark on this island."

As he turned away from them and started down the steps, he continued, "I also took care of another problem for you, Jacob." By this time Jacob was so uncontrollably shaking, he fell back into his chair again and had trouble breathing. "Down the road a piece, your overseer was talking to some niggers in a field . . . *my* field! He asked if they'd seen a runaway slave that belonged to you . . . name's Caleb, I understand. So being a good neighbor, I thought I'd help you track him, find him, and bring him back to ya . . . no thanks or compensation is necessary though, Jacob." As he spoke he was walking around the back of his wagon. Jacob wasn't sure what was going on, but all at once Ethan Jordan dragged Caleb's dead body out of the wagon and dropped it in front of Jacob and Laura. They were horrified. Such unbelievable savagery they had never seen before coming from one man.

Next, as if the last several minutes had never occurred, Ethan Jordan walked up the steps to the veranda and grabbed Jacob's bottle of rum. He said, "But I'll take this as a small token of your appreciation for my assistance." He got on his wagon and told Jacob, "Now you know how to treat yo' niggers properly, *Massa Marcus*!" He very calmly tipped his hat and drove away. Laura and Jacob were in shock.

Mary still lay on the ground *alive* and started to cry as silently as she could. When Ethan had stood over her, she never made a move, uttered a word, or cried. She even tried not to breathe but was in great pain. She now saw Caleb's body and he was not moving. She knew he was dead. It was all too much for her. She passed out from physical and emotional shock. Jacob rose and rang the dinner bell for Andrew. He heard it . . . but it was too early for lunch. He knew it must be an emergency. He gathered the boys and locked them in their cabin and raced to the house. Jacob told him to go get Alex.

As fast as he could, he unhooked the horse from the wagon and left for town to find the doctor. Laura was tending to Mary on the ground, trying to wake her. Jacob saw blood under her dress, lots of it. Laura and Jacob decided to leave her where she was until Alex got there. They brought out a pillow and blankets for her. The ground was hard and dusty. They tried to keep her warm. Laura tried to clean her up but also kept her eye on Jacob. He could be Alex's next patient if he wasn't careful. All he could do was sit on the steps, slightly holding his chest, breathing funny and watching Laura while waiting for Andrew and Alex to get back. He also thought of Jed.

Andrew found his uncle at the apothecary store and pressed him to come immediately. They were not long, and when Dr. Brookes got there he had Andrew help him get the girl onto an old couch in the back sitting room that was hardly ever used. Mary had awakened and was in full labor by now.

Alex estimated that she was seven months along, and the baby was not going to wait. He was very alarmed. He was starting to see the baby now, and its cap was a brown-grayish color. It was dying, or dead. There was no internal movement anymore. Mary screamed as the pain turned into one long agonizing contraction.

Jacob wondered if he should let Jed come up to the house to be with her, but the doctor said it was best if he was not in or near the house. Andrew was told to take the boys out to the field to continue working and to take Jed with them. The pain was torture for Mary. Jed would be terrified to hear her screams.

Alex brought his black bag with him. When he placed his stethoscope over Mary's heart, he heard it was racing and strong. He was relieved. When he placed his stethoscope over her uterus, however, he was supposed to be able to hear the baby's heart. He wasn't sure, so he added the new extension to the wooden stethoscope, which screwed into the chest piece. With this new section added, he was supposed to be able to hear the baby's heart much better. There was a faint beat, and it was getting fainter. Baby heartbeats are supposed to be strong and fast. This was far from it. The baby was in serious distress, and Dr. Brookes was not sure it would survive delivery, let alone coming out of this with no brain damage from the fall.

Mary was small. She was, after all, still a child. Her delivery canal was not large enough to handle the fetus, but it had turned and needed to be delivered . . . *now*! Alex had to cut her to make more room for the baby to come out. The episiotomy he performed would need four or five stitches to close afterward. Mary could no longer bear it; she passed out from the pain. Alex brought out some forceps and placed them around the baby's head. He had to turn the baby so that its head was in the anterior position. This made it easier to deliver. Mary could not help, so Alex had to pull it out with the forceps. He gently twisted and then pulled. The baby came out, and just as he feared, it was now dead. Mary had given birth to a very small stillborn mulatto boy. She was now hemorrhaging. Alex discovered that Mary had placental abruption. The placental lining was torn away from the uterus. It was a very bad tear, and her uterus was badly damaged from the fall. Alex was concerned for any other children she may have in the future, if she could have any at all.

They moved Mary into an extra bedroom upstairs in Jacob's house. Laura moved out of her and Andrew's cabin and into the main house to look after her. Alex left Laura some morphine for Mary's pain. When she awoke, she needed it.

Dr. Brookes was there at the plantation for quite some time that day, and he witnessed some of Jacob's symptoms. The shaking and jerking motions Laura told him about, stuttering when he spoke, and sometimes not able to put his sentences together. She also told the doctor that he'd been choking on food lately. Alex knew there was something seriously wrong and needed to run tests on him.

When Jacob felt better and steady on his feet, he and Alex went to tell Jed and the others what happened. Jed was scared but, in some small way, relieved that it was all over. He asked God to forgive his thoughts, but maybe they could get on with the rest of their lives and, God willing, have their own family someday.

It was a terrible day for everyone on the plantation and so soon after Mary and Jed jumped the broom. It wasn't bad enough with their punishment and emergency with Mary: But Jacob now had to tell everyone about Caleb's murder. Jacob expected the others would want some kind of funeral for him, or at least, he would say a few prayers, which he would make sure to include the 23rd Psalm.

Later that day, Alex examined Caleb carefully and reported to Jacob how he died. "Jacob, my friend Caleb was shot in the back. The front part of both feet were cut off by what looks like an axe. I don't think he died right away, Jacob. I think he bled to death slowly and painfully. He was whipped and his back is a mess. I'm so sorry, Jacob. I know what your boys mean to you," Alex had told him as gently as he could. Jacob's body went into a violent spell, a seizurelike fit. His limbs shook, he couldn't speak, and as he tried to walk toward Alex, he fell to the floor. Jacob clutched his chest and passed out.

When Mary finally became fully conscious the next day, Laura was by her side. Mary looked toward her and asked, "Where's Jed? Where's da baby?"

Laura looked at her through tears and told her, "Jed is working but has visited. Your baby died from the fall you had." Mary thought for a moment and started to remember Mr. Jordan visiting and throwing her down the stairs.

She looked at Laura and said, "Why was the man mad, and why did he throw me down the stairs? I doesn't understand, Laura-Ma'am. What did I do? I try to be a good girl. What I done to him?"

With tears in her eyes still, Laura held Mary, rocking her, saying, "Mary, there are going to be people in your life that will hate you and hurt you and your friends. They can't tell you why they hate you; they just do. Mr. Jordan is a mean, bad man. A murderer! He thought since the baby was not Jed's or Jacob's, he would take care of the problem by pushing you. That is what killed the baby.

It's sad, Mary, but there are no laws to protect slaves. Jacob has promised to never allow that man around here again. He feels really bad for you, Mary. After this happened to you, Jacob and I stayed in this room with you all night." She did not tell her about Jacob passing out too.

Jed was allowed to see Mary that morning and was happy to see her awake. He hugged her as gently as he could. They held each other a while without speaking. Laura let them have a few moments alone.

Alex dropped by to check on his patient. He was relieved to see her awake. Alex wanted to talk to Mary and Jed together, so his timing was good. He said, "Because your uterus—the place where the baby's food supply is and where the baby grows—tore really bad during the fall and suffered much damage, I have to tell you that it is very dangerous for you to have more babies. You would likely bleed really badly again, and you may not live if you try to have one. I'm not even sure you can ever get pregnant again, if you tried." They both were shocked and did not know what to say.

He told Jed to go back to work while he examined his wife. Alex was pleased with her condition. It was improving already. Being young and healthy, she had a good start on her recovery.

He told her, "Mary, you are a very lucky girl. You're going to be okay. Jed is very worried, but I'll tell him you will be all right. You can move back to your cabin tomorrow, and the day after that, you can get up and start to work around the cabin, but don't walk too far without help."

Jacob was now standing in the doorway of her room, and he said, "Alex, I think she should stay up here for a few more days. That way we can tend to her better."

Alex said, "Well, Jacob, that is entirely up to you. If you want to keep her here, that is fine."

Laura was glad that Jacob decided that.

Jacob said, "Alex, I've decided to let you take me for those tests now."

The doctor said, "Jacob, that's wonderful. I'm going to take a walk to the field to see my nephew. You get some things packed, and I'll get you when I come back up. I'll take you to the hospital myself, and we can start the tests to see if we can figure out what's ailing you, my dear friend." Jacob anticipated that Alex would want him to go right away and was already half packed.

On his way to the field, Alex went out to the barn to see Jed, who was tending the animals. He told Jed, "Mary will be fine, Jed, but you have to be gentle with her. You must not have relations with her for a few weeks. She needs to get her strength back. Jacob will be keeping her in the big house for a few more days. Maybe he'll say it's okay to see her at lunchtime. I know you are all still being punished, but with the way things have turned out, he may give his permission for you to see her at breakfast, lunch, and supper while she is up there. Remember, she is still not strong, and *you* must follow my orders too." Jed listened to the doctor intently and nodded his acknowledgment.

Alex walked out to the field to visit with Andrew for a bit and give him the news of the house. Andrew was just as concerned as the others about Mary, and his uncle let him know that she was going to be okay. Alex gave Andrew a fatherly pat on the back and asked when he would be coming back to deliver a baby for him and Laura someday. Andrew blushed and smiled, telling his uncle, "We really want a baby, Uncle Alex, whenever God sees fit to bless us with one. It's in his hands."

Andrew was surprised about Jacob and sighed with relief, saying. "I am so pleased that you have coaxed him to finally go to the hospital!"

A look came over Andrew's face, and Alex asked him, "What's wrong, son?"

"Is Jacob dying, Uncle Alex?" Andrew asked. He was afraid of the answer but needed to know.

Alex looked worried. "I don't know, my boy. I just don't know yet, but while we're doing the tests, the best thing we can do for Jacob is to run this plantation for him the best we can, look after his family, and pray, Andrew. He needs our prayers!"

When Andrew and Dr. Brookes returned from the field, Jacob was sitting on the veranda.

He had a small valise by his side. He had packed pajamas, shaving soap and a razor, and his robe and slippers. He had also packed his Bible. He would need it for comfort and strength. Jacob gave last-minute instructions to Andrew and Laura, and he was off to town with Alex to be admitted to the hospital.

Chapter 6

Potato Farm Beginnings

AFTER LEAVING THEIR WAGON AND animals at the livery with Adam White, John and Diana wearily went into Catherine's Eatery and Hotel and ordered food from a menu. Not from a river, stream, lake, or store—a real menu. They didn't have to clean it or cook it—just order it, wait for it to be served, and eat it! It was going to be the most glorious meal they'd eaten in over two months.

Catherine's Eatery and Hotel was the finest place for miles around. The hotel was modern, and the couple inquired about a room, just in case they didn't have somewhere to camp for the night. They decided to treat themselves to some luxury instead of the covered wagon, and Adam had volunteered to put up their animals for the night at the livery if they needed to. The deskman at the hotel assured them there were enough rooms, and they would hold one for John and Diana.

Since it was midday, they thought maybe they would like to have their large meal now, and if they didn't want to cook in the evening, they wouldn't bother. It was nice not to worry about stopping, setting up, making a fire, and cooking if they didn't feel up to it.

John ordered pot roast. It came with potatoes, carrots and green beans, as much bread as he wanted, coffee, and a slice of any homemade pie they had for his dessert, all for the inflated price of thirty-five cents. He thought he was in heaven! Diana was less hungry. She ordered a steak, almost two pounds worth, as she found out when it was served. It also came with three eggs, any way she liked, a huge portion of fried potatoes and onions, all the bread she wanted, coffee, and any kind of pie for dessert. Her meal was twenty-five cents. They were getting used to Canadian dollars instead of British pounds, shillings, pence, and so forth.

Before they began to eat, they gave thanks to the Lord, for they knew He saw them through their long journey, for guiding them to this new land, and for His many blessings.

John and Diana ate their lunch. They were so happy to be sitting in a warm room, on beautifully hand-carved wooden chairs, and having someone serve them a great meal, even if they did have to pay for it. It was worth it!

John had a big smile on his face as he devoured his huge plate of pot roast and vegetables.

As he ate, John was like an excited child and had every confidence that they could make the farm deal work, and he hoped Diana agreed with him. They made all of their decisions together, no matter what they were. It turned out she was just as excited as Johnny was. They were exhausted from their long journey, but they needed to discuss the farm business to see if they were not about to take too much on too soon. They hadn't seen the property yet, but to John, it all felt right!

Diana couldn't eat the whole steak. John smiled. He knew she'd never handle eating the whole thing. She had the kitchen wrap it in paper for her to take home. They gladly did it for her. They were used to it. Most women ordering their steaks could rarely finish them.

Diana started talking. "Johnny, m'love, it sounds perfect, I know, but do you really think that we can walk onto this farm and handle working it by ourselves? Four hundred eighty acres is a lot of land! We're so lucky to be looking at an existing farm. But do you really think we should buy the other two 160 acres around both sides? Remember, it is just you and I and 480 acres. Are we daft?"

As John stopped eating long enough to take in some coffee, he replied, "Sweet darlin', we won't have ta build another house or barn if they're not needed since we would be living on the center land, which is fully developed. Remember what Jeffrey told us? All we'd have to do is prepare the land and plant crops within the three years . . . of course we're daft, darlin'!"

They were told that the acreage was side by side by side. To the back of the lots was a road, which was becoming well used. There would be no other farms backing onto their property. And to the front of their property was the Thames River. It sounded so perfect.

Diana looked at her husband. He was so enthusiastic she did not want to spoil his excitement. She said as they laughed together, "Well, m'love, let's get Mr. and Mrs. White over here. They look like they've finished their lunch." John got up from his chair and went over to Jeffrey White's table. Jeffrey introduced his wife, Christina, to John; and John asked them to come and have their coffee and dessert with him and his wife. The three of them went to the table where Diana was waiting. Introductions were made and they sat down.

Jeffrey was beaming and said, "Christina just gave me the most wonderful news, and you are the first ones we want to share it with. We are going to have a baby!" Diana was envious but so happy for them. She began with maternity questions to Christina while their husbands talked property and farming. After an hour and the men had two pieces of pie each, the ladies turned to them and asked if they were going to spend the rest of the day sampling every pie in the restaurant or if they were going to look at property.

Diana said, "Christina, you must come with us and we can talk more. Now Johnny McDonald, let's go look at our new home and magnificent farm that we're to own." They all got up from the table. Johnny paid for the Whites' bill, as well as their own, as a gift of thanks and congratulations; and the four of them walked back to the livery to collect their wagon.

Adam had the animals fed, watered, and rested. He asked his brother, "Are you showing Property, Jeff?" His brother told him that he was taking this lovely couple out to the newly vacated property and farm and hoped that they would like it and settle.

Adam said, "Well, Mr. and Mrs. McDonald, I certainly hope you do stay. This is a great area to live and lots of great people live around here, white and black folks. You may be wanting some farm hands. I can tell you about a few black farmhands who are great workers. They work cheap and hard. If you have the notion, you could also let them have a small portion of your land to plant foods to provide their own families with. This would make the wages much less, and they do appreciate it. You just ask me, and I can give you some good recommendations. Would you be wanting a milk cow, Mr. McDonald? I just acquired a big beautiful Holstein this morning, and since Jeffrey nor I need one,

I'm at liberty to sell her, and she'll be needing milking this evening. You could have her for five dollars. She has a lovely black-and-white coat and is also in the family way, if you get my meaning!" Everyone laughed. John was very happy and immediately said yes and paid him the five dollars.

Adam continued, "Now are you all going out in Jeffrey's carriage, or are you taking both his carriage and your wagon? If you aren't taking your wagon, I'll release these magnificent Clydes to rest them a bit more."

Jeffrey said that if John and Diana wanted to go with them that would be fine, but maybe they should take the wagon. If the deal was made, he would help Diana and John unload their wagon, and John could just come back into town a little later to pick up the cows and ponies. John told Jeffrey, "Lead on, sir, we're right behind ye."

Jeffrey and Christina led the way. The farm was just a ten-minute ride outside Chatham. As they drew near the farm, the McDonalds became excited. On their way, they saw vast farmland with people working in the fields and others putting up barns and houses. They came upon the road that Jeffrey mentioned to them, and they followed it until they saw a huge beautifully built two-story farmhouse with a large barn and drive shed. There were rail fences all the way around the center property that could be expanded around the other two properties with no problem.

They all pulled up to the house and got down from their wagon and carriage. Diana could not believe her eyes. The house was beautiful. There was about a six-acre area where the house, barn, and drive shed were situated. There were about five or six huge trees for shade on the property.

Jeffrey showed them the area where the hay and straw was already starting to grow and, beyond that, the empty part of the lot that needed plowing and planting for whatever crop they chose.

John and Diana were amazed at the size of the barn. Jeffrey told them that the family that moved on was a family of twelve: mother, father, grandma, and nine children.

Jeffrey walked with John toward the barn and drive shed and gave the house keys to his wife. Christina and Diana went inside. There was a front door that faced the Thames River. This door was rarely used. The back of the house faced the road. The back door would bring you into the kitchen. This was the door used the most. There also was a side door that opened into a stone summer kitchen. This housed the laundry room and the tub room. This had a large bath tub for personal use, a special stove just for boiling water for bathing and laundry, and lots of room for large washtubs for laundry. Just outside this door, a double clothesline was strung. With the large family who had lived there, the clotheslines were long and always in use.

The summer kitchen exterior door was the one used by family or farmworkers coming in and out of the barn. They would have to leave their dirty boots, shoes, and shirts in there when it was mealtime, etc.

John was thrilled at the number of stalls that were in the barn. More room than they needed. With the former owners having such a large family, they needed a larger barn for their horses and such. The family also left a few barrels of oats along with the hay and straw. This was such a bonus. Their animals were going to have a feast and straw to lie on. It had been a while since *they* experienced such comfort also!

John was amazed at how perfect this land was; it was almost ready to be plowed and planted in. Jeffrey told him that Adam could get almost every farming implement he would need, second-hand, from people who sold and moved on. These were lower priced than new, but he could also order new machines and supplies from town with no problem. It would just take a while for delivery by train. John was happy to hear that, but he told Jeffrey they had brought a standard-sized plow for the Clydes and a slightly smaller plow for the Shetlands.

Jeffrey gave him an overview of the lot on each side of the property. The area was a little rocky and had a few trees on the one lot, and the other lot had several trees that would be in the way of planting. Jeffrey even told John that he'd be able to help him on weekends to help clear the land.

John said, "Thank you very much for your offer. I'd be obliged and forever in your debt.

We usually observe the Sabbath to rest and thank the Lord for all our blessings, which have been many, but I think he'll understand the urgency to get the planting done. I'll be thankin' ya so much for your help, and I'll take you up on it, and our ladies can visit and do what womenfolk do when they're together." The men chuckled and walked back to the house to meet up with Christina and Diana.

John noticed that much of the Thames River was still covered with ice. A bonus! He asked Jeffrey if there was a cold room or icehouse to store ice and food in so as not to spoil. Jeffrey assured him of the existing large cold room. John smiled with some relief—one more thing he didn't have to build or dig.

Diana was so excited about the house. There were five large bedrooms upstairs; the largest one still had a double bed in it, but the other four were empty. On the main floor was a large farm kitchen with a big double cooking stove. The family left their large dining room table but no chairs. There was a lovely parlor, just like you would read about in books and magazines. The parlor had a small fireplace. There was also a really large living room that had a big beautifully handmade stone fireplace with a huge hearth. There was a small library, which could be used as an office. The family had also left a beautiful hand-carved desk and a chair on small wheels. Diana laughed, for she had never seen this type of chair before. This room had a wood stove, but with the rest of the house being heated by the fireplaces and kitchen stove, there was really no need to put it on, except in winter.

Christina told Diana about the long cold winters, and Diana said their winters were the same in Scotland. Jeffrey heard some of their conversation about the size of the place, and as they neared the house, he quipped, "The outhouse is large too. It's a three-seater!" They all laughed.

When they all were together in the kitchen, John and Diana looked at each other and nodded. John said, "Well, Jeffrey, did you bring all the papers with you?"

Jeffrey grinned and said, "Of course! I brought everything we need to legally make these properties yours." John reached into his billfold and drew out $120 and gave it to Jeffrey. He filled in the papers and handed them to John. They exchanged money for contracts and a signature.

They were the new owners of this wonderful farm and the adjoining one hundred sixty acres on each side. Diana was so excited that she jumped in John's arms and gave him the biggest kiss he'd had since on the golf course at St. Andrews on their honeymoon.

Jeffrey suggested, "Well, folks, why don't we unload that wagon? It shouldn't take that long.

Since the bed is already here, you probably want to cancel the hotel room in town. After we unload, you can come back to town, pick up the animals, and I know Adam can arrange some straw and hay you can purchase when you need it. He'll tell you where you can buy full loads you will need until your crops are ready." John thanked him for the information.

John walked out of the house for a moment, went to his wagon, and went inside it to find something. He emerged with a hammer and something tucked under his arm. He went back in the house and asked Diana which door they should put the horseshoe over. She smiled and said, "Why don't we put it above the main kitchen door? The kitchen is the room where the most activity is, and we'll put the marriage kerchief in our bedroom. That all right with you, m'love?" John smiled at her and agreed. He'd found the kerchief with the horseshoe and put them both up. As John put each item up, Christina asked about the story of the marriage kerchief. Diana told both her and Jeffrey. They were touched by the tradition.

John and Diana were so grateful for all of Jeffrey's help. They could never have done all of this without the Whites—Jeffrey, Christina, and Adam. They would be friends for life!

Diana stayed behind and started cleaning while Jeffrey, Christina, and John all headed back to town. Diana found her supplies and started to pump the water in the kitchen sink. It took many pumps to get it started and for it to come out clean. She immediately put the cooking stove on and started a pot of coffee and put water on for tea. There was a lot of dust to wipe away even though the family had only been gone a week. She decided, since she had the ingredients, she would start to make bread first. She was so happy to be in her own new kitchen. On the long trip, she had longed for the day she would again be making bread and coffee and doing housekeeping. It was glorious to her. She danced as she worked. She was so happy, she felt silly!

When John got back to town, he canceled their hotel room. The desk clerk congratulated him on purchasing the land, welcomed him, and said he hoped he would see them again. Everyone seemed to be so friendly. He next went to the livery. Adam was there waiting for him. Jeffrey had to take Christina home because she was tired.

Adam had the animals ready for the last few miles of their trip. He told John where he could go to buy hay and straw until his crops were ready and, if there was anything more he could do, to just ask. John assured him he would be back very soon. All of a sudden, Adam remembered something. He said, "By the way, are you needing a plow? I have one that's only been used about three years. It is only a few dollars, if you want it. If you don't want to purchase, I can rent it to you until I have a buyer." John told him about bringing his own. They said their good-byes, and John was on his way back to his new home, his new farm . . . and a new start!

It took more than an hour to reach the farm this time. The new cow was the reason. John wanted to make sure he did not lose her, the milk, or the calf inside her. He drove at a slow pace for her. When he finally reached the house, Diana was washing the windows in the kitchen and came out to help her husband. She grinned at the new cow . . . "I guess she is the reason for the slowdown, m'love?" John reminded his wife about the cow's delicate condition. They smiled at each other as Diana helped John get the barn ready, feed and water the animals, and milk the cow. The cow provided a large pitcherful, and they were happy to have it.

As they worked, they talked about getting their seed potatoes the next day, and John said he would try to find someone who would sell them some chickens and eggs. The eggs were just for a few days, until they owned their own layers. There was an existing henhouse and chicken coop with four-foot-high fencing. John wasn't sure how many chickens they would need. Maybe a few female layers, a rooster, and some ready-to-eat birds too.

After everything was done in the barn for the night, they looked at the time. It was getting late into the evening. John put out the lanterns they were using in the barn and closed the doors for the night. He and Diana walked hand in hand back to the house. When they arrived at the side door, there was a big lamp inside the summer kitchen door. John lit it; they washed up and went into the kitchen. They were hungry.

When they got in the kitchen, John smelled fresh bread and coffee. He had no problem finding his way around the kitchen since Diana had set it up the same way as their home in Scotland. This kitchen was just on a much larger scale. He found a large cup and filled it with coffee and sat down. The bread smelled incredible. There was no butter, but they were happy to eat it anyway. Diana also had the leftover steak she couldn't eat at the restaurant that she had brought home with her. As she warmed the steak, John decided that he would do the reading this evening.

He first thanked the Lord for their new home, and he read from the Bible until the steak was ready. They were quite satisfied with the steak, the bread, fruit they still had from their trip, and the fresh milk. They noticed the night air was cooling, and they put the milk in the summer kitchen to keep it chilled. Diana planned to make bread pudding in the morning with some bread and milk. What a treat it would be.

They were getting tired but decided to take a tour inside their new house. After John helped Diana tidy the kitchen after supper, he picked up the lamp and they started their tour. John showed Diana the large pull-up trap door in the summer kitchen that revealed stairs down to the cold cellar. It was huge and perfect for them. They could keep their vegetables and preserves in there year-round; meat too. There was already ice in there that had no fear of melting soon. John grabbed the milk and set it on the top step and then they left. Diana had her laundry tubs and washboard set up in the summer kitchen already. She had planned on doing the wash the next day. She even found her bag of clothes pegs, and they were ready to go! The trip was long and dirty, and she washed clothes in creeks or rivers on the trip. She was glad she was going to be doing a proper wash now.

Diana showed John through the living room. He took a look at the beautiful large stone fireplace and hearth. He was impressed with the workmanship. They had some tables with them for this room and oil lamps. The rooms were big, and it would be some time before they would all have proper furnishings. They realized they would not have the spare time to enjoy this room right away.

There was the parlor, in which John said, "I must say, m'love, this is now considered your room for visitors, sewing, knitting, and the things you like to do and so on. I can't see m'self in here too often with my dirty old farm clothes on." He smiled!

Diana said, "After it's furnished, I better *not* see you in here with your dirty clothes on, Johnny McDonald." She paused. "Johnny darlin', could we maybe find a couch and chair for this room soon? We have that smaller table for here and lamps. I'd like to have somewhere comfortable for Christina to sit when she visits. I know we need kitchen chairs first, that's the priority. What do you think?"

John told her, "I saw chairs for sale in a store in town. We'll go in tomorrow and pick some out. I don't want to pick anything without you though, darlin'. We'll look around for a couch and chair, but you may have to wait a bit to get it. When the families put money together for our new life, it was most generous and a blessing. We've been frugal with it, and yes, we still have plenty to get on with, but we have to budget now, until we get a cash crop at the end of the season. I know we'll make it just fine here, m'love. I don't mean to be sayin' we're broke—we're not. I mean we have to watch it and buy in accordance to need." Of course, Diana knew and understood this. They were never impetuous with their money.

Diana took John upstairs. In the hallway ceiling there was another trap door. John wanted to see up there and check for a breeze coming through for holes in the structure. He pulled the stairs down and climbed up. Diana handed him the lamp. Up in the attic, he couldn't believe his eyes. He yelled excitedly, "Diana, you won't ever believe this. You've got to come up here. Give me your hand. Watch your step now, darlin'." Diana and John were standing there with mouths agape. With the lantern, they could see a lot of belongings that had been left there by the family. They saw not one but two wooden hand-carved cradles, two hand-carved wooden rocking horses, and a rocking chair. There was also a large dresser and three big mirrors. They found a box of children's toys, and leaning up against the wall were two boxes. In each box was a complete set of golf clubs made for a man and a woman. They looked at each other and had the biggest grins they could muster. Diana took a club out of the woman's box, and she held it and swung it like she was on a course. She loved it. It fit into her hands perfectly.

Diana excitedly said, "John, there must be a course near here. We have to ask Jeffrey! I know it will be a while before we can get out, but we can surely hit a few balls around on Sunday. Oh please, John, take these down, so we can look at them in the morning. Do you remember that broken club I had at St. Andrews during *The Game?*" They laughed, as they regaled the memories.

John smiled and replied, "Oh, I remember *The Game*, my dear! I'll never be able to forget it. You'll never let me, will ye?" It felt like their day couldn't be more perfect. They sat there on the attic floor for some time, talking, reliving memories of their home in Scotland and their honeymoon.

Diana said, "You know, darlin', I'd like to let Christina use a cradle and horse, if it's okay. We could loan it to her and Jeffrey. Or, for all their kindness, we could maybe give one of the sets to them. What do you think?"

John smiled as he said, "I think maybe loaning would be in order. I hope we have to use them ourselves someday . . . soon!" He put his arms around her and kissed her passionately. They looked around at everything again and, once again, thanked the Lord for more blessings. John had Diana bring the lamp closer to the cradles, and they assessed if they needed any fixing or painting; the same with the horses. They were all in sound shape, and he grabbed one of each and had Diana pass them down to him through the attic door. He set them aside.

John climbed back up and saw his lovely wife intently standing, looking at herself in one of the large mirrors. He just watched her for a moment, not wanting to disturb her. She had not seen a reflection of herself in a few months. She didn't know what to think. She had lost some weight, but as long as her Johnny still loved her, that was good enough. He broke the silence. "Love, is that the one you'd like in our bedroom?" She was startled, but she told him yes, it is the one she liked the most. She loved it. It had character. She tried to move it. It was heavy, so John hopped up to help.

He moved it to the trap door and got down the stairs and lifted it down.

Diana looked around the room some more. In the corner of the attic was something with sheets over them. John came up again, and they both walked over to them and lifted the sheets. When they did, Diana started to cry. She was speechless. He held her from behind. She turned around, put her arms around his neck, and held onto him as she wept with happiness.

When she contained her composure, she turned and said, "Johnny, it is the most beautiful sofa and chair I've ever seen in m'life. The material looks like new, and the hand-carved legs and arms are incredible. Johnny, I can't imagine why they left it here. Who would leave this behind? Let's try to move it tonight, love, please?" she pleaded.

John looked at her and said, "I know I won't get my night's sleep until I do." She smiled again through tears. They were able to get it to the opening. The chair made it through fine, but the sofa was very heavy, and Diana could not handle the weight. John told her he'd ask Jeffrey to help the next time he was over. As they talked, they figured that even Jeffrey didn't know all those things were up there. Their farm purchase was well worth it. John said, "Diana, I'm really tired. Can we please go to bed? All of this will still be here in the mornin'." She pouted but agreed.

They came down the attic stairs and closed the door and took a look at the things they brought down. It was so dark, and the lamp helped, but they needed daylight for better inspection of their new belongings. John took Diana's hand and sleepily said, "Darlin', just point me to our room, please." She forgot that he didn't know which room was theirs and pointed toward it. He asked her to grab the lamp. In the hallway, Johnny took a moment and passionately kissed Diana, picked her up, and carried her across the threshold of their new bedroom since he had neglected to do it this afternoon, when they bought the house.

They kissed again as she pushed the door open with her foot. She held the lamp up to reveal their new bedroom. John was awestruck at its size. It was as large as their kitchen. In the center of the room, against the wall, was a double bed, fully made up with their own sheets, blankets, and pillows. She decided not to worry about curtains for tonight. They could see the moon and the stars through the window this night. John was surprised to see the bedroom made up. He set Diana down and he looked in amazement. She smiled at him, and he had a tear in his eye for a change. He believed he was the happiest man on Earth tonight. He put out the lamp.

They slowly undressed and both sat on the bed. John drew her near him and kissed her again. They lay in each other's arms for a few seconds but could not contain their excitement. As he helped Diana lie down, he slowly climbed on top of her and he felt her wetness. He slid into her easily. They made love passionately for what seemed like hours and eventually fell asleep, still in each other's arms in their new home!

Chapter 7

Death Comes Calling

JACOB WENT ALONG WITH ALEX to the hospital in town to undergo neurological and vision tests that were of some worth but were still in their infancy. Dr. Brookes had seen patients when he lived in England with some or all of Jacob's symptoms. He was communicating with other doctors at that time in Europe, Canada, and America who were dealing with the same symptoms as Jacob's. No one could be sure what the disease was, but it affected men and women in adulthood only. Some patients were in their twenties when it started and others in their thirties. There seemed to be multiple symptoms in common with all of these patients but no answers.

After Jacob was settled into a room, a nurse did the standard pulse, temperature, breathing tests, and such: all were normal. She asked him how he felt and he said, "I really don't know why I'm here, dear. Dr. Brookes seems to think that s-something is wrong with me, and I'm real-ly just here to make him happy, you know how it is? I came for a short vacation." He and the nurse laughed. His slight stuttering was frustrating him, and he started to choke a little as he laughed and then coughed uncontrollably. His arms started shaking, and he couldn't control them.

The nurse called out, "Dr. Brookes, quickly, please!" Alex ran into Jacob's room and was alarmed to see his friend struggling like this.

As he tried to get Jacob to breathe slowly, Alex held his hands for a few seconds for comfort and told him, "Try to breathe slow,

Jacob. Please, try to calm yourself . . . that's right, try to slow your breath . . . that's it . . . good . . . now relax."

When Jacob slowed his breath, he stopped coughing, but his arms were still shaking. Jacob was calming down more, but he felt strange. Just like the way he always felt every time this happened to him—disoriented, dizzy, and he had some vision disturbances. He had soiled himself and urinated during his episode. He was embarrassed because he never wanted Alex to see him like this. Alex now knew what Andrew and Laura saw on the plantation. Jacob had been trying to hide what was happening to him.

"Now, Jacob, how often does this happen? When did it start?" Alex asked.

Jacob *had* to tell him now. As he did, he never noticed the nurse helping to clean him. He said, "Well, it's happened many times. The first was about a y-year ago, then the next was a few weeks later, the next only ten days later, then they became more frequent, once a week, and now it's once or twice a day." He paused and then continued, "Alex, some . . . times it's my legs too." Alex grew more concerned for his friend. Jacob sat up and asked him, "Alex, what do you think it is? What's happening to me?"

Alex replied, "I'm not sure, Jacob, but I'm going to try my best to figure it out. I'm talking to other doctors who have patients with all or some of these multiple symptoms." He held out his hand to shake Jacob's, but Jacob could not visually line his hand up with his. As much as he tried, his eyes and muscles wouldn't cooperate. Alex took Jacob's hands and asked if he felt strong enough to stand for a moment. Jacob said he could. As he stood shakily, Alex held him up. Alex now told Jacob he was going to let go of him and wanted Jacob to stand on his own and take a few steps for him. As much as Jacob tried, he was too dizzy and weak to stand, talk, or walk. Alex caught him and helped him lie down again.

The next day, Alex checked Jacob's vision first. It was poor. Alex could tell it wasn't just aging. There were other optic and sensory tests that Alex would perform. The results were not a good sign. After a day of all the tests Alex could perform, Jacob was tired and needed rest. A while later a nurse came in with his dinner, and she asked if she could straighten his bed and help him to get comfortable. As she began, she noticed that the bed was wet again. Jacob felt ashamed about his uncontrollable urinating. The nurse didn't say anything either but knew she had to tell the doctor.

The nurse asked Jacob, "Well, Mr. Marcus, aside from all the tests you've been through today, how are you feeling?"

Jacob smiled and he started to talk. "Well, I'm t-tired and glad to be resting again." He was very embarrassed about his stuttering, but he couldn't control it. She would have to report this to Dr. Brookes too. He wanted to know *everything* the nurse observed.

After Jacob was in the hospital for a few days, Alex wired the doctors that he had been in touch with previously about Jacob's case. He wanted to know how their patients were doing so he could compare their symptoms with Jacob's and find out how advanced these other patients' symptoms were. He let Jacob rest for another week or so in the hospital, just to monitor him. At least that's what he told Jacob for the time being. He didn't want him to go home until the answers were in from the other doctors. This also gave Andrew and Laura time to prepare the house before Jacob came home too. Alex advised them of alterations to the house that Jacob was going to need.

Alex brought in his chess set so they could have at least one game each day, and Alex would stay in the evenings and play if he wasn't busy with patients in the community. He wanted to keep Jacob's mind occupied, and it gave Alex the opportunity to witness more symptoms firsthand.

Alex had been to the farm to see Andrew and Laura. They told Alex to let Jacob know everything at the plantation was fine. Everyone was really worried about their Jacob-Sir, but it was work as usual. On the couple of Sundays Jacob wasn't there, the painting and renovations Alex suggested went really well, but they weren't going to mention it to Jacob; it would be a surprise. Mary was recuperating fine, thank the Lord. She was a young and strong girl, and Jacob was happy to hear she was getting better.

Jed worried about his wife, but Andrew kept him busy. They all missed Caleb and were still horrified by the way he died. Thankfully, there were no visits from Ethan Jordan. Alex knew Jacob wanted to keep it quiet that he was away from the farm. This would be for the best, mostly for the slaves' safety.

During the time Jacob rested in the hospital, Alex did not tell him that he was waiting for other doctors to respond to his queries. They did. All were reporting that their patients were having, and had, the same problems as Jacob. Some told Alex that Jacob will lose the use of his legs soon, and he will likely be in a wheelchair and then bedridden. Some developed pneumonia, others had strokes, and death came to them, as it would to Jacob. There was no way to stop it, and no one knew or understood it completely. Alex had to tell his best friend he was going to die!

Along came Friday, over two weeks after Jacob arrived at the hospital. Alex sat on Jacob's bed and told him, "After I see some patients in my office and conduct rounds here, I'll drive you back home today, Jacob."

Jacob looked at him and said, "You haven't told me what you think it is yet, Alex. Is it something bad? Is it going to go away, or can it be cured? Am I going to get worse? Please, tell me the truth, Alex. I need the t-truth, my friend. We have always been honest with each other." Alex turned his head away from Jacob so he couldn't see the tear rolling down his cheek.

Alex cleared his throat. He wiped his cheek and turned to face Jacob. "Well, my dear friend, you have what specialists have been trying to find answers for, for some time now. There are many people suffering these multiple symptoms like yourself. They are, and were, living with these same ailments as you, but there is no clear diagnosis yet."

"Alex, what do you mean 'were l-living with'?" Jacob asked.

There was nothing but silence in the room now. Alex took a long breath. He couldn't help it; another tear rolled down his cheek unexpectedly. He felt very unprofessional, but this was the best friend he ever had. Even growing up in England as a boy, Alex was concerned more about school and helping in the family business. He made no time for friends. Jacob was truly his *best* friend. Alex continued, "I believe you are, um, were in the first stage of deterioration over a year ago, starting with your vision, dizziness, numbness, and shaking. But now you seem to be slipping into a second phase, with your legs giving out on you. I feel that taking you home today will be good for you, but I am going to have to insist that you use a wheelchair from now on . . . no arguments."

Jacob raised his voice a little. "Why on earth do I need a wh-wh-wheelchair, Alex. My legs work . . . most of the time!" Alex looked into his eyes, and Jacob lowered his. His friend was right; it was inevitable. He knew a wheelchair would make life easier. Jacob asked again, "What did you mean other patients *were* suffering?" Again, Alex looked away. He stood up and walked over to the window and stared out. He saw some beautiful island birds in the tree just outside Jacob's window. They seemed to have an egg in their nest. Alex stood at the window, not saying a word, and hadn't noticed his patient had gotten out of bed and was struggling to make his way toward the window too. Jacob rested his hand on Alex's shoulder.

Alex turned to him, and the tears were rolling down both cheeks now. He started, "Jacob, let's get you back on the bed. I don't want you to fall. Not that I wouldn't catch you, you know." He wiped his cheeks and took Jacob by the arm and helped him back to bed.

"Jacob, my dearest friend, there seems to be no cure," Alex finally told him. "Eventually, the next phase after the wheelchair, you will be bedridden. Your body will become rigid, and soon you won't be able to eat, and then . . ." Alex tried, but he just couldn't finish. He had to clear his throat again and wipe his eyes. This time Jacob took Alex's hands.

"I'm going to d-die, Alex, just like the others, and nothing will change it." Jacob's voice was quiet when he said it. There was nothing else to say. They both sat in silence. After Jacob thought a bit, he told Alex to go to the office and see his patients, do his rounds, and he'll be ready for him to go home after he was finished. Alex smiled and left the room, telling him he would see him around four o'clock. Jacob thought after Alex left. He spent a good part of the morning thinking and watching the birds outside his window. There seemed to be some action in the nest. He wondered what was going on. He watched and thought some more and then smiled.

Four o'clock came. The nurse told Dr. Brookes that Jacob's lawyer had been in to see him.

Alex smiled and thought to himself that Jacob was accepting things and preparing. Jacob's bag was Packed, and he was sitting by the window with a smile. Alex hated to interrupt but asked, "Jacob, are you ready to go home?"

Jacob asked, "N-not just yet, Alex. Give me a minute? I want you to come and see what I see. Look at the nest. What do you see?"

Alex said, "It's the same two birds that were there this morning."

"You're w-wrong, Alex," Jacob told him. He continued, "Look harder, Alex, look harder.

Do you see it?" Alex looked harder. He smiled. Jacob said, "It's life, Alex. It's a brand-new life out there!" They smiled at the new baby bird in the nest, and Jacob said, "Let's go, I'm rea . . . dy." As they turned, there was a wheelchair behind them, and Alex helped Jacob into it.

It was a beautiful day for the drive, and the sun was shining. Jacob was glad to be going home. His mind kept going over so many things he wanted to do. He thought all the way home, not saying much. Alex just left him alone with his thoughts.

As they reached the Maisy-Lee, Jacob saw an addition to the house. The side door of the main house had a brand-new ramp built just for Jacob's wheelchair. He smiled. It was touching that they thought of it. Obviously, Alex told them, and he should have been annoyed with the doctor, but he knew it was out of deep caring and concern. Alex had it planned all along that while Jacob was in the hospital, he would be leaving in a wheelchair. So they all had the time to get the house ready for him. Jacob started to think about how he was going to get upstairs to his bedroom, but there were other things to take care of first.

At the front veranda, lined up were Jed and Mary, Laura, Andrew, Esther, Amelia, Thomas, Isaac, and Timothy. They all had big smiles for their Jacob-Sir. Jacob got in the chair, and Laura came up to him and hugged him with great affection and a tear. She tried not to cry but couldn't help it. He was like another father to her by now. Jacob was touched by Laura's tenderness and hugged her back.

All his boys and girls, as he still liked to call them, gathered around him and said their hellos. Jed and Mary were holding hands, and after the way was clear for them, they both stood before Jacob and told him how much he was missed. Jacob looked to Mary and asked, "Are you all right, young lady?" Jed and Mary looked surprised that he asked. They thought he'd forgotten her abuse at the hands of Ethan Jordan and subsequent loss of her baby. He held out his hands to both of them. They reached to him, and he held both their hands, saying, "I remember, and am s-so sorry you were hurt so bad, Mary. You are better?"

Jed responded first. "Yessir, she be feelin' better, sir."

Jacob turned to Mary and asked again, "Are you feeling bet . . . ter? I know your husband said so, but I would like you to tell me."

Mary was still a little shy but told him, "Yessir, Jacob-Sir, I'se feeling much better now. It still hurts me some, but I'se back working with

Laura-Ma'am. She says I'se doin' real good at my chores again, now ain't dat right, Laura-Ma'am?"

Laura agreed, "Yes, Mary, that's right, but remember what I taught you about using proper words?" Mary shyly nodded.

Jacob told the slaves that he was back in charge now, but they still had to mind Andrew and Laura and their instructions. Jacob looked tired. Laura asked if he needed to lie down. He said, "I am a little weary. You know how it is, waiting on a certain d-doctor to drive me home made for a long day." Alex smiled! He knew it was in jest. Jacob told his workers they could go to their cabins for the night and have their supper, but before that, he had one thing more to say.

Jacob started, "Now you boys and girls better not be g-getting any notions like poor Caleb. He was spirited and r-ran off, not knowing the dangers out there in the world. He found out the hard way. Andrew has been locking you in your cabins for your punishment." There was a hesitation while he caught his breath; his chest was starting to hurt. He continued, "Starting tonight, those doors won't be locked. Now mind, I'm putting a whole heap of trust in the lot of you not to w-wind up like poor Caleb. I am also going to move Jed and Mary into the main house to be closer to me, if I need help." Everyone was surprised by this.

Andrew asked Jacob which was to be Jed and Mary's room. Jacob told Andrew to put them at the end of the hall, away from his room, at the top of the stairs but close enough if he needed them through the night. Andrew smiled at Laura. They knew this was not the final word on which room would be theirs.

Andrew told the slaves they were dismissed so they could go and make their supper but reminded them, "Heed what Jacob-Sir told you about your doors not being locked starting tonight."

Laura took the handle at the back of the wheelchair and pushed Jacob around to the side entrance where the ramp was, with Alex following. Jed and Mary were to gather their possessions because they would be moving after supper. They all headed to the cabins right away to have their supper. They were sad because they knew he was dying; it didn't occur to any of them about what this meant to their own futures.

As Laura, Andrew, and Alex accompanied Jacob in his wheelchair, they pushed him into the outer kitchen first. There were no obstacles there. There were just the washtubs for laundry and a little table and chair. This is where Mary and the girls had always been allowed to eat their noon meal. After the outer kitchen, they entered the main kitchen. In there, they had moved the large butcher block that stood in the center of the kitchen and put it against a wall so the wheelchair would have good access. Jacob, as a rule, wasn't in the kitchen much, but now with the ramp being on that side of the house, he would probably be going through several times a day . . . at first. They wanted Jacob to feel free to go wherever he could inside his house. He was pleased.

Laura said, "That's not the only thing for you, Jacob." Next was the dining room. They did not need to move around any furniture or make renovations to this room. They walked clearly through with the chair. The main sitting room and library were big, but the furniture was rearranged to fit the wheelchair at his large oak desk, which he treasured so much. It belonged to his father. Jacob brought it with him when he moved from Mississippi. The space under the desk was large enough that Jacob did not have to transfer into another chair; this one could fit the wheelchair underneath with no problem.

Jacob said he was sorry, but he was very tired and he'd like to rest a while before supper. Laura and Andrew were beaming. "Now what is it with you b-both?" Jacob asked. They opened the door of the large sitting room at the back of the house. It had been turned into a good-sized bedroom for Jacob. He looked, and he blinked his eyes, not sure what he was seeing; but he saw every piece of furniture from his own bedroom upstairs, and there was still room for the wheelchair to move around. There was even room for his favorite reading chair; he had also brought it with him when he moved from Mississippi. It was a large yellow floral, stuffed winged armchair. It was his beloved mother Maisy-Lee's favorite, which she used all the time. He was astounded everything was moved downstairs, and it all fit.

Alex had also thought ahead. For Jacob's personal convenience, he purchased a commode for him. It was a beautiful hand-carved piece of furniture that looked like a dresser. The top and front opened to reveal a toilet hole with a removable pot, which can be emptied anytime. He was a little embarrassed but happy about the gift.

Jacob had lots more in store for the plantation, but that would come after they ate dinner, and only if he felt well enough to talk. Before he lay down, he told Andrew, "Put Jed and Mary in the bedroom directly at the head of the stairs. They'll be able to hear me if I need them, I'm sure."

Right then, in front of Jacob, Uncle Alex, and Andrew, Laura couldn't contain herself anymore. She blurted out, "We're going to have a baby!" They were speechless. Andrew finally picked her up, swung her around, and kissed her.

Alex said, "Now, now, Andrew, I know this is exciting, but please set her down and let her breathe!" Alex was really thrilled and Jacob was too. They all smiled with the exciting news.

Jacob said, "It's going to be fun to have the pitter-patter of little feet in this house. If w-we can celebrate after I nap, I'd appreciate it. I've have enough excitement for right now. I also need to have a serious talk with you after I get up. Alex, re . . . mem . . . ber what we witnessed today in that bird's n-nest? I knew it meant this. I felt it."

Alex held Jacob's hand for a moment and said, "Yes, old friend, you knew. Today there was a birth of several kinds." Not knowing what they meant, Andrew and Laura were puzzled but felt there was something very strong between the men, a new stronger bond that they shared.

Almost the moment Jacob's head hit the pillow, he fell asleep. Laura finished preparing dinner. They did not have the heart to wake Jacob up. Alex told them not to bother. He said, "With the day he's had, I think we should let him sleep. Now, Andrew, after Jed and Mary get moved this evening, we need to instruct them about what they will have to do for Jacob's care. For the next while, I'm sure they'll knock on your door for assistance. I'm surprised that Jacob didn't move you in to the main house too. I guess maybe his thoughts were to let you keep your privacy in your own house for now."

As they ate their supper, Andrew had a furrow to his brow and seemed to be drifting. Laura asked, "Dear, what's wrong?" She waited and then repeated, "Andrew, what's wrong?"

Andrew looked at her and then looked at his uncle. "What do you think he wants to tell us? We already know he's going to die. I'm worried."

Alex spoke up. "I'm not sure myself. Maybe he wants us to be clear on his final wishes to bury him. He may want us to transport his body to Mississippi to be buried with his family. Or maybe he wants to live out his last days there too. I know he has a cousin with a very large successful cotton plantation there, one of the largest in the South. He could want to go there. Maybe he wants to tell us he has to sell the plantation. He called his lawyer to visit him in the hospital today. He's likely helping get his affairs in order."

They were a little surprised things were happening so fast. Laura said, "I guess while he waited for you today to drive him home, he had time to think. I'm glad he called for his lawyer. Alex, why doesn't he show any emotion? For a man that's just been told that he'll die, he's quite calm. Is he giving up already, or do you think he has accepted it?"

The doctor in Alex came out all of a sudden. He said, "Well, children, this is part of what I wanted to explain to you both. You see, there are five stages of death. First, there's denial. After that is through comes the anger. The third stage is to bargain. He will try to bargain with God. Depression follows soon behind. Then the patient finally accepts that he is going to die. Jacob seems to have, or is going through these stages quickly. There is no set time per stage. He's always embraced the Lord and all his gifts! I'm sure he wants to leave us instructions and maybe help put his affairs in order."

Andrew said, "Wow, that's a lot for a dying man to handle!"

His uncle replied, "Jacob's the man to handle it, son! You can be sure of that. He will go through it with dignity, like a gentleman. Andrew, now that I've talked you both through dinner, will you please go down and get Jed and Mary and their belongings?"

Andrew came back to the main house with them, and they were showed to their room. They were so thrilled and lucky to be living in the main house but knew they were there to help with Jacob's care.

Andrew and Laura would explain their new duties to them after Alex left. He asked Mary if he might examine her before he went home. She still was very shy about showing her body. Even Jed had never seen it yet. They hadn't even consummated their marriage yet. Mary could not make love to Jed while she was pregnant with another man's baby. He'd been so patient with her. He never had sex with anyone, and he patiently waited for Mary. He wanted his Afua to be his first, one and only, for life! He loved her that much. They would lie together at night, and if Jed was aroused, Mary did not object to him masturbating.

One night when Jed was masturbating, his erection did not relax. It took a few hours, and it was painful. He couldn't understand what was happening to him. He never had this happen before, and he never got any sleep that night due to the pain. Was this a one-time problem, or was it a smaller sign of a larger problem? He wondered. He would keep this to himself for the time being.

Alex and Mary went up to her new bedroom. Alex did an internal exam, and he found that she was healing very well. He asked if they had sex since the loss of the baby. She started to cry.

"Doctor, I ain't never had Jed. He da mose patient, kindest husband, but I just can't. I don't know when I ever can. What do I tell him when he wants me? I'se so afraid ta lose him. I does love him so."

Alex was surprised at her confession. "Now, dear, I'm sure you'll make love someday. You can try anytime, and whenever you want, you can talk to me when I'm here, or I'm sure Laura will listen to you if you need to talk or get advice. I'm sure it will happen when you're ready. Jed will wait. Now let's go downstairs. I have to get on my way before it gets too dark." He took her hand and patted it gently.

They went downstairs, and Alex said good-bye and got in his carriage and started for town. Andrew, Laura, Mary, and Jed sat down in the dining room, sipping coffee and having pie, a real treat for Mary and Jed, and they all had a long talk. All instructions on Jacob's care were given before they all retired for the night, since they still had not heard a peep from Jacob.

They all were sleeping through the night peacefully, when suddenly, at 4:00 a.m., there was a loud knock at the front door of the main house. It startled Jed. He threw on his pants and ran down the stairs and opened the door. There was a black boy Jed thought to be about fifteen years old. He said he needed to talk to Jed's master and overseer. It was an emergency. Jacob did not rouse, so Jed told him, "Come wit' me." The boy followed him to Andrew and Laura's house. There was no need to knock on their door. They were both up, as usual, at that hour.

The boy said to Andrew, "Sir, you'se needed in town. I'se tole by my massa ta fetch ya. It's you'se uncle, da doc. He be foun' lass night in da ditch on da main road ta town. He been beat up real bad, sir. He tinks some white men done it. He in po' shape, you'se gotta come. He be in da hospital."

Andrew and Laura were shocked. They couldn't leave the farm together. Laura had to stay behind and keep an eye on things. Andrew didn't bother to hook up the carriage; he just mounted a horse and rode as fast as he could to town. He let the black boy ride with him, and he dropped him off at his plantation—Ethan Jordan's place. Andrew tied up his horse at a hitching post at the hospital and ran inside. There he found Alex lying in a bed with bruises on his face, two black eyes (he was barely able to see through only one), a split lip, a fractured jaw, broken arm, and several broken ribs. It was the most brutal attack Andrew had ever seen in his life.

Alex was awake. He saw Andrew come in the room, and he tried to smile but couldn't.

Andrew asked him what happened. Alex found it was very painful to talk, but he was able to slowly tell him about being ambushed by a few men on the road on his way home from the plantation.

After the attack, the men told him to stop tending to and treating niggers. He was a white man's doctor, and if they heard that he ever treated one more nigger, he would be dead. They threw him in the ditch and left. It took a couple of hours to climb out of the ditch, and he passed out on the road. At least he knew that he would be found then. He told Andrew to go back to the farm and that he would be okay. He needed to rest for the day. As Andrew rode back to the farm, he was still in shock at the sight of his uncle. Alex told Andrew that maybe they shouldn't tell Jacob. It might be too upsetting for him. Andrew agreed but thought maybe Laura had already told him by now.

When he returned to the plantation, Laura had breakfast ready. Jacob was awake and sitting at the dining room table. Jed and Laura had gotten Jacob out of bed, and Jed had washed him and helped him shave and dress. Jacob would never even consider appearing at the dining room table for any occasion without being properly shaved and dressed.

Jacob's coffee was in front of him. He was trying to put his hand around the cup but was having trouble. His hands were both shaking. Not from anger, but from the disease. Laura helped him hold the cup to take a sip of his coffee.

Jacob lowered his head into his hands, not understanding how someone could attack Alex. He was a good and kind man. When Andrew went into the dining room, he knew that Laura had told him.

Jacob said, "Well, w-well, is he all right? Please tell us he's all right. Do you think it was Ethan Jordan? The vicious bastard?"

Andrew told him everything, and Jacob said he wanted to visit him. Andrew mentioned that Alex wanted to sleep for the day but told Jacob he would take him in to visit the next day. He'd probably have more strength by then. They agreed to wait until then. Laura had tears in her eyes and so did Mary.

While Andrew was away, Laura told Jed to get the food to the others so they could have their breakfast and get ready to work. Jacob added to let them know what had happened. So Jed let the others know that they would be starting work late and why. They had to wait until Andrew came back from town.

Timothy and the girls went up to the main house to ask Laura if she trusted the boys to go to the field and start work on their own. They promised they wouldn't run off. Under the circumstances, they wanted to help Andrew the best they could. They knew he would be upset, and they wanted to help in some way. Laura wasn't sure at first, but Jacob was up; she let him decide. Jacob let them go to the field on their honor. The girls started to work immediately too.

After breakfast, Andrew went out to the field and was impressed with the progress the boys achieved. They asked about his uncle, and they spoke about it while they worked. Laura and Jacob got on well through the day. Jacob's symptoms were not too bothersome, which was a relief for a change.

Everyone on the farm went on with their day, mostly in silence and thought. Alex was on their minds. Also, what did Jacob want to talk to Andrew and Laura about? They'd have to wait.

Chapter 8

Hired Hands

J OHN AND DIANA AWOKE WITH a start at dawn. They looked at each other in disbelief. There was a shrill, loud crowing of a rooster. They jumped out of bed and looked through the window. They didn't realize it, but they owned a rooster! They looked at each other and laughed loud and hard. They figured that he had been hiding in the coop all day with all the activity going on. Diana couldn't stop laughing as she said to John, "Would you like chicken for supper, dear?"

John chuckled and said, "Well . . . apparently it's dawn on this lovely Tuesday morn, m'darlin'. I suppose it is just too much to hope for to find any eggs left behind in the coop too!" They joked about it as they got out of bed to start their day. Diana put the coffee on while John went out to milk the cow who would be delivering her calf soon. He made a mental note of asking Adam about a veterinarian in town. In Scotland, he helped birth cows, horses, ponies, and even goats and sheep on occasion for neighbors. But just in case there was an emergency, he wanted to know who was available to help him. He fed the animals and let them out for their day.

Diana had breakfast ready about the same time John came in from the barn. While she was making breakfast, she also started heating large pots of water for laundry. Whatever hot water was left over, they both would enjoy for bathing!

When John came back to the house, he noticed that there were a few early crocuses and daffodils. He stopped to pick them, and he brought them to the house. He set them down in the summer kitchen while he washed up. After he dried his hands, he gathered them up and tried to arrange them. He knocked on the kitchen door. Diana wasn't expecting anyone but wiped her hands on her apron and answered the door. There stood Johnny holding the most beautiful spring bouquet she'd ever seen. She hugged him and they kissed. She told him, "Just for that, you get a special breakfast, m'darlin."

They made plans for the day over breakfast. There was so much to do. It was still early, so Diana had time to wash clothes and hang them before going to town. John said, "Why don't we mount the horses and take stock of our new property, Mrs. McDonald? I'd love to show it to you."

Diana replied, "Okay, darlin'. Why don't you saddle them, and I'll quickly do the dishes and clean up." John left for the barn while Diana cleaned the kitchen. After they finished, they mounted and left on a tour of their new farm. It had been a while since either of them rode the Clydesdales. Their large size with their custom saddles were much larger than normal horses, and it'd take some getting used to again.

They headed first for the acreage to the east. There were rocks that would have to be removed and only about a dozen trees. The west field had no rocks protruding the surface of the land, but in the southeast corner of this lot, they noticed at least fifty to sixty trees. John decided to work the west field first. He was going to remove all the trees, except for maybe a few for shade, and replant the rest along the north edge of their property. This row of trees would act as a breaker in the winter, against the cold north wind. It also would give privacy. The road used to get to their farm was the only major road to the south. It took you to Windsor and the Canada / United States border. It was getting to be a very busy road.

John thought to himself that with Adam and Jeffrey's help and a hired hand or two, maybe he could get most or all of the trees moved before winter, maybe even in a few months. He needed to order a special hook for getting the rocks out. They already had the horsepower.

He would work the east field the next year. The priority though was to concentrate on the existing field and plant the potatoes and Diana's vegetable garden. There was a lot to be done. Next on the tour came the workable field that the former family had developed. They left a field of hay and straw. There were just about fifty acres of each.

Diana and John wished they had known this family to thank them for the work they had done and their generosity in leaving so much behind for them to get their lives started in their new country.

There had been a few cold nights since the family left, so John thought plowing would take quite a while. They both dismounted and tied the horses to a tree. Walking hand in hand, they used their feet to push the soil. It was much softer ground than expected. Plowing would be easier than first thought. John was thrilled. They had so many seed potatoes to plant in fifty acres.

To plant their fifty acres of potatoes, he would need to purchase and plant over five hundred thousand seed potatoes. Surely the seed store would not have that much in stock and would likely have to order more. This could cause a delay in planting too. He had to plow fifty acres but feared it'd go slow, even with Diana's help. It would likely be a late crop. He knew they'd have to hire help to plant, or he'd be planting for weeks. John also set aside two acres for Diana's vegetable garden.

The other fields of 160 acres each would be just for potatoes, with the exception of some more hay and straw, and they might try wheat for their own flour if they chose to in the next couple of years. John imagined them being one of the largest potato farms in Canada. But Diana didn't dare dream yet. If it was meant to be, it would.

After looking everything over, they went into town to get their planting supplies and groceries. The first stop was the livery to see Adam White. He was happy to see them. The men talked about where to get everything John needed. Diana went to Lavalle's General Store. They had everything you could think of. There was food, of course, some furniture, material for clothes, as well as a selection of ready-made clothing. They even carried wine and spirits. Diana bought meat, cheese, flour, sugar, coffee, tea, and so much more. She also looked at their tables and chairs. She asked if she could buy chairs without a table.

The owner of the store, Mr. Rene Lavalle, told her that was not a problem. His wife was behind the counter and told her husband, "Why don't you take Mrs. . . . Mrs. . . . ."

Diana extended her hand to the lady and said, "Mrs. McDonald. Please call me Diana, and you'll meet my husband shortly. His name is John. We're from Scotland, as if you couldn't tell from the accent."

Mrs. Lavalle smiled and shook Diana's hand and said, "Emilie. May I present my husband, Rene?" Diana noticed a French accent in both of them. Their ancestors hailed from France several generations ago, she would learn. Diana nodded a friendly hello. His wife continued, "Why don't you take Diana out into the storage room and show her the chairs we have in stock. How many are you looking for, dear?" Diana explained that she would like six for now and maybe more later. She told them where she lived, and they understood; they knew the large family. Emilie had heard they had to leave some furnishings behind. Rene and Diana went to the storeroom. There were a few styles to choose from.

The door to the storeroom opened up and in walked John. He said, "Hello, Mr. Lavalle, may I join you? I'm Diana's husband, John." Rene happily shook hands and told him to come and join them.

Diana told John which style of chair she liked, and he agreed he liked the same one. They were similar in style and wood grain as the table they had. The cost of the chairs was $1.25 each. John agreed that was a fair price. They bought six and said they would be wanting four or six more later. That was fine with Rene, and he helped John carry the chairs out to the wagon.

Emilie and Diana talked while the men loaded everything in the wagon. John paid their bill, and the Lavalles welcomed them to Chatham and hoped they would be friends and that they would remain in the area for a long time. Also, if they needed credit at the store in the future, it would not be a problem.

The seed store was next on their agenda. John asked Diana if she knew what vegetables she was going to grow in her garden. She told him, "Well, m'love, I want a lot of root vegetables since they last long through the winter. I want gourds and lots of corn." In Scotland, she learned from other farmers a drying method that you can use for corn on the cob to preserve it over the winter. Whenever you wanted to have corn, all you had to do was pop it into boiling water, and it would rehydrate, and it was good to eat. They brought quite a lot of it with them.

When they went into the seed store, John introduced them. Mr. Yablonski was the proprietor. They learned he'd immigrated to Canada from Poland five years earlier. He had everything Diana wanted for her garden and lots of seed potatoes but had to order more because they ran out with John's order. They had two-thirds of the supply he'd need but would have to come back in a few days for the rest. They also purchased hoes, shovels, sickles, and all the implements they would need. They went back to say good-bye to Adam.

Before they left the livery, they told him to say hi to Jeffrey and Christina and would love to see them at the house anytime. The invitation also included Adam, whenever he had the time.

Adam said, "John, I know this is a bit forward of me, but I have arranged for you to have five black workers for five days for right now. If you want them longer, I'm sure they can accommodate. They are fifteen cents each per day, plus meals, and maybe in a few days I can rent out another team and a plow to you. They can plant fast! For seed potatoes, I'd say they could each plant about twelve per minute. They'll work whatever hours you want. They live here in town, and I can show you where, or just let me know what time you want them, and I'll make sure they get there.

"But I'm warning you now, if you pay any of them daily, you'll not see them the next day. They'll take their money and buy spirits and never wake up in the morning for work. You pay them at the end of the five days or however long they work for you." John and Diana were shocked Adam had done this but very happy.

John said, "Thank you, Adam, that's wonderful. There will be a couple of acres to start planting by tomorrow. I'll have some plowing done this afternoon and be ready for them in the morning. While they're planting, I'll continue plowing. I'll have to go buy a few more hoes. Oh yeah, the seed store had to order more seed potatoes to fill my order. When it comes in, if they don't see me in town, I asked them to let you know they're in, and you could maybe get the message to me. I hope that was okay, Adam?"

Adam nodded and reached inside his door of the shop and pulled out a large handful of used hoes. "I think I have enough to loan you." They all laughed.

John said, "How about I take them now, and that'll save the workers from carrying them to work?" John had already bought three new hoes, and he borrowed three from Adam and tossed them in the back of the wagon. John also got the name and directions to the other farms to buy straw and hay from before his fields were ready to harvest. Adam also gave John the names and directions to the best chicken farmers around. One happened to be on the way home.

John and Diana thanked Adam again and went on their way. They found everyone to be so pleasant and were delighted to find that the chicken farmers were from Edinburgh, Scotland—Mr. and Mrs. Maguire (Michael and Eileen). John and Diana stayed and chatted for over an hour. When Eileen asked them to sit for lunch with them, they were happy to join them. During lunch, the McDonalds told them all the happenings in Scotland. The Maguires were happy to hear the news and changes. They'd been gone for eight years. The Maguires had heard about the smallpox and the potato blights through newspapers.

After a great lunch with new friends, they got ready to take home two dozen fresh eggs and ten laying chickens, as well as a few chicks. Michael also threw in a month's supply of chicken feed.

They already had a rooster waiting for them! After telling Michael and Eileen their strange rooster story of the morning, they all laughed uncontrollably.

John and Diana were happy with their purchases for the day. They returned the invitation to the couple to come to their farm someday soon for a visit. Michael had asked John if he'd be needing help to plow and get his crop in. John was thankful and said, "If you can see your way clear to come and help, I'd appreciate it." Michael told them he would be at their farm the next morning by 10:00 a.m. with his team of oxen and a double plow. John told Michael that he wanted his furrows twenty-four inches apart. Michael told him that was not a problem.

They said good-bye and headed home. They were astonished how well their day was going. Everyone was so friendly and helpful. Diana unloaded the kitchen supplies while John put the chickens in the coop. The rooster seemed to enjoy his new company. Diana still giggled about the morning wake-up call. She started to put things away in the kitchen while she got ready to bake more bread, scones, and, for dessert, some apple pies.

She'd purchased several large beef and pork roasts they could use for several meals and would be able to keep in their cold room. She also purchased a ready-to-cook chicken from Michael and Eileen that was freshly killed and cleaned that morning. They would have this one for supper. They also bought some chickens that were already frozen. She needed the extra food with five workers and themselves to feed for the next few days. She didn't mind the extra work. She liked a full house. It reminded her of home, growing up.

There was so much ice in the cold room that meat could actually freeze and stay frozen for long periods of time. John would be sure to harvest more ice from the Thames before it all melted away. He was glad he brought their skates and his hockey stick with them, although it might be too late to play this season. Temperatures were climbing, so he was worried that he would not make it in time to get the last of the spring ice into the cold room. The method they used for keeping ice cold longer in the cellar was to add straw to act as insulation.

John came into the kitchen and told Diana, "I hooked up the Clydes and plow, m'love. I'm going to go out for a few hours and hopefully get an acre or two ready for the hired help tomorrow." She offered to come out and use the ponies, which she was skilled at, but he declined. She had enough inside work to do herself.

The afternoon seemed to fly by. John plowed almost three acres on his own. Before they knew it, dusk was coming. John headed to the barn, fed the livestock, milked the cow, and soon they both were sitting down for a late supper.

They woke up at dawn, and by 8:00 a.m., they had Adam with five black boys on their doorstep ready to work. Both John and Diana went out to greet them. Adam said, "Good morning, folks. I'd like you to meet Don, Ned, Gerald, Rolly and Frank. Boys, this is Mr. McDonald and his wife, Mrs. McDonald." They each nodded when their names were mentioned, and John and Diana both welcomed them. It never occurred to either of them about a possible language barrier. They simply never ran across a black person until they came here. They were relieved to know they spoke English. However, there was a deep Southern slang to their speech, which took some getting used to.

Adam said he'd be back for them any time John wanted. John told him 8:00 p.m. That gave Diana time to give them a good supper before going home. Adam said he'd be back then. John told him to come at seven so he could have a good supper too. Adam grinned and said, "I'll see you at seven, folks, and thank you!"

John took the boys to the barn to get the horses and wagon full of seed potatoes and then out to the field. The five boys took their own planting sacks, which they had over their shoulders, and filled them up off the wagon and replenished when needed. Each one was given a hoe, and Adam was right. They were great workers. Once they got themselves into a routine, they could plant twelve seed potatoes per minute. John was amazed how quick and thorough they were. He had all five boys planting the three acres of the field he plowed the evening before while he kept plowing more.

Michael was true to his word. At 10:00 a.m., he arrived with his team and double plow.

Diana offered him coffee, but he declined and headed straight for the field and John. They discussed the plan for the day. Michael was able to stay for about six hours. He used his double furrow plow and just kept on plowing until he had to leave, only stopping for lunch with the rest of them. Diana had invited him to stay for supper, but he had told her Eileen would have supper ready for him when he arrived home.

For every acre John could plow, Michael would plow two. This pace would keep them well ahead of the five boys planting. When Michael was leaving at four o'clock, John tried to give him money for his help, but he refused. He said, "Now, now, John, there's no need to pay me. We Scotch lads have got ta stick together! I can lend you about four hours Thursday and some on Saturday, if you like." John was grateful and accepted. Michael headed home.

John looked skyward for a moment and said silently to himself, "Thank you, Lord. I know now I took on too much, but you saved me, and I be thankin' ya for the rest o' my days. Just don't be tellin' the wife, please." A lone tear rolled down his cheek as he got back to work.

Diana had time to look over the rocking horse and the cradle they brought down from the attic. They both were in good shape. They didn't even need painting. She cleaned them both and set them in the parlor for whenever Christina dropped by. Diana hoped she would come Saturday, when she knew Jeffrey was coming.

After Michael left, John and the boys worked until about six thirty, and then he gathered them and the horses, left the plow where it was, and the boys helped John with the evening chores. Adam arrived; John and the boys washed up for supper.

By Thursday, Diana was very organized, and she decided that she was going to start her garden. She asked John if he would hitch up the Shetlands and the small plow for her. He had no problems with his wife plowing; she was very skilled at it. John had put stakes in to mark off the garden area he set aside for her. It took her several hours on Thursday and Friday, and by Friday night, she had her two acres plowed and seeded. John stopped plowing two hours earlier each day; the boys were still seeding the potato field, and he helped her finish her garden.

When Jeffrey White arrived Saturday, Christina and the five boys were with him; all the men went out to the field to work right away. Jeffrey would help plant today with the boys. The ladies stayed in the kitchen for the morning. Diana was doing her usual baking and preparing a good lunch for the men while also doing laundry. It was a beautiful sunny morning with a breeze, and the washing would not take long to dry.

Michael showed up to work too and went directly out to the field after saying good morning to Diana and Christina. Christina pitched in to help, which Diana was a little concerned about, with her condition. Christina told her not to worry; she would stop and rest if she needed to.

The guys got quite a lot of planting done while John and Michael were always able to keep ahead of them, plowing. They went in for lunch and quickly went back to the field afterward.

There were some dark clouds rolling in, and the wind was getting up. The *Farmer's Almanac* advised that there would be some rain and storms around this time. The men knew, by the look of the sky, their afternoon could be short. They worked quickly, and by 2:00 p.m., they started to hear thunder in the distance.

Michael spoke up to John, "I'd best be goin', laddie, before I get poured on. Hope you don't take offense, lad." John told him he understood and told everyone it was quitting time due to the incoming storm. Michael continued, "Tomorrow will be a good day, ye wait an' see. I'll come back an', m'wife said she'll come and help plant—that is, if your Mrs. takes no offense to her bein' in the field and not the house. We also have a teenage boy, Toby, who'll pitch in too." John was flabbergasted. He couldn't believe the generosity of his neighbors and friends and said Diana would take no offense to an act of kindness.

Michael smiled and said, "Good-bye, John, Jeff." Since his farm was halfway between town and the McDonalds, he said to the boys, "If you boys would like a ride back as far as my place, you wouldn't have to walk so far to town."

They looked to John, and he said, "That'd be mighty nice of you, Michael. Is that okay with You, boys? You can get home before the storm comes too. Oh, boys, my wife will give ye some food to take home, seein' as ye won't be eating here tonight." They all smiled happily and nodded in grateful appreciation. They had been working hard and would enjoy the afternoon to themselves.

John said to them, "Adam said he'd bring you 'round 8:00 a.m. to start again tomorrow."

Michael went on his way with the five black farmhands while John and Jeffrey worked until they saw lightning. Right then and there, they got everything gathered up and rushed back to the barn. Just as they were getting back to the barn, it started to pour. The animals all headed into the barn too, and the chickens were not to be seen anywhere. They were safe and dry in the coop. The winds rose, and the men ran back to the house. As they entered the side door, they quietly washed, and Jeffery changed his clothes as to not drag dirt into the house. John would change in the house when he went in.

They heard Diana say, "If those two have any sense between them, we can only hope they come out of the storm and call it a day." The guys heard them and smiled.

John opened the kitchen door and asked his wife, "Now, darlin', how many brains does it take to come out of the rain? Maybe as many as to figure out we own a rooster?"

Diana replied quickly, "That's not fair, Johnny McDonald. You didn't know about him either." There was much laughter. John excused himself and went up to the bedroom to change into clean clothes. When he came back down the stairs, Diana whispered to him that she had not shown Christina anything yet. John smiled.

After dinner, while Diana was getting tea and fresh apple pie, John said, "Darlin', do ye think we'd be more comfortable in our—pardon me, I mean your—parlor?" Diana smiled and agreed while bringing in a tray with the tea and dessert.

Jeffrey and John went first. Jeffrey saw the cradle and rocking horse in the middle of the room. He quickly said, "Don't tell me that you two are in the family way too?" Before John could answer, Jeffrey grabbed his hand and shook it, congratulating him.

John said, "No, Jeff, we aren't yet." Christina came in the room next and saw the cradle and rocking horse. She was surprised to see the cradle and rocking horse. She asked Diana where they got them.

Diana told them as she poured the tea, "From the attic. We went up there the other night and found this and another set just like it. We would like to loan you these two pieces, if you'd care to use them for your baby."

Christina and Jeffrey were so touched. He told them that it was just the day before that they had talked about buying a cradle or making one himself. They added that they would be ever so grateful for the use of both items. Christina asked, out of curiosity, if there was anything else up in the attic that the family left behind. Diana said, "Yes, they left the two cradles and rocking horses, exactly the same. There were three large mirrors, which you can have one if you like. There were some toys, two sets of golf clubs, and this beautiful furniture we're sitting on, this rocking chair, and they also left a bed in the master bedroom and a chest of drawers. Oh, we are so blessed, I must say, and I'm sure my husband agrees. Ever since we landed here in Canada we have been so lucky." Everyone admired the lovely furnishings left behind.

Christina said, "Thanks, but my mother gave us a beautiful mirror for Christmas last year." She commented on the fabric and design of the furniture, how lovely it was and how it belonged in that parlor. The rocking chair was a big cozy platform-style chair. Diana imagined rocking a baby . . . all their babies to sleep at night in it. Its fabric didn't match the sofa and chair set, but it was a beautiful solid color that accented the other two pieces nicely. All the pieces were in very good shape.

Right about then, something occurred to Jeff. "I remember now. The family had a set of identical twins, that's why the double cradles and horses." Everyone laughed.

Diana asked Jeffrey, "Oh, Jeffrey, I wanted to ask you. Is there a golf course around here? They left behind a complete man's and a woman's set of golf clubs."

Jeff nodded and said, "There are two courses in the area, one's just down the road a mile. But before you go, maybe, let me know. I'd love to come out with you, if that's all right." John and Diana said they'd love it, but with planting, they wouldn't get around to it for some time.

Diana said, "We've golfed ever since we were young, and we spent our honeymoon at St.

Andrews Golf Course, Scotland. Have you ever heard of it? It's the oldest golf course in the world, and it was so much fun to play there. We had this competition going between us on our honeymoon, and I won—"

John interrupted, "Now, dear, they don't need all the details of our honeymoon golf game. It would just bore them." Diana gave her wicked smile to her husband and he smiled back. Christina was getting tired, so Jeffrey put the rocking horse and cradle in their wagon, and they went home, telling John and Diana they would be back in the morning.

Jeffrey said he would bring the boys out with him, and he told John he'd let Christina sleep in. Adam said he would be able to come and work a little later in the morning and would bring Christina with him then. John said, "Now my beautiful wife, would you like the guest list for tomorrow?" She paused and looked at him, thinking that he was kidding . . . he wasn't!

John cleared his throat and started the count. "There is you and I, of course, the five boys, Jeff, Christina, Adam, Michael and Eileen Maguire, and their teenage son, Toby, and, oh yes, Michael had specific instructions that you were not to cook any meat. Eileen is bringing roasting chickens, all dressed and ready to cook. All you have to do is potatoes, vegetables, and the sort of stuff you'd like to add to dinner." Diana was speechless but appreciative for all their friends and their help.

Diana and John rose at dawn, according to their rooster, which by now they had named Old Reliable. Diana quickly got things started in the kitchen, and then she met John out in the barn to help him get everything caught up so when their company arrived, John would be ready to go into the field. By 8:15 a.m. all the troops arrived, except for Adam and Tina. By now, she overcame her shyness and asked everyone to call her Tina, just as Jeffrey preferred Jeff.

Eileen came with one of the biggest roasting pans Diana had ever seen. In this pan, she had five chickens dressed, ready to roast. Eileen's large pan just fit in Diana's oven. She was able to close the door with an inch to spare. Eileen apologized for not having larger chickens right now, but she thought that five would make enough for supper for the amount that were coming. Diana had cooked a roast beef, roast pork, and lots of extra bread on Saturday so that she could make a lot of sandwiches for lunch Sunday. She had lots of coffee and tea (hot and iced), milk, and fresh water. She started to bake cookies, a few pies, a large bread pudding with a brown sugar sauce, a cake, and scones for Sunday desserts and breaks.

The group greeted one another and left for the field. The rain from the day before made the soil soft to work in. At least it did not ruin this day's planting. Around 10:15 a.m., Adam came with Tina. To save John a trip into town, he also brought the rest of the seed potatoes that were ordered for him. They had come in on the train Saturday night. Tina went in the house to see Diana.

Adam asked if Diana needed anything heavy done before he went to the field. She got him to go into the root cellar and bring up a large pot she had there and fill it to the top with potatoes she was storing down there. She also asked him to fill a large cauldron with water and put it over the fire pit at the back of the house and light it for her. This was for the corn on the cob they brought from Scotland.

Diana thought back to when they were getting ready to leave home. When John was loading so much of it to bring with them, Diana told him they didn't need to bring so much. John joked with her, "You never know when we might be feeding the neighbors, darlin'."

She giggled to herself, remembering this as Adam brought the corn out of the cellar. She and Tina heard another wagon. It was a covered wagon; coming down the road was Rene and Emilie Lavalle. They were coming to help their new friends as a surprise. The store was closed on Sundays.

Emilie went into the house, and after the cauldron was put on to boil for the corn, the two men went out to the field, taking the morning refreshments. Diana shouted, "Please tell Johnny that lunch will be at twelve thirty, and thanks again for your help, Adam, Rene. Adam, don't you be forgettin' my pitchers and cups. We'll be needin' them for lunch." Adam waved his arm back at her to acknowledge.

When everyone came in for lunch, Diana was ready for them, but she did not know where to seat them all. There were only the six chairs that they bought earlier that week at Lavalle's. She thought they should sit down and eat in shifts. Right then, the Lavalles asked John and Diana to go out to their covered wagon with them. When they looked in the back of their wagon, there were eight matching chairs to go with their set. "Consider it a welcoming gift, folks. We heard how many people were going to be here and decided that the chairs were needed. Please accept them as our housewarming gift, and we also brought six bottles of our finest wines, hoping no one takes offense to this, being the Lord's Day." Diana and John didn't know what to say, except to tell them thanks so much for their kindness and all their hard work.

John said, "I'm sure the Lord will forgive our indulgence on this glorious day, Rene, Emilie.

Thank you."

By the end of the day, there was so much done. The last few acres were plowed while everyone else planted. When John was finished plowing, he planted too. Almost half of the fifty acres was planted in by the end of Sunday. John was overwhelmed. They had just bought and moved into the farm on that Monday.

As they all sat down for supper together, thirteen around the table, John and Diana took their glasses of wine and stood together with their arms around each other's waist. John raised his glass. "To our new friends and to our new neighbors, to our new home and country, we'll never forget everything you've all done for us. We can never fully repay you for your hard work. But Diana and I decided that, and we don't want arguments from anyone, our first crop is going to be shared with you all! Cheers to you all, and again, thanks so much for everything!" They all rose and lifted their glasses in cheers.

John continued, "Now we mean no offense to any of you. We know that you all need to get your own farming and business taken care of for yourselves, and as much as we appreciate your hard work, I've arranged with our fine young colored lads here that they and I will finish the field. We feel we can get it done in ten days or less. Now that being said, Diana and I will come and help any of you with anything you need. It matters not when, where, or what it is. We will be there for you all in a moment's notice to help each and every one of you." Everyone raised their glasses to John and Diana. No one took offense.

He then asked everyone to put their glasses down so he could ask the Lord for his blessing for the food, their new friends, their new home, and their crop. Dinner was filling, and there was enough food for this small army of workers.

After supper, the wind was getting stronger, so everyone decided that they should get on their way while there was still a bit of daylight left. The women all insisted on helping clean up before they left while the men had some more wine and a smoke. Everyone was a little tired, but they were glad to help.

After they were alone, the McDonalds were just as tired as everyone else, but both went to the barn and coop to tend to the animals. While they were in the barn, John asked Diana, "Do we have an abundance of eggs, love?"

Diana answered, "We're a dozen ahead. Why do you ask?"

John continued, "Rene said if we have excess, they would buy them, just as he does from Michael and Eileen, at the same price. If I go into town, I told them I would bring whatever we didn't use or need. What d'ya think, m'love?"

"Why, that sounds great, darlin'!" Diana said. "I'm sure we can start soon. Let's just wait until we're finished feeding the five hired hands we have and Adam. We must keep them fed and healthy, dear."

John continued, "And, darlin', you can keep all the money that the eggs bring in for hobbies and things you'd like for yourself or the house. Maybe you could save up and buy a beautiful dress for yourself or some golf balls. How does this sound to ye?" There was no need to answer; she hugged him warmly and kissed his cheek. There was such tenderness between them. Their love always showed.

When they retired, Diana read the scriptures for a while. She had a feeling Johnny wasn't listening. He lay beside her and he just stared at the ceiling. Diana elbowed him in the ribs. "Are you listening to me, Johnny?" she said.

All he said was, "Hmmm." Diana closed the Bible, set it down, and elbowed him a little harder this time to the point where it broke his concentration on the ceiling and asked her, "What'd ye do that fer, woman?"

She raised her voice teasingly. "Don't you woman me, Johnny McDonald! You tell me what's so darned interesting on that ceiling? So interesting that you can't even listen to the Good Book? You just wait, Johnny. The Lord is going to be mad at you for this. First he'll tend to you, then I will . . . and you'll not soon be forgettin' it!"

He rolled on his side and rested his head on his hand while propped on his elbow. He started, "I think that we should seriously consider hiring permanent help. I know our friends pitched in today, but this large farm needs a permanent farmhand. The blacks work hard and cheap. We just have to pay and feed them. I just don't know who to pick. Adam gave a good reference for them all. They are good. What d'ya think . . . woman?" He tickled her under her chin as he said the last part, knowing he was looking for trouble.

Diana sat up straight, grabbed her pillow, and started a pillow fight. This was always her way to fight with her husband ever since they had married. John grabbed his pillow, and they went into a full-blown pillow war, with both pillows breaking and all the feathers flying around the room. When the pillows were both empty, they stopped and looked at each other and went into hysterical laughter. John took his wife in his arms and kissed her passionately. She responded. They lay down on the feather-covered bed and made love.

Afterward, they were too tired to gather the feathers, so she said that she would do it in the morning. They both fell asleep, to be awoken by Old Reliable, who was a little late this morning.

It was an hour after dawn! The sun was shining brightly through their window. They looked around the room, saw the feathers, and laughed again. She told John that she would clean up after the downstairs work was done. As they washed and got ready for their day, John said, "I guess Old Reliable isn't too reliable today. He must be really happy with all the hens we bought for him!" He smiled a devilish grin and she replied with hers.

They still never had time to talk about a permanent farmhand, but John needed help. He could not run this farm by himself. They would talk later. Meanwhile the five boys were delivered by Adam by 8:00 a.m., as usual. Adam said he'd be along at seven, if the offer still stands for supper.

John told him, winking and smiling, "We'll see you for supper, Adam. Take care and thanks."

It was a very productive day. Diana got the pillows put back together with the help of Eileen and a lot of her feathers since she didn't have enough. As they ate supper, John said, "Love, I think we'll have the crop in by ten days, or my name isn't Johnny McDonald. These five lads here are some of the best workers I've ever had the pleasure of knowing. These boys say they'll work for us anytime. What d'ya think of that?"

Diana smiled and nodded her approval toward the boys. "Now, m'love," she began, "I am glad the potatoes are more than half planted. That's our first goal. We'll have a huge crop for sure. But don't you be wearing these boys out. Remember, you want to start clearing the west field soon, but give them a break, dear."

The boys all shook their heads as Rolly spoke. "No, ma'am, no, ma'am, we needs no break. We likes workin' here, we does. Y'all treats us fair, y'all treats us good. We likes y'all. Canada been good ta us too. Not like plantation works, no, sir, not like dem plantation works at all. Da whuppins an' beatins we's all taked. It be bad dere, Mrs. Diana. You never believe, if'n we tole ya."

Diana replied, "Please tell us, if you can."

Frank spoke for them all. "Well, missus, we all be from different plantations in da Sout'. Me and Gerald is from Mississippi, Don and Rolly be from Alabamy. Ned be from Wouisiana. We's all been born'd in our real home, Africa. We misses it so." He ate a little dessert.

Frank continued, "We's all been whupped many times. Sometimes in da fiels, overseer may fire a shot from his gun, it go right by you'se head, an' he juss do it fo' fun, and den laughs 'bout it.

Sometime a slave might take da notion to runs away . . . you juss gets captured agin an' brung back.

Some massas kills y'all when you'se gits back, most juss whups y'all real bad. We hears tole some slaves gets deys feet or juss toes cut off wit' da axe, ma'am."

Diana, John, and Adam were appalled to hear these stories. Such cruelties for a human to endure. Rolly spoke up. "Ma'am, sir, dat not even half o' it. 'Dese tings is punishment for simple stuffs. Like stealin' a chick, 'cause you'se starvin' ta deat' or makin' babies wit' a kitchen wench you'se love. Meals, we'se only ate two times ever'days. Sometimes da massa gives us rotten food an' we'd has ta eats it or starve. We'se not gits any more till da rotten stuffs be gone. Den some would gits sick from it or dies.

"I gits whupped on da boat I comes on from Africa. Juss for talkin'. On da boats, people dies from sickness. We git sick or dies, dey juss trows ya overboard ta da sharks."

Diana asked them not to tell them anymore. She was in tears thinking about all of this. She could never imagine a human treating another human being this way. The injustice was too much to bear. It also brought to mind the story she heard on the *Destino*. She and John heard about the little African girl being repeatedly raped by the crewman. She shed more tears.

Chapter 9

So Much Death . . .

S ATURDAY CAME AND THE MORNING work was done. The boys had worked hard and not only filled their quota, but they also cut a lot of extra cane for Jacob that week. Andrew promised Jacob, after they went to get paid for the week's sugarcane, he would take him to the hospital to see Alex.

Jacob and Laura were anxious to visit Alex. Jacob and Andrew went to talk to the boys before they left for town first. The slaves were all sitting outside their cabins, finishing their lunch. Jacob cleared his throat and began, "You all know Dr. A-Alex has been in the hospital. Now Andrew is taking me to town to visit him for a while. But I have a problem. Although Laura has not said anything, she is very sad because she can't visit too. Someone has to stay behind and make sure you'll stay here. I'm thinking if I asked you to not run off if all three of us go to town, maybe you could take heed and stay put. Remember C-Caleb? There are people out there who catch slaves and kill them. You've seen that. I don't want to lose any more of you. You all make me p-proud of the work you do. Can I trust you all if Laura, Andrew, and I go away for a few hours this afternoon? Can I trust you all to be here when we get back?" They were surprised. In all the time they'd lived on the plantation, Jacob'd never left them alone before. They stared, dumbfounded, and couldn't speak.

Jacob didn't wait for an answer and said, "Now there is another approach I can take if you're not answering my questions rightlike, I can lock you all in. What do you all say?"

The slaves promised Jacob they would be there when he returned later in the day. They understood the ramifications. Timothy spoke on their behalf. "Jacob-Sir, we's come ta love y'all, an' we promises we doesn't do nothin' ta be bad. We misses Caleb, he goin' away like dat, an' bein' killed by dat bad man. We don't want we should end up like Caleb, an' y'all doesn't need ta lock no doors, Jacob-Sir. We'se gonna stay fer sure, we promises! Y'all can truss us, sir."

Jacob smiled. He turned to Andrew and asked, "What do you think, Andrew, my boy? Do you think the three of us can go n-now?"

Andrew smiled and said, "Well, Jacob, I think we should go to the house, get my wife, and go see Uncle Alex. Now you boys and girls mind what Jacob-Sir said. We trust you to stay here this afternoon."

Jacob felt good. He wanted to trust his slaves and was giving them an opportunity to stay or run. He was sure of the choice they would make. He smiled as he spoke. "Now I don't expect you to cause d-damage around the place either. I'll inspect things when I come back. Jed and Mary are going to come down here when we leave, and I'm locking the main house. I'll see that you get your supper food. How does chicken sound?"

Timothy bowed his head a little and said, "Yessir, that'd be right fine, sir. We'se like yo' chickens a lot. We likes ta have Jed an' Mary wit' us too. We'se misses dem. Y'all has a nice trip, an' please tell Dr. Alex we's tinkin' 'bout him, and we's prayin' fer him. We knows he be wit' us soon agin. Tanks agin, Jacob-Sir . . . fer trussin us. We'se not be lettin' ya down, sir."

As they started their walk back to the main house, Jacob's face changed a bit. He thought for a minute and turned and said to the group, "I hate to say this to you because you want to enjoy yourself while we're gone, but I'll have to ask you n-not to play or sing any of those African songs that tell stories. If s-some . . . one over on the next few farms hears it and you say something about being alone, someone may come and do harm to you. Y'all going to heed this warning too?"

Isaac spoke for the group this time. "We not tink of dat. Tank you, sir, fer da warnin'. We'se be real quiet 'bout bein' here 'lone. What does we do if'n we has someone come to da farm, Jacob-Sir?"

Andrew spoke up this time. "If you see someone on the property, no matter who it is, you all should run into the cane field as far as you can and still be able to breathe properly until they're gone. That way they can't harm you. Now do you all understand that Jacob-Sir and I are trying to keep you safe? It is not a punishment, it's for safety."

Jacob said, "That's good advice. You mind what Andrew-Sir said too. We'll see you later."

As they both started back to the main house, the five slaves all took Jacob's hand warmly, thanking him for his trust and said good-bye and wished them both a good afternoon. They were so thrilled with their little bit of independence. As they watched them leave, they saw Jed and Mary coming toward the cabins to join them. Andrew and Jacob went to the house to collect Laura. She was surprised and delighted that she was going to be able to visit Alex too.

Andrew placed the wheelchair in the wagon, and they went on their way town. Jacob hated driving by Ethan Jordan's plantation. He usually got Andrew to go faster when they drove by. Today was no exception. As they rode by, they didn't see Ethan outside anywhere. They were relieved! But Ethan saw them. He saw Jacob and Andrew, and he was quite certain that the woman he saw was Andrew's wife. Right then, Ethan Jordan started devising the most diabolical plan for the afternoon that was to horrifyingly destroy so many lives.

Before going to the hospital, Jacob collected his weekly sugarcane money. He was still getting prime dollar for it and sometimes a little extra since his boys took such fine care cutting it and Andrew so carefully looked after it and transported it. Other farmers didn't know he was getting more for his crop than theirs—that is, except for Ethan Jordan!

One night while getting very drunk at a local pub in town, Ethan was sitting with a man who works where Jacob sold his sugarcane. This worker was as drunk as could be, and he told Ethan the amount of money Jacob made weekly.

Ethan was livid, absolutely seething mad! He mumbled under his breath, "That man will Pay . . . in lives this time!" He would not let this go by unpunished. There were no other witnesses to his threat. The destruction of Jacob Marcus's Maisy-Lee Plantation and anyone around him was Ethan Jordan's one and only goal now.

*　　*　　*

It was such a beautiful afternoon to be outside. Laura didn't get out to town much, only about once a week to shop for Jacob or visit her parents. Sometimes Andrew and she went there for supper on Saturday evenings. Her parents wanted to keep an eye on her pregnancy too. It was their first grandchild and they were excited. Today was a great opportunity for Laura, Andrew, and Jacob to enjoy life without a concern, except for how Alex was doing.

When they arrived at the hospital they were having a happy discussion as they entered.

Andrew was teasing Laura about whether she would be able to fit through the doors when the baby got bigger. She slapped her husband on the hand and said, "Don't you dare say things like that. You're so cruel.Remember, you're the baby's father, you scoundrel!" Jacob smiled, enjoying the banter going on between them.

Andrew said, "Oh, here's his room. He's out of bed. This must be a really good sign. I wonder where he's toddled off to?" They were still smiling and having a little fun when Alex's doctor walked into the room. Andrew continued, "Good afternoon, Doctor. May I present my wife, Laura, and Mr. Jacob Marcus. Where has my uncle gone? I swear that man can't lie still for a moment. Did he run away from you, or is he chasing nurses?"

Dr. Reid said, "I'm sorry, Andrew, your uncle died about a half hour ago." The three of them were in shock. Laura started crying, almost in a hysterical state.

Andrew shook his head, saying, "No, I can't . . . won't believe it. He wanted you to say this, and he's hiding somewhere. Uncle Alex, you can come out now. This is not funny." A nurse came in the room crying. He looked out at the desk and the other nurses were crying too. It was really true; his uncle Dr. Alexander Brookes had died of his injuries from his attack.

Jacob's chest started to hurt a little. He asked the doctor, "Exactly what killed him, Doctor?"

Alex's doctor started, "It was what we call a subdural hematoma, a large bruise on the brain that bleeds. If the bleeding doesn't stop, it causes too much pressure and the patient dies, unless he has decompression surgery. That means to drill holes in the skull to relieve that pressure.

He started having symptoms of subdural hematoma, and we were readying him for the surgery when he had a major seizure and died. We couldn't stop it or bring him back. Andrew, I know you all loved him, and we here at the hospital loved him too. I'm so sorry. What do you want to do with the body? I assume you are in charge?"

Andrew was in shock. He couldn't believe his uncle Alex was dead. He loved him so much.

Andrew shook his head back to reality and said, "Yes, I guess I am. I'd better get his lawyer to get his instructions so I can help fulfill his final wishes. He . . . um . . . he never told me. We never talked about it. We thought we had lots of time . . ."

The doctor sent a messenger to Alex's lawyer to tell him what happened and to come there to meet with Andrew. His office was just down the street from the hospital. Andrew was sure the lawyer would have his uncle's will and final instructions. As they all stood by Alex's bed, they just stared at its emptiness . . . and the only thing on the table were his broken glasses. The authorities expected that during the beating, his billfold and gold watch were likely stolen.

Alex's lawyer arrived in minutes with Alex's papers. He said, "Andrew, I am so sorry about this. It's a terrible shock. Andrew, he left specific instructions upon his death. He has donated his body to medical science so that student doctors have someone to practice on. I know that probably upsets you, but he insisted on it. There are provisions to hold a memorial service. You can plan it, and I'll have the money in a couple of days for you. I will get everything in order for you. Everything he owns goes to you. Andrew, there is quite a lot of money left for you.

"All the medical equipment in his office has been donated to the hospital. I can, or we can, attend to packing it all up. I have the keys to the office and his apartment above the office. He didn't own that building, but I'm sure the landlord will give you time to remove everything. Andrew, are there any questions?" He shook his head no, still not believing what had happened.

Laura was kneeling by Jacob's wheelchair, weeping on his lap, Jacob just staring into space while patting her head. His best friend in the world was gone. He couldn't believe it. It had to be a dream. All of a sudden, he felt something wet on his leg. Laura was weeping so hard her tears fell on his knee. It broke his stare, and he started weeping too.

Andrew put one hand on Jacob and one on his wife. Jacob looked at Andrew and sadly asked, "Can we leave now? Would that be okay with you both?" They nodded through their tears. Andrew pushed Jacob's wheelchair out of the hospital for the sad journey home!

As they neared the plantation, there was something in the air—*smoke*! Andrew put the whip to the horses and told Laura and Jacob to hang on. All three of them could see the smoke, but what part of the plantation was burning? They weren't sure. As they drew nearer, they didn't see flames, just smoke. It became clear to them now. The slave cabins had burned down. Two out of the three cabins were completely burned to the ground. They were worried about the slaves, but Andrew said, "Remember, we told them to go into the cane field and hide." He was sure that's where they'd be.

They drove the wagon as close to the cabins as was safe for the horses. All three of them saw devastation. As Andrew covered his mouth and nose with a cloth, he entered both cabins. Inside the cabins he counted five burned corpses. Five out of Jacob's seven remaining slaves had been murdered, but which ones? Who was safe or still alive? Laura was crying hard and holding onto Jacob for support. Andrew was being so brave, considering. First his uncle died and now this. He felt that both tragedies were the deeds of Ethan Jordan! There was no doubt in his mind or in his soul about this.

The three of them hung their heads and began to pray for the souls of the five slaves. Suddenly there was rustling in the cane field. Slowly, out came Mary and Jed. Mary ran to Laura and cried hard. She was shaking uncontrollably. Jacob took Jed in his arms, and they both cried too.

Jacob composed himself and said, "There's nothing we can do for them now. Let's all go to the house and find out what happened here today."

Mary asked, "How is Dr. Alex today? We was hoping you had some good news. When can he come to visit again?" Laura looked at her husband and Jacob, and they nodded to each other.

Jacob looked at them both and said, "Jed, Mary, Dr. Alex d-died just before we arrived at the hospital." More tears filled the dining room that day than any other time in its history. Jacob was exhausted, but he needed to hear what had happened at his plantation that afternoon.

Andrew and Laura sat with Jacob, and they listened to Jed and Mary's horrible story.

The slaves never saw anyone coming, and then Jed told them, "Mary an' me went fer a walk ta be 'lone. We'se walkin' t'ward da cane fiel', when we hears screamin' an' a gunshot. We's scared an' 'cides we should outta hide 'stead of goin' back ta see what be wrong. We walks along in da fiel' an' watch dat bad man. Dat man dat almos' kills my Mary. He be here wit' 'nother man I ain't seen afore. He rounds up Timothy, Thomas, and Isaac and locks 'em in da cabin. Da udder man watch da girls. We'se too scared ta come out o' hidin'. We stays in da cane. Den we hears screams. It be Amelia. I don't know what dat man be doin' ta her, but she screamin' lots.

"Da bad man be sittin' at our table outside wit' Esther. It like he be guardin' da place an' Esther. Few minits later, da udder man an' Amelia comes out o' da cabin an' she ain't got no clothes on. Right den, dat bad Ethan man takes Esther in da cabin an' we hears her screamin' too. He mussa done da same ting, 'cause she comes out buck naked too!

"Da men, dey juss laughs. Dey grab bote girls and trows dem back in da cabin an' locks da door. Juss like what dey done to da boys. Dey has a rum bottle wit' 'em. Dey's drinkin' an' a drinkin'. Finally, dey gadder up some dry cane stalks dey finds. Dey was nearer to us now in da fiel', and we holded our breath . . . but dey not seen us. Dey lit da stalks on fire, broke da windas in bote cabins an' trowd in da burnin' stalks. Da two cabins juss went up wit' dem all inside! Dey's all screamin', it be a horr'ble soun'. We was cryin' as quiet as we'se can.

"Den dat Massa Jordan says he's hurt y'all in da worse way poss'ble. Dey laugh an' laugh an' keeps drinkin' an' left da same way dey come, I s'pose—tru a fiel' behin' da cabins. We'se so scared, Mary and me, we not come out of da cane fiel' till we sees y'all!"

Mary was crying all the time Jed was telling the whole story, so was Laura. They were holding and comforting each other while listening to him.

Jacob hung his head. He was gently crying too. He also urinated in his pants. He couldn't control it and became embarrassed. He felt responsible for their deaths. He had bought them to give them a good life with him, only to be murdered by a jealous, maniacal plantation owner. They could prove it was Ethan. Mary and Jed were eyewitnesses, but there was no way police or the court would believe a slave. It was no use at all to tell anyone.

It was quite a day of mourning. First Dr. Alex and then five slaves. Andrew would take care of Alex's arrangements, and Jacob wanted "his kids" buried with Caleb.

Jacob was in quite a state. Jed took him to his room and washed him and changed his pants. Then he helped Jacob to lie on his bed but ran to the dining room. He said, "I tinks Jacob-Sir not be well. He done look like a beet, all red an' hot an' breathin' funny."

Laura got up and checked on him, and she agreed with Jed. He was flushed and clammy and holding his chest, breathing hard. Laura screamed, "Andrew, get in here quick!" They both looked at him, and Andrew quickly opened his shirt so he could breathe better and propped his head at an elevated position. Jacob's eyes were not focused on them; they were just staring. He couldn't talk due to chest pain and his breathing. They wiped Jacob down with cold cloths to lower what seemed like a fever, and it helped.

When they left the room, Andrew said, "I'd best go to town and get my uncle to . . ." He stopped and realized what he said. He hung his head and started to cry. Laura held him while they both cried.

Andrew told Laura to keep an eye on Jacob, to make sure he was okay. He was going into town to find another doctor to come to the plantation. He quickly rode to town bareback. He sped by Ethan's farm. He felt contempt for him and was outraged because going by his plantation was the only way to get to town quickly.

In town, he found Dr. Reid, the same doctor who looked after Uncle Alex. Andrew told him what happened. Dr. Reid said, "I'll ride with you, it's quicker." Andrew agreed. As they rode together, Andrew explained everything from the afternoon after they'd left the hospital.

As they arrived at the plantation, the doctor could smell the distinct odor of burned flesh on the grounds. He would look at the bodies later. When the doctor and Andrew entered the house, they heard no crying. What had happened? Everyone was in Jacob's room. He was conscious and talking slowly with labored breath and now a slight slur. The left side of his face drooped now.

After Dr. Reid examined Jacob, he said, "His heart's palpitating irregularly and a little too fast, but his breathing's better now than you described. I think Jacob may have had a heart attack. The irregular heartbeat, or cardiac arrhythmia, could have even caused a transient ischemic attack, or slight stroke, but he should recover. This falls on all the other symptoms Alex diagnosed too. Keep him in bed for a couple of days, he needs rest, and give him aspirin if the fever comes back. Now, boy, we have to get those burned bodies in the ground before disease becomes rampant. I'm sorry."

Andrew, the doctor, and Jed walked to the burned cabins. Jed got three shovels and they started to dig. Andrew and Dr. Reid discussed how to bury them, each in their own grave beside Caleb or altogether. They asked Jed, and he told them, since they were all so close, to bury them all together with Caleb. Jacob would want it that way. All three men got busy with their shovels.

After digging a while, Dr. Reid finally said, "I think we can stop now." They had dug around Caleb so they could lie in peace together. Friends . . . family, forever! Jed went to the house to get Laura and Mary to come down for a bit of a service. Jacob knew what they planned and wanted to attend since he felt strong enough now. Dr. Reid said it was okay, but he had to get back in bed right away after the service.

The grave was filled with the bodies by the time Jacob arrived. He brought his Bible. He opened it, and he very slowly, somberly, recited the 23rd Psalm. Afterward, he hung his head and started the Lord's Prayer. Everyone joined in.

After, Dr. Reid said that he wanted his patient back in bed. Mary and Laura said that they could manage on their own. When they left, the men started to fill in the grave. After the girls got Jacob on the bed and comfortable, he reached up with his right arm and patted Laura, and then Mary, on their cheeks. He would have lifted both arms but couldn't. He couldn't feel his deadweight left appendage; it was numb, and he lost the use of his muscles. He didn't want them to see him now, not even his doctor.

Jacob told Laura, "When the guys come back to the house, I want to talk to you, Andrew, Mary, and Jed. It's important." As the girls left the room, tears began to roll down Jacob's cheeks. He knew he didn't have long, and he needed to speak before it was too late.

After about forty-five minutes later, the men came in. Dr. Reid said, "I'm going to look in on my patient before I leave." He went to Jacob's room and asked Jacob how he felt. He lied and told the doctor he was fine. Dr. Reid checked his heart again, and it sounded worse than before. He told Jacob to stay calm and rest. If Jacob needed him, he would come back through the night. But really, there was nothing Dr. Reid could do for Jacob. Jacob smiled and said good-bye to the doctor, shaking his hand, knowing this was the last time they would see each other.

Dr. Reid went into the kitchen and said to the others, "He's not doing well! He could have another heart attack or stroke anytime. He needs to stay calm and rest, to slow that heartbeat down. You come get me if you need me, and Jacob wants to talk to you all."

The four of them went into Jacob's room after the doctor left. Jacob smiled, happy to see who he had left of his family. He started, "Come, please sit with me so I can talk to you about what's going to hap . . . pen around here." As he labored to get his words out, they sat nervously. He continued, "Mary, Jed, when I found out I was going to die, I took the lib . . . er . . . ty of writing a letter to a cousin of mine, and Alex mailed it for me. His name is Jeremiah Marcus, our daddies were brothers. I t-t-told him about you, that I wanted to give you a better life. I want you to go to the United States, where there are so many opportunities.

"My cousin owns a successful cotton plantation in Miss . . . iss . . . ippi. He will take you in. Now cotton work is different from farmwork and housework. I told him that you're my best workers. Mary, I expect you'll work in the house, and maybe Jed can do some of the jobs for my cousin he does for me.

"I really believe that someday soon, there'll be no slavery there. You'll be able to go where you want and live anywhere, and you'll need money. I'm giving you five hundred United States dollars." Everyone gasped with surprise! Jacob stopped to take a few breaths. He was sweaty, warm, and very flushed. They wanted him to stop and rest, but Jacob knew it was near the end. He put his good arm over his chest and tried not to let the others know he had chest pain again.

Heavily breathing, he slowly continued, "Now L-Laura, I need you to do somethin' special for me." His bulging eyes were noticeable, but they didn't know it was from high blood pressure. If it didn't lower, surely he'd have another heart attack or a stroke at any time. His eyes blinked away tears as he bravely looked at Laura and continued, "Dear, please roll the money up as small and tight as you c-can, and sew it into some old piece of material and make Jed a belt with it inside. Make it a tie-up, one to look like a belt other blacks wear, and no one will think nothin' of it.

"Now, J-Jed, you keep this belt on you *always*! Only take it off to bathe or sleep, put it un . . . der a pillow or somewhere safe. You tell no one you have that money, and you'll be fine, son. There are folks out there that think blacks can't survive living off a plantation. Well, I think they're wro-wrong. You have the right to have a happy life, and this money will help.

"In light of what's happened today, I think you should get out of here as soon as An . . . drew can find safe passage on a ship for you. You'll have to leave when he tells you. I know you don't want to, but it's for your safety, and you still have so much liv . . . ing to do. I'd like it to be in a land where you can have your free . . . dom eventually. My cousin will treat you right, the way he should. I made him swear to it. I'll die knowin' you'll be happy some . . . day, having adventures and babies. Andrew, please m-make sure they get to his plantation safely." He smiled warmly at Mary and Jed as they cried. He took his good arm off his chest and beckoned Jed and May to his bosom. Jacob hugged them both and then slightly pushed them away, saying, "Here, here now, it's Andrew and Laura's turn."

Jacob turned to Laura and Andrew and started, "Your uncle, my dearest friend, was to have money from my estate. Now that money goes to you both. With a new babe coming, you'll need to buy things for him or her. On the more serious side, you're probably wondering where you are going to l-live. Well, you're going to live in your new home: The Maisy-Lee Plantation. I signed everything to your names. The place is yours. I'd planned on your workforce still being here to help you. No one could have fore . . . seen what happened today. I'm sorry, Andrew, but you'll have to hire help, if you p-plan to stay. The other option is to sell the place and t-take the money and start a new life somewhere else. It's *all* yours. I had my lawyer draw up the papers while I was in the hospital. What do you think, you two?"

They knelt by Jacob's bed, cried, and said, "Jacob, we don't know what to say. How could we ever thank you for the trust in us and your kindness?"

Jacob was having more chest pain but refused to tell them. He felt the urgency now to say everything before it was too late. His heart beating faster, he asked, "Do you kids think you'll stay?"

Andrew and Laura said, "We'd love to stay, Jacob. We'll hire field-workers." Jacob smiled a sigh of relief. He was happy to hear they were staying.

Jacob calmed himself, his breathing slowing, and said, "I'm happy you're stay . . . ing. I want to be buried beside my children. Promise me that, Andrew!"

Laura spoke as Andrew was starting to cry again, "Jacob, we'll bury you right beside *your* children, but there's lots of time yet to . . ."

Jacob shook his head. He started to get worse pain in his chest, his heart racing. He had to get his last words out. "Think of me now and again with good thoughts. I've l-loved you all." He took a last shaky breath, clutched his chest, and winced in pain. His body froze and then slowly relaxed. He passed away with a tear in his eye. Their beloved Jacob Marcus was dead!

The sobbing in the room was loud and went on for some time. This was the most horrible day of their lives. The grim reaper had taken his toll: Dr. Alex, the slaves—Timothy, Thomas, Isaac, Esther, Amelia—and now their most beloved Jacob. It was an unimaginable tragedy that befell the Maisy-Lee Plantation all within twenty-four hours. The four sobbed into the night and woke up on the floor of Jacob's room. They had all cried themselves to sleep.

Chapter 10

Funerals and a Getaway

L AURA, ANDREW, JED, AND MARY had a very rough few days. There was a memorial service in town for Dr. Brookes. It was very well attended by many respected businessmen, doctors, nurses, Laura's parents . . . almost the whole town. Even Ethan Jordan showed up. Mary and Jed were allowed to attend, but they had to stand upstairs, at the back of the church, and thankfully, he never saw them. The four of them were shocked Ethan had the nerve to come at all. But the worst was yet to come.

The day after Alex's memorial, there was another; this one was held at the Maisy-Lee Plantation. There was a service for Jacob, who was obviously respected just as much as the doctor. Farmers came from miles around and the townspeople too. Jacob was a good man, revered by most.

Rumors had spread around the island about the fire and death of his slaves. Were they true? Was it arson and murder? People were naturally curious about the slaves' deaths, but that was not the reason for their attendance; Jacob Marcus was.

As people arrived, Jed was at the mouth of the driveway, and he told everyone where to park their carriages, wagons, and horses. He was very busy, and he thought he might miss the service. Just when he thought there would be no more people coming, he heard another horse on the road. He waited to take care of this one, and then he would be going to the grave site with everyone else. As he took the reins of this horse, the man dismounted. Staring into the face of Jed was Ethan Jordan. Jed became scared.

He shook with fear. Ethan Jordan had a most evil look. Ethan said, "Well, well, well, what do we have here? I guess one got away. Where was you hidin', boy?" Jed was shaking too much to speak. Mr. Jordan had not taken care of *all* the slaves. Somehow, this one got away from him. He was angry with himself for his mistake.

Everyone went to Jacob's grave, where the service was to be conducted. Jacob's favorite minister officiated. As the service started, they all prayed for Jacob's soul. Some wondered if the rumors were true as they looked past Jacob's grave and saw a much larger area that had been recently dug. Were all of Jacob's slaves burned to death and buried nearby Jacob's newly dug grave?

As Andrew and Laura stood together, they saw Ethan arrive. Andrew was furious and wanted to tear him apart, limb from limb. Laura saw the anger in her husband's eyes and squeezed his hand so he wouldn't cause a scene. Ethan now had a look to him of almost pride. Pride in his murders and that he had hurt as many people as he did.

He looked past Laura. Directly behind her was Mary. Ethan did not kill her either when he pushed her down the stairs. He clenched his teeth in anger. She was alive too! He hadn't finished the job. But then, he thought to himself, he did hurt Jacob in the worst way. He didn't intend it to cause Jacob's death. That, he thought to himself, was a bonus! Ethan was such a hateful man.

Andrew saw him glare at Mary, and right then, he knew he had to get Mary and Jed off this plantation as soon as possible, even tonight, if he could. Their lives depended on it. He would have to move fast to get them to Mississippi. He knew Ethan would try to kill them both.

After the service, everyone retired to the main house for refreshments. Mary and Laura had left a few minutes earlier to get things ready. They had a beautiful spread of sandwiches, tea, coffee, and desserts, pretty much the same as the day before after Alex's service. Everyone was giving Andrew and Laura their heartfelt condolences. People just whispered to each other about the slaves' deaths, but Jacob Marcus was the topic of the day.

All of a sudden, Mary became very frightened. She looked to Laura and said, "Laura-Ma'am, he's in here. The man that hurt me, the man that killed the others is here. I'se so 'fraid. Do I have ta serve him?"

Laura looked to Mary and replied, "No, dear, you don't have to. Andrew or I will do it. I just can't believe that he has the gall to show his face around here. Andrew wants to make him pay for everyone dying, but we only have your word about Ethan being responsible, and the police won't believe a slave."

While people were enjoying the food and drink, they were having a pleasant time even under the circumstances.

There was a sudden loud voice from the back of the room. It startled everyone. He asked, "So tell us, Mr. Brookes, what is to be done with the plantation? If you're going to sell it, I'd like to put the first bid in. I aim to expand my plantation. I'll even give ya'll a right fine price fer it too. I'll even let you and your . . . *wifey here* . . . stay on and help by runnin' things for me." He was sneering as he was mentioning Laura. Everyone in the room went silent. Ethan was smoking a cigar and tapping the ashes on the floor. He continued, "Now I also see you're short on slaves 'round here!" An evil grin came to his face as he went on. "Oh well, I see you have a couple left . . . *fer now*. I'd be happy to sell ya a few for a right good price. Or *is* the plantation even being put upon the block?"

Laura could take no more. She cut him off and said, "Mr. Jordan, what is being done with the plantation is none of your business, but I'll tell you anyway. Jacob Marcus was a kind, sweet, and generous man. My husband and I own the plantation now." Everyone was still quiet, with a few gasps of surprise.

After a few moments, people started to move around and chatter quietly, but they didn't want to miss anything. Ethan tossed his cigar on the floor and mashed it into the floor with his boot. He said to Andrew as they were now nose to nose, "Looks like we'll be neighbors then. I'm sure there won't be no trouble between the two farms. Do you want me to arrange some slaves fer ya, boy?" His grin gave shivers down the spines of all.

Mr. Jordan went to the liquor cabinet, which was locked, so he put his elbow through the glass and took out a full bottle of rum. People were disgusted by his behavior. They started to fear him after witnessing this act of barbarism. The visitors went silent again.

Ethan stopped in front of Laura and spat in her face, saying, "I told you before, bitch, don't you never talk to me like that! Next time, it might be your turn to join your precious Jacob Marcus in the ground! Remember, Mr. Brookes, I said you only have two slaves left . . . *fer now*. What are you going to do?" He laughed loudly as he exited the room and left the plantation, bottle of rum in hand.

People were shocked at Ethan's behavior. Andrew said, "Ladies and gentlemen, he's gone and I don't think he'll be back. Please stay and enjoy more sandwiches and coffee. Remember, we're here to honor our great and wonderful friend, Jacob Marcus."

Andrew stood beside his wife and thanked everyone for everything, for their kindness and concern. He extended an invitation to all to feel free to come back and visit sometime. They would be welcome. People thanked them in return and wished them well.

After the house was empty, the four of them cleaned up. No one said a word for several minutes. Andrew was formulating a plan to get the two away from the plantation right away. He was sure now. It had to be tonight. After the dishes were cleaned and put away, Andrew said, "Let's grab a coffee, sit down, and I'll tell you my plan."

As they sat, Andrew continued, "Jed, Mary, you know I have to move you off the plantation as quickly as I can. It is the only way we can save your lives. You've got to get to Mississippi. Mr. Jordan will come back to try and hurt or kill you. I don't know when he will try, so that's why you have to leave right away." Mary let a tear fall down her cheek. She knew this day was coming but not quite this soon.

Jacob had given Andrew directions to his cousin's plantation in Mississippi. Andrew knew that the best way to get two endangered slaves to the States safely was by traveling with a white man or a couple, pretending to be his slaves all the way to Mississippi.

He told them, "I want you to pack your belongings, and we'll leave tonight. All four of us will go to town, but you two will be hidden. All anyone will see is Laura and I. I'll take you to Uncle Alex's flat, and I'll find someone to take you on a ship. Don't worry."

After dark, they put their belongings into the wagon, and they set off for town. He told them, "We're going to speed up to go past Ethan Jordan's, so just keep low and we'll do fine."

They seemed to be successful at getting past the Jordan farm without being noticed.

When they got to town, Jed and Mary were let in the back door of Alex's office. There was a staircase to get upstairs to the apartment. Andrew was sure this was the best place for them to hide—right in plain sight! But they were cautioned to not light any lanterns for their own safety. In the dark, Andrew showed them the bedroom, but he made them feel their way around the large bed and where the chamber pot was. These were the necessities until morning. Laura and Andrew had to get back to the plantation and come back then.

Andrew said, "I'll be back in the morning. I'll make it look like we are cleaning the flat out, and I'll bring breakfast too. I must find someone tomorrow to accompany you on a ship. As the girls started crying, Andrew said, "We really have to get going, love. We can't stay."

Andrew and Laura left and made it back to the plantation without incident. Laura still had tears rolling down her cheeks. "Andrew, I feel like I'm losing a daughter, a best friend, and a sister." He felt the same way about Jed.

Bright and early in town, there was so much noise that Mary and Jed awoke. There were no farm sounds, and it sounded odd to them not to hear the animals and the plantation rooster. It was about nine forty-five when Andrew and Laura arrived. Laura had their breakfast and Jed's belt with his money rolled up in it. Andrew was moving things around in the wagon, making it look like he was clearing it for Alex's belonging. They couldn't chance for Ethan Jordan to find out their plan.

Dr. Reid was on his way to the hospital to do his rounds and stopped by to talk to Andrew. Dr. Reid said, "Andrew, m'boy, how is things today? I thought that both services were very good, and lots turned out for each one. Those are two men who will be missed around here. Cleaning out Alex's stuff there?" Andrew shook his head. He wanted to take the doctor into his confidence . . . he felt he could trust him.

Andrew took Dr. Reid into the flat to have coffee and he asked, "Dr. Reid, would you be knowing anyone who is traveling to the United States on a ship tomorrow or the next day?"

Dr. Reid asked, "This is about that Ethan Jordan fellow and Jed and Mary . . . isn't it, son? I don't know anyone who can handle him. I imagine his slaves are sick sometimes but won't let them get any treatment. He makes my skin crawl, and I don't mind saying it."

Andrew said, "Dr. Reid, I need this kept very confidential. What I am going tell you can't leave this flat." Mary, Jed, and Laura were in the bedroom and heard Andrew talking to someone.

They were scared, until they realized it was Dr. Reid.

Dr. Reid finally responded to Andrew's question. "Well, lad, as a matter of fact, I do know someone sailing in two days. I am! My wife and I are just about to go to visit relatives in Mississippi.

My wife's parents are there and a couple of sisters. We go at least twice a year. Is there something I can help you with, Andrew? Anything?"

It would be the most perfect solution to their problem. Andrew explained about having to get Mary and Jed out of Jamaica before they were murdered too. Andrew told Dr. Reid about everything they'd gone through with Ethan Jordan, how cruel he was and the murders that he almost bragged about. He was the one that had his uncle Alex beaten, just for treating Negroes.

He told Dr. Reid that Jacob willed these two slaves to his cousin in Mississippi. He wanted to give them a better life in the States. Andrew told him about Caleb and about Mary and her baby too. Dr. Reid was horrified. He had no idea how mean Ethan Jordan *really* was.

Dr. Reid said he and his wife would gladly escort Mary and Jed to Mississippi. Andrew showed him the map to the cotton plantation. As Dr. Reid looked at it, he realized that it was on the delta, only forty miles south of where they were going, and it was on the way. He said he and his wife would be glad to do this favor for them after all they'd gone through, and he wanted to help in some way.

Right then, Dr. Reid had to be getting to the hospital, so Andrew accompanied him so they could talk more. Andrew tried to give Dr. Reid the money for Jed and Mary's passage; he wouldn't take it. He would gladly purchase the kids' tickets, but they had to do everything in secrecy. If Ethan found Jed and Mary before they left the island, they were as good as dead! Andrew also tried to give the doctor money for his help, but he wouldn't take it either.

The day of their departure, they would try to get the young couple on the ship without any problems. When it came time, Andrew and Laura had to *really* say good-bye to Mary and Jed. This would be very hard. They did it in Alex's flat, not out in the open. Dr. Reid took the couple under his wing as they left Port Royal, Jamaica, quietly . . . for the last time.

On the ship, Dr. and Mrs. Reid paid for two adjoining rooms—a large stateroom connected to a smaller room meant for children and maids or nannies or for a butler or a valet. Mary and Jed had never seen such luxury before, not even at the Maisy-Lee.

This was the first time they had been on a ship since the *Destino*. Mary and Jed were both upset being on a ship again. It felt like it was a lifetime ago, but only a few years had passed, and the terror that was in Mary's head was as fresh in her mind as if it was yesterday.

By the time they arrived in Mississippi, Mary had told Mrs. Reid about their lives and how kind Jacob was, especially about him sending them to America to have a good life. Mrs. Reid was pleased to have the two along on the trip. Jed and Mary ended up having the time of their lives with Dr. and Mrs. Reid. They happily smiled, which was something neither of them had done recently.

When the ship docked, the stagecoach the Reids hired was standing by. The land journey was about an hour to the plantation. As they drove past large fields, there were many blacks working in them. They saw the vast cotton fields of the Deep South. When they arrived at the Marcus Plantation, it was near lunchtime. They were getting really nervous about their new home. Would the plantation owner like them and keep them doing the same jobs they did for Jacob, whom they missed so much?

The coach stopped at the main house, and all four got out. Dr. Reid rapped on the door. When it opened, there was a man who looked much like Jacob. Dr. Reid said, "Mr. Jeremiah Marcus, I presume? My name is Dr. Reid, and I am delivering the two slaves that your cousin Jacob arranged to give you upon his death. We're sorry you couldn't make it to your cousin's memorial. It was a lovely service and very well attended. Well, sir, let me introduce Jed and Mary Allen."

Mr. Marcus shook hands with Dr. Reid and his wife, saying, "Please, it's Jeremiah. Would you both like to freshen up and have lunch with me? Please, your driver too." They were delighted to be invited to dine with Jeremiah. Their coach driver was white, so Jeremiah didn't mind inviting him to come in, wash, and eat with them too.

Mr. Marcus then gave a rather loud shout to someone named Betty. She was a large black woman who cooked and oversaw the house staff. She was told to take Mary and Jed away and get them settled, and they were told to say their good-byes now since they would be too busy later. Mary and Jed thanked Dr. and Mrs. Reid for helping them to get there and said their good-byes. As Betty was ushering them out of the room, Mary asked that they say hello to Laura and Andrew for them and let them know that they got there safely. As soon as Betty got them out of the room, they were expected to work right away. Betty asked their names, and Jed replied, "My name be Jedediah, and dis be my wife, Mary. You'se can call me Jed. Our lass name be Allen. Is we goin' ta be in da same room t'gedder?"

Betty laughed. "What chew tink dis is, boy? A hotel? Y'all sleeps where you'se put, you'se juss 'nudder pair o' niggers 'round here. You may not even see one 'nudder all day long. Git used to it."

Just then Mary started to cry. "Why can't we see each other? We do nothin' bad. We's good workers. We has a letter here from Jacob-Sir 'bout our work bein' good."

Betty said, "Ain't no use showin' dat ting to me, girl. You'se know it agin da law fer niggers ta be readin' an' writin'. Dat's da law an' dat da way it be's here. It agin da law ta even teach blacks ta read an' write." Betty told the two of them that if they knew how to do either, don't let da massa know.

Jed spoke up then. "Who da massa?"

Betty threw her arms in the air with frustration. "Don't chew know . . . dat man dat let you in, dat da massa. What he say an' do to ya be his law. He axe ya to do somtin', ya best do it right away. Y'all don't sass him none. He be hittin' ya an' whuppin' ya. I 'spect you'se Jed will go out in da fiel' an' pick cotton wit' t'others. Mary, ya may be in da house wit' me, don't rightly knows yet. But one ting's sure, you'se young an' pretty, he gonna want ya in his bed befo' long!"

Jed became mad. "No one ever gonna touch my wife. She be mine an' no one gits at her!

Why won't we be bedded t'gedder?"

Betty laughed again. "You'se sure you'se comes from 'nother plantation? Don't seem like you'se knows nuthin'. Don't rightly knows fer gospel trut' yet where you'se workin'. We's findin' out after lunch . . . oh gracious me, I gotta git lunch out dere. You might as well start workin' now, girl. Carry dese two bowls an' faller me."

Mary did what she was told and followed. She served her new master and his guests, and he was pleased with her. Mary had given him the letter from Jacob to read.

After the Reids went on their way, Mr. Marcus told Betty, "Keep her here in the house. She can be a kitchen wench for you. The boy can report to the gardener." They were both pleased about his arrangements. They would have to get used to more rules here, but maybe it was going to be okay after all.

Midafternoon, Jeremiah took both new slaves outside and tied Jed to a tree—his whipping tree. He tore open the back of Jed's shirt and saw a few well-healed scars. He sneered, "I thought as much." He took up his whip, and he whipped Jed ten lashes. Jed tried not to cry out in pain, but eventually he had to. Mary was screaming for the massa to stop, but he just glared at the girl. She stopped.

Next was Mary's turn. He tore open the back of her dress and whipped her eight times as Jed wept for her. He then made them both stand in the warm sun, bleeding for an hour. They had to be silent too. Mary was still crying. They both had to use the outhouse. Mary could not last. She urinated, and the master saw this and said, "Well, little girl, you just earned yourself another hour out here." Jed held his bladder until he was told he could go.

Betty came out with a salt rub for Jed's back. She put it on him, and he managed not to scream. It was difficult, but he was more worried about Mary. She could never stand this. He really feared for her safety *now*. The master made Jed stand the rest of the time, watching Mary suffer.

When Mary's next hour was over, she got the salt rub from Betty; it was too much for her to take. She passed out. Jed ran to her to put his arms around her, but the master had his shotgun. He let a shot go in the air, right by Jed's head. Jed stopped dead in his tracks. Jeremiah Marcus was staring into his eyes, deep. Jed saw that same look in Ethan Jordan's eyes once.

How could his Jacob-Sir be so wrong about his own cousin? They had been told that they would be looked after by Mr. Marcus. Jed had to start today to learn from others and plan their escape. He was devastated by seeing Mary hurt like that. He had to save her. He must get them out of this hell on earth . . . *soon*!

Jeremiah told Betty that Mary could sleep in her room. She had a bed with a drawer that can be pulled out to reveal another smaller bed. That is where Mary would sleep. He told Betty he did not want any of the male slaves to get to her. Jeremiah told Betty to get the gardener to come up to the house immediately. She set off right away to get him. Mary was still in pain from the salt rub and the whipping but conscious now.

Jeremiah told them in a gruff, stern voice, "Mary is sleeping in the house, and Jed will work and stay with the gardener and barn boss. While you're here, there will be no sexual relations between you." He couldn't have known that their marriage was still not consummated. But they still wanted to be in the same room.

Jed really feared for Mary now. She would be near the master, and he might not be able to protect her. What was going to happen to them now?

The boss of the gardens and barn staff came right away, and Jeremiah told him that he had a new worker. He said, "This is Jed Allen. I believe I've taken care of his notion to run away! Jed, this is your boss. His name is William, but you will call him boss." Jed was relieved to see his boss was black. Jeremiah continued, "Don't be getting notions that he's going let you get off without hard work. He has a boss too. The overseer is Mr. Jackson Wylde, and he's a mean son of a bitch! He will be addressed at all times as 'sir.' You'll meet him later. You do whatever you are told to do, or the punishments get worse every time you cause a fuss." Jeremiah laughed and smacked Jed on the back, right where he was whipped and treated with salt, fully knowing what pain he would be in. It was agony, but Jed didn't utter a word.

William took Jed into the barn first. He asked Jed what he did on the other plantation. Jed said, "It was my job ta keep da gardens pretty an' lookin' nice. I also looked after da barn chores an' I done look after dem animals. Jacob-Sir liked da job I done on dem."

William said, "Who be dis Jacob-Sir you'se talkin' 'bout?"

Jed continued, "He be your Jeremiah's cousin. Why he be so mean, dis Mr. Marcus? What did Mary an' me do ta get whupped?"

Jed's boss said to him, "Dat be so you'se don't run. You'se better get tings right here, boy.

You ain't on no easy plantation now, boy. You heed what I say now. You'se and dat girl be workin' hard here."

Jed interrupted, "She just ain't no girl. She be my wife, Mary. Why can't we live in our own cabin an' sleep t'gedder? Whas wrong wit' dat?"

William laughed. He said, "Married, you'se ain't married while you'se here. Massa don't 'llow it here. An' as for havin' a cabin t'gedder, you'se never have it here. What his cousin like anyhow? It soun' like you'se was workin' fer a soff kinda man, not a hard man like da massa here."

Jed was about to tell him about Jacob when Jeremiah walked into the barn. He overheard the last part of the conversation. He laughed, "I'll tell you what Jacob Marcus was like. He was soft, all right. He was a mama's boy. He didn't believe in punishing, like he was brought up seeing. No, on his plantation, you were treated right, am I right, Jed?" He nodded. Jeremiah continued, "Yeah, that's exactly what I thought. He was a man that was God-fearin' and easy to work for. He had no punishments."

Right then Jed stopped him and said, "Dat be wrong, Massa. Jacob-Sir punish us once, when one o' da other slaves runned off. He lock our cabins . . ."

Jeremiah shouted at Jed, "Don't you never interrupt me again . . . you'se gonna learn not to sass me, interrupt me, or talk to me without bein' asked to! You got it, boy?" Jed nodded his head again. Jeremiah grabbed him by the arm and took him to the whipping tree and tied him there once again. He was whipped five more lashes. Jed was in severe pain now, worse than before. Jeremiah said that Jed was to go back to William, shut his mouth, and get to work.

When Jed went into the barn, William was shoveling manure out of the stalls. He got Jed a shovel. Jed had tears rolling down his face but did not utter a sound. He worked hard until he heard a bell ring. William said, "Dat's da end of our day, boy. You come wit' me an' I'se take ya to da cabin you'se gonna live in."

They walked down to where the cabins were. There was a spare bed in William's cabin. He liked Jed, and he felt that he needed much guidance. Jed told him thanks, and he was going to try to not be any more trouble.

William had to give Jed the rules of this plantation. "Now, boy, I'se goin' to make our supper. Dere be no food for you till tamorra, but you can has some o' mine."

Jed said, "I did miss lunch, I guess."

William said, "No, you didn't, boy. There ain't no lunch 'round here. Not for slaves. You eat in the midmornin' an' ya eat in da evenin'. Dat be it for ever'day." William did not want to be mean to Jed, but he had to toughen him up to live here, or he'd die for sure. By the sound of it, Mary wasn't going to handle it well either. Every pretty girl that comes to this plantation has to go to bed with the master eventually.

As William started, Jed listened very intently. "Now pay 'ttention an' remember dese rules.

Once a week you gets yo' food. Tamorra be da day. We each gits fourteen herrings, or sometimes we gits a bit o' pork. Remember dis has ta lass ya a week. We also gits a few pound o' cornmeal each. Dis food ta lass you all week too. We slaves has a garden dat we grow vegibles in. We shares dem, but we don't has much time to tend 'em. We share da work in da garden, but maybe da massa let you do it, since you loves it so. We has 'tatoes, carrots, peas, beans, onions, okra, an' tomatas. Sometimes we's also be gittin' salt pork, coffee, and, once in a while, an egg, if we's been good an' dey has plenty left over.

"Each cabin has ta make deys own meals. We can take our food out ta eat wit' ever'one an' talk. If y'all wants to do dis tonight, I can show you to da udders."

Jed said, "I tink I best be stayin' in here wit' y'all to learn me some more rules. Dat be okay wit' you?"

William smiled. "I tink dat be bess, boy. Learn stuff now an' meets 'em tamorra. Dey's lotsa time for dat, lotsa time indeed. You'se prob'ly gonna gits some more clothes. Dese ones is gittin' a might bit small. You'se gonna git one set an' dey has to lass. We only gits 'em twice a year. You'se gotta always 'member, when da massa talk at chew, you'se pays 'ttention, an' always address him as massa . . . nuttin' else, just massa. When he say jump, you ask how high, Massa! You do ever'ting he say, or you get whupped.

"You make sure 'at you'se don't says nuttin' more 'bout da girl bein' you'se wife, dat just give him a better 'scuse to bed her down, an' make no mistake, he gonna tell you how good she be.

He may want to keep her for all time."

Jed was getting mad. "He better not be tryin' my Mary, I'se kill him wit' my own hands."

William could see the truth in Jed's eyes; he would kill him to protect his Mary. William continued, "We's not allowed to sleep wit' da girls here, only he is. Massa wants no chil'run 'round da plantation. Any girl gits wit' chile, she sold or killed, an' . . . da boy who dun it gits killed too. He won't even let wenches birth to see if dey's his own chil'run.

"We rises at dawn an' we starts workin'. At 'bout ten in da mornin', we gits called in to brekfass. We gots ta make it an' eats it an' clean up in one hour. If'n you'se don't gits it done, you'se gits da whip. We work after we eats an' till da bell go at six in da evenin'. Den da time be ours. Dey's no drinkin' here, 'cept fer da massa. He be mean an' he juss as soon kills you if'n you crosses him bad 'nuff.

"We has ta keep our cabins clean, clothes washed an' no talking in da fiel' neither. You'se gonna meet da overseer tamorra mornin'. He be da one to rattle our cabins an' gits us up fer work. Da cabins be locked ever' night an' unlock when he be gettin' us awake. Dat overseer, Jackson Wylde, da massa tole ya 'bout. He wasn't kiddin'. He be da meanness son of a bitch on dis here eart'. You don't *never* cross him, I means *never*! He juss as soon shoot ya betwixt da eyes. Keep clear o' him, you gots all dat, boy?" Jed nodded his head, probably more from fear.

Mary was getting the same lessons in the house. She was told she was only allowed to see Jed when he came up around the house and only for a couple of minutes. There was no reason for her to go out to the barn or the gardens. She knew about the no-baby rule and felt comfortable that no other slaves would bother her like that sailor did. While Betty was busy, Mary drifted back to the Maisy-Lee and their own private cabin.

Mary wanted Jed but just couldn't bring herself to make love to him yet. She was still traumatized so bad with her first experience on the *Destino*. When they lived at Jacob's, Jed had been so kind to wait for her, and she didn't mind him masturbating if that was what he needed until she was ready.

She remembered the time his erection didn't go down for an hour or so. They didn't know what was happening to him and were concerned because it was painful for him. It happened again a few more times afterward. He didn't even need to be aroused. A couple of times, working in the barn or garden, he would become erect, and it would not release for a couple of hours. Each time, it became more painful, and it seemed like it took longer to go down. He was too ashamed to mention it to Andrew, Alex, or Jacob; and he even tried to hide it from Mary too but couldn't.

Betty called out to Mary and broke her thoughts. She told her about the food situation, both for her and for Jed. She would eat better than him. She could have three meals a day with Betty after serving the master and his white staff.

Mary was to spend her days with Betty, cooking and cleaning the kitchen and serving meals. She would rarely have time to even get out of the kitchen to take a walk, if she was allowed.

After their first day at the new plantation, both of them were tired and scared. Mary wondered what Jed was doing right then, and he wondered the same about her. She spent a little while in bed telling Betty about the misadventures in her short life. Betty thought she'd heard it all, but the sailor on the *Destino* and that Ethan Jordan were the worst men she'd heard about in a long time! Betty listened to every word while she was tending to Mary's back. Somehow she knew in her heart that this beautiful young Ashanti girl was telling the truth. Betty took the child to her bosom and wept, "Oh, chil' y'all dun suffer so much already! I pray ta God ta looks after y'all an' you'se husban'. I sees it in ya, you'se likely gonna run, I'se do what I can an' he'p y'all, but we cain't talk 'bout it now."

Mary looked up at Betty while still in her arms and cried. From her bosom, Betty took out something that Mary had seen once before. Laura-Ma'am had one. Betty had a beautiful linen-and-lace handkerchief tucked inside her dress. Betty took it out and dried Mary's tears as she fell asleep. She was safe for tonight. Betty would start passing a message to a faraway place in the morning.

William and Jed were talking until late too. Jed was exhausted but glad to be on a one-inch mattress, even if it was on a rickety old cot. His back was really sore. The overseer was told to put bandage supplies in the cabin for him to use. William fixed him up the best he could for the night. William said, "Jed, you'se Mr. Marcus, he soun' like great man. He mussa love you an' Mary so." Jed smiled a weak smile, nodded, wept, and finally fell asleep.

Chapter 11

Hiring Permanent Help

AFTER THE MCDONALDS' CROP WAS in, they were finally alone and able to talk freely and not fall asleep on each other. They talked about hiring help. John didn't know who it would be. He liked the five boys who were working there but did not know who they should hire.

Diana interrupted his thought. "I've been thinkin', m'love. What do you think of hiring a couple first? We could have a helper for you and one for me in the house. In return, if it works out, we could offer them the use of a portion of land on one of the other fields for growing food for themselves, sort of like crofting back home."

John rubbed his chin in thought. "Well, I think that might be an excellent idea. And to go even further, we could build a small house on whichever field we let them use. They could stay and live here on the land. I would still pay them too but not as much as we'd pay if they were coming here daily. What do you think? After, if we need more help, we could hire the other boys as we need them, but they would come in the mornings and leave in the late afternoon. Does this make sense to ya, darlin', or am I reaching at stars?"

Diana smiled. "That's wonderful. So we would look for a couple first and make the proposal, which I can't see anyone turning down. It is a wonderful opportunity for anyone we choose. Oh, John, we could make some couple very happy. Let's get Adam's recommendation soon.

But can we afford the expense of building a small house for them? I never thought of that."

John told her, patting her hand tenderly, "We'll make it, lass. Don't ye worry, we can do it.

We'll go into town in the morning and do our errands. Right now, I'd like to set to paper a design for this little house we're going to build. I guess until it's built, the couple will be going back and forth to town. For this big project, I may ask Jeff, Adam, and some of the boys for help, as well as the couple we hire, to build the house."

Until the house was built, Diana suggested that since they had extra rooms in the farmhouse, to let the couple sleep there in their house. This is if the couple they choose doesn't already have a place to live and prefer not to live on the farm. It would be more convenient having them there permanently.

Diana found John something to write on so he could design and figure costs. By bedtime, he had things worked out, and he was proud of himself. They went to bed, happy with themselves and very proud of their new potato farm.

The next morning was raining, so they used the cover on the wagon and tried to keep themselves as dry as possible on their trip to town. Diana said John should see Adam while she was at Lavalle's with some eggs to sell and to do her shopping at the same time. He dropped her off at the store, and he went to the livery. John got off the wagon and said, "Good morning, Adam, and again, thank ye fer your hard work lately. We never would have gotten as far as we did without your help.

"I was thinking about hiring blacks permanently. What we would like is a couple. Maybe you could recommend a couple for us, and we'll talk to them. Do you know of a couple we could talk to? We'd like to employ a husband and wife, if possible."

Adam replied, "I don't know of a couple already here just yet, but I hear there may be a couple heading north from the States. I'll let you know what I hear. It won't likely be for near four or five weeks yet. It could be more. They are young, maybe about your age. Slaves on a cotton plantation in Mississippi. Before that, they were on a sugar plantation in Jamaica. They have a history of being hardworking and will be good workers for you. John, this couple has been through a tortured life, for the most part, especially the wife.

"They originally come from Africa. The man is a gardener and barn worker and does well with farm animals, and I hear he happens to be a jack-of-all-trades. That was on the first plantation they lived on, and the second one, he had much of the same jobs. The wife has always worked around the kitchen and in the house. They're going to need a place to stay too. How does this sound? They're names are Jed and Mary Allen. We hope, God willing, they will be able to make it up here to safety."

John said, "Well, let me know when they get here, and we'll look them over and give them a try. By the way, when they get here, if things work out, do you think you could help me put up a small house for them? We wouldn't mind them living on the property." Adam smiled a big approving, grateful smile and nodded.

John was wondering how Adam knew so much about this couple and when they were arriving. It seemed strange to John. He went to join his wife in the store, where she was picking up necessities. John and Rene started talking, and Emilie was helping Diana to get everything on her list. John was ordering two special hooks that would help with removing rocks and trees. There would be one for the Clydes to use and one for the Shetlands to use.

Rene told him he could order one but to ask Adam first if he had a used one. John went back to the livery and asked Adam about the hook, but he didn't have one. John told him he'll buy new ones, but if anyone wanted to borrow them, they could. Adam said he'd keep that in mind. John turned to leave, but he came back, saying "Adam, how did you know about the couple that's coming here?"

Adam smiled and replied, "The Lord works in mysterious ways, John." He turned and went back to the store and ordered the hooks, which would be a week or so on the train. Just then, Christina came into the store to buy some soft wool for making baby clothes. The ladies were gabbing and giggling.

John excused himself from the store again and his wife, who was too busy talking to notice if he were there or not, and went to see Adam one more time. John asked, "Adam, how *do* you know about the couple traveling here? I'd really like to know." Adam had a feeling that John and Diana could be trusted. Adam closed the doors of his shop for a few moments while he and John had a discussion.

Several minutes later, Adam opened his doors, and John went back to the store to collect his wife, who was still talking. He tapped her on the shoulder and said, "Darlin', the farm won't run itself, you know." She turned to him a said that she would only be a minute, which she said a few times. John didn't like to get annoyed with her, but he wanted to get home and do some work since the rain stopped and the sun came out.

Diana said good-bye to the girls. John had already paid for the supplies and food and was waiting on the wagon for her. He grabbed her hand and helped her up to sit beside him. She got very busy telling him about Tina and knitting outfits and how good she looked and that her and Jeff will be at their place on Saturday and Sunday, weather permitting, for taking out trees and rocks.

John mentioned that the couple they would consider will be there within the next several weeks and that they were coming from the United States. Adam will let them know when they arrive.

While John and Diana awaited the arrival of the couple to come from the United States, Tina, Adam, and Jeff had been out to the McDonalds' on the weekends because the men were helping John remove trees on the west field. They would pull the rocks as they went along too.

His rock-pulling hooks had only taken a week to come in from the day he ordered it.

The Clydes were working hard, pulling larger trees and rocks out, while the Shetlands were taking care of smaller ones. Adam came to help when he could and so did Michael Maguire and his son, Toby. He was usually chopping and stacking wood for all their houses to share.

John needed more help during the week, but everyone they knew had to work their own farms and had jobs. Diana tried her best to do some of the fieldwork with John through the week, but it was heavy. He hired the colored boys again. Not all could come every day. Sometimes one would come, sometime two or three. Whoever was available and wanted the work came in the morning. It was the same arrangement as for planting. They were paid fifteen cents per day for nine hours, two meals included.

Diana helped. She could maneuver the ponies well enough, and John guided the Clydes. She needed more rest than usual lately, and she was feeling sick when she cooked breakfast for John every day. He wanted to take her to the doctor, but she refused. While she was out in the field one midafternoon, she fainted. That was it! John placed her on the wagon and drove her and the ponies back to the barn. By the time he got her to the barn, she had regained her composure and was starting to argue with him . . . all the way to town.

Dr. Marsh was in his office and not traveling around to patients, so they were in luck! He only had one patient in the office. He was a long, lanky sort of fellow with a wife and children. His most prominent trait was that his glasses were always on his head but he could scarcely find them. All his patients were amused by this.

John said, "We'll wait right here, Diana, m'love. You'll see him if I have to hog-tie ya!" He was worried, but she kept telling him she was fine and didn't need a doctor. The other patient left, and Dr. Marsh called her in. She told him her symptoms and he examined her. He was able to come to a conclusion quickly.

Dr. Marsh told her, "Mrs. McDonald, you are going to have a baby!" She was shocked and happy at the same time. She was so thrilled she started jumping up and down. All of a sudden, she stopped and looked at the doctor. "Oh dear, I guess I have to stop doing this." He grinned and told her she could be excited and jump but not too high or too long, to tone it down a bit. He told her to start seeing him once a month and *no* fieldwork whatsoever. She got dressed when he left the room.

John asked, "Well, Doctor, is she all right? Is there something wrong with her?"

Dr. Marsh said, "Well, Mr. McDonald, her symptoms are real enough and, at first, maybe a little alarming, but . . ." Just then Diana fluttered so high out of the examination room that she barely felt the floor beneath her at all. She looked so much better than she had in days.

She had a great big smile, and as she gently took her husband's face in her hands, she said, "My dear sweet Johnny, the Lord has blessed us with a babe!" John looked so surprised, and he couldn't speak. He put his arms around her waist, lifted her, and swung her around in joy.

"Now, Mr. McDonald, you be careful how tight you squeeze her," he kidded. "I've told her she has to see me once a month until it's close to her time, then I'll see her every week. If you have a problem getting here, I can come out to see her." Before they left his office, they paid for their appointment. The doctor was pleasantly surprised when John paid him in cash. Most people gave him vegetables, fruits, chickens, and baked goods, bartering for his services.

He was happy with cash for a change. Not that he would deny anyone treatment, black or white. He took what he knew families could afford to give. Dr. Ian Marsh had a family of his own to feed, and he was grateful to get cash.

After Diana and John left the doctor, they went to the Land Registry Office and told Jeff. He was so excited. It was almost closing time, and he asked if they could stay in town and have supper with them and Adam. He wanted them to go home with him, because he wanted to see the look on Tina's face; since there was no supper prepared at home for John and Diana, they said they'd love to come. Diana was anxious to see Tina.

While waiting for Jeffrey, the two strolled over to the livery and told Adam. He congratulated them too. They told him they are going with Jeff when he goes home so they all can see the look on Tina's face when they tell her Diana is pregnant too. Adam was going to close up when Jeff did and go with them too.

Tina was so surprised to see John and Diana come in with Adam and Jeff. Everyone had grins on their faces. Tina was delighted to see her friends coming in with Jeff. They didn't speak right away. Tina said, "Now what in the world have the four of you got up your collective sleeve? You've all been up to something, now what is it? C'mon, someone tell me now, or there's no supper for any of you." Diana smiled and rubbed her lower abdomen to see if she got the hint. She didn't.

John said, "That Dr. Marsh is really pleasant, isn't he?"

Tina replied, "Oh yes, we've never heard a bad word about him. I really like him and I think Jeff and Adam do too." All of a sudden she became concerned. "Is someone sick? Who went to see him?"

John said, "I had to take Diana today. She fainted out in the field."

Tina became alarmed. "Oh no, what's wrong?"

Diana stepped in. "Well, it's something I'll have to see Dr. Marsh every month for, for a while then every week for a month. The whole process takes about nine months." She was still rubbing her abdomen while she was speaking.

All of a sudden Tina got it! "Oh praise Jesus, *you're* having a baby too? Oh, Diana, get off your feet, girl. Sit down, and . . . oh my gosh, Jeffrey, I don't have enough food for everyone. We're having the leftovers from last night. What can I do?" She was in a tizzy!

Jeff had the solution. "Well, I think since Diana and John were with us for the good news of our having a baby at Catherine's Eatery, I think we should take them there. We can all celebrate. How does that sound to everyone?" All agreed it would be a great idea. So they walked toward the restaurant, and on their way, they saw the Lavalles. They had just closed the store and were on their way to Catherine's for supper too. John spoke up and told them the news. They were ecstatic for the couple too.

Jeff said, "Why don't you join us?" They said they'd be delighted to celebrate with them, and they all walked into the restaurant together. The staff had to pull a couple of tables closer so they could be seated together. Adam told the restaurant owners, Catherine and David, the good news that they were celebrating. They too congratulated Diana and John on their wonderful news.

Everyone had a good time, but after a couple of hours, Jeff said, "I think it is time for all good little mothers-to-be to be getting to bed. They need their rest." They all said good night and parted.

The next morning, Diana was surprised to see her husband sitting at the bottom of the bed, holding a tray with coffee, juice, three eggs, bacon, fried potatoes, toast, and a small bouquet of flowers he had just picked on his way back from the barn. She had slept in a bit, but John was happy she did. That way, he would be able to surprise her with breakfast in bed. Diana sat up. She looked at the love of her life through misty eyes and lots of love and said, "My dear sweet Johnny, I love you so. And you made breakfast too." He placed the tray on her lap and sat with her on the bed. He had brought his coffee up to be with her. Diana said, "I love you, Johnny McDonald. I know we'll be great parents because we had great parents." She paused. She missed her mother. A longing tear fell down her cheek. She wiped it away and continued, "Johnny darlin', I know your heart is in the right place, m'love. But I can't eat all of this. What say you eat the eggs and the rest, and I'll eat one piece of toast, juice, and coffee, if I can get it all to stay in place. That would be a welcome feeling. I'm sure you're hungry, love. You've already been working for a while."

John put his hand gently on her still-wet cheek, and they looked in each other's eyes. There was still the unmistakable bond they shared that had been there since childhood. They ate breakfast together, and Diana was relieved that it stayed down. It was time to tell John about morning sickness!

Diana was about to be spoiled for the next several months. John was so thrilled. He was going to be a father. He didn't get as much work done as he should have in those next few days. He kept running into the house to check on Diana. Every time he came in, she looked at him and said, "I'm fine, m'love. Now you just get back out there and tend to your business, and I'll tend to mine. I'm not the only woman in the world that has ever been in the family way. We women have been having babies for thousands of years, and I'm no different. Now *get out* of here before I shoot you across the backside with my broom and sweep you out the door myself!"

While Diana worked in the house, she constantly was thinking about the nursery she wanted to prepare. She wanted it to be in the bedroom, right next to hers and John's. Of course, she thought to herself, the baby will sleep in the cradle in their room at first. She'll move it when it sleeps all night.

John was outside working with Rolly and Gerald most of the time. The others came one or two days a week to help when they could. They were quite thrilled for Mr. and Mrs. Johns. Mr. Johns was so happy he whistled and sang all the time while he worked. The boys were always laughing. They never heard such silly dirges, as John called them. There was a fun atmosphere working with John these days. When he was in the house asking how Diana was, he was comfortable leaving the boys to continue to work. When visitors came to the farm, for that first while, they noticed John's behavior, and it was a delight to see an expectant father so happy.

Jeff and John would exchange stories about their wives' condition and progress, and they laughed all the time when they got together. It wasn't mean-spirited; it was the hilarity of a father-to- be's observations. One day Jeff said, "You know, John, I think we should write a book on this. I think we have something here."

John started laughing hysterically. "Come now, lad, you know they'd kill us! Could you just see the look on their faces if it were to be published?"

Jeff continued, "We have to let other fathers-to-be know about all this . . . stuff they go through. We'd be millionaires, John."

John said, "Well, lad, I think we should keep this on the back burner for a day, when we're not so busy." As they kept working, they laughed more.

When Jeff was at the farm, Tina always came with him. She and Diana would spend hours in the house, baking or sewing, knitting, doing laundry . . . everything that needed to be done. They both were so happy spending their time together.

Tina loved being at the farm. She was born to farmers too and loved the life. It was quite an adjustment moving to a town when she married Jeffrey. It took her a while; it was dusty and loud all the time. There were saloons to contend with and gambling. But Chatham was a small town. She couldn't even imagine how noisy and busy a city was; she'd never seen one, but then they met the McDonalds, and then she was so happy to be living in Chatham, Ontario.

Chapter 12

Escape Plans and Murder

D AWN CAME TO THE MARCUS Plantation as it did every day
with the crowing of a rooster and animal sounds. Mary was
kind of happy to hear it again.

Betty said, "Come, girl, you wash up now an' I'se start cookin' fer
da massa. You gits right down to da kitch'n quick like, an' he'p me
now." Mary got her Kente cloth robe and asked Betty if she could
maybe put it on and wear it while she worked. Betty took a look at
it and said, "No, girl, da massa don't want no tings roun' his house
lookin' like Africa. You'se bess hide it right 'way, or you'se never sees
it no mo'. You'se jus' wear da dress I done gives ya. You'se mind now,
you'se hafta keep it clean, you'se only gits two a year. Dat 'cludes da
apron I gives ya, gal . . . two a year an' you'se keep it as white an' fresh
as can be. Da massa hate ta sees dirt an' he wants ta sees a clean dress
an' apron all da time."

Mary put the dress on after she washed. Her back was still sore,
but Betty dressed her wounds daily. But the memory of the whipping
would last longer than the pain.

One day Mary asked Betty about her handkerchief. Betty was
surprised that Mary even knew what it was. Betty said, "Had me a
husban' once, an' he gives it ta me as a gift fer our weddin.'" She said no
more about it but looked sad. Mary just left things alone but thought
it was so beautiful anyway.

Mary decided, with this new day and Betty beside her, she was going to try to be happy. She skipped down the stairs and ran right into Jeremiah at the bottom. He had his newspaper in his hand, and she made him drop it. She was terrified, but she couldn't say anything. He didn't speak to her first. Jeremiah said, "Now look here, young lady, look what you've done! You made me drop my paper."

Mary got her courage up and said, "I'se sorry, Massa. I won't do it agin." She picked it up and handed it over. As she did, she continued, "Massa, I didn't mean no harm, sir. I'se so sorry I bump you, sir. Please forgive me, sir." Betty was on the other side of the door listening to them, and she was so proud of Mary for being smart enough to try and find her way out of this situation herself.

Jeremiah cleared his throat and said, "Let's just see that there is no more running or jumping in the house, shall we!" He let her go past and get in the kitchen with Betty. They both had big smiles on their faces. Maybe today will be a better day, but she wondered how Jed was.

Jed heard the roosters in the mornings when he woke up every day too. For a minute, some days, he thought he was still at the Maisy-Lee, until he rolled over onto his back. The pain made him remember. William helped get him dressed and changed the bandages daily. He was healing as well as Mary. He thought about Mary and what pain she must be in too. But he worried most about Jeremiah and what he might do to her! He didn't have much time to worry about it though, because he had to get to work.

His first order of business each day was to milk and let the cows out to graze for the day.

Next was egg collection. He worked alongside William, and before he knew it, the breakfast bell would be ringing. Everyone ran off to their cabins to get their food. This was after working about five hours, starving. After breakfast it would be another seven hours before the end of their day and supper.

As the days went on, neither of them felt the whip again. Things were going well, and Jeremiah was satisfied with their work so far. Jed especially loved working in the gardens. He always had. His favorite was the vegetable patches. His favorite vegetable was potatoes. Eating, planting, and harvesting. Carrots were close behind. As he worked away, he wondered if this day would be good for them. It would.

In the afternoon, William told Jed to take a large wheelbarrow-load of carrots, cucumbers, and potatoes up to the kitchen in the big house. Jed was beaming from ear to ear at the thought of seeing his Mary.

William told him, "Now don't you linger up dere. Da massa git 'spicious an' fin' you'se messin' wit' yo' wife, dat be bad fer ya bote. You'se bote git whupped fer sure, an' he takes her to do . . . you'se know!"

Jed took the vegetables up to the kitchen. William showed him where the side door to the kitchen was, and he knocked on it. Mary answered it and was so happy to see him. After he set the vegetables down, she jumped into his arms, which was a little painful for them both, but they didn't care. Betty saw them and pulled them apart.

Mary turned to her and said, "I'se sorry, I forgits the rule. I'se just so happy to see him, I can't he'p it." Betty looked around to see if their master was there. He wasn't. They were extremely lucky.

Betty said, "You kiss her good-bye and gits outta here, boy." He held her tenderly and kissed her. It was emotional and sweet. Betty sympathetically smiled for them, just a little.

Mary whispered in his ear, "Betty is helpin' us get a plan to run. You hear about it from William? It be soon, I hope. You okay with that, Jed?"

Jed was glad she knew about it already. He was happy. "You sure we can do it?"

Just then William was at the door and grabbed Jed by the scruff of the neck, saying, "What da hell you'se tink you'se doin', boy. You gits yo' nigger ass back to dat garden now before da massa sees you'se t'gedder!" Jed reluctantly went back to the garden. Not even being called a nigger could ruin his day. He had the biggest grin since he first set his eyes on Mary in Port Royal, Jamaica.

William had been on the Marcus Plantation for over six years and was always a barn worker and gardener. After William was only there two years, Jeremiah shot and killed his boss for stealing a chicken to eat. Jeremiah gave the job to William, reminding him, with a whipping, that he better not do anything to make him regret it. One of the first tasks William undertook was to start a tunnel. This was a personal task. It took a while because he couldn't trust anyone to help him. So he worked on it himself. It didn't have to be a long tunnel, just big enough for a man to crawl through and get off the plantation under the fence and to the other side. He finally completed it after four years. No one had ever discovered it. Not Jeremiah or the overseer! William never told anyone about it, except Betty.

She had been there about the same amount of time as William. They were sometimes sold together, growing up, and a couple of times, they wouldn't see each other for a year or two, but they always seemed to meet up again.

William and Betty never really had plans to use the tunnel themselves, unless things became really unbearable for them. They could take a lot. It was mostly for someday if they met someone who really needed to get out and had to take their chances. After a slave escaped through the tunnel, Betty and William would know nothing, say nothing, or do nothing to cause suspicion after they fled. They now knew what their mission was. They were meant to meet Jed and Mary so they could help them escape to a better life . . . and they put the word out in the system immediately that a young married couple was escaping to Canada. Ontario was the destination everyone agreed to guide them to. The farther away, the safer they would be. The message traveled quickly, right to this town called Chatham, which was to be their haven!

Both Betty and William had chastised the kids about Jed staying at the house too long. Jed and Mary both took a great risk with each other, but they were liked by Betty and William a lot. They did whatever they could to help arrange a visit with each other a couple of times. They also had to help them get away from this plantation to live as husband and wife somewhere safe.

Normally, Betty and William saw each other daily for one reason or another. They whispered their plans to get Jed and Mary off the plantation. They both agreed to get them onto what was known as the Underground Railroad.

The Underground Railroad was a series of safe houses where slaves could stop along the way after their escape from plantation life or to just escape from servitude. At these houses were people who hid the escapees, fed them, and let them rest. Abolitionists would pass the slaves on from one place to another. It could take between two and three months to get from Mississippi to Canada.

This means of escape was dangerous for many reasons. Traveling through the different states, they might come across poisonous snakes, alligators, infectious mosquitoes, not to mention the large amount of slave hunters. They would roam the land to see if they could find a runaway slave. They were usually paid handsomely for their captures when returned.

Sometimes a family would travel the railroad, but they would be split up to go. A couple, like Jed and Mary would go together. They would be two of the thirty thousand slaves who would use this . . . *railroad.*

Slaves journeyed mainly at night and slept during the daytime hours. Safe houses were about fifteen to twenty miles apart. Travel was often on foot, but slaves were also hidden on wagons or carts with false bottoms. There would be times when they had to get across swamps and rivers. There wasn't always a boat to row them over it, so they would have to swim or walk through it.

Betty taught Mary everything she knew about the system, and William taught Jed the same.

William and Betty made sure they told them the same things, or it might cause confusion for the kids, as they were now referred to.

But something new was up in the house. Betty was now afraid of a situation about to happen. One day, Betty figured that they had to get moving fast because the master was casting his eye in Mary's direction. Betty was worried that he would take her into his bed in the next few days.

The plan had to be acted on fast. It had to be tonight; Betty wasn't sure how long the master would wait. William and Betty were confident the kids learned enough, that they would successfully be delivered to safety. They had to believe in them, or it would mean Jed's and Mary's deaths.

Mary was still a little naive when it came to men. She didn't think her master was interested in her. She just thought he was being nice to her, instead of the gruff way he usually treated her. She thought that maybe he wasn't bad after all. Then she remembered the whipping! After the breakfast dishes were done, Betty said that they had to go tonight.

Mary was shocked and scared. "But why Betty? Is we ready 'nough to go? Does Jed know we'se leavin' tonight?"

Betty told her, "Jed's bein' tole by William dis very minit. Y'all can't brings nuttin' wit' ya, but don't fergit dat pretty robe ya made all by yerse'f. You wears it under you'se udder dress an', for a bit more warmth, keep da apron on too." Mary got teary, smiled, and hugged Betty; she was going to miss her. William popped up to the house around midday and told Betty everything was on for that night. Jed was ready, and Betty told him that Mary was too.

This was the evening their master usually went into town to play poker and drink. He was usually gone by eight o'clock and didn't usually get back until just before dawn. It was the perfect time, except something was different tonight. He started drinking at home before supper.

It was uncommon for him to change his routine. Betty was worried but could not let William know. The next time they would see each other was going to be at the escape hour. They had chosen 9:30 p.m. for their departure, and there was a new moon, so the escape would not be witnessed easily.

After dinner, the master stayed home. William always had his horse saddled and ready for him when he left each week. But William and Jed hadn't been watching, and they didn't realize that the master's horse was still in the barn. When nine fifteen came, William and Jed had slipped out of their cabin, unnoticed by anyone.

William had a way to get out of his cabin, even after Jackson Wylde locked him in. He had a hole in the back wall of his cabin that was hidden outside, and he had things piled up inside to hide it. His cabin was never inspected carefully. The master and overseer trusted him not to run.

The men went directly to the kitchen, and William whispered out Betty's name. Even though he thought there was no one else in the house, he would not take a chance of anyone hearing him. His life was at risk too. There was no reply. He whispered a little louder—nothing. He and Jed crept through the house and they heard a noise. William knew where Betty's room was and he opened it. That was where the noise came from. The master had locked her in the wardrobe.

Betty told William, "The massa be in his bed with Mary!" Jed didn't hear this. He went back in the hallway and heard more noises, which he followed down a longer hall that led to another wing of the house. Slaves were not allowed to go in this wing, other than to clean it.

While Betty was telling William about why the master didn't go out, Jed was following the other noises, when he came to what he figured was the master's bedroom; the door was slightly open.

Jed saw Mary naked on the bed with a rag stuffed in her mouth, and her hands and legs were tied to the bedposts. Jeremiah was sucking the nipple on one of her firm breasts, and he was not all the way inside of her yet, but he was trying. She was struggling as hard as she could and made it very difficult for him. He was very drunk too. She was terrified!

When Jed saw this, he couldn't stand it. As Jeremiah continued to enter her, suddenly he fell on top of Mary, hard and heavy. Jed had picked up the poker from the fireplace in Jeremiah's bedroom and brought it crashing down on his head, killing him instantly. William and Betty ran into the room and saw what was going on. Betty cried out, "Oh Lawdy, you poor chile, looky what he done here ta po' Mary."

Jed was just staring at the blood flowing from the master's head. The three of them looked at each other and then took Jeremiah's body and tossed him onto the floor. Jed was in shock about what he had done. He'd killed his boss. Surely he would be a dead man now.

Betty grabbed a blanket and put it around Mary as quick as she could. William and Betty untied her and took the gag out of her mouth. Mary was hysterical, but she had to be quiet. Betty pushed Mary's face to her bosom a little to muffle her loud sobs. It worked. Mary felt safe in Betty's arms and calmed down. Betty helped Mary get dressed.

William said, "It has ta be now! You two has ta leave now. It cain't wait. We's gonna leave da body dere, and when dat mean overseer Jackson Wylde be comin' up early fer brekfass, Betty, y'all juss pays no mind ta da time an' den you or him's gonna go up an' finds da body. Now let's git y'all to da tunnel. Mary, girl, you'se gonna be okay? We's not likin' ta do dis to ya tonight, 'ciderin' what he done to ya and all, but it hasta be right now. Jed, y'all jus' ain't no runaway nigger slave no mo', you'se a murderer of a white man. You'se very own massa. You'se gonna has a price on yo' head an' you'se gonna be hunted down, Mary too!

"Jackson Wylde ain't gonna let you gits 'way wit' dis neither. Now, we's gonna give a message to ya ta take. You'se gives it ta da firs' station master, den he's gonna pass da message on befo' you gits ever'wheres else. It'll travel faster den y'all. Dey be all knowin' you'se story before y'all gits to where you'se goin'. Dey has to know what y'all done, so's dey can make ya safe on yo' journey."

They quickly went to the tunnel and gave their hugs and good-byes, and then Mary and Jed Allen were gone. They stood up at the end of the tunnel so Betty and William could see them and make sure they made it all the way through the tunnel. Betty started praying for this wonderful young couple. Jed knew his instructions inside and out. He knew where the first safe house was. They should reach it on foot, through the woods, within an hour. It took them only forty-five minutes to reach it. Fear always has a way of making you move faster.

This was the start of their long journey, which would usher them along the Underground Railroad to a new life. William and Betty had told them about Canada, the promised land. "'Cross dat border, it be your chance ta live an' be free an' happy." These words Betty said before they left rang in both of their ears as they fled!

The horrendous trek meant they would travel hundreds of miles through Tennessee, Kentucky, Ohio, Michigan, and, finally, Canada. The relief of crossing the national border would mean that they truly would be in the promised land . . . and free!

They had to endure raging rivers and go over hills and dales, and all their trips between safe houses had to be done only at night since there was now a $750 price on Jed's head, and Mary had $250 on hers just for being with him.

By the time they made it to the fifth safe house, the conductor told them about the attempts to capture them and the reward for both, which was started by Jackson Wylde. It was no surprise to Jed and Mary. The other news they received at the same time was that there was deaths at the Marcus Plantation. When they asked the station master who it was, he told them, "It seems the overseer found the tunnel on the property that you two escaped through and finally figured the gardener made it. Since you were the kitchen wench that escaped, Mary, he figured the kitchen boss was in on it too.

"These two slaves claimed they don't know where you two went or how, and the overseer didn't believe them. It seems that he hung the slaves named Betty and, uh, William." They would not give any information on you two."

They both gasped in horror. Jed asked, "Is you tellin' da trute?" Jed asked the station master.

He continued with the story he heard. "Everyone knows Jeremiah Marcus don't let his slaves marry and have young'uns. Well, it seems, after many lashes to both slaves and they was about to hang, I heard it told that William asked if he could kiss his wife of twenty years, Betty, good-bye. Mr. Wylde let out a laugh and let them kiss and hung 'em both together." Mary and Jed were hurt that they were dead but happy to find out they were really married so long without anyone knowing, especially the "great" massa, Jeremiah Marcus!

During their route, there were bloodhounds barking in the distance wherever they went. Trying to sleep through the day was hard. Several places they stayed, there was pounding on doors from the law or bounty hunters. They all would take a look around to see if the pair was there. They were, but they were never found. No one caught up to them but had been so close. None of the hunters even knew that the door they were knocking on was a station of the Underground Railroad.

Other hazards they really met up with were poisonous snakes, alligators, and quicksand. They paid heed to every station master along the way. Sometimes a conductor would tell them they would meet a shepherd for some bad terrain they had to travel through, which was so hard to navigate in the dark, except for those who knew that part of the country. Jed and Mary never saw so many people care about what happened to them before.

From station to station, they were kept updated as to how far Jackson was trailing behind them. Everyone kept telling them how far they had come and how far they had to go, but station masters were not allowed to say much more than that. Not even the station masters knew the whole route; it was for their own safety. If ever found out, a station might close down, but usually it was replaced. If caught, a white station master would go to jail and have a large fine to pay, but if blacks who ran stations were caught giving aid to anyone, it meant death!

As Mary and Jed neared the end of their journey, they heard that Jackson Wylde turned back when he hit Michigan. He knew by then that they were going to Canada . . . there was no point going any further. A man like Jackson enjoyed the hunt and the kill, but he was too far away from the plantation and hoped it was still in one piece when he arrived back. Other plantation owners were helping by looking after things for him, so he finally gave up and went home.

The station masters had to be very cautious at the national border. Recently, Canada was cracking down on imports, not letting all wagons cross over. Canada was starting to grow more potatoes and other vegetables but still needed some brought from the States until their own crops were ready. Luckily, Mary and Jed were hidden under a large wagon of potatoes going from the Detroit area to Windsor, the first city you came to when you cross over into Canada on this particular underground route.

The driver said aloud to himself, "Well now, Canada sure is pretty, yessir, I might like to live on this side of the border someday." That was the signal to let Jed and Mary know that they had made it. They were in Canada. All they had to do now was get from Windsor to the town of Chatham, Ontario. The farmer bringing the load of potatoes unloaded in Windsor. Jed and Mary still had another couple of hours to get to their new hometown of Chatham.

Chapter 13

Treacherous Journey Relived

WITHIN A COUPLE OF MONTHS after Adam told John about Jed and Mary, they were finally delivered to the livery in Chatham, their final destination on this "railroad of chance and great risk"!

They were let out of the false bottom wagon. It had taken sixty-seven days to reach their new hometown, the same time it took Diana and Johnny to arrive from Scotland.

At the livery, they were immediately introduced to their "brakeman," Adam White. It was late in the day, so he closed shop and took them over to his brother's home for supper. Jeff was just getting home from work too. The five of them ate supper together . . . at the *same* dining table. The black couple couldn't believe this. During supper, Jeff asked what their jobs were on both plantations and told them they had heard some worrisome stories about them, and they would like to hear the truth from them.

Jed began to talk first. "I'se special at gard'nin', flowers an' vegibles, an' tendin' barn animals, sir. Y'all knows like cows an' horses. I'se has to tell y'all, someday me and my Mary here, we's gonna be 'tato farmers, yessir. It be my favorite vegible ta work wit'. Does ya tink we's gonna make it here, Massa, me and my Mary?" They all smiled at each other.

Jeff answered with a sincere smile. "Now, Jed, please remember, you and Mary are no longer slaves. You can call people by their Christian names here. No one here is a massa or master, not even your employer. He'll let you know what to call him and his wife. Please call me Jeff, my wife is Tina, and you know my brother, Adam. You are a free couple here, and although you are, it's against the law for blacks to buy land here. You can work on a farm and get paid, but not as much as a white man. I know it's disappointing not to be able to buy land now, but in time, that law will change. There are some farmers here who let you stay and live with them and feed you too. How does that sound?"

Jed just burst. "Den dat's da ways we's gonna works it! We's gonna be rich here someday, but not juss right 'way, like. We waits. Do y'all knows of any place like y'all done just said? We wants ta do dat."

He turned to Mary and continued, "We's gonna work real hard on a farm, Mary, juss you wait an' see. Yessir, we's gonna work real hard on a farm, you an' me! We's gonna work real hard an' own our own place someday. We ain't never gonna be da cause o' no trouble, no sir! We be no trouble at all, we's gonna be real good here, ain't we, Mary?" She smiled a great big grin, nodded, and they hugged each other. This indeed was the promised land for them.

Tina, Adam, and Jeff smiled at each other, and they were all thinking the same thing—John and Diana McDonald would take them in and give them a chance.

Adam asked, "What about the other stories we've heard about you? The real reason you ran so quickly?"

When the euphoria settled down, Jed and Mary lowered their eyes for a moment. Mary patted Jed's hand affectionately and said to their waiting hosts, "That might be a problem that maybe gonna change tings. Now you go along, Jed, you tell 'em the trut'."

Jed looked at Mary, and he took a breath and started, "I hope you'se all listen careful, 'cuz I'se tell y'all what really happen. Da real trut'. We had dis plan to run, wit' the he'p of this couple dat lived dere. I went in the plantation house on da night we's gonna run. We tink da massa was away.

He weren't. I finds him pesterin' my Mary. She be tied to a bed an' he on top o' her. Doing . . . tings to her. I cain't stan' to see my's Mary under him. I takes a fire poker an' I'se smash it on his head. I'se kill him right dere on dat very spot. We had to get out of dere right away. We was followed through da route we was taked on by our overseer and bounty hunters, but da bad men after us, dey turn back an' goes home juss befo' we gits to Canada. What chew say now?"

All three were listening, and this was the story they had heard about them too, but it was still a shock. They didn't know what to say at first. It was quite a confession of murder. When they didn't say anything, Jed and Mary felt they'd have to move on and fend for themselves. They got up from the table to leave, but to where? They were in a new country and didn't know what to do.

Christina spoke first. "Please, have a seat and tell us what your lives were like?" The two sat down again and explained everything about their lives from Africa to Jamaica and Mississippi to Chatham.

Based on that, the three decided that under the circumstances the killing was justified, and they felt if Jeff or Adam were to explain everything to this particular farmer and his wife, they might still give them a try on the farm. Adam knew of the bounty on their heads, but only in the United States. It did not apply in Canada, so he felt they should be fairly safe. Jeff decided he would speak on their behalf. He told Jed and Mary that he thought the McDonalds would likely take them in, and they'd be safe on their farm.

Jeff mentioned at that time the McDonalds owned a large potato farm. Jed began to grin again, so did Mary. The two felt they had a chance. They were invited to stay at the Whites until everything was settled.

In the morning, Jeffrey and Adam went out to see John and Diana. They came along to tell them all they could about the young black couple and their clandestine arrival via the Underground Railroad. As Jeff explained the situation, Diana's heart wept for them and felt they needed to take this couple in and protect them.

Suddenly, Diana smiled and said to John, "Darlin', it's meant to be. Remember last night when you read from Deuteronomy? You know, 23:15–16? 'Thou shalt not deliver unto his master the servant, which is escaped from his master unto thee: he shall dwell with thee, even among you, in that place which he shall choose in one of thy gates, where it liketh him best; thou shalt not oppress him.'" She continued, "Johnny, this couple needs us. They need a chance at life. Remember, dear, they know potatoes, and we can put them up in one of the bedrooms until we build the little house, and—"

John stopped her by putting his hand over her mouth. "My sweet Diana, take a breath." John grinned at her and they both agreed! Jed and Mary would come to live and work with them as soon as possible.

The start of Jed and Mary's new life would be this very day. They had survived so many tragedies and cruelties in their short lives things could only get better. John and Diana could hardly wait to meet the couple!

Jeff and Adam went back to town. Jeff had to show a property. Tina was tending to Jed and Mary's needs, and she learned so much. Mary told her about her Kente cloth and the rapes from the sailor and the whippings for no reason.

Jeff dropped by quickly to say, "We're going to the potato farm this afternoon. The McDonalds want to meet you both, and you're to bring all your belongings!"

Tina stopped him. "Dear, after their bath, I'm going to take them to Lavalle's to get new clothes and shoes. The poor dears have nothing."

Jeff was in a hurry but continued. "That's fine, love." He turned to Jed and Mary. "You're going to stay there for a month for now. They're going to try you out, and if things go well, you'll be there permanently. If things don't work out, maybe Adam could find you another place to work in the area. But I have confidence that things will be fine." Jeff knew it would work out . . . Jed and Mary Allen would be staying with the McDonalds!

He continued, "You'll live in their house with them until they see how things go. If you do well, they'll make more permanent plans for you. Oh, by the way, Tina, I told them we would bring the bed that Jed and Mary slept on here last night. They don't have a spare one at their place yet, so we're loaning this one. I hope you don't mind, sweetie." She didn't.

Jeff figured he would be out with the interested buyers for around two hours or so. Tina wanted to take Mary and Jed out to Lavalle's and buy them proper working clothes, shoes, underclothes, hats, and everything they would need to start their new lives. They only escaped in the outfits that they were wearing. Mary was wearing her Kente robe underneath the plantation dress, like Betty suggested. By now, their clothes were almost in tatters from their travels. Mary's Kente cloth robe had seen better days, but Tina promised her that if she left the robe with her, she would repair it for her.

The bathing tub Jeff and Tina had was a bit unusual. It was not your typical one-person tub.

It was really large. In fact, two medium-sized adults could fit in it quite comfortably. It took lots of water, which Christina had been boiling all morning. By the time they got around to having their bath, adding the cold water, it was perfect.

While they were undressing, Jed was quite shy. Tina said she wouldn't look. Mary smiled.

Tina handed him a towel to put around his waist, and Mary wrapped hers around her too. Tina added liquid soap to the water, which made bubbles. They had never experienced this before and were amused. She also gave them a bar of soap and a scrub brush to clean each other. She gave them special soap for their hair called shampoo. Jed and Mary had only washed themselves in ponds and rivers with homemade soap.

While Tina was gathering their clothes, Jed remembered his belt. Tina thought it should go out with the other clothes. Mary and he looked at each other with a scared look to their faces. Tina asked, "Whatever is wrong, I think we should get all of these clothes and burn them." They both lowered their eyes, remembering what Jacob's instructions were. Don't let anyone know you have the money. They whispered to each other and decided that they could trust Tina.

Jed said, "We cain't trow da belt away . . . Jacob-Sir make us promise dat we never tell anyone 'bout da belt."

Tina asked, "Is there a special meaning for it?"

Jed continued, "We has five hunerd United States dollars sewed in it."

She was shocked as she smiled at them and said, "Your Jacob-Sir must have loved you two dearly to do that for you. How about while you're having a bath, I carefully take the belt apart and get the money out of it for you? I promise it will be safe. We can get you a billfold to put some of your money in, and maybe you can open a bank account to put the rest in." They had no idea what she was talking about!

Tina asked, "Do either of you know how to read or write?" They went silent again. "Oh, I see. It's against the law for blacks to read and write in the United States. Correct?" They both nodded.

She went on, "It's okay to tell me. It's not against the law here. And we're going to teach you anyway. Is that okay with you?" They grinned and nodded their heads. Mary kind of thought of Tina as fondly as she did Betty, and Jed thought of her as his beloved Laura-Ma'am.

Mary said, "I can write my name and Jed's name, and I can spell a couple of words, like 'kitchen,' 'cow,' 'horse,' 'barn,' and stuffs like that. I can reads some too. Jed can spell his first and last name, that 'bout all. Oh yeah, he can spells my name too."

Tina said, "That's all right. Like I said, Diana or I will teach you to read and write really well. Diana, uh, Mrs. McDonald wants to be a teacher, so you'll learn. That means you too, Jed."

While they were both getting cleaned up, Tina carefully opened the belt, and sure enough, inside was four one-hundred-dollar bills and five twenty-dollar bills in US currency. It was weathered but spendable. This made them very wealthy, as far as blacks go. They had no idea at all about money or the value of things. Jacob was trying to teach them, but unfortunately they ran out of time. Tina was so happy for them that they had money to start their new lives.

She threw away the old clothes and burned them. She stood for a long while, just staring at Mary's Kente cloth robe. She was imagining a little African girl getting instructions from her father, whom she adored. She felt emotion welling up inside her. She shed a few tears for this young couple. In their short lives, it seemed they had lived many decades.

As Mary and Jed started to clean themselves, Mary took the soap and brush and washed Jed. She was careful not to scrub too hard. The bristles of the brush were stiff. He didn't mind. She put the shampoo on his head, like Tina told her to do, and scrubbed hard. The water for rinsing was beside the tub where they could reach it.

Jed scrubbed Mary gently. He was so tender with her. As he washed her back, he kissed her neck. Mary felt something inside her stir. This was such a new feeling for her. She never experienced these feelings before. She liked it! She was smiling while he continued to kiss her. He poured shampoo on her hair and scrubbed it for her. She turned, and they faced each other. As she put her arms around her husband's neck, she kissed him like she never had before. The stirring in her was intense. She wanted Jed to do the things that had been done to her by the sailor and Master Marcus, only more gentle and tenderly. She had a feeling this time, with Jed; it was such a pleasurable feeling. She wanted him. Mary was ready to consummate their marriage.

Tina called out, "Everything all right in there?"

Jed said, "Uh . . . yes, Tina-Ma'am, we'se juss rinsin' off." Tina let them use Jeff's and her own clothes temporarily so they could go to the store. It felt so good to them to be clean and wearing clean clothes, even if they didn't fit exactly right or belong to them.

Tina took the Allens over to the general store. They were surprised when Tina told them that they would be going inside the store with her, that they were allowed to walk in. In the States, most slaves were only allowed to wait for their masters outside a store, even in inclement weather. Here they were walking into a "white store." Their emotions were mixed—scared yet excited at the same time. They didn't know what kind of reception they would get.

Tina led the way. Next, Mary came in, and then Jed. They were looking around in wonderment. They saw so much food, clothes, tools, and household goods. There was so much to take in.

Tina put her arm around Mary's shoulder and tapped Jed and said to Emilie Lavalle, "Mrs. Lavalle, this is Mr. and Mrs. Allen, Mary and Jed. They are new to the area and are going to be employed by the McDonalds."

At that time, Rene came in from the storeroom. Emilie said to him, "Rene, this is Mr. and Mrs. Allen. They will be working for the McDonalds."

Mr. Lavalle asked, "Are you from the States?"

They were too afraid to talk, and Mary tried to hide behind Tina as she talked for them. "They are just new to Canada. They lived in the United States, in Mississippi. They are trying to start a new life here. Now we need to buy clothing and shoes and everything else a new Canadian needs to live and work here on a farm. Can you help us out with that?"

Emilie turned to them and said, "We're pleased to meet you both, and I hope you get on well in our country. I'm sure we can fix you up with some proper clothing. Let's see what we can do.

Rene, why don't you fix up Jed, and I'll tend to Mary here." Mr. and Mrs. Lavalle had many black customers over the last few years, and they treated them just like any other customer that came into their store—with respect!

Rene put his hand out to Jed to shake it, and he took it shyly and said, "Good day, sir, and I'se be thankin' y'all fer yo' he'p."

Rene told Jed, "Please, it's Rene. If you're uncomfortable, then feel free to call me Mr. Lavalle. The McDonalds are friends of ours, and we hope to get to know you both and become your friends too. Now, Jed, what will your job be? Barn, field . . . ?"

Jed shrugged his shoulders, saying, "Don't rightly knows, sir. I'se s'pose I'se be in da fiel', in da barn wit' the animals, in da coop wit' da chickens an' I does real good work in gardens too, Mr. . . . Rene, sir." Rene realized then that they were slaves who had come from a plantation, and it would take them a while to be casual with people.

He started, "Okay, here are some working clothes to try on. Jed was thrilled with such luxury. He was fitted with three pairs of pants and three shirts, two light and one heavier. Undergarments were next, as well as suspenders, socks, a belt, and a working hat. He was also fitted with working boots.

Rene turned to Tina and asked, "Tina, do you know if they need Sunday clothes?"

Tina thought for a moment. "I expect we should get some and appropriate shoes too, please." Jed wasn't sure what Sunday clothes were. Rene brought out a suit for Jed to try on. It was black and such nice soft material; he grabbed it and went to try it on right away.

Rene said, "Hold on there, my boy. You have to put a proper shirt on under that suit." Rene grabbed a white shirt off the shelf and brought it in for Jed to put on under the suit jacket. He loved it. Every time he tried something on, he came running out of the dressing room and had to show Mary and Tina. Mary giggled upon seeing Jed wearing white man's clothing, just like he was a master himself. He made an impressive picture. She thought he looked very handsome, and there was a sparkle in her eyes he had never seen before. He felt a warm feeling come over himself. It was like things were changing so quickly. And it was a wonderful feeling!

Tina said, "Jed, those clothes look great on you. Rene, please wrap all of Mr. Allen's purchases for him. Oh, by the way, could you please show him your leather billfolds. He can pick out whichever one he likes." Jed was beaming with pride about the treatment he was getting. He felt very important, a feeling he'd never had before.

Mary told Jed, "You'se gotta see dees dresses, Jed. They'se so pretty. I ain't never seen such dresses." She selected two lovely floral ones for working around the house. Very durable material!

Tina said, "Emilie, could you also get her two aprons as well? She'll need them." She was fitted with bloomers, petticoats, corsets, a regular bonnet, as well as a Sunday dress, gloves, a bonnet to suit it, and a small drawstring purse to carry things in while on an outing. She tried on regular shoes that would be suitable around the house and for working in and a pair that were fine enough for Sundays and special occasions.

She was also fitted with a small pair of men's trousers, working shirt, and proper boots in case she had to work in the field sometime, during harvest time in particular, which is the busiest time of year.

Rene was totaling Jed's purchases. His bill was already up to $16.25. Just then a customer staggered in. Rene stopped what he was doing to deal with him. He was an ignorant man who hated blacks and was always drunk. Emilie nervously took over wrapping their purchases.

The customer looked around and saw Jed and Mary with decent clothes on. He drunkenly said, "What the hell is going on here? You be sellin' to coons now? What are these niggers doing in here?" Jed heard that word! He thought they got away from that word when they came across the border, but it was still there.

The customer became more obnoxious and belligerent, staggering and breaking things. Rene really didn't want to serve him but did, just so he would leave. He was making Mary and Jed very nervous. It brought back bad memories . . . of Ethan Jordan.

Rene politely asked him what he wanted. The town drunk and resident bully, Bartholomew Knox, demanded a bottle of whiskey. Rene reluctantly gave it to him. The next thing they all knew, he threw money on the counter, and as he left the store, he spat in Jed's face.

Rene was horrified, and Emilie could not apologize enough about this man. They were so angry and embarrassed. Jed and Mary were shook up over the incident, so was Tina.

Emilie finished wrapping Mary's purchases, and Rene started to total them up. Mary's total was $17.95. Added together, their bill was $34.20, which seemed like a lot, but they had so many clothes and shoes and boots, it was well worth the money. It was spring, and they didn't need to buy coats. The weather was getting warmer, but dawn in the springtime could be quite cool, as were evenings after dusk. The heavy flannel work shirt Jed was buying would come in handy during these times while Diana and Mary would likely not be outside during the cooler times of the day.

Tina started to get her purse open to pay. Jed tapped her on the shoulder and whispered in her ear, "Tina-Ma'am, could we's use our own monies ta buy da clothes?"

Tina thought for a moment, and she answered, "Well, Jed, if you really want to, that's okay. It is your money to use for anything you want. What do you think Jacob might have wanted you to do?"

Jed grinned. "I'se tink dat he be wantin' us ta pay for da clothes. Dey's our clothes, so we should oughta pay for dem an' look after dem proper like."

Tina smiled and said, "Then you do whatever you and Mary like." They wanted to pay for their own purchases and were so proud to do it.

After they purchased their clothes, Tina took Mary and Jed to the bank across the road from the Land Registry Office. As Tina walked in to the bank, she said, "Good day, Mr. Eliott. How are you today?" He nodded to her and her party, letting them know that he'd be with them shortly. There was one customer ahead of them who was just finishing his business. After the customer left, the three of them stepped up to the counter.

Jed extended his hand toward Mr. Elliot to shake it and said, "I'se Jedediah Allen, an' dis be my wife, Mary. We's be workin' fer . . ." He froze. He was so excited and they'd had such a busy day he forgot the farmer's name.

Tina interjected, "John and Diana McDonald." She was smiling with pride that Jed took the initiative to introduce himself and Mary. She was pleased with his progress for their first day here.

Jed smiled again and said, "My Mary an' me works fer da McDonalds. What do I'se have ta do ta open me a a-account? I'se never seen one afore. I don't knows how ta gits one. Ever'body keeps sayin' we needs one. We's bote knows our numbers an' how ta count, but I don't know what ta do next."

Tina was surprised. It never occurred to her to explain what they were talking about when they kept saying they need to have a bank account.

The banker was surprised that a black man wanted to open an account. After all, what black person has enough money to actually want to open an account. The banker was shocked when Jed pulled out almost $500 in United States currency from his pocket.

Mr. Elliot said, "Well, Mr. and Mrs. Allen, a bank account is a place to put money, but it is nothing you can hold or touch. How about I tell you about it? Would that be okay with you both?" They nodded and were grateful for the time and care he gave them. He told them about the process. Mr. Elliot told them that it is customary to keep a couple of dollars with him most of the time, that you never know when you'll need it. He suggested that he give Jed $40.00 to keep in his new billfold.

After Jed and Mary sorted the banking out, Jed went back to Lavalle's. Jed asked Mr. Lavalle to show him a couple of other things. He picked out a small bottle of Lily of the Valley cologne and a beautiful linen handkerchief with lace edging. It was so beautiful; Mary was going to love it. He asked Mr. Lavalle to suggest something small that he could purchase as a gift for Mr. McDonald. It was a thank-you gift for hiring them. He told Rene that the perfume was for Mrs. McDonald.

Rene said, "I have just the thing for him. I know that he likes to smoke a pipe occasionally. Here is a pack of his favorite pipe tobacco." Jed thought it was perfect. As Rene wrapped each gift separately, he gave a kind smile to this young man's thoughtfulness and sincerity. It was rare. Rene knew right then that Jed Allen would end up being a respected, true friend to many in the area, no matter how long or short his life would be.

When Jeff was done showing property to a couple, he took them out to lunch at Catherine's.

He did this as a courtesy, usually to seal the deal, as it were. Tina was used to this, and she counted on it most of the time when he had a morning appointment. It helped. They bought the 160 acres of property for the usual $10. They were a nice couple from England.

After Jeff was done with lunch and the paperwork for the new owners, he picked up Mary, Jed, and Tina to take them to the McDonalds'. Jeff unhooked the carriage and hooked up the wagon. He and Jed loaded their double bed onto the wagon to take with them. Mary and Jed rode in the back of the wagon. They couldn't be more excited if they tried. Here they were, a free young black couple about to live and work in a new country in a white world. They were excited and so nervous.

Jed took out two of the small packages that he bought without Mary seeing. He showed them to Mary and described each one. She was so surprised that he had thought to buy thank-you gifts for each of the McDonalds. Sometimes it felt to Mary that she didn't know her husband at all. He was a puzzle to her at times. She loved him so much. She put her arms around his neck and tenderly kissed his cheek as he smiled at her.

She said, "Jed, you looks after me so good an' you'se so kind to people. We's gonna has a good life, and I'se gonna love you forever . . . so dat be it now. You'se gotta live forever!" He smiled at her and kissed her lips.

Jeff said, "Jed, Mary, why don't you peek your heads out here for a moment." They moved to the front of the wagon and looked out. Jeff stopped the wagon so that he could show them and continued, "Look at all this land. All this land belongs to the McDonalds. In the middle there is their house, and that's where you'll be living for now."

Jed saw the size of the barn. "Is dat barn full?" he asked hesitantly.

Jeff laughed, "Not yet, but maybe someday. Right now it has three cows, two horses, and two ponies." Jed sighed with relief. Jeff went on, "There is two large fields to finish clearing. Do you think you two can handle living out here?"

Jed said, "Sho' 'nuff be a big place, but we been workin' on larger plantations. Is me an' Mary da only workers?"

Jeff said that for right now they were. He told Jed and Mary that there were many colored people in the area. Most boys and men did farmwork unless they had another skill they could perform and make a living at. There were five boys in particular that John often hired by the day or by the job. He told them that they would likely meet them later in the week. He told Jed the main field was already planted with potatoes, so he would be helping tending to many other things around the place or watering the field if a drought happens. He also mentioned that Diana also put in a fair-sized vegetable garden too. She'd be needing help with it since she was with child now and couldn't do all the work as time goes on.

They continued on to the house. John and Diana came out of the house and helped Tina off the wagon. She and Diana hugged. They also helped Mary get down too. Jed jumped off after Jeff and John came over to him. Tina made the introductions. "Mr. and Mrs. McDonald, I'm very pleased to introduce to you Mr. and Mrs. Allen. Jedediah and Mary." They all shook hands.

John said, "Please, you may call us John and Diana. If we're going to be living here together, we may as well start off friendly. We are your employers, but we are casual folks and are sure that we all will get on well together and become friends." Diana nodded in agreement. She was so happy to have Mary and Jed there finally.

Jed reached into his pocket and handed Diana the bottle of cologne, saying, "Diana, me an' Mary jess wants ta say tank y'all fer takin' us in an' 'llowin' us ta live wit' cha an' be workin' fer ya." He took the tobacco out of his other pocket and approached John. "John, here be a little sometin' fer y'all too, jess saying tanks fer givin' us a real chance at a good life!" Mary smiled and nodded along with him. Tina was fighting back a tear. She had no idea that Jed had bought these gifts. Diana and John were taken aback. They never expected anything like this. It certainly wasn't necessary, but the gifts were well received, and they would never forget the gesture of this young black couple who came to work for them and live with them. Their lives would be much richer for knowing each other now.

Chapter 14

Africa and Scotland Come Together

A FTER INTRODUCTIONS WERE MADE, DIANA suggested that they all go into the house for tea. Mary was so shy she stayed near Tina, but Diana tried to make her feel at ease right away. Jeff, Jed, and John followed the women into the house.

Diana showed her guests to her parlor. She used her best china and her beautiful silver tea service, which her father had given her as wedding presents. They had belonged to her mother and her grandmother, like the wedding dress. Jed and Mary were not used to sitting on such luxurious furniture. Jacob's was nice but more masculine. It was a very intimidating experience for them. Mary followed Diana around, from kitchen to parlor at one point, asking what she was supposed to do.

Diana said, "Mary, I would like you to relax today, and let's get to know each other. Dear, you don't have to do anything but sit and enjoy your tea and your afternoon." Mary felt awkward.

She should be doing the serving, not the Mrs. of the house. Mary had never had anyone serve her tea before, especially in a parlor with such beautiful surroundings. She still felt like a misfit, wondering if she would ever fit in!

Jed was talking up a storm with John and Jeff. When he was excited, you couldn't stop him. He just went on and on . . . mostly it was about farming, potatoes, gardens, and his Mary. John was glad to hear his enthusiasm. He was going to be great to work with. John also found him amusing, as most people did. It was a very endearing quality in him. Jed was definitely motivated. He wanted to go to the barn and to the field right away. John said he would take him to the barn later, to do the evening chores.

Diana had started supper and asked if Tina and Jeff would like to stay. They said they'd be delighted. Diana thought she saw a sigh of relief from Mary when Tina said they'd stay. Mary was comfortable around her. She liked Diana, but it would take her a little while to relax in their new home.

Diana said, "Why don't we show you to your room? Do you have a traveling bag with your clothes in it to bring in the house? You can unpack later, after supper."

Jed said, "Yes, ma'am, I'se git it." He got up and went to get it. When he returned, Jeff and John were just getting ready to go out and get the double bed from the wagon. The ladies went upstairs to the bedroom Jed and Mary were to have.

Mary was wide-eyed and gasped. "Lawdy, Lawdy, dis here room is bigger than our whole cabin at the Maisy-Lee! Looky here, Jed," she said as he was coming up the stairs. "I doesn't believe it. This room is juss for me and Jed?" The bed was being brought upstairs by the men. As they reached the top of the stairs, Jeff heard what Mary said.

He said, "Oh, by the way, Jed, Mary, Adam heard some news today about your Maisy-Lee Plantation, well at least from around there. We try and keep up on slave news and those wanting to travel north." They placed the bed in the room and the traveling bag on a small chest of drawers Diana picked up in town for them.

She washed the sheets and quilts and dried them fresh on the line that very morning when she heard they were here and coming that afternoon. She had already prepared two pillows for them with feathers she had gotten from Eileen. She did not have enough from her own chickens to make two pillows. In their room they had their own oil lamp and a window that could open, and it even had curtains. The young couple was feeling like royalty. Diana and John wanted them to feel at home and comfortable.

Everyone went back to the parlor and had a bit more tea. Jeff continued his story. "It seems there was a neighbor, uh, what was his name?" He scratched his chin for a moment, trying to remember the name. "Uh, Ethan Jordan," he said suddenly! Mary choked on her tea and scone and spit a bit out. She was horrified.

Mary regained her composure and said, "Oh, ma'am, I'se so sorry, ma'am, I'se so sorry. I din't mean it."

Diana said, "Oh, Mary, are you all right, dear? Take a deep breath."

Mary said, "I's so sorry, ma'am. I'se better now. It juss I heard that bad man's name." Diana went over to Mary and patted her on the shoulder and gave her a small hug. Mary was afraid but wanted to hear more. "Mr. Jeff, what was that you was sayin' 'bout that Mr. Jordan?"

Jeff told them, "Well it seems that his slaves got hold of the news that he was the one who burned the slaves at your place and killing the runaway you had. This Mr. Jordan's slaves did not take it too well. One morning they didn't get out to the field on time, so he went to the slave cabins to see what was up. He opened the door of the men's cabin and he went in. They surrounded him and jumped him. First of all, they gagged him and dragged him out into the yard. The biggest slaves did most of the work while the others kept him down.

"With every slave watching and helping when they could to make sure he stayed quiet and still, first, they cut off the front of both feet with an axe. Then they chopped the rest of both feet completely off at the ankle. Next, they dragged him to the whipping tree. By this time the overseer was there, but they were ready for him. They jumped him too and grabbed his gun. They shot him in the head and killed him instantly.

"Meanwhile at his whipping tree, Mr. Jordan was lashed to the tree and as many slaves that wanted to got to whip him. He was scarred from top to bottom, they say. The next thing they did to him was their last. They put a rope around his neck and lynched him right there off the whipping tree and set his body on fire! He was burned alive. All the slaves then started the crops on fire as well as the house, the barn, everything. The Jordan Plantation was burned to the ground."

Mary fainted. Jed ran to her side and held her, fanning her. Diana and Tina were so appalled to hear this; they were nearly on the floor with Mary. When she was revived, she apologized for fainting.

Tina was in tears. She looked to Mary and Jed and said, "It was him that threw you down the Steps, wasn't it?" They both nodded. Jed had tears in his eyes too.

He held Mary, and they both cried, saying, "We's free, we's free from dat man! We's free!"

They hugged and laughed a sigh of relief, and Tina joined them on the floor, hugging them. Diana realized there was a lot to this young couple they'd figuratively adopted. She smiled, knowing that their lives were now really saved. Jeff apologized for retelling the story; he didn't know it would upset them so.

Jed got up and went to Jeff, holding out his hand until he took it. Jed smiled. "Don't you fret none, we's be okay. We's glad ya tole us. We's never knowed if ya ain't done tole us. Dat man's like a ghost dat be followin' us. You'se got rid of him fer us. We's thanks ya! Is dere more news from Maisy-Lee?" Jeff said that Laura and Andrew had twins, a boy and a girl. Their names were Jedediah and Mary. Jed and Mary smiled and hugged. They were so happy to hear this. Mary cried some more.

Jed said, "Heck, Mary, ain't y'all ever gonna stop cryin'?" Mary told them these were happy tears. They all laughed.

Jeff said, "Jacob Marcus left enough money for Andrew and Laura to buy the burned-out Jordan Plantation, and since it was connected by only a fence, they now have the biggest sugar plantation on the island of Jamaica. It's now called The Jacob Marcus Maisy-Lee Sugar Plantation. They have hired so many local people they have the biggest workforce on the island. They are paid well and can live on or off the farm. They are employees, not slaves."

Jeff continued, "Some of the Jordan slaves were captured and put to death without trials, but they were happy to be free of that man too. Some went into hiding, and Andrew tried to save as many as he could. He found about two-thirds of the Jordan slaves and hired them to work for him and swore to protect them all."

Diana and John were appalled that the treatment of slaves was so bad that they had to kill or be killed. Adam usually kept Jeff informed when he heard any news. Jed asked, "If you'se hears mo' 'bout da Maisy-Lee, would y'all tell us? We likes to know 'bout Laura-Ma'am an' Andrew-Sir an' now 'bout da young'uns dey done named after us. Ain't dat so, Mary?" She grinned. Jed liked to see her smile for a change. It had been so long since either had much to smile about.

The afternoon seemed to fly by, and chores in the barn needed to be done, so John took Jed out. Jeff followed behind but was reminded by his wife not to get his suit dirty. He did not bring his working clothes. He turned and saluted Tina. She raised her foot and kicked him in the behind.

Mary was shocked. She thought Tina might get a whipping but realized those days and people are behind her. She lived in Canada now.

The three ladies went to the kitchen to finish getting supper ready. With John and Jed working together, chores would go faster. Diana suggested just the barn chores tonight and leave the field tour until tomorrow. John agreed.

After the men got back, they all sat down for supper. John asked, "Would you all please bow your heads and hold hands as we pray? Dear Lord, we thank thee for this glorious day and this food we are about to receive. We thank you also for family and friends. We are truly blessed that you have brought Jed and Mary into our home, and may they both find peace and happiness with us on our, on their farm . . . Amen." Everyone felt sincere emotion as they repeated, "Amen."

They talked and enjoyed each other's company. Mary and Jed were finally fitting in as a couple. They were losing their apprehension, and Mary was now laughing and talking with the ladies.

She was still a bit intimidated by the men but understandably so. After supper, the men went outside in the cool air and had their smoke. John reached in his pocket and pulled out the package of tobacco that Rene sold to Jed to give as a gift. Jed was proud. His boss liked his gift. While the men were outside, the ladies talked more and cleaned up the kitchen.

Jeff came in a little bit later and said, "Tina, my girl, we'd best be heading home before it gets too dark." She agreed. They took their leave, and the four were now left alone to start their new life together. Mary started to get tired, so Jed asked for permission to take her and go to bed.

John said, "Jed, you don't need to ask our permission to go to bed. This is your home now.

If you want to go to bed, you just go. I know it will take a while to get used to us and for us to get used to you as well. But how about starting tomorrow, we are John, Diana, Jed, and Mary? Is that okay with you?"

They both lowered their eyes. Jed spoke. "We's sorry, we ain't never been 'llowed ta, we's fergit. We's try our bess ta remember, sir."

John continued, "Jed, that also means that we are not sir or ma'am, okay?" He nodded, and Mary did too. John and Diana bid them a good night and a very good sleep.

Diana gave both Mary and Jed a very warm hug and said, "Thank you so much for coming into our lives. You will be safe here. You are now part of our family." They went up to their room. It was the first time in a long time they were able to relax. They had a new home and family.

After Jed and Mary went upstairs, John pulled his wife over to sit on his lap and said, "Well, dear, how would you feel about telling them about our plans for them and start building their new house tomorrow? Is that okay with you, Mrs. McDonald?" Diana nodded her head in agreement and was so happy to hear him say this. She kissed him, and they just sat like that in the dark. Not saying any more, just . . . being together. When they went to bed, Diana read from the Bible, and they also thanked the Lord again for bringing Jed and Mary to them. They, and their families to come, would forever be protected by the McDonalds.

Mary really wasn't tired. She just wanted to go to bed with her husband. She still remembered the way she felt when he kissed her in the bath that morning. She was aroused again when she thought about it. She got into bed with nothing on. She always slept in a long night shirt, but tonight was different. She wanted to make love to Jed. She climbed on top of him and kissed him, gently at first and then with a little more passion. It didn't take Jed long to respond. She was so warm all over she couldn't wait. She guided him inside her and he was so excited. It didn't take long for both to reach their climax. After the excitement subsided, Mary got off of him, and Jed got up out of bed.

At first, Mary was upset that he got up out of bed. She thought she had done something wrong. He went over to the traveling bag where their clothes still were waiting to be unpacked. He opened it up, and from a small compartment, he pulled out a little package. Jed turned to her, and she saw the small package of brown paper. There was a string on it, tied in a bow. Jed got back into bed, and he handed Mary the package.

Mary took it from him and untied the bow. Inside the brown paper was the most beautiful linen handkerchief with handmade lace around it Mary had ever seen. Mary was so shocked she was speechless. She put her arms around her husband and just laid in his arms for the rest of the night, occasionally wiping a tear of joy with her very own handkerchief. She was now a lady, just like Laura-Ma'am and Betty.

Old Reliable woke them all at dawn the next day. Jed and Mary hurried to get washed and dressed. All four of them went down to the kitchen, greeting each other. Diana asked if they slept well.

Jed looked at Mary, both smiling, and said, "Diana, we has the most glorious sleep we's ever had since we was chil'uns in Africa!" Diana smiled back, telling them she was glad to hear it.

Diana delegated a job to Mary. It was now going to be her responsibility to collect the eggs every day. Just as John had told Diana she could keep the egg money to use on herself, Diana now passed this job and privilege on to Mary. She thought that Mary needed to have some money of her own.

They loved hearing the news at breakfast about their very own house that was going to be built for them. After John and Jed completed the feeding, milking, and cleaning the stalls, they went out to the fields, where John explained all the work that must get done. Jed looked over the potato field. John was waiting for his expert advice, smiling while he was thinking this.

Jed looked about and finally came back to John and said, "Sproutin' juss fine, John. Juss fine. Two feets 'part and two feets 'tween rows, huh? I tink you'se makes da right choice, John.

Dat give lots o' space fer dem ta grow big, not too big, mind y'all. Dey be a good size fer sure, an' tasty, no doubt. It be good we's on a riverbank. If we has ta water dem 'cause of drought, is we's ready wit' 'quipment? What chew has fer waterin'?"

John said, "Well, in Scotland, we mostly used prayer." He sheepishly smiled.

Jed said while looking at John as an almost equal, "You'se all got any backup plan, John? Da Lord could be busy dem days. You'se gots some big barrels 'roun' da place, don't cha? Oh yeah, I sees a couple by da barn; dat ain't gonna be 'nough, but it be a start. We gots ta keep dem ready an' full o' water. We can catch da rainwaters if ya perfers, but da river water's juss as good. We gots to find us some tin plates, like pie plates or some type o' waterin' can we's can make out of whatever you'se gots lyin' 'bout here.

"We best get dem barrels ready soon, looks like it might rain in da next day or so. I feels it in my chest. Dey's water comin'. Dat be good, mind y'all. God be waterin' da fields as we's juss c'llectin' water fer when he be mad at us.

"Been tinkin' 'bout a water system from da river. I'se draw it out fer ya. You'se buys supplies I be needin', an' I'se show ya how we done water crops from a river in Africa. We's needs it fer da trees dat we bein' trans . . . trans . . ."

John humbly replied, "Transplanting."

Jed came right back with, "Oh yeah, I fergit dat word—transplant. Dey needs lots o' water when we's moves 'em. I 'spect wit' dem, we needs more water, but we's can git it from da river when we wants.

"Now dem rocks may be a bit bigger dan y'all tinks. Dey can be real big below da surface, as big as a house, ya know. What chew gots in mind fer dem?"

John looked at Jed a new way. Jed was not simply a black teenage kid he hired to work on the farm. He was a farmer with great knowledge and deserved the respect due him. John was going to be good friends with Jed. He felt it, he heard it, and he knew it.

After they came back from their discussions in the fields, Jed and John went into town to start ordering building supplies. They were able to bring the materials to start the frame of their new house.

Many days went by, and things were going very well in the main house, the barn, and the potato field. John and Jed also started to pull more trees out of the west field. They had made preparations along the north side of the properties to put his fence of trees in. They started with smaller trees and put them at the outside edges, and the bigger trees were to be put in the middle for maximum winter protection.

John and Jed could handle the small trees by themselves. The big ones, he needed more help with, and it was going to be a very slow process. He hoped by winter, the trees would all be moved. Adam, Jeff, Michael, and the boys he used for planting would come when available. Michael wandered over with his oxen at least once a week to help with the rocks and trees. Toby was always with him to help too.

All five black boys came to work on the trees one day after Jed and Mary arrived. They were happy to meet Jed and Mary, and as miracle would have it, Rolly was Ashanti too. But that wasn't the only surprise! When he and Jed looked at each other, they smiled. He was Berko's best friend growing up in Ghana and one of the young boys who was playing with him the day he was kidnapped from his village in Africa.

Rolly and Jed embraced with tears in their eyes. They were so happy to see each other they hugged for what seemed like a lifetime. This was as close to ever seeing their home again as they would ever get. They started to talk in Twi, and it felt wonderful for Rolly and Jed—and for Mary too. She missed their native language.

Rolly was kidnapped about five months after Berko was. He was held in Elmina Castle for a while before going across the ocean too. He was not on the same ship as Berko and Afua were, the *Destino*; he was on another ship. This must have been much bigger than the *Destino* because Rolly told him, "We had us, muss be 'bout seven to eight hun'erd niggers in dem holds." Berko's eyes looked down. That word—could he ever escape from that word?

He asked, "Why you'se call us dat fer. We's people, juss people. Nuttin' more, nuttin' less."

Rolly started to understand that Jed may have had a little easier time of things than he did.

He was whipped on the ship and on the land. Wherever Rolly went, he was a no-good nigger, so he decided he'd never be anything else. He smiled at Jed and said, "Where you'se landed when ya come?"

Jed and Mary told them about being in Jamaica first and then Mississippi. Rolly had been sent directly to Mississippi to a mean massa, Mr. Waters. He told Jed that was his last name now. They all feared this man, and you had to behave or die. There were no punishments on this plantation, just life or death. He too escaped by the Underground Railroad about eight months before Mary and Jed did. They had so much to talk about.

Diana and John were delighted that Jed's childhood friend was here. Diana overheard them talk about the *Destino*. She wondered if it was the same ship she and John were on. She made a mental note to ask Mary and Jed later about the boat that they came in on. They really hadn't had much time to talk about the past yet, but Diana's curiosity had been piqued. She remembered a few stories on their own trip and wanted to ask if they knew anything about them. It seemed so coincidental.

Jed said to the boys, "'Dis be my wife, Mary. Her Africa name be Afua Kakira. We's livin' here on dis land, an' we works perm'nent here now. See dat house down yonder bein' built?" He pointed to the west field, and they could see the partially built house from where they were standing. "Well, dat be our house. Our very own! John and Diana is building it so we's can live where we's works. Dat's what chew gonna be he'pin' wit'. We move trees in the mornins and builds our house in da afternoons." Every day that Rolly was working, he and Jed were talking constantly about everything. It was so wonderful for them both that they had each other again.

At least two boys came every day to work, sometimes on a rotation basis. But there were also days when more could come. They were a great help with the trees and the few rocks they had to remove from this field, and they all pitched in to complete the house for Jed and Mary. John figured at fifteen cents a day each, it was well worth it. By the standard of the day, it was a lot of money for most, especially a black man.

The potato crop was well on its way. Diana's garden was thriving and so was the garden that Jed and Mary put in. The season was turning out to be hot but had enough rain to sustain all the crops so far.

The two-story house was built in about a month and a half. There were five rooms: two bedrooms (one larger, one smaller), a large kitchen, a summer kitchen (like Diana's, used for laundry, pantry, bathing, and storage), and a decent-sized living room with a beautiful large stone fireplace and mantle. They loved it.

Until the kitchen was furnished, Diana suggested that they could remain eating at their house, since the kitchen would be the most expensive to set up. Jed decided that it made more sense to get the cooking stove and a wood stove for the summer kitchen first, along with the table and chairs for the kitchen.

Below the summer kitchen, they had their own cold room and root cellar. It was the wrong time of the year to put ice in their cold room, so they would share Diana's since hers was well stocked to keep food frozen. They already had bedroom furniture for themselves. Tina and Jeff told Mary and Jed they could keep the bed that they loaned them, and Diana let them keep the chest of drawers. They would be able to sleep in their own house finally.

Diana loved having Mary in the house, and John enjoyed having Jed work with him. They were going to miss not having them in the house all the time. One day, while in the kitchen, Diana asked, "Mary, when we came over here from Scotland, we were on a ship called the *Destino*. I heard you mention that same name of the ship you both came on. Is it?" Mary shamefully nodded. Diana continued, "We learned on our trip coming here that the ship used to be a slave ship years before. Do you think it is possible that it may have been the same one that you and Jed traveled on?" Mary shrugged her shoulders but thought for a moment.

"Diana, I'se don't like to talk of it much. There was a punisher man on that ship. At night, he sneaked to my part of the ship and unchained me. He take me up on top. He done things that hurt me. He took my Kente robe off, an' he wash it. He wash me too, all over my body. Then he lay on top o' me, and he done things like husban' an' wife does." She started to cry, remembering it and retelling it.

Diana continued for her, "You were twelve years old, and after the first night he took you up top, he took you many times more and did those same things, washing your robe each time he saw you. He washed your body before and after he hurt you."

Mary's eyes were so wide. Diana was telling Mary her own story. How did she know? Diana came over to Mary and put her arms around her and hugged her with tears. Mary cried too. They hugged for a minute and cried many tears. Diana felt terrible. The horror story Diana and John heard from the sailor on their *Destino* was the same punisher of Mary on her very same *Destino*.

Both ladies fell silent for a while. They smiled at each other often that afternoon. There was a new level to their relationship now, the best of friends, and Diana would always do everything she ever could to make Mary feel protected, safe, and loved by her new family. They were never to talk about her experience on the *Destino* again.

After reading in bed with John that night, Diana let him know what she and Mary discovered that day. John was shocked and sickened to hear that the horror story they heard on the trip about the little twelve-year-old slave girl who was tortured by this sexual molester was their Mary. They held each other and said an extra prayer for their dear, sweet friend. They prayed to God to help them to protect and care for Mary and Jed and all their generations.

Finally, Mary and Jed had their very own house now. It wasn't a village hut or a slave cabin or a room in a plantation house . . . it was a home. They both couldn't believe it. Jed and Mary Allen had a real house to live in. They could eat, sleep, keep warm, pump their own water, and, eventually, God willing, have a family.

The first night they spent there, they danced and sang and talked for hours. They made love. They never thought of Jamaica. They never thought of Mississippi. They never thought of the Underground Railroad or anything but themselves for a change.

Everyone became closer to each other. There was happiness, hard work, and friendships. By now, the potato crop was thriving, the east field was almost cleared of trees, and the first hay field was ready to be harvested.

Diana and Mary were becoming very close, and Tina too. Tina was almost ready to have her baby. Jeff was a very nervous father-to-be. Tina's parents didn't know they had a cradle and bought a brand new one for their first grandchild. They were very grateful and gave Diana and John's back to them. Tina's father was also hand carving a rocking horse. So Diana also got theirs back. Tina and Jeff felt bad, but John and Diana were not offended in the least; they understood.

The three girls were busy with making baby clothes, getting diapers ready, and helping Tina out of chairs! She had gotten so big in these last couple of weeks. She was always saying that she was as big as a house. One morning when Tina was out at the farm, she told Mary, "Mary, I finally got your Kente cloth robe mended. I wanted to wait to give it to you after I finally matched all the thread colors to repair it." Mary was so thrilled. She was getting it back, repaired. Tina brought out a box wrapped in paper. Mary unwrapped it. It was like getting a special present.

When she opened the box, she lifted the robe out carefully. It was beautiful. Mary cried and dropped to her knees and wept on Tina's lap as Tina patted her head gently. Mary was so happy that she had it back. Tina mended it perfectly.

Diana said, "Mary, it's so beautiful. Is this the robe you made beside your father?" Mary looked at Diana through her tears of joy. She nodded her head, wiping her eyes. All of a sudden it had a familiarity to it. But what was it? Diana was in silent thought for a moment. All of a sudden, she jumped up out of her chair and ran upstairs. She looked in the bottom drawer of her dresser. There it was! She hadn't taken it out of the box since their wedding day. The McGee tartan sash her mother made for her wedding. She ran down the stairs as quickly as she could, saying loudly and excitedly, "You won't believe this, girls!" She popped around the corner of the kitchen and showed them her sash . . . the colors were identical to Mary's Kente robe. All three were speechless.

Diana picked up the sash and the robe and held them together. She chuckled and said, "Well, Mary, I guess we have the same favorite colors . . . hey, you could even call it common threads!"

They all laughed. Diana continued, "Mary, it's just like both of us sailing on the *Destino*. That is another thing we have in common . . . I think our families were meant to meet. It truly is our *destino*.

That's the Spanish word for 'destiny.'" All three ladies just sat and could not believe the coincidences they discovered that afternoon. What other parallels could there be in their lives or would show up in the future? Diana was sure these similarities were what brought them together, and they are what will always keep them together as a large extended family, like Jed and Mary had in Africa.

John, Jed, and Jeff had been out on the north side of the property and were replanting trees one summer Sunday afternoon. The sky had become a scary shade of greenish black. They dropped the equipment and let the horses and ponies go toward the barn. John knew they would have to take their chances if the weather became really bad. The doors to the barn were left open for each to make up their own mind as to their safety.

The thunder and lightning was more severe than just a regular summer storm. They were in the middle of tornado season, according to the *Farmer's Almanac*. They heeded the advice and ran toward the house as the sky opened up, and they heard the deafening rumble coming toward them. John yelled, "Everyone to the root cellar now!" There was just enough time to grab the girls and get below. They had just enough room in John and Diana's cellar for the six of them. Jed and Mary did not have time to run to their own.

They heard the terrible rumbling and the ground shook . . . and then . . . silence. John peeked his head out of the trap door after all went quiet. He climbed up, followed by Jed and Jeff. All three went outside to look around. Nothing seemed amiss; nothing had been disturbed—at first glance. All the animals were accounted for, and not one thing seemed out of place. John had thought a tornado hit. Was he wrong? He'd never experienced one before, so it was just a guess.

Then it was confirmed; a tornado caused some property damage after all. John, Jeff, and Jed discovered some of the trees they replanted on the north side of the property were uprooted. After examining them, John decided they could be replanted again, but it would have to wait until they made sure their neighbors and other folks in Chatham were all right.

Others in the area, John surmised, may not have fared as well from the storm. He told Jeff and Jed to come with him; he was going down the road to check on other people and their farms, and then into town. They let the girls know they were going after making sure the three of them were fine and after bringing them back up into the house. Both houses were still standing, thank the Lord.

Diana, Tina, and Mary agreed that the men should go and see if anyone needed help and that they would be perfectly fine while they were gone. Diana said, "M'love, what on earth could happen here that the three of us couldn't possibly handle together? You just get going to see if you're needed to help anyone. I love ya, darlin'!" She kissed her Johnny, and the three men headed down the road to help their neighbors and friends.

As they ventured down the road, now littered with many tree branches and debris, they saw quite a lot of damage. A tornado certainly struck a path of destruction through their neighborhood! John couldn't believe it had missed their farm almost completely.

They first came to Michael Maguire's farm. It was damaged somewhat. One of his chicken barns, which held about one hundred laying hens, was no longer there. Neither were the chickens . . . at least, none were alive. They were scattered everywhere. Michael was indeed upset but was more concerned for his neighbors. He was so glad to see his friends safe.

Michael said to the three of them, "We're all fine here. Let's get into town and help where we can, lads. I can clean this up later!" As they entered town, they heard that it was a twister for sure.

There were a few buildings that had completely disappeared, and some were damaged. They heard a few cries in tangled heaps of wood and shingles. They saw arms waving from below these piles of rubble. People were alive.

Jeffrey found his brother, Adam. His livery and blacksmith shop was unharmed, but he had been physically hit by some flying debris. His arm was badly bleeding, but Jeff bandaged him up, and he was able to help with rescuing others and the recovery of bodies.

John stood after helping pull people out of the rubble and looked around.

Suddenly he asked, "Where's Lavalle's General Store?" Everyone stopped what they were doing and looked about. There was not one trace of the general store that had been there that very morning.

And where were Rene and Emilie? After everyone who could be saved was saved, they all looked around for their friends.

Not too many places got severe damage, but they still hadn't accounted for a few people. Rene and Emilie were not to be found anywhere. John, Jeff, and Jed headed back home after telling people they would be there to help them in the next several days. They had to go make sure their wives were all right. They hurried back to the farm, stopping to tell Eileen and Toby that Michael was fine and staying in town to help search for people. Eileen told Toby to go ahead and help in town; she would be fine. John said it was fine for him to go; he would be okay. He left to go help his dad.

After the girls came out of the root cellar, telling the men they'd be fine, it started. Not bad at first, but it quickly got worse! Tina was in labor! Diana got her up to a bedroom. Everything they needed was in the house. Sheets, hot water was still on the stove, scissors to cut the cord. Mary chopped some ice to keep Tina comfortable during the worse parts . . . but they would have preferred there be a doctor too. None of them ever participated in a birth before . . . at least, not a human one. Mary was unconscious when hers was born. No one wanted to leave to try and find Dr. Marsh and thought he might be needed elsewhere anyway.

Tina's labor was going fast. When Diana checked after about thirty minutes, the baby was right there. Tina had to push. The head came out fine, but the shoulders were a little stuck. Diana gently put her hands around the baby to move it into a better position. It worked. The rest of the baby came out fine. With Tina crying, she asked, "Diana . . . Diana . . . what is it?"

Diana finished tying and cutting the cord, and then she held up a very large baby boy. All three were crying now. Tina took her son in her arms and held him tight. Mary tended to cleaning Tina and the baby. Their tears had now turned into giggles. This day was certainly going to go down in history in that house!

While they waited for the men to return, Tina felt well enough to sit up. They washed the boy completely now, and Tina was so happy. They did get to use Diana and John's cradle for Tina and Jeff's baby after all. Tina was so thrilled. Diana was too!

"What's you gonna name him?" Mary asked. Tina said she'd rather not say until Jeff was with her to tell them all together. Mary wanted to bring some water or tea up to Tina and Diana, who sweat almost as much as Tina did. Tina would not hear of it. She wanted to go into the kitchen; they could bring the cradle down there too. Diana was concerned, but Tina promised she'd lie down again if she needed to. She had borrowed one of Diana's nightgowns and prettied herself for her husband for when he arrived.

Suddenly, from outside came some very strange noises. Mary heard it first and then Diana. Tina heard something too. Was an animal trapped? Diana took her shotgun and started outside toward the noise, with Mary close behind her. It was coming from the barn. The door was open. She could see the two Clydesdales; the two Shetlands were nearby and so were the two Anguses. They were all fine, thank the Lord! What else was there making that noise? She was in the barn more than halfway when she saw Petunia the cow lying on the barn floor. She was in labor and starting to deliver too.

"Lord Almighty, have ye no done enough fer today without addin' this to the pile too?" Diana said as she looked skyward. "Oh well, what's one more to our family? Mary, have you seen a cow born before?" She shook her head no. "Well, love, there's a first time for everything. Hanging on the doorway of the barn is a very long pair of gloves. Please get them for me. I'll have to try to turn the calf; it looks backwards."

Mary wasn't sure what the gloves were for, but she found out in a few minutes.

Diana stuck her arm in the cow and tried to turn the calf around for easier passage. She knew she was doing it right, but she wasn't quite as strong as John was. Mary had run back to the house to let Tina know they were fine and what was happening. She and the baby were doing well.

Tina now felt well enough to make a pot of coffee and some tea for everyone when they all got in.

She worried about her husband and brother-in-law and the others, hoping they were all okay in town.

Diana had a hard time with the calf. She could not get close enough to the cow because her own pregnant belly was getting too big, and it was just starting to get in the way of things. As she pulled the calf, she started to laugh. She couldn't stop and said, "Oh Lord, when you put the three of us girls in this situation, I know you were just having fun, but the twister too—I think that was a bit too much!" She could not stop laughing as she pulled. All of a sudden, the calf emerged, wobbling and soaked with afterbirth but looked in good shape. Diana, on the other hand, was another story.

When she had a good grip on the calf, she didn't let go, but when she started to laugh, she knew one way or the other the calf was ready to come out. When the calf slid so quickly, Diana lost her grip and flew backward into a large pile of manure, which the men were going to clean out that afternoon. She was covered from head to toe. But she was still laughing. Mary worried about her falling, but Diana assured her there was enough dung to cushion her landing and was fine.

Mary could no longer stand it; she let out the biggest laugh. They both tried to get Diana up out of the pile, but she kept slipping backward, and there was more laughter.

The three men were at the barn door all of a sudden because they heard laughing. They came in to see a cow tending to her brand-new baby calf. John was surprised. "Was it a hard birth, love?" John asked.

Diana replied, still giggling, "No, dear, I just had to insert one hand to bring him out, instead of the usual two." The men were proud of her for doing it and then realized that Diana was sitting, pregnant, in a very large pile of shit! They tried not to laugh, biting their cheeks, but it didn't work.

They all laughed as they helped her up to her feet, out of the manure.

Jeff looked around and asked, "Where is Christina? Is she in the house? Is she okay?" Diana waved her hand around to let him know she was fine and motioned him, all of them, to come to the house.

"You're not coming in my house looking and smelling like that, woman!" John teased. She tossed him a look that he'd seen before.

"When was the last time you filled the pillows, dear?" John asked, trying not to laugh. He smiled that smile; he loved to provoke his wife so much. All of a sudden, when they were in the summer kitchen, everyone heard a baby cry.

Jeff looked wide-eyed at Diana. "No, you don't mean?" All of a sudden, Tina was standing at the door between the summer kitchen and the kitchen, and she was holding their bouncing baby boy. Jeff let the tears out, apologizing for not being there with her. "Oh my sweet Tina, are you all right? Is it a boy or a girl?"

Tina said, "Papa, meet your son. Mr. Benjamin Jeffrey White. We estimate him to be about nine pounds, but I'll check at the doctor's office when I take him to his first appointment."

They all smiled and said hello to this very sweet baby, born on such an eventful day. Jeff could not take his eyes off his son and his wife. He loved them both so much.

John hated to turn the mood sour on such an occasion but had to let the girls know. "Darlin', Michael has lost one barn and about one hundred chickens. Some are scattered, dead on his property, and he is letting people come to take them home for food, if they like." Diana realized then that each of the guys had two chickens a piece in their hands. She tried to suppress another giggle but couldn't. They looked so funny, just standing there with dead chickens in their hands.

After a moment, John told them, "There are buildings torn up and some missing in town. There are also some people dead, but we helped save some. M'love, Lavalle's General Store is gone. There's no building, no merchandise, no Rene or Emilie!"

Chapter 15

Aftermath

T HERE WAS MUCH DISBELIEF AND sadness after the surprise twister. The most damaged parts were north of Chatham and around London and Woodstock, Ontario. Chatham folks were pulling together to help wherever they were needed. The potato field and vegetable patches at the McDonalds' fared well. After transplanting the many trees on the north edge of their lot, several were ripped out by the roots. They would be replanted as quickly as possible after other more important jobs were completed.

Some farmers lost grain, hay, and straw crops, and then there was Lavalle's General Store.

There was still no sign of Emilie or Rene. No one understood why they could not to be found. Were they maybe traveling and were lost or killed on the road? Why couldn't they find their friends?

There were other stores to buy from, but they weren't Lavalle's. Adam had plans to rebuild the store for them. If they did not come back, he would legally buy the property first, but if they returned, he would give it back to them. If not, he would arrange to run it himself.

About a week after the twister, men from all over came to help. They started to clear away the rubble that fell into the basement of Lavalle's. There was a large piece of stone and cement that was lying down. They needed to get it out, but it would take much more than manpower; they needed horsepower. They gathered as many horses and ropes as they could to remove the huge slab. It was an all-morning-

and-half-the-afternoon job to set the job up properly, but by later in the afternoon, they were ready to pull it up. As the horses worked and the men guided the slab up, underneath were the bodies of Rene and Emilie Lavalle. They were lying on their stomachs with their arms around each other's waist.

Everyone was horrified. The condition of the bodies was poor due to the hot days, and there was obvious decomposition to both, but they couldn't lose the momentum of the horses during the lift to stop and take a closer look. It took about eight minutes to bring the slab out and lay it on the ground beside where the store used to stand. No one said a word. Everyone just stared into the hole where Rene and Emilie spent their last tragic moments together.

Everyone was saddened by the news. As soon as could be, there was a large funeral for them. They were buried together. The priest in the town knew them well and performed a lovely service, which was attended by almost the whole town.

After the twister there was plenty of rebuilding needed. Everyone helped out all they could to get folks on their feet again. It was truly a great Christian community. They really did "love thy neighbor." Then it became very busy on the farm. It was harvesting time.

One day, Mary became sick. Diana suggested that she take her to the doctor. Her monthly appointment was the next day, so she could take Mary with her. Mary was relieved. She was worried.

Jed was so worried about her it affected his work. He was making mistakes and couldn't concentrate. Many times his chest really hurt, and the two of them thought it was just stress and worry for his wife, but was that the real reason?

Suddenly, Mary started to have a lot of pain in her lower abdominal area. She and Jed were very worried. It was as painful as the fall down the steps when she lost her baby. Diana thought maybe she should be seen now. Diana told Jed to grab a horse and get to the doctor immediately; Mary shouldn't be moved. She was bleeding vaginally. Jed had no idea what was wrong and was scared. He looked tenderly at his wife and asked, "Is y'all sure you'se ain't fallen down no stairs?" She shook her head no. He left to find the doctor while Mary lay in her own bed in their house, not moving much. Every time she moved, she was in pain and bled a little more.

On the trip back to the farm, Dr. Marsh had gotten as much information as he could about Mary's medical past. Jed told him everything. Ian asked if she was pregnant. Jed looked wide-eyed and said, "No, dat doc in Jamaica tole us we cain't or shouldn't have no babies. It be too much for my Mary's little body ta take. He say she be in danger if she be wit' chile. She be tellin' me, Doc, wouldn't she?" Jed started to shake his head, saying, "No . . . No . . . she cain't be, Doc . . . I'se surely know! . . . Wouldn't I be knowin' . . . Doc?"

Dr. Ian (as he liked his patients to call him) confirmed it. Mary was pregnant! Jed just shook his head and kept repeating, "I guess dey's juss sometin' in da water here. Firs' Tina, den Diana, now my Mary . . ." He just kept saying it over and over for a moment as he paced back and forth. All of a sudden, he stopped in his tracks. He looked so shocked. "Mary, you'se with chile, I mean a yung'un, I mean you'se gonna, we's gonna . . . a baby?" Jed fainted.

As sore as Mary was, she laughed, "That be my big brave, strong husban'!" Everyone laughed with her. Jed came to, and the doctor confirmed it for him again.

Jed went to hug Mary, but the doctor told him he had to be really gentle. He told them they couldn't even sleep in the same bed. Mary could only move slightly and not get up. She had to stay in bed for the rest of her pregnancy. The damage that Ethan Jordan caused was now torturing her tiny body again.

Dr. Ian's advice was that Mary sleep alone in the bed, and Jed could sleep beside her on the floor or get another bed in the same room. John would see to it for them. Ian told them he would be coming to see Mary every week, and more if needed. Diana did not need to come to her own appointments in town anymore; he would see her when he came to see Mary. Mary's would be the most delicate pregnancy he would ever care for in his career. And it was all because of an ignorant, selfish, evil man's senseless tyranny! How could someone brutalize such a sweet, lovely young woman like Mary? He would never understand Ethan Jordan's brutality for as long as he lived.

Diana looked after Mary now. Christina came out when she could to help, always bringing Benjamin with her. He usually cheered Mary up. Diana's time was also coming, so that kept Mary's thoughts busy. Diana would go to see Mary several times a day. She had brought the cradle and rocking horse over to Mary and Jed's place as gifts. Mary just prayed her baby would survive to use them.

The vegetable gardens and the potatoes were now being harvested. John hired the five boys to work every day. He decided to pay them at the end of each week. He knew they could get hangovers and may not come the next day to work, but he took his chances with them. He wanted to trust them to be responsible to get to work the next day.

Diana was out in her garden one afternoon when she felt a pain. She went down on her knees. She thought it was a bit soon for the baby to come. It was not quite nine months yet. Was it labor? She got herself back up to a standing position; she felt better. She continued to work. She was pulling mature vegetables in, and after about ten minutes, she felt another pain but was ready for it. This time she stayed on her feet. She started to think maybe she should return to the house . . . or should she go to where John and the boys were working in the field and tell him? She thought for a moment and decided to go to John. That way he could bring her back to the house, and she'd feel better with him by her side.

As she walked through the harvested part of the field, she had another pain. This one hurt more than the others. She was becoming convinced that she certainly was in labor now. All of a sudden, she cried out, "Johnny." She paused. Again, she called out, "Johnny, come help me, darlin'." She screeched louder this time, but there was no response. Ned was the closest to her. He was in the straw field. He stopped chopping the straw. He listened carefully. There was nothing. He started chopping straw again, and several seconds later, he heard it again. He stopped chopping again and listened. He was sure this time.

Ned yelled to John, who was in earshot of him, "John, yo' missus be callin' to ya. She soun' bad, she do." Everyone stopped working and ran toward the shouting. John found his wife sitting on the ground, leaning on a straw mound for support. John crouched down to see how she was. She told him her pains were maybe ten minutes apart or so. They both knew it could take quite a while before the baby was born.

The boys got the wagon from where it was sitting, down the field a piece, and brought it to Diana. John picked her up and carried her. Diana said as she smiled, "My sweet Johnny, there is no puddle to carry me over." She smiled, referring to the golf game at St. Andrews when he picked her up and carried her over the puddles on the golf course. He smiled and kissed her on the nose.

The next pain came after around another ten minutes. She decided that this could be a long day. As John carried her to the wagon, she remembered her mother telling her that she had been in labor for fifty-four hours before Diana herself was born. She crossed her fingers and hoped for the best. She was ready for whatever God had in store for her.

John asked if she wanted Dr. Marsh yet. She told him, "No, not yet, love. I'm okay." When she got back to the house, she didn't want to lie down; she just wanted to putter around in the kitchen and do some baking. She promised him that she would sit down or lie down in the parlor if she couldn't handle the pain. John said that he was going to stay with her. She argued with him and won. He told her she was the most stubborn woman he'd ever known! Diana said, "I know, darlin'. That's why you love me, remember! I'll be fine, love."

The next pain came along, still within another ten-minute interval. She sighed, and after the contraction, she started her scones. John suggested that maybe he could have Tina come out to be with her. Diana liked that idea. Since Mary was laid up with her delicate pregnancy in the other house, Tina could keep an eye on both of them, and John could get back to the field. John said he'd send one of the boys to fetch her. It would be a chance to test out the new carriage and one of the new thoroughbred horses he bought from Adam a few days earlier.

John let Rolly go to get Tina from town. The horse pulled the carriage very easily, and it was a smooth ride. The new carriage seated four comfortably. After about twenty minutes, Rolly was turning into the driveway, delivering Tina and Benjamin. He unhooked the carriage and put it back in the drive shed, let the new horse out in the field with the other animals, and headed out to the field to work.

John had reluctantly gone out to the field while Rolly was away getting Tina, but when he saw them coming down the road, he quickly walked back to the house to talk to her.

John asked Tina to keep an eye on both ladies and to ring the bell if he was needed to come back. She was glad to be there to help and assured him she would let him know as soon as he was needed. He felt much better and went back to work after checking on Diana and

Mary one more time. John told Jed that he had checked on Mary, but he thought Jed should see her for a few minutes, just to reassure her, as well as him.

Jed returned to see Mary and told her the news that Diana started into labor; she wanted desperately to be with her. She asked, "Jed, does you think you could gets me over to see her? Do you tink we could do it? I wants to see her so bad, Jed." Jed started pondering the situation. All of a sudden, his chest was getting sore again.

He talked with Mary as he sat holding her hand, trying to catch his breath from his chest pain. He said, "Maybe I'se should see da doctor 'bout my chess an', well, ya know . . . da udder ting." He had been having several more erections that would not release for an hour or more. They were getting more concerned lately because both symptoms were very painful. He decided, after talking it over with Mary, he would see Dr. Marsh next time he was in town or next time Ian was at the farm checking on Mary. He also told her he would think of a way to get her over to Diana's to be with her. But he had to make sure she was safe. He kissed her tenderly and told her that he had to get back to work, but Tina and he would be checking on her through the day. She smiled and reminded him to think of a way to get her over to Diana's to be with her through her labor. He smiled, promising her he would, and left for the field.

The end of the workday was almost three hours early this day. John wanted to be at the house with Diana. They had been working so well, and he wanted to reward them for doing such a great job, so he gave the boys the rest of the afternoon off and paid them all. He also told them they didn't need to come in the next day, but in two days. They wished Diana and John well and were all concerned for them.

As they passed by Michael Maguire's farm while walking back to town, they took the initiative to stop and ask if he needed any work done and to tell them about Diana. Michael was thrilled to see them, for them to help with his harvest. He hired them for the rest of the day and the next day, and they would stay until dusk each day.

Eileen popped out of the house to see what was up with the boys, and she found out Diana was in labor. She was told Tina was there, but with a baby herself, she might need help. She told Michael and Toby that they could warm last night's leftover chicken stew for supper.

She also left the makings for fresh dumplings. She decided to walk over since it was really not that far, just a mile and a bit. It was not an emergency at this point, and the walk was just what she needed. When Eileen arrived, Diana was at the counter making pies. She looked at her and said, "For a woman in labor, you sure look fine, young lady!"

Diana said, "Hi, Eileen, you're just in time for tea with Tina and me." She just popped a strawberry rhubarb pie in the oven when she started to cry out. Another pain came along, still at the confirmed ten-minute interval. She was not making much progress, but it seemed like real labor, even if it was a bit early. She figured it had to be false labor since she wasn't having the pains at closer times.

Eileen told her about her own false labors with Toby. She had them twice. About a week and a half later, Toby was born with no problems with five hours of real labor, which she thought was false again.

Diana was a little disheartened to hear it might not be real. She prayed something would happen soon. Her Johnny was staying close to the house now. He wanted to be there if she needed him. During that first day, he paced in the barn, in between working. He wished he could do something for her.

John and Diana received a surprise guest. When the boys walked toward home and then decided to work for Michael, Rolly continued into town to let the doctor know that Diana's time seemed to be here and that Mary was getting very worried, almost to a frantic state. He mentioned this to the doctor because Jed had told Rolly in private that even her worrying could be bad for their baby.

There was no one in Dr. Marsh's office. He was getting caught up on paperwork, organizing his schedule and ordering supplies, so when Rolly burst through the door and told him what was happening at the farm, he grabbed his black bag and got into his carriage.

Ian took Rolly and dropped him off at Michael's to work. On the short trip, Rolly told him as much as he knew about Diana's labor and Mary's anxiety. The doctor sped up his horse. He quickly let Rolly off and promised he would get word to him about what was happening at the McDonalds'. Rolly went back to work, telling Michael and the boys that the doctor was on his way to the farm. They all went back to work, saying a prayer for the McDonald family.

When Dr. Ian arrived at the farm, Tina met him outside, and she took him to Diana. He found her sitting in the kitchen, having a tea with Eileen. It was obvious she wasn't ready for him, so he decided to go see Mary. Both John and Jed came to the house when they saw the doctor arrive. Ian told them that they had to do everything they could to keep Mary calm. He agreed with her idea that she would be much calmer if she could be in the other house with Diana. She was so worried about her and wanted to be there for her.

John and Jed asked the doctor if they could move Mary over to the other house; he said the only way would be to move her over, mattress and all. They sized up the situation. They picked up the mattress and Mary, and the three men moved her. It was a chore to get through doors, but they were determined.

Diana was so happy so see Mary coming through the door; she didn't even notice that her next contraction was coming along. She was pouring tea for everyone and sat down to have hers, and then this one hit. This next one was stronger than the others. Still, she thought it might be false, but it had come in seven minutes. Finally she was making progress. Ian decided to leave and told them where he was going to be over the next day and that he'd come back as soon as they needed him.

Since the contractions started, it was over twelve hours, but there was no sign of it happening soon. The next day, Diana busied herself with getting breakfast for everyone who stayed at their place overnight. While standing at the stove, her water broke. She laid down on the parlor sofa now. She thought it would progress faster now. No such luck. The pains were still six to seven minutes apart. This went on for another six hours.

Finally the pains jumped to four—to five-minute intervals. Jed rode a horse toward town to let the doctor know but came across him on the road and told him about Diana. They both rode back to the farm.

Dr. Marsh told them that she could have it any time that day, or sometimes women can be in labor for three or four days before the baby comes. She prayed that it would happen soon. John was holding her hand and was so concerned; he never left her side that day.

After another four hours, a total of twenty-two hours of labor, Diana gave birth to a baby boy, who they named George. John was so excited. He never left the room, even for a second, when the baby was coming.

John held his tiny son in his arms, and he was the proudest papa on Earth at that moment. He looked at Diana tenderly with a lone tear in his eye and said, "Thank ye, darlin'. I do love ye, my bonnie lass: My beautiful Diana McGee." He raised his eyes and said, "Thank ye, Lord, for deliverin' a bonnie baby boy safe in our care now!"

Tina was a big help to the doctor; so was Eileen. They also kept Mary calm and tried to get her to stop worrying, assuring her that Diana and George were just fine. Then Mary couldn't help but worry about herself and her own baby at this time. Would they make it too? She wondered.

She tried not to show Jed how she was worrying, but he saw it in her eyes. He put his hand over the baby inside her, reassuring her that the baby will be fine, and she would be too. Jed promised he would look after them both.

John was so thrilled with his son. He watched him sleep that night in the cradle, right beside their bed. Mary had been moved back to their house a few days after George was born, and Diana brought him to visit Mary every time she went to check on her several times a day. Mary was nervously awaiting her time. Jed still was not sleeping in their bed with her. It was too risky for her condition.

It was now coming up to winter; the fields were harvested, and every one of their friends shared in the potato crop, just like Diana and John said they would. The McDonalds' crops were successful. John, Jed, and their hired hands were able to clear the whole east field and finish replanting the trees along the north side of the property. Just as John hoped it would, the trees blocked the cold north wind. John and Diana were so proud and happy with their farm! Life had changed so much for them.

One winter day in 1860 came Mary's time. Jed was not with Mary as much as he wanted to be. He had many chores but tried to see her at every opportunity. Mary cried out to Jed early one morning, when he came in from shoveling the barn. He was washing his hands and heard her. He ran to her without drying his hands. He came flying around the corner of the bedroom and found Mary holding her abdomen; there was blood coming from under her nightgown.

He didn't know what to do. He didn't want to leave her, but he needed help. He screamed at the top of his lungs, "John, Diana, come, it's time. She be in a bad way, git da doc . . . hurry." He didn't hear any reply. They didn't hear him. He remembered the bells John put up for both of them by their front doors to alert each other during emergencies. He rang it fast and furiously. He was desperate. They heard it! John came running, and Diana wrapped George in a blanket and ran to their house too. Jed cried, "She be in a bad way, Diana. She be bloody. She's bad." Diana gave George to John and assessed the situation. She told John to place George in Mary's cradle and to go get the doctor and Tina or Eileen to help too. It had to be fast! Jed was by Mary's side. He held her hand as she screamed in pain. When she moved, she bled more. Diana pushed on her lower abdomen the help try and slow the blood down.

John quickly jumped on a horse and went to town as fast as he could, not even saddling up first. By now, they had a couple of thoroughbreds. They were great for fast trips. On the way, he stopped at the Maguires' and asked Eileen to go quickly to his house. Michael was on his way back from town when he stopped on the road and heard the news from John. He sped home and let Eileen up onto the wagon to take her to the McDonalds' as quickly as he could. Eileen told Toby to go into town and let Tina know what was happening for John. John found the doctor on the road too. He was just on his way out to check on Mary.

When Tina heard Mary was having the baby, she had Toby run to tell Adam because Jeff was showing property. Adam closed the shop and drove Toby back to his house and Tina and Benjamin to the McDonalds'. He said to wish them the best and tell them he's sorry couldn't do anything to help. He told Tina he'd let Jeff know where she was as soon as he returned to town.

Jed tried not to cry, but the tears came. He couldn't stand to see his Mary in pain like this.

He didn't know that having this baby would mean so much pain for her. Dr. Brookes, in Jamaica, told them she could go through pain like this if she ever got pregnant. They never realized how bad it could really get. This baby was a blessing to them. They wanted it so. God gave it to them, but Jed was afraid he might take it back and his Mary too. Jed let go of her hand and clutched his chest in pain again.

Dr. Marsh could not diagnose Jed's problems yet. All he could do was give him morphine powder for the pain. Dr. Marsh wrote to some doctors in Toronto, hoping they could shed light on his medical problem. He was waiting their reply.

In the meantime, the task at hand was to deliver a baby from a very tiny body that had severe uterine damage. It was going to be delicate, and at first, the baby seemed to be in position when the labor had started. Mary was in great pain, slowly passing in and out of consciousness, and she was bleeding more now. The doctor told Jed to press on her lower abdomen so Diana could be ready to help him. It helped slow the blood flow some. The baby now showed, but to the doctor's horror, it was not head down but feet down. When the baby came out, it likely would kill Mary, and the baby might not have a chance either.

Eileen arrived and the doctor was glad. He had called on her to assist him a few times with deliveries out in the county. She was experienced. She and Diana were now his nurses. He would tell them what to do to help, and they followed instructions the best they could. He asked Tina to go out of the room, since it was not large enough to accommodate them all, but to please stay in the house in case she was needed. She and Ben went in the kitchen and started to clean up. She decided to start some baking for the Allens. It was the only thing she could think of doing while she was waiting.

Ian had only been in practice for six years. This was only his fourth breech baby. All other three mothers were lost unfortunately. If there was time, he could do a caesarean section, but not in the house. She would have to be in an operating room. He didn't have time to get her there, and he was afraid they would both die on the trip. He asked Eileen and Diana if they could handle this difficult delivery. Both responded that they would be able to help and accept what happens, if they must. They knew he needed their help. They would be strong. He was grateful.

Ian wanted Jed out of there, so John was now taking care of him in the kitchen. He tried to calm him by being jovial. They had tea while they were sitting, waiting. The doctor didn't want Jed to know what he was doing. It would upset him too much, and the shock may be too much for him and his own medical condition, whatever it was.

Diana was unaware that Jed had anything wrong with him. He kept his symptoms and doctor's appointments to himself. John knew some of it but not everything. Only what he witnessed in the field and in the barn while Jed was working. Jed asked him to keep it to himself, because he knew Diana would talk to Mary, and it would upset her. Jed didn't want to upset anyone, especially his wife.

Mary was passed out, but he needed her to push. Diana was swabbing Mary's head and talking to her, reassuring her, hoping she could hear. Eileen was at the other end with the doctor to help with the baby.

John had Jed and George still in the kitchen. He asked if Jed knew how to change a nappy.

Jed had no idea what he was talking about. John said, "Sorry, lad, I meant a diaper. In Scotland we call it a nappy." Jed shook his head. George needed changing, and John thought there was no time like the present. He decided to show Jed how to change him as Tina watched with a grin. After the wet diaper came off, the chill of the air made George urinate. The stream was a perfect shot, and it landed right in John's tea. They laughed so hard they cried. It broke the tension.

John let Jed take over and actually placed the diaper on him correctly. When Jed picked up George, the diaper fell off him completely. George was always smiling and is such a good-natured boy he cooed and giggled through it all. John couldn't help but laugh more. Tina burst out laughing with him.

John smiled and said, "Let's try that again, Jed. I think you need more practice." John let him try again, and this time the diaper stayed on the baby. Jed gave baby George a hug and looked to John. There was tremendous screaming from upstairs now. Jed got scared! John had to hold him back from going up to the bedroom. He tried to break free and go, but John held firm. Then there were no more sounds from the bedroom.

After several seconds, John called out, "Is everything okay up there?" He said a quick silent prayer as he asked the question. He, Tina, and Jed waited with great concern. There was more silence, and then a *smack*. A few more seconds passed, and then they heard it—the loudest cry they ever heard!

Diana called back, "Oh, darlin', things are fine."

Jed was afraid but smiled at the sound of the cry. John and Tina both smiled at the sound and held Jed, congratulating him. He was a father finally. After a few moments, Jed called out, "How's my Mary? She be okay?" As he asked the question, Diana brought a bundle into the kitchen.

She handed it to Jed. Diana and John were so happy for them. Tina too. Jed and John looked at Diana with worry.

As she was handing Jed the baby, Diana said, "Jed, meet your son, and don't worry, Mary's fine. She's asleep now. The doctor has to put what he calls a lot of packing in her to stop the blood, but she made it. Your son came out backward, you know. He was rough on his mama. Doc Ian had to cut her a little to make the opening bigger to get him out, but here he is, Papa."

When Mary woke up, she looked around the room. She saw Diana, and John was holding George. Eileen was there beside the doctor, and Tina and Benjamin were also there, squeezed into her bedroom. Jed was sitting on the bed beside her, holding their son. She didn't even know what she had yet. She looked at Jed and saw the tenderness in his eyes, just as many times as she had seen before. He was selfless, true, and strong. They had a bond stronger than none, with all they had been through in their lives.

Mary went to speak but Jed shushed her. She needed her strength. She wanted the baby. He stood up beside her and placed the baby in her arms. He looked around the room at everyone smiling and waiting. He would not tell anyone his name until Mary woke up to share it with their best friends. Jed let a tear roll down his cheek, and Mary did too.

Jed said, "You folks is the bess folks we ever has wit' us, 'n' dat ain't no lie. But dere be one udder dat he'p us a might. Dat man we be workin' fer in Jamaica. He taked us in an' give us a comfer'ble life. He da man dat name us. First, we git our lass name from him. Da boys' lass name be Allen. Dat be fer his dead brother. An' he calls me Jedediah. From da Bible! When da girls come, he give dem da lass name Belle, after his dead sister. When she come, he named my Mary.

"Now we wants our baby ta have his name. Dis be our son. Jacob Marcus Allen. An' Mary, Doc say he be healthy!" Everyone gave a little giggle. They all choked back the tears a little. They were all so happy to know Mary and Jed, and now Jacob.

They all hoped to hear many more stories about the older Jacob Marcus. Mary and Jed loved him so, and it was obvious that he loved them. It seemed like an honor to this baby and to Jacob's memory that life had turned out the way it had for them. Jed continued. "Juss as we's remembers him, now wit' our very own Jacob ta love, he does remain wit' us ferever."

Chapter 16

A New Career

T HE McDONALD FARM WAS NOW a registered business and had grown so much. They were on their way to becoming a name you could count on for their quality potatoes.

It seemed that the years were passing by so quickly. The boys were around four years old.

Where had the time gone? Diana and Mary had grown very close. They were almost like twins, finishing each other's thoughts and sentences at times. The same could also be said for John and Jed. Even the kids were to be friends forever.

Diana now had time to think of herself. She had wanted to become a teacher ever since growing up in Scotland. She studied and wrote the examinations to receive her teaching certificate to teach anywhere in Ontario. She had no trouble passing. She excelled in everything. During the time her mother was sick and dying, she had to leave her own high school education to run the house. She earned an even greater education in life over the past few years than could be taught in any school. She had a lifetime of thirst for knowledge. Her sisters finished their high school studies while Diana took over in the home and cared for their mother until her death from smallpox. That seemed so long ago. Now she could have a satisfying career and be a wonderful mother too.

Her first students were Mary and Jed. She taught them both to read and write fluently. They were slowly getting away from their

Southern, Mississippi plantation slang. They were grateful for the lessons because they wanted to correspond with Laura and Andrew in Jamaica whenever they could.

Diana's first young students had been Benjamin, Jacob, and George. She taught them so much as babies and toddlers, with help from their mothers, Mary and Tina. Now she was ready to reach out and teach other young minds in her community. Diana's dream of being a teacher was like John's dream of becoming a doctor, but only one of their dreams came true. There were no regrets on either part. They were so happy in the life they chose together in Canada.

Diana was hired to teach at a new elementary school just outside of Chatham. It was a one-room school for grades one through eight, for which she was licensed. She was not licensed to teach high school. She was much happier teaching the smaller children anyway. She had a chance to give their young minds a good start in knowledge and in life. Diana read a quote by Hippocrates once: "It is through error that man tries and rises. It is through tragedy he learns. All the roads of learning begin in the darkness and go out into the light." She would always believe in this. She wanted to be this light and instill this in all her children.

There were now so many people moving into the Chatham area that they had to build several schools in the district to educate the children. They also had to form a school board. The school Diana was in charge of was situated between her home and Chatham. She knew all the children under her charge, either through their parents or by teaching them in Sunday school in their church. She loved and enjoyed teaching them all.

She had a district supervisor who circulated around the region to look in on all the schools in his territory and was in charge of funds and expenditures for the schools. He was always pleased when he could visit Chatham District Public School 101. Mr. Johns always felt that Mrs. McDonald, Diana, made an excellent teacher. The love was mutual between students and teacher. Mr. Johns was a funny, slightly rotund older man who admired Diana a great deal. He always granted her requests first in the district but kept that secret to himself as a courtesy to her. She was not demanding nor did she have expectations with her requests, but he never failed her.

She once put a request in for some new, updated McGuffey Readers, or McGuffey's as they became known. These were the readers that were commonly used all over North America. When they built the Chatham school, they could not afford to buy new texts for all the students. They could only buy a few for each school. Most children had to share, two or three students per text. They contacted other school boards in Ontario that had been around longer and were richer. When these other school boards bought new books for their own schools, they gave Chatham their old ones.

Diana's school seemed to inherit the texts that were in the worst shape. When she asked for new books, instead of excuses, as Mr. Johns would sometimes make to other schools, they arrived the next week on the train. He would, in turn, take her old books and give them to other schools in the district that could still use them.

For mathematics, or arithmetic, the school board preferred to use Thomas Dilworth's *The Schoolmaster's Assistant: Being a Compendium of Arithmetic Both Practical and Theoretic*. Diana always got a chuckle out of the long title of the book. This text covered whole numbers, four operations, weights and measures, common fractions, decimal fraction operations, roots up to fourth power, annuities, and problem solving. It covered what everyone should know as a basic need for daily life.

In their area, English wasn't the only language spoken. There were so many people that emigrated from France and spoke only French. In the Chatham and Windsor area, it was spoken just as commonly as English. The school board decided that all the children would benefit from learning to speak French. Once a week, there was a French teacher who visited all the schools in the district.

Mademoiselle Marcin would teach French at each school in this district for one hour each week. At Chatham Public School 101 she would arrive after lunch on Tuesdays and would teach French from 1:00 p.m. until 2:00 p.m. Diana stayed in the classroom and also took the lessons. She wanted to become fluent in the language too.

Diana was also expected to teach good manners, religion, and penmanship. Each school was provided with the Holy Bible for religion class. She held recitations, oral quizzes, and drills usually before the children were dismissed to go home in the afternoons. She was also required to assign projects to be completed by each student, according to their grade, twice each year.

Along with the regular studies set out by the school board, she also taught whatever she thought the students were capable of understanding about the Civil War happening in the United States. She taught them right from the first shots fired on Fort Sumter to the present day. It was expected to come to an end very soon since the Confederacy was faltering and had very little money left to support their war efforts. She would explain to the children what the Civil War was all about.

She told her students that the President of the United States, Abraham Lincoln, wanted to free all the slaves in their country. The North agreed with him, but the South disagreed. The South, who had their own president, Jefferson Davis, was so set against freeing the slaves that they started the war. The other issue Diana wanted to address was slavery. She wanted the children to know about the fact that the Negroes in Canada are allowed to have an education. In the United States it was illegal for a Negro to learn, and it was illegal for a person to teach them. They were sometimes punished by death, if either was caught. She also wanted to teach them about segregation of the peoples of the United States.

She thought they should know about slavery and the Underground Railroad, which she had personal knowledge of. She reminded Mr. Johns that Chatham was the last major stop for so many. He thought for a moment, rubbed his beard, and said, "Well, Mrs. McDonald, in this case, you do make a strong argument. But keep in mind, what one school teaches, they all should within the district."

Diana replied, "Why shouldn't the other schools teach it, sir?" He had the last say on these matters, and he said he would discuss it with the school board and get back to her soon. That was the best answer she could expect for now. But she would not be put off. She was going to take up to a half hour each day, when lessons were done and they copied their homework, to talk about the war. She did not have a lesson plan, but she felt that if she were to take the newspaper and read the stories about what was happening in the war, they could discuss it as a class. The smaller children didn't always understand but listened to the stories with interest. She felt there was no harm in approaching the issue this way until she heard back from Mr. Johns.

All the schools around the area, including Diana's, were built by the community. They also maintained the school, cleaned it, and supplied the wood for the cold winter months. The stove was started by one of the closest neighbors who was hired as the caretaker. He would start the stove by 6:00 a.m., so it would be warm for when Diana and the children arrived.

There was no bell tower atop the schools. It was felt by the board that it was an extravagance and therefore did not build them, saving money. So when it was Diana's first day in the new school, John gave his wife the most beautiful brass handbell to bring the children to class and to use at recess. To her surprise, John had her favorite Hippocrates quote engraved on the inside of this bell. She was never so touched by a gesture of love as she was the day her Johnny gave her this bell. She would cherish it all her life.

All Canadian schools were supplied with a Royal Union Flag since they were under British rule. Each school also had a portrait of their sovereign, Queen Victoria, who was now in secluded mourning after losing her husband and consort, Prince Albert, many years before.

The student desks, as well as Diana's, were made by the community carpenters. The workmanship was the finest around. There were large blackboards. They were still made the same way as they were when they were invented sixty years earlier.

Each teacher was expected to discipline the children who got out of line or talked back to Her . . . or for any disobedience in general. Each school after 1850 would be supplied with a leather strap. Diana remembered the *tawse* in Scotland schools, although she never received punishment from it. The other methods that had been used in North American schools were hickory switches, which the students cut for the teacher to use on them, and the ruler to the hand. Disciplining girls was not common at all. It was primarily the boys that tested their teacher's patience. Diana had a few boys who tried to see how far they could go with her. She had a lot of patience and never used the strap in all her years of teaching. She used the "standing in the corner" method for the most part and would always assign extra homework and an essay on why the child was being punished. The length of the essay would reflect the child's age and grade level.

Around the time Diana was teaching, goose quills and ink were used by the older students to write with, which Diana was expected to whittle herself. Actually, she let Jed make them. He loved doing it for her. It was also the teacher's duty to make the ink. The recipe for the ink was not easy to make. You needed tannic from an oak tree mixed with light oil from swamp maple bark and copperas. The farmers around always make sure Diana had a sufficient supply of these ingredients at all times. Mary took care of mixing the ink for her. The newer apparatus of the day was a slate and a pencil for the other younger, inexperienced students. The writing slate was made with a wood frame around it, and the pencil was made of slate too.

Most children stayed at school for lunch. Lunch started promptly at noon. The children took this time to talk since there was no talking allowed during class time. Diana would eat in the classroom at the same time the children did. After the children ate, they went outside for a forty-minute recess and played. Diana would use this time to correct papers or write the afternoon lessons and homework on the board. This was very time-consuming, and she sometimes needed the whole lunch hour to prepare these lessons for each grade level. She was always finished just in time to call the students in from recess.

While Diana was out teaching every day, Mary was at the farm to look after their boys. John was very supportive of Diana's dream to be a teacher. Mary was very happy doing the housework, cooking, and baking for both families while looking after both kids. As she watched the children, it took her back to her own childhood. She had siblings whom she thought of once in a while.

She would wonder the rest of her life about them and what their lives were like. Right now, however, she was becoming very concerned about her husband.

Jed's symptoms became more of a concern in the last few months. Even though he had been having symptoms all through the years, he was not telling anyone about them. His chest had become more painful, and the time in between flare-ups was getting shorter. It was not just the lungs that was causing pain; his abdominal region was hard, sore, and swelled at times.

Dr. Marsh surmised it was swelling in the liver, spleen, or both. If they were to remove the spleen, maybe the pain might be more tolerable or gone. But often with a splenectomy, there was also a very high risk of Jed picking up any or every infection going around, and that could easily kill him too. They had to weigh the pros and cons to this action.

He was also still experiencing the problems with erections lasting a long time. He didn't have to be aroused, but when they would occur, they lasted a couple of hours, and the pain was increasing with these episodes too. Dr. Marsh told Jed these episodes were called priapism of the penis. He was now seeing Jed about every two weeks. Ian and Jed had decided against the surgery for now.

Sometimes Jed would drive into town to see the doctor. He would hook up his Clyde some days and go to town to see Dr. Marsh, but if Dr. Marsh was out in their direction, he would stop by to see how he was doing.

John and Diana were quite concerned for Jed's health too. He hadn't looked good for a while. But in Jed's own way, he persevered and never let on the extent of his pain. He was taking small doses of morphine, but only when the pain became unbearable. His strength started failing, and John was trying not to give him heavy jobs to do. John knew something was very wrong with Jed. At first he didn't want Mary or Diana to know how bad Jed actually was feeling. John hoped it would pass.

By now, Jed and Mary owned their own Clydesdale, a Shetland pony, and a female calf that was born to John and Diana's Holstein, which they acquired from Adam a few years earlier when they moved to Chatham. John let the Allens buy the first offspring of each of their stock.

John never charged Jed too much for the animals, but anyone else would have to pay a full but fair price. Jed and Mary were so proud to now own their own livestock. They were kept in the McDonald barn since it was so large. Jed saved their money and was even able to buy his very own wagon.

John and Jed talked a lot while working in the barn and fields, which by now, between developing the east and west fields, had grown over 275 acres of the best Ontario potatoes in the southern region of the province. Their farm had grown so quickly after that first harvest. They also expanded their hay and straw crops and included wheat and oats.

Diana's and Jed's vegetable gardens were enlarged and were thriving too. They were selling their fruits and vegetables in smaller quantities, but their main crop was their high-quality potatoes. They had indeed become a very successful, self-sustaining farm business.

There were another 160 acres for sale right beside their farm. It was fully cleared and usable right away. John decided he would buy it up and use it for fruit crops. There was a house and barn on the land, which they kept. They decided, since the farm was growing so big, that they might have to hire more people to work there who could live in the extra house they now had. They knew they could make a go of it, growing fruits and other vegetables. They would also plant hay and straw on that property to keep their growing number of animals looked after. Chatham was a great area for Chatham was a great area for growing apples, pears, cherries, plums, grapes, and a variety of melons because of its rich soil. Jeffrey was still into the real estate business and sold the land to John for a really good price.

Now when planting and harvesting, John hired many people to work on the farm. They were not needed all year-round, just at these busier times. The hired help were Africans, Italians, French—all nationalities that had moved into the area. The farmland was quickly getting bought up and developed. There were farms cropping up everywhere in Southern Ontario. There was wheat, potatoes, tobacco, hay, and straw, along with the finest vegetables and fruits around. This was a money-making land. Ontario and the rest of Canada had certainly been the place to emigrate to.

Most of the land was perfect for planting, and with Europeans moving here, they were bringing foods they grew and ate in their home countries and introducing them to Canada. They brought their foods, their livestock (which included breeds of animals new to Canada), and their craft and expertise of a vast number of professions. There was enough space in Ontario to sustain the many people who were now flocking to Canada's shores.

There were new doctors coming and setting up practices everywhere. Hospitals were built in towns and cities. The McDonalds and Allens were going to have firsthand knowledge of the hospital in Chatham. It was small but adequate. Most patients with serious cases, who could not be looked at in Chatham, were sent to the Windsor hospital. The good thing about the Chatham hospital was that Dr. Marsh worked there. He was the most familiar with Jed's case. He had been looking after Jed ever since he and Mary arrived in Chatham by way of the Underground Railroad.

One morning, Jed couldn't get out of bed. Mary ran across the yard to get John. He ran to see Jed trying desperately to get up. Mary was alarmed. He had a different look to him. His face was contorted with pain, and he could barely breathe. Dr. Marsh had never been able to diagnose Jed's problem, but he was convinced that Jed had been born with it. But what was it? A few years earlier, he heard back from doctors in Toronto that they had only seen or heard of these symptoms in young people of African descent. All the patients who had it had died with varying degrees of their symptoms, and not one of them made it past the age of twenty-five years so far. None of the doctors had ever come across any white patients with it.

This morning, John quickly left the farm with Jed, Mary, and the two boys. John dropped the kids off at Tina's place so he could take Mary and Jed to the hospital. Diana had already gone to the schoolhouse.

The grade eight pupils were doing written and oral exams this afternoon, and she wanted them to be prepared. They agreed to arrive before class began so they could get ready for them. These exams were not held in the classroom; they were held in a separate building in town. The school board members and Mr. Johns conducted these exams. All the district schools sent their grade eight students for these exams.

Not only did the students get advanced to high school, but there were also awards for excellence and a friendly competition among all the district schools to see which school got the highest combined scores.

Each school had at least three grade eight students who were being tested this year, and the award would be calculated by the board. They would take the three highest scores for each school, to make it more fair with the schools that had more than three students participating in the examinations. Diana's school had won the district prize for the last couple of years. She was so proud of her students. The winner of this competition would win a prize for their school. This year the school board decided that the winning school would receive an updated new dictionary and a new world map.

When John stopped to drop the kids off at Jeff and Tina's, they saw how bad Jed looked.

Dr. Marsh met John, Jed, and Mary at the hospital. There was a bed for him in the critical infirmary.

Jed was now in severe pain and nearly unconscious; he could barely breathe. His chest hurt him so much that he felt like he was being crushed.

After the nurse got Jed onto the bed and Dr. Marsh saw his face, he asked the nurse to get John and Mary to wait in the visitor's room down the hall. They placed a screen around Jed's bed for privacy. He was not looking normal due to lack of oxygen. The doctor was worried that he was going to lose Jed. All of a sudden, Jed stopped breathing and his heart stopped. He was clinically dead. Ian started to give Jed what was called mouth-to-mouth resuscitation, combined with chest compressions, to get the lungs breathing on its own and the heart pumping again. Dr. Marsh did the mouth-to-mouth, and he had a nurse perform the chest compressions. He told her to set a pace of twenty compressions per minute.

It took about five and a half minutes before the nurse saw Jed's chest rise and fall on its own. She told the doctor, and he stopped the procedure to see for himself. Somehow, it worked. Jed's normal color was returning to his face. The nurse assisting the doctor was so good with her chest compressions she actually broke two of Jed's ribs. This was commonplace during these situations. Jed was alive; that was all that mattered.

After Jed was breathing on his own, he was allowed to see Mary and John. Mary had a tear in her eye due to worry, and the doctor did not tell her right away about almost losing him or that he was clinically dead for over five minutes. He wanted Mary to see that he was okay first. Mary was still an emotional young lady, with everything she had been through in her life. Dr. Marsh tried not to upset her whenever he could spare her, but she needed to know what was happening.

Jed's symptoms were getting so much worse, and there was no way of knowing what this disease was that was making Jed's body slowly fail. He was now on regular doses of morphine for the pain to keep him comfortable. He was kept in the hospital for a week. During that week, Jed was getting stronger very slowly, but the doctor told John that Jed could no longer work around the farm. He had to stop doing strenuous jobs. He was not even to do the gardening in their own garden patch.

It would possibly kill him to do this work, and Mary wanted to make sure he would stay around a long time.

So after he returned home in the afternoons, while the boys took a nap, Jed stayed at the house to watch them while Mary weeded and watered their garden. She would help in Diana's garden too as much as she could. John also helped keep it up. Diana missed not spending much time in her garden in the springtime, but on weekends she took total charge. Fortunately, schools were closed in the summer, so she could devote more of her time to her vegetables and flowers.

John stopped collecting rent from Jed and Mary after about two years and gave them the land (two acres) and house legally. Jed built his own chicken coop; John gave them a few chickens of their own to raise. He built a play area for Jacob and a swing, which he attached to a large branch on one of the big trees in front of their house and then put one up for George too so he wouldn't feel left out.

John and Diana really had little time to golf, so they decided to make a driving range. They used about 350 yards in the west field. They built a couple of small hills to make it a little challenging. Diana and John taught Mary and Jed to drive and putt a few years earlier; they hoped they could all go out to the local course and play sometime. They enjoyed it, but Jed's chest became too sore for him to participate. He enjoyed watching Mary learn and practice. Jeff came over a few times to practice his drive too. The next year, they added a putting green.

John had the disappointing task of replacing Jed with someone to work for them full-time.

He was saddened that he had to do it because he felt Jed was indispensable, as well as his best friend. He hired the best man he felt he could to take over. He hired Rolly Waters, Jed's childhood friend, to come and live with them at the farm. John said he could live in their house, but Jed and Mary wanted him to stay with them. Rolly chose to stay with Jed and Mary. He would sleep in Jacob's room. Diana and John were not offended; they understood. The boyhood friends wanted to be together again.

Rolly moved in and helped John with the entire farmwork and also tried to help Mary to nurse Jed back to some reasonable sense of health. But they had no way of knowing that Jed would never be in good health again. Dr. Marsh had explained what he had done to save Jed in the hospital, and he taught the others on the farm how to do it in an emergency, when he couldn't breathe.

Mary worried about Rolly needing companionship. He told her that it wasn't a problem; he had a girl in Chatham. Her name was Sally. Her father didn't like him, so they didn't see each other often, but they were still satisfied occasionally.

Jed spent his days mostly sitting outside, watching. Watching the world, wondering what will be and what has been, worrying about his Mary. He worried about leaving her behind. Would she be able to stand the pain of his dying and leaving her a widow with a toddler who might also die of this same ailment someday? He wondered what God wanted from him. Did he mean to put this all on Jed's shoulders for a reason? What was the purpose? Was he just testing Jed's love for him? He wondered.

Jed had no doubt he would eventually go to heaven. The Allens and the McDonalds went to church every Sunday that they could. They each prayed so hard for Jed's life. They all prayed to the Lord to spare Jed. He was needed here by his son and his wife. Jed, the little African boy once called Berko, was needed by his family and friends.

There was very little sadness in him. If he had never been kidnaped and brought across the ocean he never would have met and fallen in love with his Mary. Afua was the love of his life. He felt his life slipping away. Although he was only in his early twenties, he knew his life was coming to an end, and no one knew why or how to help him.

He would spend his days with his precious son, Jacob Marcus. He also would play with George. Mary liked having Jed around the house so she could keep her eye on him. She watched with happiness at seeing father and son together. It warmed her heart. She was so in love with him, but she also knew he was dying. Dr. Marsh told them at the hospital that whatever was ailing Jed was congenital; therefore, Jacob may also inherit it and may display symptoms at some time in his life.

At this prospect, they feared for their child. They knew Jacob was going to be their only child, but Mary couldn't stand the thought of losing her son the same way as his father. That, she surely would never survive, she thought.

John liked having Rolly around. He was a strong and excellent employee. Jed was slightly jealous that he couldn't do the work in the fields. He missed his beloved potatoes for some reason.

He could only watch John and Rolly go to the fields and come back. One day Jed asked John, "John, do you tink I'se can go out wit' cha to da fiel'? I'll just sit on da wagon or walk around. I'se promise I won't work or nuttin'. I won't git in yer way, I'se promise." John thought about it and asked what Rolly thought and what Mary thought too. Mary was a little apprehensive, but Rolly thought it was a good idea. John and Rolly told her they would watch him carefully and made sure he did nothing!

Mary said, "You can go, but *no* work!" Jed was like a little kid again, all excited about going to the potato field. He climbed up on the wagon, and John gave him the reins. He told Jed to drive them out to the field. John sat right beside him in case he needed him. You couldn't have seen a happier man.

When Mary awoke the next morning, she didn't want to disturb him, so she quietly got up and dressed. As she was leaving the bedroom, she looked lovingly at her husband. His face was so different today. He had a big beautiful smile on his face like she'd never seen before. It made her glad to see her husband so happy. After a few seconds, her smile vanished . . . Berko Yaba was dead!

Chapter 17

Celebration of a Life

MARY WAS DEVASTATED. ALTHOUGH SHE had known that her true love was dying for some time, she never expected it would be this soon. She prayed, and she hoped that Jed would last longer than he did, but God was not to answer her prayers. Mary asked John and Diana, "Why would God take such a lovin' man like my Jed? I don't believes he be thinkin' right when he took him. Why? Jed loved everyone . . . Why?" She kept asking them over and over again. They could not answer. They could only hold her while she wept and help her with Jacob.

His innocence tugged at their heartstrings when he kept asking, "Where my papa? Where my papa go?" All John or Diana and Mary could tell little Jacob Marcus was that Papa has gone to be with God. He wanted him in heaven, but he will be in his heart forever. And then John remembered something Jed told them after Jacob was born. Jed and Mary wanted him to know about the other Jacob Marcus, whom he was named after.

John set little Jacob on his knee and asked, "Did your papa ever tell you about another Jacob Marcus?" Jacob nodded his head innocently. John continued, "Mama and Papa gave you that name because they wanted to always remember him. He was a very kind man to your mama and papa. He looked after them as best he could for as long as he could. Your parents loved him very much. And Jacob loved them very much too. That's why they gave you his name. Well, your papa is now in heaven with God, but you know what?" Jacob shook his head no. "Your papa is not only with God, he is also with the other Jacob Marcus, and I know that your papa is being looked after again by him.

"So you see, Jacob and your papa are going to be together forever. You never have to worry about your papa again. Jacob Marcus and God will look after him. Do you know what else?" Jacob was carefully paying attention to all that John was telling him . . . he gazed for John to continue. He did. "Well, you know that Papa had a hard time breathing and had pain all the time?" Jacob nodded again. John went on, "I think that heaven is the best place for your papa now because there is no pain in heaven. He is in heaven with Jacob, and God is looking after both of them. You will always love your papa, and he will always be watching over you, whatever you do or wherever you go. He's always going to watch over your mama too. You know, I think your papa will always be watching over the whole farm and all of our families now and all the families to come after us. He will always be in your heart, in Mama's heart, and in our hearts too. Even in the hearts of all the friends he made and the workers we've had here . . . you know, Jacob, I don't know anybody that won't miss your papa. He was a special man to so many people." Jacob smiled a warm, happy smile as John hugged him tight and kissed his forehead.

Mary overheard John talking to Jacob. She listened to John tell her son about Jacob, and it made her smile. She was so warmed by the story John told him that she stopped crying. She took her son to her bosom and held him tightly. She bent over and gave John a kiss on the cheek and took Jacob outside and put him on his swing and played with him for a while, thus forgetting her troubles.

John and Diana were equally shocked that Jed died so early in his life. Dr. Marsh had been to the house to declare that Jedediah had died in his sleep of respiratory failure.

The doctor told them all that he knew about Jed's illness, but it really wasn't much. There was no medical explanation for it. Maybe someday there would be, he hoped, so that he could be sure that little Jacob wouldn't suffer with it too. Jed just stopped breathing in his sleep, beside Mary in bed. She was asleep when he slipped away, and she was to blame herself for the rest of her days that she never woke up in time to revive him. Although she seemed okay after John's talk to little Jacob, she would never be the same in her mind. A big part of her died too, but she knew she had to go on, for Jacob's sake, but she would never be the same woman without Jed by her side.

John and Diana had talked about Jed dying in previous days. They knew it was inevitable but would never bring up the subject of a burial for him to Mary. Remembering the past history of buried bodies in the kirkyards in Scotland being stolen for science, John wanted to make sure both families were going to be forever safe on the farm. They decided that they would designate a portion of their 640 acres for a personal family cemetery. It would be for all the McDonalds and all the Allens, now and their future generations. When they approached her about it later in the day, she was overwhelmed with such love and respect for her friends' generosity. Jed was to be the first of both families to be buried there. This way, Jed would always be close to her. She was happy that he was going to be near her and Jacob, watching over them.

John washed Jed's body and cleaned and changed him into the outfit that Mary had chosen for him. She chose his first suit, which they bought at Lavelle's with Tina, on their way to meeting John and Diana the first time. Diana gave him a manicure and shaved him so he looked nice. Mary was touched that they would take such care to do all this for him.

John said, "I can't send my best friend off to heaven in a shabby condition now, can I?" She smiled. They laid Jed out in the parlor at John and Diana's house since there was more room there, and that way, Mary wouldn't feel that she needed to attend to everyone's needs or fuss over them.

She could just sit at John and Diana's house and talk with everyone who came to pay their respects to her and Jed. Diana, Christina, and Eileen would see to the food and drink for everyone.

The last time Jed went to town on his own, about a month or more before he died, he stopped by the livery to see Adam to ask a favor. Jed poured himself a cup of coffee Adam had heating on the stove. There was always a pot of coffee on Adam's stove. All the people around Chatham knew they were always invited to have a sit-down and a coffee there. Adam was very popular, and he went through a few pots each day, not to mention the county gossip he heard.

Adam was always discreet and never contributed to the chatter. He just took it in stride.

Jed had sat down on a beautiful handmade saddle that was straddling a rail in the shop. It was the latest acquisition Adam made. A widow was parting with her late husband's belongings, so Adam bought his horses and saddles to sell off. Jed took a deep breath and said, "Adam, I wants ya ta measure me up." Adam stopped working for a moment and looked up at Jed.

Adam said, "You want me to what?"

"Measure me up," Jed replied. "I needs ya ta measure me up 'cause you be doin' nice woodwork as of late, an' I knows I can truss ya ta keep it to yerse'f. I wants ya ta makes me a coffin fer . . . well . . . ya know."

Adam was shocked by the request and said, "If that's what you really want, Jed, I'll do it, of course. But you're not going anywhere for a while, dear friend!" Jed just looked into Adam's eyes as he began to breathe a little harder than normal. There was nothing more to say. Adam took a measuring stick he had in the shop and started to measure Jed's height, width, and depth and wrote the figures down.

Jed's breathing went back to normal quickly. Both were relieved. He told Adam, "Ya sees, in Ghana, where I'se from, dere be a b'lief dat when a man dies, he goes on to 'nudder life. I don't knows where dat be, but I pray it be where I'se s'rounded by what I loves. We's also believes dat a man's coffin should reflect da man. What he stood for an' what was important and dat, which all folks would know, made him da man he be." By this time, Jed had a suspicious, devilish smile on his face. Adam watched him, and he started to smile too.

He said to Jed, "Well, Jed, of course I'll do what you ask, but I'm sure I'm about to carve the very first potato-shaped coffin in the world, aren't I?" They smiled, which turned into laughter, and they shook hands. Jed wanted to pay for it, but Adam wouldn't hear of it. Jed had already sought out and found the tree that Adam was to make it from. It had plenty of knots in it. Knots can be troublesome when doing fine carpentry, but Jed wanted them left alone. He decided that the knots in the wood would act as the eyes of the potato. As he showed the wood he chose to Adam and explained, they both laughed and it became a humorous project, for that's what Jed wanted it to be.

He and Adam were to laugh about it several times when they were to see each other. The coffin was kept a secret from everyone, even Mary.

Adam could only describe the work he'd been doing on it since Jed could not see it often.

When someone took him into town, he would make an excuse to see Adam and tried to go alone so he could see the work Adam had been doing for him. Adam had expanded the livery by this time, and he had a large extra storage room in the back, which no one went into. He carved in there at night and whenever he could find the time. Jed was so happy with his work. It was going just the way he wanted it to. The two of them laughed about it a few times, but Jed wanted it, and everyone who knew him would understand.

When Dr. Marsh returned to town the morning of Jed's death, he stopped by the livery. He got down from his carriage and went in to see Adam. Jeff was with him, having a coffee. He told them that Jed had just passed away that morning and, if they could, to please pass the word along to friends and the townsfolk who knew him. Adam would make sure that all the black workers that knew Jed would hear the news from him. Adam had cared so much for them; he counted them among his best friends. He helped most, if not all of them, with their escapes on the Underground Railroad. They found salvation from slavery, into Adam's care.

They were not surprised but were saddened by the news, especially Rolly. He had come to town the night before to stay and have a good time with some friends, spend the night with Sally, and to give Mary and Jed some privacy.

He started walking to the McDonald farm right away, stopping at the Maguires' to tell Michael and Eileen. They both hopped in their wagon and invited Rolly to join them in going to the McDonalds'. He gratefully accepted the lift. None of them spoke on the way. There was nothing to say.

Jeff walked over to his own house to tell Tina the news. He opened the front door and said, "Tina . . . honey?" Ben ran to meet him at the door. He jumped into his daddy's arms. "What are you doing here, Daddy? You went to work?" Jeffrey tenderly hugged his son.

He said, "Where is your mommy hiding? I bet doing laundry, huh?" He put Ben down as he nodded his head to let Jeff know he was right. He found her out back, hanging the sheets on the line. She was surprised to see him. He looked at her and smiled. They were told by Dr. Marsh that their new baby could arrive any time now, and Tina was ready . . . she was two weeks overdue, and large! Jeff said, "Honey, Jed's gone." She hung her head. She knew it would be soon, but the tears still came. Jeff held her, and Benjamin jumped up to be held again. Jeff took him in his arms and, holding Tina too, they had a silent family hug.

Tina wiped her nose and tears and asked, "Darlin', can you run me out there? I'd like to help out and see Mary." Jeffrey nodded and allowed them to get ready. She took up the baking she had done in the last day, packed it, and took it with her. She knew food would not be on their minds, but she would help in any way she could, even if it was just making sure everyone kept up their strength by eating. She would help see to it.

When Rolly and the Maguires arrived, John and Diana greeted them. John took Rolly aside. He took him over to Mary's house. He wanted to talk to them both about a wake and burial.

Rolly held out his arms to Mary as he walked through the door. She came to him and he hugged her.

No words were passed between them; they just knew he was better now, and there was no more pain. John asked, "Mary, Rolly, I wondered, would Jed like some type of African ceremony or just a standard burial? I'm not sure. What should we plan?"

Rolly looked to Mary first and then to John and said, "Adam ask me to tell you dat he be bringin' da coffin. He say he 'xplain when he gits here. If Mary say it be okay, I tinks Jed would like a African wake. It be juss like what dey has here, da body lay out so dat people can 'spects him, but dere be lots o' music 'n' singin'. Dey celebrates his life, not be sads 'cause he dead. Den da next day, he be buried where his missus wants him ta be. What chew tinks, Mary?" She nodded in agreement and it was decided. When Adam brings the coffin, Jed would be placed in it, and he would stay in John and Diana's parlor so people could pay their respects, followed by wine, music, and song.

After Jeff had dropped off Tina and Ben and paid his respects to Mary and Jed, he went off to town to tell everyone that the wake was going to be held at the McDonalds' that night and burial would be the next day. On the road Adam came along Jeff, while driving toward the farm. Jeff asked what Adam had in his wagon that was covered over. Adam said, "Well, dear brother, Jed commissioned me to do a work of art for him before he died." Jeff had a quizzical look on his face. Adam had a strange smile on his face, and even though he was saddened by Jed's death, he still smiled. He thought he'd give his brother a sneak peek.

They both got down from their wagons and walked to the back of Adam's. Adam pulled back the tarpaulin. There, on his wagon, was a very, very large wooden potato, equipped with it's eyes and a lid. Adam was grinning, and Jeffrey burst out laughing. Adam started too; they couldn't help it. It was a sight to behold!

Jeffrey blurted out, "Adam, what in blazes is that monstrosity?"

Adam grinned. "It's Jed's coffin, of course!" Jeff stopped smiling . . . Adam was serious. Adam slapped his brother on the back a couple of times and told his brother the story of when some Africans die, it is customary to shape their coffin to exemplify what the essence of that man was. Everyone knew that Jed's favorite thing on Earth, besides his family, was potatoes. As Jeff learned about the coffin, he laughed, and so did Adam. They did, knowing that Jed would not have been offended by their laughter; he would have joined them.

When Jeff got back to town, word was spread about the plans that everyone was welcome to come to the McDonalds' farm after the supper hour, where they could join the family in celebrating the life of their African friend, Berko Yaba . . . their Canadian friend, Jedediah Allen, a loving husband to Mary and father of Jacob.

Adam pulled the wagon up close to the house when he arrived. Jeff had already told him to take the coffin to John's place, where Jed was resting. He stopped the wagon. John, Mary, Rolly, the Maguires, and Tina came out to the wagon. The kids were playing together in the yard without a care in the world. Adam got down from his wagon. He turned to Mary and said, "Mary, some time ago, Jed came to me to ask if I'd carve his coffin. He explained to me about the Ghana-African custom of a man being laid to rest in a coffin of his own design. This portrayed what his life meant to him. I want you to know this is exactly what he wanted. He saw it last week after I was finished working on it, when he and John came into town. He chose it, and he knew after the initial shock of seeing it you'd understand." Mary was confused but wanted to see the coffin. Adam got John to help him pull the tarp back to reveal the coffin. Mary's eyes grew wide. She could not believe what she was looking at.

Everyone was silent, except for gasps. Mary walked around the side of the wagon to get a different view. Then she hopped up on the wagon with Adam's help to get an even better look. She put both hands over her mouth, sat on the side of the wagon, and roared with laughter. Everyone sighed and joined in the laughter! Mary jumped down from the wagon and said to John, "Y'all better measure it up to make sure ya dig a big 'nough hole for it, John." The kids ran to the wagon and looked.

Jacob said, "Mama, what dat big 'tato doin' here?" She smiled, and she told him it was the box that his daddy would go to heaven in. Jacob shrugged his shoulders and turned to go play again. They all laughed. There was no tension or sadness in the air anymore. John and Rolly got to work measuring the soon-to-be famous potato-shaped coffin. Rolly suggested to everyone that if someone could go to town, they could maybe round up the other blacks to come and help dig so they'd get it done faster. Eileen told them she'd go get them and some more shovels.

Adam told her to get new shovels from his store. He had kept the name, Lavalle's General Store, in memory of their friends Rene and Emilie. Adam had married in the last few months, and his wife, Jennifer, was now running the store. He told Eileen, "You just tell Jenny I said to supply the shovels needed for the job." Eileen was off on her errand while Michael, Rolly, and John finished measuring the coffin.

When they were done, they took the coffin into the parlor to place Jed in it. Although she needn't have worried about it, Mary came along to make sure her Jed was put in with care. She hated not to be near him, even in death. Jed seemed to be comforting her, like he always tried to in life.

Eileen was back from town within about thirty minutes. There were many volunteers to help dig. The African boys, as they came to be known, rather than the "blacks," came out from town and helped dig the grave for Jed. John decided that the grave should be eight feet long, six feet wide, and they should dig down at least seven feet down so when the spring thaw comes the coffin wouldn't surface.

Rolly had a few tears through the day when he thought no one was looking. Diana noticed.

She went to him and said, "Rolly, let's go for a walk." He said that he'd like that. Diana and Rolly left the house, and she started walking toward Jed's beloved potato field. They walked in silence for a while. Diana grabbed hold of Rolly's hand and squeezed it while they were still walking. She stopped, turned to Rolly, and said, "What is it, Rolly? I know there's something. Please tell me. Maybe I can help." Tears were rolling down his cheeks by this time. Right in the middle of the potato field, he dropped to his knees and wept. Diana was still holding his hand.

Through the tears, he said, "Diana, if I'se only stayed here lass night, he be alive. It be my fault, Diana. He died 'cause I went and stayed in town wit' Sally . . . I knows it. If I stayed home lass night, he be here t'day. Why did I have to leave him lass night?"

Diana pulled this large muscular man to his feet and scolded, "Rolly, how dare you think that! You have a life to live, and you have a right to live it however you want. Yes, Jed died through the night. You would have been sleeping, just like Mary was, and she was right beside him. You wouldn't have known he died until this morning! There is nothing that you or Mary could have done. Don't you dare blame yourself! We all know how much you and Jed loved each other. You've been friends since you were little boys in Africa. He loved you dearly and was so happy you lived with them in their house. He was so happy the day he saw you come to the farm to work in that first potato field. Oh, he loved you so much."

Rolly wiped his nose and stared at the ground, shyly kicking the dirt. He said, "Yess'm, I s'pose you'se right, but I still wished I be here juss da same." He wept some more. Diana put her arms around him and held him. She let him cry for a while, when all of a sudden . . . he started laughing. He wiped his nose again and said, "Ain't dat da biggess, funniess 'tato you ever dun see'd in yo' life?" Diana started laughing, nodding her head. She and Rolly sat down in the potato field and just kept laughing till they were ready to go back to the house.

Diana, Eileen, and Tina prepared lots of food for supper. Adam supplied the spirits and wine from his and Jenny's store while the African boys brought their moonshine. Mary did not eat much. George, Jacob, and Benjamin ate and were tired from all their playing. Their moms bathed them and laid them down for the night in George's bedroom at John and Diana's house. They were all asleep within minutes. The ladies fed everyone who had shown up through the day and had remained for the evening's festivities. Diana wanted supper and the dishes done before anyone else arrived.

As dusk was approaching, people started to arrive. There were wagons full of people; many had covered wagons so they could sleep in them overnight. There were people on foot, walking. You could look down the road toward town, as well as in other directions, and all you could see were some flickering lights from lanterns to light their way. There was the sound of music and singing coming along the road. It was truly an awesome sight with such sounds in the air. It was joy, such a procession. There were so many visitors to see Jed and to talk to Mary. Many of the African workers brought their musical instruments, and the music would go on all night while everyone regaled stories about Jed. There would be lots of laughter and smiles, remembering him. No one could ever say a bad thing about Jed Allen. He was funny and sincere, the best friend anyone could ever hope to meet in their lifetime.

Mary had no idea that Jed even knew that many people or touched that many lives. She was amazed. There were lots of room for everyone to park their wagons and carriages in. John, Michael, and Rolly made sure everyone's horses and ponies were looked after, as all, or most, would be staying far into the night. John had lots of hay, oats, straw, and water ready for the animals whenever it was needed.

Everyone came through Diana and John's house to the parlor. Mary was in there and they all greeted her. No matter how difficult it got, she tried to smile for everyone. They all saw the coffin. Some of the white townsfolk were slightly confused and felt that the potato was strange, not to mention shocking! But John, Rolly, Michael, Adam, and Jeff circulated the story of the potato coffin. After they had heard the story they understood that it was what Jed truly wanted. Everyone knew about his love for potatoes.

People laughed and had fun with it. They commented on Adam's good carpentry work.

Some of their African friends, Ned, Frank, Gerald, and others, had also brought their musical instruments and played. They played

African songs, songs from the Deep South, hymns, and whatever tunes everyone wanted to hear and participate in. Everyone sang along while they ate and drank. They all listened to stories of Africa from when they were young boys.

Rolly talked about playing, hunting, and learning lessons in Africa. He told them about Berko's family. Most of the people there never knew that his name really wasn't Jed. Rolly talked about Berko's brothers and sisters, his parents, and all the extended family he could remember in the village. Rolly had tears a couple of times, and he would get a little choked up. Mary was grateful Rolly was there to tell people about his young life. He also included the day that they were playing the hiding game in the brush outside the village, when Berko disapeared. They searched for so long, but they couldn't find him. His family and the rest of the village searched for three days for him. His mother was torn. She knew her boy would never be found, that he was gone on a long trip, never to return. People were amazed that this man they respected was once a boy, so happy, but was torn away from his family and taken to Jamaica to be a slave.

When Mary could talk between little sniffles and the occasional tear, she filled people in on the life that she knew about. She told them everything he told her about his trip on the *Destino*; she told them about Jacob Marcus buying him and looking after him. She talked about Jacob treating Jed like a son. "After a year or so," she told them, "I was snatched from my village and brung to the same place an' went on the same ship, right to Jamaica. When Jed seen me on the boat, he liked me right off . . . he said so. He liked me so much, Jacob-Sir bought me. He say he bought me for Jed, and he called me Mary. Jed wanted to jump the broom with me, and he let us. We had our own marriage cabin and everything."

People hung on every word Mary told them. There was shock and disbelief at some of the treatment they received. Most white people in Canada had no idea how bad it really was for the slaves. They sometimes cried; a couple of ladies had to move away from the crowd and get air.

Darkness made way to light, and before they knew it, people who did go home through the night came back. It was time to bury Jed.

The minister from their church came early. He wanted to see what Mary wanted for a ceremony. She asked Diana and John and Rolly what they thought. They did not want to talk her into anything, so they let her decide. She said to the minister, "I know Jed liked yo' sermons about lovin' neighbors, and he liked hearin' about heaven. Can you talk some 'bout that and pray for his soul?"

Reverend Knight said he would love to talk about what she knew Jed would want to hear. He went into the parlor and gasped! There was a loud noise. John ran into the parlor to see what it was. Reverend Knight had passed out from shock. It was plain to see that he had never come across a Potato-shaped coffin before. John and Diana helped revived him. They explained about it and couldn't say he completely approved, but he understood.

A few of their African friends and other appointed friends went to go into the parlor. It was time to take Jed to the grave. They were met at the door by John and Diana. They told the men that Mary was not ready to let him go yet. They would have to wait a bit. She needed to say good-bye.

Diana went out to the crowd and said that they will start as soon as Mary was ready, and it wouldn't be long.

Mary had changed into the Kente cloth robe she had made. She wanted to honor her Berko in the African way. She, as the wife, was dressed in her finest and was to be the one to lead the coffin to the burial ground. She took his hand. It was cold, but at the same time, it was warm to her. She smiled. John knocked on the parlor door. Jacob was looking for her, and she let him come in. She picked him up to see his father one more time. "Mama, is Papa going to heaven now?" Jacob asked her.

She kissed him on the forehead and held him cheek to cheek, letting a tear roll down hers to meet with his. It seemed like a lifetime, but it was only seconds. She said, "Yes, Jacob, Papa has to go now. God, he be ready for him now." She set Jacob on the floor and he held her leg. She bent over and kissed her husband on the lips one last time. John told her to come and get him when it was time to close the coffin, and he'd do it for her. He took Jacob out so Mary could have a last private moment.

There was one more thing she wanted to do. She took a sharp knife, which she had sneaked into the parlor when no one was looking. She did not want anyone to see it. She slowly took the knife and aimed it at her abdomen. She held the knife and looked at her stomach. She wondered where the best position would be.

She fumbled with her Kente robe a little, and she said in a whisper, "There . . . that is the best spot for sure." With knife firmly in hand, Mary started to cut. She let out a slight whimper as though in pain, and a tear rolled down each cheek. She cut a small piece of her Kente robe and laid it in Jed's hand. He adored her robe, and now he was taking a piece with him.

She placed the knife back in the hiding place for now and would put it back in the kitchen later. No one would know she cut her precious robe; she was able to find an excess piece around the waistline that would not be missed as she wore it. She would mend it later.

She now took a long slow painful breath, and she closed the coffin herself. She opened the parlor door and asked John to come in to nail it shut. He did. Mary wanted the coffin to be rolled out to the cemetery on their own wagon, using their own Clydesdale. Jed would be so proud.

Mary led the procession. She walked hand in hand with their son into the beautiful morning Sunlight, down a path to where John had designated the area where the family cemetery now was. The wagon was next. Reverend Knight walked behind it. She asked John, Jeff, Adam, Rolly, Michael, Frank, Ned, and Gerald to carry the coffin from the wagon to the grave. She asked eight to carry him since the potato coffin was quite heavy. Diana, Jeff, Adam, Tina, George, and Ben were next, and everyone else followed behind.

As the minister spoke, he told the group of mourners to be happy. They should be happy that their friend was going to be with the Lord Almighty. He said, "Although I'm not sure the Lord is quite ready for the vehicle Jed chose, but you can't have too many potatoes in heaven, can you?" Mary cracked up laughing. She couldn't stop. John started next, and then Diana, Rolly, Adam, and shortly the whole crowd was giggling. Mary stopped laughing after a minute or two. They all knew the minister wanted to continue.

Reverend Knight started, "I asked our dear sister, Mary, here, what she thought Jed would like me to talk about. Well, she told me two of Jed's favorite subjects . . . after potatoes, of course." There were a few more giggles. He went on, "Jed loved his neighbor and loved to hear about heaven. Now the Gospel according to St. Mark 12:30–34 teaches us, 'Love the Lord thy God with all thy heart, all thy soul, and with all thy mind and with all thy strength, then the Lord said, "And the second is, namely this. Thou shalt love thy neighbor as thyself, there is none other commandment greater than these." And a scribe said unto him, "Well, Master, thou hast said the truth; for there is one God and none other than he. And to love him with all thy heart, and with all the understanding, and all the soul and all thy strength, and to love his neighbor as himself, is more than all whole burnt offerings or sacrifices." And when Jesus saw that he answered discreetly, he said unto him, "Thou art not far from the kingdom of God. And no man after that durst ask him any question."

Reverend Knight paused for a moment and then went on. "I have known Jed and Mary almost since they arrived in Chatham. In conversation with Jed, he truly believed and lived by the commandments. He is now in the kingdom of God. As anyone here can attest to it, Jed loved his neighbor. Think of last night, I hear the procession of visitors came from miles. Look around at how many of you there are here again today. You are his neighbor. He clearly loved you with all his heart . . . it seems clear by your attendance you loved him too." Mary smiled; she liked what he said.

Mary spoke up as she turned to the crowd and said, "Jed really loved every one of you. He's talked about y'all with a carin' heart, for all o' ya." She wiped her nose and looked to the minister to continue.

Reverend Knight started again. "St. Matthew 13:31–32 tells one of Jesus's parables. 'The kingdom of heaven is like to a grain of mustard seed, which a man took, and sewed in his field. Which indeed is the least of all seeds; but when it is grown, it is the greatest among herbs, and becometh a tree, so that the birds of the air come and lodge in the branches thereof.' I have to say this parable describes Jed. He planted the seeds of potatoes here on Earth and now is in heaven. His planting is done."

Reverend Knight held his Bible to his chest and said, "Jed hoped to go to heaven. I don't know about you, but I think he made it. There was never a better man, father, husband, and friend! Heaven is greater for having our loss." Mary wasn't sad when she saw him being lowered into the large hole. She took a handful of dirt and threw it on the coffin once it was firmly in the ground. Little Jacob Marcus took a handful and did the same, although he didn't know why. Mary asked the crowd to please take a handful and help her bury her Jed. Everyone obliged, and when the people were all finished tossing the dirt, the coffin had a complete thick layer of dirt covering it. He had that many friends. The men would come back later to fill the rest of the dirt in.

They all went back to the house for more coffee, wine, food, songs, and music. It was the second day of celebrations for Jed's life. He was gone. But he was still here, a short walk away.

Chapter 18

Farm Changes,
Life Changes

T HE 1860S WERE BUSY; THEY were good years for some and bad for many. The United States Civil War ran for five years before General Lee, who was in command of the Confederate troops, surrendered with President Jefferson Davis's permission. There was very little money left to fight with, and the South lost so many soldiers there were just not enough people to fight for their cause.

The president of the United States, Abraham Lincoln, first issued the Emancipation Proclamation in 1862 and then in 1863; many slaves were given their freedom. Most headed North, and then something unexpected happened. The government decided that they would let the colored men sign up and fight to help preserve the Union. There were over two hundred thousand colored men that joined the Union Army and helped turn the tide of the war. The Confederate Army was soon not able to compete with the number of soldiers that were signing up to fight them.

Even in Chatham, many Africans were happy about the freedom of their brethren. Many emigrated back to the United States to help the cause and fight with the Negro troops. They were in full support and glad to be helping defeat the South.

Abraham Lincoln was not to see how his country would eventually unite. He was shot while watching a play with his wife in Ford's Theater in Washington. He succumbed to his wound and died the next day, April 15, 1865. The United States and Canada were devastated. His assassin, John Wilkes Booth, was surrounded, captured, shot, and killed two weeks later.

At the farm, just after Jed died, Rolly asked John if he could clean up and use the house on the newer lot he had bought. John couldn't see why not but said that there would be a small rental fee; Rolly agreed. He had no other bills to pay. He felt that moving out of Jed and Mary's house was the proper thing to do. He did not want to compromise Mary's reputation—new widow, still living with her late husband's best friend. Mary thought it was very kind of him to think of her like that. So did Diana and John.

John and Diana were busy with getting ready for the planting, and after Jed died they hired Frank and Gerald. They moved into the house with Rolly. Rolly was the one who offered them the house to live in so they could share the rent. They were full-time, permanent farmhands now on the McDonald farm and very proud to be there. Everything was doing well, and they now had the most successful potato farm in Southern Ontario.

Mary was really busy too. Diana was at school all day, and their kids were now students in her school. The school board had decided to accept five-year-old students this term. Both boys were five years old now. Benjamin had to go to a school in Chatham because his parents lived there. Mary was glad the two very active boys were away during the day with so much cooking, baking, and housework to do. Diana kept her own place up, and Mary, hers; but the men needed help in their house. You could certainty tell they were bachelors. Mary cleaned and cooked for them too. They tried to keep their house neat, but sometimes they were very tired and had to rely on Mary to do it for them.

Mary really had no time to feel sorry for herself after Jed died. Life went on, and they all remembered him fondly with a chuckle and a smile. Rolly, Frank, and Gerald were invited to take meals at John and Diana's now. Mary felt there was no sense in cooking for Diana, George, and John and then cook for herself and Jacob and then for the farmhands. It was decided everyone would have meals together as one big family. She liked feeling so useful and needed by everyone.

Frank and Gerald had found a couple of young eligible ladies who lived in Windsor. They drove there every Saturday night and would come back to the farm on Sunday. Their relationships were turning serious, and both men, who seemed joined at the hip most of the time, decided to ask for their ladies' hands in marriage. Diana almost burst when she found out! There would be wedding plans in the air—as a matter of fact, a double wedding. John and Diana offered the use of the farm.

When the ladies were proposed to, the men brought them back to the farm to meet Diana and John. Beulah was Frank's fiancée, and Cora was marrying Gerald. Diana and John liked them both right off. They wanted to get to know the girls since they were going to be employees' wives, living on their farm, and they would likely hold jobs there as well. Both women worked in a button factory in Windsor, and they were currently assigned to making buttons for soldiers' uniforms, but they were glad to be moving away. They were both born on a plantation in Southern Alabama and had been friends all their lives. Both of their parents had been killed, and they were left with other slaves to be raised. They each had a hard time in their teens. Many times, as they were blossoming into young women, they were raped by their master and overseer repeatedly. When they had enough of this cruel treatment, they successfully ran and made their way north. Like most escaping slaves did, they did not know where they were going or where they would end up.

They also put their lives in the hands of the conductors of the Underground Railroad. They made their way to the end of the line and were delivered into Adam White's hands at the livery in Chatham. He took them to Windsor, where he had arranged jobs for them in a factory and a room in a rooming house, and that's where they lived. They worked with and lived in a house with white and black folks, which shocked them. They expected to have some resistance and "nigger" treatment, but they were met with kindness and very little rudeness or intolerance.

The two women really missed farm life and would love to get back to it. Diana was so happy to hear this. Mary was fussing about with tea and scones for their guests and listening to them talking. Jacob and George were out playing in the yard since it was a beautiful day. As Mary served the tea, she poured herself a cup and sat with everyone. Gerald and Frank had told their ladies about Mary and even Jed and the McDonalds; they felt that they already knew them and felt Jed's loss.

Diana said, "I guess our family is just getting larger and larger, isn't it, dear?" John agreed with a smile. The ladies were so shocked to be visiting the McDonald farm. They had heard that there was this large "white" potato farm around Chatham that employed blacks. They were not slaves but were paid employees and shared the land. Being from the worst plantation in Alabama, they were honored to become the wives of these workers. They could finally forget the cruelty they had been born into and brought up in. Diana continued, "Do you want a big wedding, or small?"

Beulah spoke for Cora too. "Well, ma'am, don't rightly know what our fellas want. We ain't talked much 'bout it yet. They tole us y'all is gonna let us wed here. Dat be so nice, Mr. and Mrs. McDonald. What chew tink, boys? Big or small?" Gerald and Frank shrugged their shoulders, smiling.

Diana sprang up off the couch. "Oh, Mary, we're going to have a wedding around here." Mary was thrilled too. She and Diana jumped around excitedly, so happy for them and their news.

John leapt to his feet and took Diana's hand. "Darlin', what did Dr. Marsh tell you about jumping up and down when you're pregnant?" She stopped, kissed John on the cheek, and then she and Mary grabbed hold of the girls and went into the kitchen to start planning. The four women put their heads together and planned a double wedding to take place in one month.

One day Diana asked Mary while working in the kitchen together, "What day were you and Jed married?" Mary thought for a moment. It seemed like so long ago, and she did not know much about calendars and such back then.

"I knows it was fall. Let me see, it was a Saturday, I knows that for sure. The day we jump the broom, that was the same day Caleb runned away. I guess that be why me and Jed did not have happy anniversaries, likes you and John does each year. That Mr. Jordan he brung back Caleb's dead body ten days after we jumped, and that was the day he throws me down and kills my baby. I remember asking Laura-Ma'am what day it be when I woke up later that day. She told me it was October 20. Don't know why she was so 'xact."

Diana turned to her with a smile. "Mary, you won't believe this . . . do you know that you and Jed were married on the same day as John and I? We were married on October 10, a Saturday. They both laughed as they worked, knowing their connection was even deeper. Mary now had a *good* reason to remember that day, instead of it being the day that led to Caleb's death. Mary chuckled.

She all of a sudden thought about Jed's potato coffin. Diana asked what she was laughing at. Mary told her and they both laughed. Mary said, "Remember the day Jed was buried?"

"Uh huh," Diana replied, turning her smile to a slight frown.

Mary said, "When I was with Jed, by myself in the room, I cut a piece of my Kente robe and put it on him. Diana, when I goes could you do the same for me? I want y'all to promise that you'll cut a piece off to put in my coffin and give the robe to Jacob. Tell him 'bout it's meanin'. I needs you to promise me this."

Diana said, "Mary, you'll be around a long time, but yes, I will make sure Jacob gets the robe and to pass it down to the next generations. That is what I am doing with the McGee tartan.

It will be passed down to George, and he will pass it to his children. We want it to be around a long time so people, our people, in the future, will know who we were and where we came from. I don't need to cut any from our sash. We have the marriage kerchief. Remember I told you half of it goes in the first coffin, and then the other half goes in the remaining person's coffin when they die? This means that the whole sash may be passed down." They both nodded at each other as Diana made her solemn promise to Mary she would take care of it.

One day, Mary and Rolly asked Diana if maybe John, Diana, Rolly, and her could give the new wedding couples a gift. It would have to be agreed on by all four of them since it *was* the McDonalds' property. Mary said, "I been thinkin' . . . there I am lonely with Jacob in our house at night. Now, Diana, I knows I can come here, but it's still lonely. And Rolly feels like he'll be in the way when Beulah and Cora move into da farmhands' house. What chew thinks that we let one of the couples' move into my house, and I moves into your house with Jacob. Rolly could move in too. That way, we be givin' the newlyweds their privacy in both houses. You got lots of bedrooms, and I'll be closer to help with the baby when it comes."

Diana thought it was a really wonderful idea. She told Mary yes. But she and Rolly wouldn't hear of it without John's okay. When they asked John later that day, he wholeheartedly agreed. They would not tell the couples until the wedding day. The four thought it would be a wonderful, unexpected surprise wedding present for both couples.

John and Diana had lots of room in their house for Mary, Jacob, and Rolly. Mary would only use up one bedroom for her and Jacob. She wanted to keep Jacob in the same room, close to her. But who was to get which house? John figured that they would flip a coin on the wedding day. Mary owned the house now since Jed passed away; and that would not change. John would see that it remained legally hers. She would collect rent on it from whichever couple lived there and keep it for herself and Jacob, just like John would collect his rent from the other couple.

The double wedding day arrived, but so did the rain. The *Farmer's Almanac* said to expect lots of rain during this time. They were right, as usual. Everyone was disappointed, but they had a plan B. John, Jeff, Adam, Rolly, and the two grooms completely cleaned and painted the inside of the barn on the farmhands' lot. The wedding that was supposed to take place outside would now take place in the festively decorated barn on the McDonald farm.

The wedding was attended by the whole African community of friends from Chatham and surrounding area, as well as Adam, Jeff, Michael, Dr. Marsh, and their families and a few friends of Cora and Beulah's from Windsor. The ceremony was to be a combination Western and African. They had Reverend Knight perform the customary ceremony, and then both couples jumped the broom. Oddly, Beulah and Gerald jumped the highest. They were to be the decision makers of their families, according to Ghana tradition. This was followed by a large feast, with music and dancing.

After everyone left, the coin was tossed; Frank and Beulah would be living in Mary and Jed's house and paying the rent to her. Gerald and Cora will move into the house that Rolly vacated.

Everyone was so surprised about the family's gift. During the morning, while helping the brides to prepare, Diana discovered that they were both pregnant. She smiled at the thought of more children around the farm in about six or seven months. Hers was due in another couple of months, she estimated. She couldn't wait. She and John were so excited to be having another child. She decided that she would work right up until the end of the current school term, and the birth should coincide with part of the summer vacation. Diana planned to continue working when school opened in September again. Mary was happy at the thought of more children around to help with too.

A few weeks after the wedding, Mary woke up with a sore throat, chills, and a fever. Since Diana had to go to school, she asked Beulah to fill in for Mary while she was sick. Mary stayed up in her room and slept a lot. She did not want anyone to catch what she had or make a fuss over her. A couple of days later, in the morning, Diana hadn't been able to check on her because she was running late for work, so she asked Beulah to look in on her. When she opened the door to Mary's room, she was shocked by what she saw. Mary was lying in bed covered with lesions on her hands and arms—smallpox! In a panic, Beulah quickly ran down the stairs and out toward the barn, screaming. It was early, and the men were just coming in for breakfast after the first set of chores.

Beulah was running, waving her arms in the air, yelling, "Smallpox, smallpox, it be da pox.

Someone get da doc." John was horrified. He remembered Diana's mother and sister. Diana was going to be devastated. Frank mounted the fastest horse they had on the farm and rode into town to get Dr. Marsh. He found him at his home, just getting ready to go to the hospital.

Frank pounded on the door of his house and said, "Doc, Doc, it be Frank. You'se gotta come to da farm right quick, dere be sickness."

Ian opened the door and asked, "Who is it, Frank? What is it?" Frank told him to hurry; it was Mary, and Beulah said it was smallpox. Dr. Marsh grabbed his black bag and mounted his horse and rode fast.

Frank went to Adam's and told him, "Adam, it look like Mary, she have da pox. Doc be on his way now to say fer sure." Adam was speechless for a few seconds. He asked if there was anything he could do. Frank said, "I'se gonna go by da school an' tell Diana. She may wants ta go home. Can Tina or yo' Jenny gits to da school an' take over for da rest o' da day?"

Adam said, "Don't worry, someone will come right away. As Frank rode to the school, Adam ran over to his brother's place and told Tina. Benjamin was already in school for the day, so Tina grabbed her shawl and little one and ran with Adam back to the livery, where he helped her up on his wagon. When they arrived at the school, Diana was shocked with the news from home and angry with herself for not taking Mary's sickness more seriously. She wanted to go home. Frank told her that someone would be here soon to take over the school.

Tina arrived in about seven minutes. Adam got her there as quickly as he could. She told Frank and Diana to go; she'd be fine with the students, and she'd just follow Diana's lesson plans. Frank had to ride the horse with Diana sitting behind him, holding onto his waist. He had to ride carefully because Diana was pregnant.

When they arrived at the farm a few minutes later, they were relieved that Dr. Marsh had made it there before they did. Diana ran up her stairs as Dr. Marsh was coming out of Mary's bedroom. Ian took her arm gently and said, "She's gone, Diana. I'm so sorry, love. I know how close you two were." Diana leaned back against the wall with a slight thump in the hallway outside Mary's room, and her body slowly slid down the wall until she was sitting on the floor, just staring at Mary's bedroom door. She couldn't believe it. Her best friend was dead. What would she do without her? What about Jacob? What would she tell him?

"I was afraid of this," said Dr. Marsh. "I was afraid of something like this happening since Jed died. I suspected that she could never survive an illness if she were to get one. She couldn't fight it. She wasn't strong enough to fight it without Jed. Now, Diana, you, John, Beulah, *no one* can go in that room right now. I mean *no one*! You may have been exposed already, but we can only hope none of you gets it. Especially since you ladies are all in the family way. You can't go in that room even for a moment to see her. Diana, I'd like to lock this room until I can make all the arrangements to take her body out and bury it right away. I'm sorry, but it has to be this way . . .

Diana." She broke her stare and looked up at the doctor with tears in her eyes, and she told him that the key to Mary's room was in her top drawer. He slipped into her room and got it; he locked Mary's door.

Dr. Marsh said, "Diana, I need you to focus now. I need you to bring the boys home immediately, and I have to examine them. I have to examine everyone that lives here on the farm.

You can't visit anyone or go to work or church until I tell you it's safe to. Diana, are you listening? Diana?" She slowly turned her head to look at him again, still in a fog, and nodded that she understood what he said. She went down the stairs and outside to the men awaiting word. She told them that Mary was dead and that John had to get the boys from school right away to be examined.

She told John they had to get hold of Mr. Johns and that he would need to close the school.

John left for the school, and Frank rode back to town and told Adam about it. He was so shocked that Mary died. Dr. Marsh didn't want the cause of death known yet. He didn't want a panic on his hands.

Frank went to the post office next and sent a Morse telegraph to Mr. Johns to let him know. Diana had written the message that Frank was to give the telegraph operator to send her boss. Frank rode back to the farm to be examined, and John was already back home with the boys. When Jacob got out of the wagon, Diana knelt down and held him to her. Everyone gathered around Jacob and Diana. Diana said to him, "Honey, you know we all love you here, don't you?" He saw how sad she was and nodded his head slowly, remembering another conversation he had with John while sitting on his knee. He was young, but he still remembered it. Jacob started to feel uneasy.

He broke out of Diana's hold and said, "Where's Mama?" He looked at everyone's faces, and it told the tale. Mama was gone now too.

Diana continued while hugging him again. "Dr. Marsh came to help her, but he couldn't get here in time." Jacob broke loose from Diana's hold again and went to Ian, and he gave him the hardest kick on the shin he could.

Jacob yelled, "It be your fault my mama be dead now. Why you not get here to help her?

You made my mama die cause you wasn't here on time!" He kicked the doctor's shin again, and John grabbed hold of him and held him while he started to cry. Jacob put his arms around John's neck, and the tears flowed. John carried Jacob into the house, and everyone followed.

Although Diana was teary and in such pain for Jacob, she smiled and asked, "Dr. Marsh, would you like me to take a look at that leg for you?" He pulled the leg of his trousers up and saw it was bloody. He had bruises and abrasions. He knew Jacob didn't mean it. He was now orphaned at the age of five.

John went into the parlor and sat for a while with Jacob crying on his lap. Everyone was still being examined by the doctor thoroughly, carefully. He could not let it spread to these wonderful people whom he had become so close to. Everyone seemed fine. There was also the possibility he could take it home and infect his wife, Nora, and his son, Mark. He now needed to examine Jacob and John.

They both went in the other room to see the doctor together. The doctor examined them both. Jacob didn't want to let go of John. After a little talk with John, Jacob told the doctor he was sorry for kicking him. After the doctor examined him, he gave him two pieces of rock candy for being such a brave boy. Jacob turned to John and popped one of the candies in John's mouth, saying, "Here, John, you'se a brave boy too." John was overwhelmed with emotion but kept it together. He loved Jacob so much. Almost like another son.

Ian sat with the group in the kitchen after examining them all, and he told them they had to bury Mary that afternoon. When they inquired about contact with her, the doctor told them they all had to put kerchiefs around their noses and mouths, and everyone also had to wear gloves of some kind until she was buried, and her room was to be scrubbed clean. As these instructions were being put into action, Diana remembered her own mother and sister. They were both alive for many days with the pox before dying. As Diana thought, she knew that the doctor was right. Mary could not survive an illness without Jed. She wasn't strong enough. Diana was sad, but somehow she had known it too. Jed had always been her protector and savior, and now he will be again, in heaven.

Dr. Marsh headed back to town so that he could talk to Adam. Adam had many requests for coffins since the potato coffin. They were normal-shaped ones though. When he got busy, he would hire some of the other skilled carpenters in the community to help out. Mary did not need a big one since she was such a tiny woman. Ian asked Adam if he had a small coffin prepared that would hold Mary. He did and told the doctor that he would run it out to the farm right away. The doctor told Adam about the precaution of a kerchief and gloves, and Adam made sure he took them with him.

Mary had to be buried that afternoon, even before people heard the news. The family all decided they would hold a great memorial for her when Dr. Ian said it was safe to have visitors. He needed to see if anyone else in the community came down with the pox too.

Dr. Marsh stopped by the Maguires' on his way back to town to examine Michael, Toby, and Eileen and tell them about Mary, but they were told they could not visit until it was safe. He next went to the school and told Tina that she could not visit there either and that she needed to close the school and send the children home after he examined each one.

The grave for Mary's coffin was dug right beside Jed's. Before the coffin was closed, Diana took a knife and cut a piece of Mary's Kente robe, and with a kerchief on her face and gloves on, she carefully, lovingly placed it in her hand as she promised she would. She never expected it to be this soon though.

Mary's coffin was lowered into the grave. Reverend Knight was told of the tragedy, and he quickly came out to the farm to give her a short service. Dr. Marsh came back out from town to attend but was not happy about Reverend Knight being there. Reverend Knight said, "I am doing the work of the Lord, Doctor, and I will go wherever I am needed. I have been guided here to our dear sister, Mary. She deserves a Christian burial, no matter how sick she was." The doctor could not say anything; he agreed and understood.

Reverend Knight left the farm without touching anyone or anything. After the service, the doctor stayed for tea and coffee cake, which Beulah had made that morning. Everyone was sad to not have had a proper funeral, but they would make sure she would be remembered with a fine memorial service. Diana was beside herself with grief. She said, "Why didn't I check on her this morning? Why did I have to get up late and ask Beulah to check on her? It should have been me that checked her!"

John was holding Jacob again and could not get to Diana. She understood Jacob needed to be held right now. Rolly came up to Diana and said, "Diana, would you'se like ta go fer a walk wit' me?" Diana smiled at him, remembering her walk two years earlier, the day Jed died. Rolly took her out the summer kitchen door, and he reached up and ran his hand along the clothesline. He continued, "I'se wonder how many bedsheets dat woman dun hung up here. What chew figgers?"

Diana took a breath and smiled. "I think hundreds." She paused for a moment to reflect and then continued, "Remember how she liked to fold the sheets in half, and she had to have them hang perfectly? The way she used so many pegs because the boys were always running through them while they were drying? She would always pretend she was mad at . . ." She couldn't finish.

Rolly put an arm around Diana's shoulder and said, "I remembers da day we walked ta dat 'tato fiel' an' I drop ta my knees an' you juss dun pick me up an' tole me dere be nuttin' I coulda done ta save our Jed. He woulda died if I be home or not dat night. It took me a while, but I believes what y'all said be true. I cou'n't save his life. Dat's juss da same as you now. Mary be dead wedder y'all checks her in da mornin' or not. Dat be God's way. We all bein' better people fer knowin' your Jed an' Mary Allen, an' my Berko Yaba and Afua Kakira."

They hugged and Diana asked, "If Mary had the choice, what do you think she would have liked Adam to carve for a coffin?"

Rolly thought for a moment. "I tinks she woulda like a cake coffin." Diana laughed and laughed until she let out a loud scream. She was dropping to her knees, and Rolly caught her. Her water broke! It was too early. The emotional stress and shock of the death of Mary, her best friend in the whole world, started her labor. Rolly picked her up and carried her back to the house and told them, "Her water, it dun broke." John was shocked.

Dr. Marsh was still at the farm. He said to take her upstairs to the bedroom. He didn't want to risk taking her to the hospital in Chatham; this was an emergency. She was crying in pain, both emotional and physical. She didn't know which was worse. As Rolly laid her down, John handed Jacob to him. That was okay with him . . . Jacob wanted to go outside and play now. Rolly took Jacob and George, and he went out into the yard with them and watched them play.

Diana was in full labor and Ian could not stop it. He did not have much time to prepare. The head was showing. She was too early to deliver. Beulah and Cora came in to help the doctor. John stayed with Diana; they were both scared.

Diana looked at him, and he held her hands. She squeezed hard and let out another yell. Dr. Marsh said, "Now, Diana, push." She pushed hard, and it only took the one push. The baby was too tiny, so there was not much to push.

Dr. Marsh said, "Mama, Papa, you have a very little boy here!" He smacked his tiny bottom and then smacked it a second time, and he took his first tiny labored breath and made a small whimper. He shivered until Cora grabbed a blanket to wrap him in. The doctor cut the cord and gave him to Diana. She looked up at her beloved Johnny and cried out, "Doc . . . Ian, he's not breathing!"

The doctor took him back, but it was too late. He was too little. Diana had turned out to be not as far along in her pregnancy as they thought. She was only around five months. Their baby was dead. He never had a chance.

John let tears fall while Diana was still in shock. Dr. Ian said, "Folks, he was a few months early and too small. Diana, I'd like you to go to the hospital with me. You're still bleeding, and it would be better if I treat you there. But you need to go *now*. We can care for you better there. You may have to stay there a couple of days. Since the smallpox was here in the house, it's best."

John left the room with all haste to hook up the wagon and two Clydes. He called to Frank and Gerald to grab a mattress to put in the wagon, which they did. John had to get her to the Chatham hospital. He pulled up to the house and went in to get his wife. Rolly was halfway down the stairs carrying her, and the doctor followed behind.

As Diana was lying in the wagon on the trip to town, the doctor kept an eye on her bleeding and applied pressure. He also needed to keep her warm; she was in shock.

Rolly rode the doctor's horse behind the wagon, back to town for him. He could not stay because of the smallpox scare at their house. He would have to wait for John to come back with news of Diana's condition. Everyone kept an eye on George and Jacob at the farm. They were quite happily out playing on the swings that Jed had put up for them. John and Diana never worried about the boys—they were always cared for and loved by all.

Neither John nor Diana heard their son cry. Diana's mom had once told her you'll know you have a blessed child when you hear it cry. They were not blessed this time. But they still had George and hoped they would make him a big brother someday. They did not want to tell George he had had a little brother, at least for the moment. John would have to bury their son in the family cemetery without Diana. She was devastated but understood.

They arrived at the hospital. Dr. Marsh jumped off the wagon and went inside to get a couple of nurses and a wheelchair to transfer Diana; he didn't want her to walk and wanted her in a bed right away. The doctor had a nurse put a fair amount of pressure on Diana's lower abdomen and pubic region, which could stop bleeding in many women. He hoped it would help Diana now. She was getting very pale and almost passed out. Dr. Ian estimated she had lost one and a half pints of blood already.

John was scared for his wife. He had to leave Diana at the hospital and go home. Ian wanted him away from the hospital because of the smallpox scare at his farm. There was so much for John to do there anyway. He could rely on his farmhands but still needed to get home to tell everyone how things were with Diana. He also needed to tell George how much he loved him and hold him for a while. Then there was Jacob. He lost his mother this day too. He thought to himself that such a sweet and innocent child did not deserve the hand he had been dealt in his less than six short years of life.

By the time John left the hospital, Diana had calmed down some. The bleeding had stopped. She was resting, and her blood was being replenished by transfusion. When John left, it was already dark outside. He drove up to Adam's livery. The doors were closed, but the lantern was burning inside. He pulled up as close to his door as possible and yelled out, "Adam!" There was no response.

Again, he called out louder, "Adam, are you still in there? It's John McDonald. Are ye there, lad?"

John waited a moment and he heard the doors unlock.

Adam opened the door and said, "Johnny, m'boy, come in. Jeff's here too."

John said, "I can't come in. The doc says I can't go near anyone until he's sure there won't be any . . . you know, outbreak. I just stopped by to tell you that, well, . . . Diana had the baby today . . . we had a boy. He didn't live because he was so small. Diana'll be in hospital for a while. Please let Tina and Jenny know. I have to go."

John turned the wagon around and was just driving away when he heard behind him from Adam and Jeff, "God be with you, Johnny McDonald! You're good people, and we know everything will be fine. You just wait and see. God be with you and your family. We'll pray for you."

John felt a warm glow within him. He thought about all the wonderful people that he and Diana had met in Canada. Although they loved Scotland, Canada was more like home to them now.

As he rode back to the farm, he asked God, "Lord, I know there is a reason for everything ye do, but how can ye take such an innocent little one so early. He wasn't ready to come, but you brought him anyway. Why, Lord? And what about little Jacob, Lord? Why take his mama?" He wept as he rode on. Before he knew it, he was home. Now he had to tell everyone the news. Diana had to have a transfusion and needed to stay for several days. She was in delicate condition.

As he drove the wagon into the barn, Frank asked, "Everything okay, John?" John nodded slightly. In the barn, he, Rolly, and Gerald were almost done with the evening feeding and bedding the animals, and John was thankful. He didn't feel like working right now anyway. They all walked back to the house. Beulah and Cora had a beautiful spread of supper ready for all of them. George and Jacob had been put to bed already. John was relieved, for he didn't know what to say to them.

At supper, John told everyone about the day's happenings. He would head to the hospital in the morning to check on Diana. He asked about the boys, and Cora told him that they were both asleep up in Georgie's bed. John was happy; the boys always had each other. It was a strain off his mind, at least for this night.

No one got much sleep. There was a storm. As he watched out the window from their lonely bed, he realized this was the first night that he and Diana had spent without each other since they were married. He had a strange feeling as he got in his bed. He didn't know what else was wrong, but it was something. There was a loud crack of thunder, and all of a sudden, there were two little boys under the blankets with him. He smiled and held them both. Then he realized what was wrong. Diana was not there to read with him from their Bible.

John asked the boys, "What's this? My two brave boys are afraid of the storm? You know, when you hear thunder, it is only God moving his furniture in heaven. It can't hurt you."

George looked up at his father and smiled. He said, "Daddy, why is God moving the furniture?"

John replied, "Well, son, he's just making room so that Jacob's mama can join his papa and the other Jacob Marcus." Jacob looked up at John and smiled. He asked John if he would tell them a story. John put the lamp on, and he took the family Bible from the table beside the bed and asked if they wanted to hear the story of David and Goliath. They both smiled and nodded. John turned to the Old Testament and looked up 1 Samuel 17.

By the time John was finished reading the story, both boys were fast asleep. He placed the Bible back where it belonged, put an arm around each little one, and fell asleep too.

After a week in the hospital, Diana was able to go home. Dr. Marsh said, "You can now have the memorial for Mary any time you like, folks, since I lifted the quarantine off the farm." He smiled and continued, "We were so lucky. We only had three cases of smallpox in the community, and those families are quarantined now. You know, in the 1600s, Great Britain had the biggest outbreak of smallpox in history; it killed millions of people, and they almost lost Queen Elizabeth herself. The quarantine was the only thing I could do to not have it spread. Let me know when you'll have the memorial, and I'll help spread the word."

Diana and John started to plan Mary Allen's memorial service as soon as she felt up to it. It would be the next Saturday. They would hold it in the barn, now called McDonald Hall, where the couples were married.

Many people came to pay their respects to Mary, like they did for Jed a couple of years earlier. There was singing and music long into the night. Diana made sure that all the stories about her were good ones. She thought Mary would be disgraced if they all knew how tragic her young life really was. She was so shy and humiliated; Diana knew she would have been hurt to remember the terrible things that she endured again.

People were asking how little Jacob was doing now without both parents. Diana and John had taken it upon themselves to start to raise Jacob with the help of Rolly and the other couples on the farm. He would be able to grow up living in the same house with his best friend, George. It was now like they were brothers for the rest of their lives. They would see each other through their weddings and their own children. The boys would always be there for each other . . . even when it would take Jacob such a long, heart-wrenching time to become a father himself!

Chapter 19

Growing Pains

AS YEARS PASSED, JACOB AND George grew and learned to rely on each other and cherish their large family. Frank and Beulah's family now had one daughter. Gerald and Cora had two boys while friends Jeff and Tina had two boys and a girl. Adam and Jenny had one girl, and both White families still visited the McDonalds often. But George was not to be a big brother yet.

Rolly died very suddenly, only a year after Mary did. It started with a bad cold. He was working in the rain with everyone else. The next day, he had a sore chest. Everyone grew scared. They thought of Jed and hoped that Rolly would not suffer the same fate. After all, he had a painful chest and found it difficult to breathe . . . and he was African! Did he have the same affliction as Jed? Everyone wondered nervously, even the doctor, when he was first told of the symptoms.

Dr. Ian Marsh was still the family doctor, but he was getting on in years and wanted to retire while he was still young enough to enjoy it. His son, Mark, studied in Toronto and became a doctor too. He came back to Chatham to hang his shingle with his dad. The senior Dr. Marsh was a very proud father. Ian took Mark with him at first on community rounds and to the hospital to get him familiar with the routine of a country doctor.

They both went to the McDonalds' because Rolly couldn't get out of bed. After the doctors thoroughly examined him, they were certain it was not the same thing Jed had; it was pneumonia.

Rolly was worried, as he was a father figure to Jacob, like John, and had just found out he was going to be a father himself. Sally became pregnant, but her father took her away one night. He never knew where. Rolly was devastated. He started to neglect his health; he was so depressed about it.

Throughout the early years Rolly had taught Jacob about the Negro ways, slavery, and their history while John taught him of white life, side by side with his own son, George. He taught them both about farming and made sure Jacob knew that his parents in heaven knew he was loved and educated. Rolly passed away of pneumonia within four days of his diagnosis, never knowing that someday Sally would escape from her father and make a life for her and their son, Rolly Waters Jr. Diana and John made sure he had a proper burial in the cemetery, just on the outskirts of Chatham, which was started mostly by and for the black community, with the help of Adam White and his family.

All the children living at the farm, which had now grown by another 320 acres, had chores. John had bought the two lots on the other side of the road. "Olde McDonald's Potato Farm" had grown so much over the years that there was enough work for everyone living on the farm to have chores, but the children all went to school Monday to Friday with Diana. John still had to hire outside help for planting and harvesting each year.

John now paid his boys, George and Jacob, to work on the farm. Ever since Jacob's parents died, both John and Diana thought of him as their son. George and Jacob were big healthy strapping lads, just like John was to his family in Scotland back in the 1850s. Both Jacob and George finished elementary school. They were both sent to Chatham High School to complete their education. Although you could still not educate Negroes in the United States, they were very slowly being educated in Canada. There were fewer black children now since the emigration of them back to the United States during and after the Civil War ended. In and around Chatham, Negroes were allowed to be in schools; integrating them with white children was no problem.

Toward the end of grade eleven, George seemed a little strange. He was not concentrating on his schoolwork or his farmwork. John wasn't sure what the problem was, until one day when Jeff and the family came over for supper on a Sunday after church. They often spent Sundays at the McDonalds', and the afternoon was filled with golfing at the farm.

The McDonalds had added a few holes, another driving range shorter than the other one so the kids could always practice. They also added another putting green to their farm. All the adults and the kids loved to play whenever they could, and they always did on Sundays during nice weather, but only when chores and church were done.

This one Sunday, John looked around for George but could not find him. He looked toward the house. Out on the swing, in front of their house, sat Dora White, Jeff and Tina' s daughter, with George pushing her gently and kissing her on the cheek each time she swung back toward him. They did not know they were being watched. Johnny walked over to Jeff, Tina, and Diana, who were talking with Beulah and Cora about happenings they heard in church that morning. He came to join them and said, "Aha, m'love, I think I can account for George's problems. Mom, everyone, look over there." He pointed at the teens.

Diana and Tina were surprised. All four of the parents were a little taken aback, but after they got over the initial shock, Diana said, "It was bound to happen sometime. They have had eyes for each other since grade school. Remember, everyone, we all married young."

Tina said, "Yes I know, but they're just childr—"

Jeff cut her off, "Now, darlin', they'll be fine. Don't fret so. They all have to leave the nest sometime. I don't think we should stand in their way. They make a good couple, I think. There's no one else in this county I could ever want my daughter to marry . . . someday."

All the parents smiled as they watched George slow the swing to a stop; Dora stood up. He bent over and kissed her once on the lips. He took her by the hand, and they walked out to the driving range. As they held hands, the parents thought they would turn the other way and pretend they don't see them. As the kids arrived near their parents, George said, "Mr. White, Mrs. White, I'd like to ask for your daughter's hand in marriage, if I may." There was complete silence. The parents just looked around at each other, not believing what they heard. They never thought it would happen this soon.

John said, "George, son, are you sure about this? What about school?"

George replied to his mom and dad and to Dora's parents too, "I was thinking that, well, Dad, you and Mom never completed high school, and I realize there was extenuating circumstances. Well, I can work full-time here on the farm. At least, I hope I still have a job here, Father. I was also thinking Dora can still go to school and complete her studies while I work. And, sir, I was thinking that we could use my bedroom until one of the houses here on the farm is vacated."

It seemed like he had it all figured out. Dora was dumbstruck. She never knew George was planning this so soon; Jeff and Tina took their daughter into their arms and hugged her and asked her if she loved George. She said, "Oh, Papa, Mama . . . I do love him so much!"

Jeff and Tina looked to each other, and then to Diana and John. Jeff said, "George, you have our permission, *only* if your parents agree to your plan too."

The teens both looked to George's parents, and John said, "I think we can add one more person to our household until we get their little house built. Unless you prefer to live in town, closer to your parents. But we certainly couldn't ask for a lovelier daughter-in-law."

With that, George knelt on one knee, just the way his dad told him he did at St. Andrews Golf Course, pulled a ring out of his pocket, and asked his sweetheart, "Dora, will you please marry me?"

She let a tear fall down her cheek as she helped him put the ring on her finger and said, "Yes, George McDonald, I will marry you. I love you so much, and I'll make you a good wife, I promise." Both mothers were crying a full stream at this point, and so were Beulah and Cora. They gathered around the couple and congratulated the bride—and groom-to-be.

Jacob was a little jealous. He was happy for his brother but a little jealous that he was going to be a married man, moving on with life; he still wanted to have more education before marriage. But did it have to be that way? He thought about it for a bit but did not want to steal George's thunder, so to speak. He would wait a bit longer. This was George and Dora's day.

Jacob was secretly in love with Beulah and Frank's daughter, Mina Brant. Every chance he had, he would try to be around her on the farm. She was so beautiful he could never imagine loving anyone else. He watched his money carefully and thought that he would save enough to buy his own home someday. But he was reminded that Jed and Mary's house rightfully belonged to him. It was the Allen house. He wanted for nothing living with the McDonalds, and he loved them like his own parents. They had loved him since the day he was born. Adopting a Negro in those times in Canada or the United States just wasn't done. They took him in as son, as brother to their son, and he kept his parents name, Allen. He would try to honor them in everything he did and whatever the future held for him.

Diana, Dora, and Tina started making wedding plans. Cora and Beulah would help with whatever they could. Dora's head was still spinning. Was she dreaming? She went to her mother and hugged her and realized she wasn't sleeping or dreaming. She was awake and it really did happen.

She was engaged to the sweetheart she fell in love with when she was just six years old. The ladies all went into Diana's house to start planning the first wedding in quite some time. Diana asked if they wanted to be married in their church, and the couple said there was no question. They would like their wedding to be held at the farm. That was fine with everyone. The men would paint the inside of the barn again and make it festive for the occasion. John and Jeffrey were actually excited about doing this for their children.

Diana told everyone that she was keeping a secret. Everyone was listening as she told them, "I brought with me all the way from Scotland the wedding dress I wore, my mother wore, and my grandmother wore. My sisters insisted I bring it with me because I was the eldest." She continued, "Since it's my son getting married, he'd look pretty silly in it, so, Dora, I would be honored if you would wear it. If you can't or your mother already has a dress for you to wear, I understand."

Tina and Dora were so surprised and accepted her generosity. Diana said, "It has brought good luck to three generations of McGees, and now I know you will have good luck wearing it too. It will look beautiful on you, love. George will be wearing the family tartan sash, in keeping with our Scottish tradition. Johnny wore the McDonald tartan sash, and I wore the McGee sash. We have the McGee tartan to hand down to our children. The McDonald tartan sash stayed in Scotland for his brothers. You could also wear the luckenbooth brooch, which was loaned to me for my wedding but was given to me when we moved to Canada. Oh my goodness, Tina, Dora, I'm so sorry to go on about our traditions, not realizing, I mean, I'm sure you have some family traditions too. Please forgive my enthusiasm. I'm just so excited." Tina and Dora were giggling at her; everyone was. They just let Diana go on and on and on, waiting for her to run out of breath.

Tina said, "Diana, my family wasn't much on traditions, but we would be delighted to follow with some of yours."

Their wedding day was a bright and sunny one. It was so nice to be able to have the ceremony outside. The wedding was attended by many friends and family. They all had a great time at the reception in the freshly painted barn. All the ladies had outdone themselves with the feast. Festivities went on into the night. Both mothers let some tears flow during the ceremony, and at times throughout the day, they reminded each other that it was a mother's prerogative.

After everyone left, George and Dora went into the house and went upstairs. He carried her across the threshold of his bedroom. Everyone else pitched in to help clean up. Jacob and Mina kept "bumping into each other." They had smiles for each other all day and evening. They danced many dances together. The only other one Jacob would dance with was Diana and, of course, the bride.

Jacob was so intent on watching Mina as they cleaned up that he bumped into a beam in the barn, fell backward on his behind, and dropped and broke the dishes he was carrying.

All movement stopped, and everyone looked at Jacob to see if he was all right. He was. There was laughter from everyone. He looked ridiculous. He was so embarrassed. Mina couldn't help but laugh too. John said, "Where is your mind, son? It sure isn't on what you're doing, lad. Might it be on the one who you've been looking at all day?"

Jacob gave a really big smile and said, "Yes, sir, it be the beautiful young lady I'se looking at that made me fall." Mina was a very shy girl. She embarrassed easily and blushed around Jacob. Beulah and Frank gave a wink to each other. They may be the next ones to have a wedding to plan.

They were around helping with Jacob's upbringing for so many years they had no problem with giving their permission if the question of marriage should come up and Jacob didn't chicken out.

Dora became pregnant right away. It was a little quick for them, but they had this large family to help them out. Dora would continue on in school and hopefully would complete her current year. George was happy but was he ready for fatherhood? He would often rely on his parents' advice.

Dora was only fifteen years old. Her body just wasn't ready for motherhood. She miscarried within the third month. She and her husband were distraught but accepted what God had planned for them. Dora completed her year at school and the rest of high school without becoming pregnant again.

She and George were so excited because John, Jeff, Adam, Michael, and the other men on the farm had built a house for them just after the wedding. It was as nice as the others but not as big as Diana and John's. Theirs had one large bedroom downstairs, with a large kitchen, living room, and parlor; and on the second floor, there were two bedrooms for children. They moved into it, and they were going to be so happy. George carried his wife over this threshold too, following tradition.

The next summer, Jacob decided to follow suit. He asked Frank to have Mina's hand in marriage. Frank looked at him, smiled, and said, "It be all right wit' me if it be okay wit' her mother." Jacob grinned, said thank you, and ran to Beulah and asked her too.

Beulah said, "What took you so long, boy?" She smiled and patted Jacob on the cheek gently and added, "You look after my baby now. I be watchin' over ya'll." She grinned at him again. He wasn't sure if she was teasing him or not. Just then Mina walked in the house with a large load of potatoes in her apron for supper. "Here are the potatoes for supper, Mama. Hi, Jacob. What chew doin' here?"

He said, "Nothin' special, just talkin' to your mama. I best git back to work now." He told them he'd see them later, and he gently kissed Beulah on the cheek and turned to Mina and gave her the first kiss on the lips he'd ever given her in front of anyone. Beulah was touched. She was sure it would be a long-lasting, loving marriage, much like her and Frank's.

Jacob went back to work and asked George, "George, you gotta help me. I want to marry Mina. How do I ask? Her mama and papa said yes. How should I ask her?" George smiled and congratulated his brother. Jacob was not sure how to do it and really wanted George's advice.

George asked, "Do you have a ring?" Jacob took it out of his pocket and showed him. George was impressed. He said, "What does she like? Walks, boats, golf, driving?" Jacob thought for a moment. He thought it should be a private proposal since she was a little shy. Doing it in front of everyone may embarrass her, and it may be a little embarrassing for him too. He was afraid he would mess it up and wanted it to be something to remember.

Jacob said, "I tink she'd like a drive in da country on Sunday after church. How does that sound?" George said that it sounded like a good plan. Jacob just hoped those who knew about it wouldn't tell her before Sunday.

Sunday arrived. John let Jacob use the carriage his dad bought and a horse to take Mina to church. She was surprised but liked the idea. He said that he wanted to drive her to church himself. She asked her parents, and they said she could go. They went on their way and met up with their families at the church. Their large extended family always sat together, and today was no different.

Reverend Collins took over in their church after Reverend Knight relocated to a new parish in Northern Ontario, where ministers were needed. Reverend Collins had longer sermons than Reverend Knight. Jacob was sitting in the pew, tapping his foot and not concentrating on what was being said, just what he was going to say to Mina. He didn't want to lose his nerve. By this time, all the parents on the farm knew about Mina's proposal happening that afternoon. They were all happy for the kids, and no one would ruin the surprise.

When Jacob finally became aware of his surroundings again, Diana was poking him in the shoulder to get up and leave. Service was over. He started to perspire, and he was getting quite nervous. This was it. He was going to take Mina for an afternoon drive and propose to her. As all the families greeted Reverend Collins, he asked, "Well, Jacob, what did you think of my sermon?" Jacob was horrified. This was the first time he wasn't paying attention and didn't know what to say. The reverend smiled and said, "Don't worry about it, Jacob. At least you had open eyes. Some people were 'paying attention' with eyes closed, right, Gerald?" Everyone laughed and Gerald apologized for falling asleep during the service. Reverend said, "Well, you can make up for it by inviting me to Sunday supper."

Everyone thought that was a wonderful idea. John stepped in and said, "Reverend, do you like golf?"

Reverend Collins replied, "I love the sport but don't get much chance to partake."

Gerald asked, "Do you have your own clubs, Reverend?" He told them he did, and they said he is welcome to bring them along and play at the farm. Gerald explained that it was not an actual course, but it was a fun time. Reverend Collins was excited, and after he greeted everyone he would go home, pick up his clubs, and head out to the farm after visiting a few shut-ins in the community.

Jacob helped Mina get into the carriage and said, "We'll be home a little later. If Mina doesn't mind, and, um, it is a nice day, um, well, Mina, can I take you for a drive?" She smiled and asked her mother for permission.

Beulah said, "Yes, but don't stay out too long. It's lunchtime." Jacob grinned when he looked at George. George grinned back and winked at Jacob as they drove away.

Jacob thought they might drive toward Windsor. Maybe not all the way to the city, and he thought they would stay on back roads because it was a little less busy. He remembered a spot not too far away near the Thames. It was a secluded spot used for spooning. He headed in that direction. As they drove close to this wooded area, Jacob noticed that there was no one there. He was relieved. He was so scared. He couldn't have asked her in front of anyone else; he was that nervous!

He tied the horse to a tree where he could munch on different vegetation from what there was on the farm. It was quite a treat for the lucky majestic Clydesdale. Jacob reached his arms up and placed his hands around Mina's slender waist and helped her down off the carriage seat. They stood there, so close together; Jacob could not resist. He took her in his arms and kissed her like she'd never been kissed before. It was very passionate. They started having feelings they hadn't experienced before, or at least Mina had never felt like this. She wanted him, and he had wanted her for a long time.

He took her to a place on the riverbank that was hidden away from the road. He had brought out a blanket with them in case they decided to stop anywhere to sit and talk. As they sat on the blanket, they were still trembling from the kiss. Mina said, "Jacob, I wants ta wait till my weddin' night. I hopes ya understan'." Jacob smiled and said that was okay with him. They weren't nervous anymore. They were relieved they got this out of the way. The sexual tension was strong, but they were still young and weren't ready just yet. But they were mature enough to realize it.

Jacob took the ring out of his pocket and looked at Mina. He held it toward her and nervously asked, "Mina, I would likes ya ta be my wife. Is that okay?" She was surprised and shyly smiled and thought to herself how cute he was right now and that she was very much in love with him.

She said, "Jacob, I would be right proud ta be yo' wife . . . yes, if it's okay with our parents!" With her answer, Jacob jumped up off the blanket and started to whoop and holler. "She loves me, Lord, and she'll be my wife . . . thank you, Lord! He pulled her up to a standing position, picked her up, and swung her around until they were both dizzy and fell to the ground laughing.

She said, "Jacob, let's git back to da farm right away. You gotta axe my mama and papa. I wanna tell everyone an' plan our weddin'!" He agreed, folded the blanket, put her back up on the carriage, and then they headed back to the farm—full speed ahead.

At the farm, everyone was just finishing lunch. Diana and Beulah made sure they kept some aside for the kids when they returned with the good news they knew about already. Diana said, "Now don't anybody spoil their news when they get here! You do and I'll throttle you!" She was glaring at the men in particular when she said this. She knew if anyone would blow it, the guys would. She kept her fingers crossed.

When they returned from their drive, the two of them went into the house, and Mina ran to her mother. Mina said, "Oh, Mama, Papa, Jacob's done asked me ta marry him!" She was hugging Beulah, and her mother started crying with joy.

Beulah just let it pop out; she couldn't help it. "I know, baby, I knows it!" Diana hung her head, smiling; the secret was out that they knew.

Mina said, "How come ya knows already?"

Beulah had to think fast on her feet. "Well, baby, Jacob had ta come an' gits our p'mission firss." Mina smiled; that was a good enough explanation for her. She didn't know that almost everyone on the farm knew about her proposal before she did.

She said to Diana and Beulah, "Can we starts plannin' now?" Then she turned to Jacob and asked if he had a date in mind. They decided that the wedding would be outside, at the farm, near the cemetery where Jacob's parents were buried. Mina happily agreed. They wanted it sometime in the summer. It was decided that the wedding would take place in two months.

The men, including Reverend Collins, all migrated out to the driving range to hit a few balls and talk among themselves while their ladies cleaned up the kitchen and dining room and started to plan a wedding. Mina told them that she knew Jacob wanted the usual ceremony that ministers perform, but he also wanted to jump the broom, like his parents did and hers too. Diana thought this was a lovely idea. She knew Mary and Jed would have been so proud to see this wedding. She wished Jacob's parents were still here to witness their son's wedding.

Diana asked Jacob when she was alone with him for a minute, "Jacob, dear, do you think you might like your bride to wear your mama's Kente robe for the wedding?"

Jacob looked at Diana and said, "Yeah, I tink dat be a beautiful idea, Diana. Do ya tink she will?"

Diana continued, "Well, there's no time like the present, darlin'. Let's go ask her and her mama." They walked into the dining room where the girls were sitting and planning. Jacob sat down beside his fiancée.

Although Jacob's language was usually good, whenever he was nervous, everyone noticed he reverted to slang. Diana had tried to teach him for years to speak proper English, but sometimes he forgot himself and spoke like the other blacks. Jacob took Mina's hand and said, "Mina, I don't know how y'all feels 'bout weddin' dresses 'n' stuff, but I would be da proudess man in da worl' if y'all would agree ta wear my mama's Kente robe fer our weddin'. What chew say? It be somtin' she made herse'f an' we's gots ta pass it on ta our chil'run. Dat be okay wit' chew?"

Mina understood the significance of the Kente robe. She'd heard the story of Afua Kakira making the robe. A young Ashanti girl working beside her father daily, designing, weaving, and sewing it and what it meant to her. Mina looked at her mother, and Beulah smiled, remembering Mary and her robe with fondness and love. Beulah knew Mary would have offered it to Mina herself since she had no daughter of her own to hand it down to. Mina understood her mother's smile. Jacob was nervously waiting for her answer. Mina turned to Jacob and said, "I be more den proud ta wear yo' mama's robe fer our weddin', Jacob." Jacob was so happy, and Diana shed a tear. Both knew that his mother and father would be so happy and proud!

It was a beautiful morning the day of their wedding, but the sky looked like it would cloud over and rain in the afternoon. The barn was repainted and made ready for their reception. There were a lot of people in attendance from the community. Most people liked Jacob because he was much like his father, Jed. Diana and John were so happy for their Jacob too.

Reverend Collins stood by the cemetery with his back to it. Jacob and Mina were facing the minister and Jacob's parents' grave. He had a warm feeling in his heart, yet at the same time he felt a slight emptiness. Diana and John were certainly his parental figures, but his mama and papa should have be there. Jacob wanted them to be there, and having the ceremony near their graves was the best he could do. He had Mina's full support, as he always had and always would, in everything he did. He loved her so, and she loved him.

As Diana watched the ceremony, with Mina wearing Mary's Kente robe, she couldn't help recalling from the Bible Proverbs 31:25: "She is clothed with strength and honor, and she can laugh at the time to come." Diana prayed that there would be lots of time to laugh. The reception was as grand as George's had been a year earlier. George was by Jacob's side for his wedding, just like he had been by George's side for his. They were each other's best man.

Jacob and Mina moved into his parents' house on their wedding day. John and Diana owned everything on their hundreds of acres, with the exception of Jed and Mary's house and gardens. It was now owned by Jacob, and it would always still remain in the Allen family forever.

Jacob lifted his bride and crossed the threshold of their house. She kissed him while still in his arms. As he set her down, they kissed harder. The sexual tension they felt the day that Jacob proposed was still there and was much stronger. The two of them just looked at each other and Jacob said, "Mina, I loves you more den anyting', an' I promises ta be a good husban' to ya!" She smiled and kissed him again. Jacob smiled back and said, "Lass one upstairs has ta make breakfass!" As they both ran toward the stairs, Mina nudged Jacob and he lost his balance. Mina was the first one up the stairs. She went into their bedroom and she sat on the bed, waiting for him. As Jacob came through the door, she started laughing. He joined her laughing . . . although his pride was a little wounded.

He looked at her again and pulled her to her feet and then he started to take his mother's Kente robe off his new wife. Mina shook with excitement and nervousness. Jacob was trembling too. As she stood before him with nothing on, she started to open the buttons on his shirt. He was now becoming more aroused and helped her. He motioned for her to lie on the bed while he removed his trousers. He was still shaking and got one foot caught in his pant leg and fell back on his behind on the bedroom floor. Mina let out a great laugh, remembering him falling a year earlier, the night of George's wedding reception in the barn, when he ran into a beam. He felt just as stupid now as he did then. He was embarrassed but joined Mina in laughter . . . again.

When he got all his clothes off, he slipped under the covers with Mina. As he lay down beside her, he took her into his arms and kissed her. She didn't want to wait; she was aroused and wanted him. They were both virgins and inexperienced. Although she was wet with excitement, it did hurt a little. They both reached climax very quickly. After making love they fell asleep, but not before Mina told Jacob what she wanted for breakfast!

Chapter 20

Jacob's Tragedy

J ACOB AND MINA HAD BEEN trying to have a baby for almost twenty
years. There were pregnancies, but Mina had never been able to
carry a fetus through to a full-term baby. They watched all the
children that were born and raised on the farm. They all grew from
fine, loving, caring youngsters right through to happy adulthood,
having babies of their own. Mina and Jacob participated in helping to
raise them, just like all the adults on the farm had done with Jacob's
raising. Jacob felt he had had the best upbringing. He had been blessed
with many parental figures in his life.

Toward the end of 1886, there was blessed news on the farm. As a
matter of fact, there was a double blessing. Dora finally got pregnant.
They had been wondering for a while if they were ever going to have
a child, just as Mina and Jacob were thinking the same thing about
themselves.

Everyone was so happy for Dora and George. The grandparents-to-be
were just as ecstatic as Dora and George were. Dr. Marsh was so
delighted that he could finally tell Dora and George that she was about
three months along.

Diana wanted to tell her own news, but she let everyone revel in
the happiness around Dora and George. After a couple of weeks, Diana
decided that she would tell everyone that she had been keeping a secret.
She called the family into her house to have tea and dessert one night,
after supper. She said, "Now I know you all are wondering what I

wanted to say. Johnny, please don't take offense that I'm doing it this way. Well, not only am I going to be a grandma, I'm going to be a mother again. Johnny darlin', I'm pregnant too." There was a gasp from everyone. Never in their wildest dreams did anyone expect this news. After all, she was forty-seven years old.

Johnny was so shocked! So was everyone else. As a matter of fact Diana was five months along. Her baby would come about two months before Dora and George's. She had been wearing heavy sweaters and looser clothing. No one had really paid attention to her figure, not even John. She hadn't gained a lot of weight and felt if she told anyone, even John, it would be jinxed. She wasn't taking any risks.

There was so much excitement now. Dora and Diana were so excited they were jumping around, hugging each other. They couldn't help themselves. This was the greatest news in such a long time!

John leapt to his feet and took Diana's hand. He said, "Darlin', remember what Dr. Ian told you about jumping around and getting excited when you were carrying with George?" She stopped.

She said, "Now, m'love, don't worry, I just forgot for a minute. I'll be fine, dear." She went to John and put her arms around his waist. He kissed her on the nose with a very big smile on his face. Just then, Diana let out loud scream, and her water broke. She and everyone else in the room were shocked. She was sure her jumping caused it. She started to cry. She was only five months along. She said, "Johnny, get me to bed now, and get Dr. Marsh. *Please hurry!*" John picked Diana up and carried her upstairs and laid her on their bed. She was crying hysterically, absolutely sure she damaged or killed their baby.

Beulah and Cora were in the house and followed them up the stairs to help any way they could. John yelled for Frank or Gerald to get to town and bring back Ian or Mark. Frank ran to the barn to get a horse and took off to find either Dr. Ian or Dr. Mark.

Diana was crying really hard now. She was so sure she killed or damaged their baby, and now she hoped that John could forgive her. John just thought she was crying with the labor. He sat beside her on the bed and held her. He tried to calm his wife down, saying, "You hush now, and concentrate on tryin' ta keep our little one inside ye. Frank is getting the doc." As he held Diana's hand, she tried to tell him she probably killed or hurt their baby. He didn't want to hear such nonsense.

Diana told John, "Johnny, I'm so sorry, darlin'. This is my entire fault. I'm so sorry. I'm sorry . . ." She cried harder, and another pain came. She felt so guilty about jumping.

John tried to keep her calm. He was sure things would be fine. He said, "Love, it's up to the Lord now. You are not responsible. Please believe me, love!" Diana was still crying. Johnny held her and they started to pray.

Diana let out another yell as Dr. Mark was coming in the house. He called up to her, "All right, woman, I'm coming." Diana and John let out a laugh as he walked through the bedroom door. As he assessed the situation, he told them, "I can't stop the labor, love. It's going too far, and I don't want to chance moving you to the hospital right now. There's no time. We'll have to deliver right here." Diana cried some more. Mark asked John to try and keep her calm.

John stayed with his wife while Beulah and Cora stayed to help in any way they could. The doctor also suggested that if Dora wanted to come in, if it was all right with Diana, she could get an idea what she is in for. Diana nodded and said, "Someone go get her, please?" Cora went to get her.

About two minutes after Dora entered the room, the baby came out. Dora was wide-eyed and nervous about her upcoming delivery.

Dr. Marsh said, "Johnny, Diana, you have a very tiny baby girl here. Now we have to get her and mother to the hospital right away." Gerald had anticipated they would need to get to the hospital since it was way too early for the birth. So he hooked up the horses and wagon, and then he and Frank put the mattress in the wagon, like they did when she gave birth to their son over two decades earlier.

John carried his wife down the stairs as she continued to cry and blame herself. Johnny said, "Now, love, you stop crying. This is not your fault." Mark also told her that her jumping around did not do this. It was just her time, early as it was.

Gerald drove as they rushed Diana and the baby to the hospital. This way, John could sit in the wagon, giving his support to his wife, along with Mark. He was afraid for her. John and Diana looked at each other with tears in their eyes. This felt exactly like the time their son died because he was too premature. This little girl was around the same size as their son.

They both were expecting that she was going to die. The doctor was tending to both patients in the wagon on the way to the hospital. The little one was still miraculously breathing. She was hanging on. Dr. Marsh didn't know how or why, but she was surviving with her tiny lungs. Her parents were praying very hard. They arrived at the hospital, and their little girl was still alive. Was she going to be a fighter?

The next hours and days would tell. Mark rushed the baby into the nursery and told the nurses to tend to Diana and that she was hemorrhaging. John was really scared for his wife and daughter but didn't want to show it to Diana. He didn't want to worry her more than she already was. As the minutes turned into long agonizing hours, both were still alive. God seemed to be answering their prayers! Was this tiny miracle going to make it? Things looked positive over the next several hours as she still hung on for her life.

The evening the baby was born, John went back to the farm, exhausted from worry. He had held Diana as she finally fell asleep. He would not leave until her tears stopped. She was so exhausted. He quietly slipped out of her room after she fell asleep, and he went to the nursery. He looked at his tiny daughter through the glass window. She was so small! Mark told them that she only weighed one pound and fifteen ounces . . . not even two pounds.

John told everyone at home the news. George was very worried about his mother and his new baby sister. Dora tried not to worry about her own child but couldn't help it. It was a natural feeling. As everyone tried to sleep that night, they all prayed.

When John went back to the hospital the next morning, he was told his daughter had made it through the night. Diana was fine but still very upset. As he went into his wife's room, smiling and happy, he asked, "Mama, don't you think we should give our little miracle from God a name?"

Diana was still crying a little. She looked at her husband with tears in her eyes and gave a bit of a smile and nodded. Johnny came and sat down on the bed beside her and gave her a warm, loving hug. Diana knew then that he really didn't blame her for the early birth. They held each other for a moment and then looked into each other's eyes. The love was still there after all this time!

She said, "Johnny, this little one needs a strong name—a name with honor and dignity. My best friend had honor and dignity. She was an incredible lady. John, I thought about Mary and the strength she had to go through everything she did in her life. Our daughter will be our own little Mary. What do you think about Mary Patricia?"

John smiled so happily. "Darlin', I think you picked the perfect name for her. And while she's growing up, we don't have to ever worry about her. With Mary and Jed watching over her, we'll know she'll always be treasured! They would have been so happy for us. I remember how Jed loved children." They looked each other again. Johnny kissed his beautiful Diana, and she rested in his arms for a while without either one of them speaking. Just in love and thanking God!

After a few private moments together in Diana's room, John helped her out of her bed, and they both went to the nursery and watched their daughter. They trusted in the Lord! They both believed if the Lord saw fit to help Little Mary Patricia McDonald survive her first night, she was going to make it. It would be a hard struggle for such a little girl, but she was going to survive.

As the next few days went by, Diana recovered quickly. They were feeling good about their daughter although Little Mary needed the sterile environment, which was scary and intimidating. Diana and John couldn't enter the nursery. Diana would not be able to nurse her own baby because she couldn't suckle. She was too little and the instinct had not developed yet. Diana watched the nurses as they tried to feed Little Mary.

Ian Marsh had joined his son, Mark, on Mary McDonald's case out of love, concern, and respect for his friends. Ian and Mark both knew Diana was pregnant but were keeping her secret for months. She wanted to make sure this baby lived; Ian really wanted this for them too. He knew they wanted more children after George but never knew it would take this long, and at the same time, George himself was about to become a father. John and Diana were happy to have both Dr. Marshes tending to their daughter. Not that they didn't have full confidence in Mark; they just trusted and respected his father for so many years, and he was a dear friend ever since they moved to Chatham. It was wonderful to see them working together to keep their daughter alive.

Both doctors agreed that they wanted Mary to have cow's milk. They felt it was the best for putting on weight. As Diana and John watched at feeding time, the nurses used a glass tube that had a hole in one end and a rubber bulb on the other. It worked on the same principle as a fountain pen. The nurse squeezed the bulb end to let out the air, and then the glass end went into the milk. Then when the bulb was released, the milk was drawn up into the glass shaft. The narrow glass end was then placed in Mary's mouth, and she squeezed the bulb again to release the milk into it. It was very time-consuming to just get a couple of ounces of milk into her, so she had to be fed many times in the day to keep her alive.

Every morning, after recovering and leaving the hospital, Diana would leave the farm very early and go to the hospital to watch their daughter being cared for by the nurses. And after chores, John would make his first visit of the day and sit with Diana for a while, watching through the glass window as they would talk about their hopes and dreams for their family, praying that their daughter would live and grow into a healthy, happy girl.

After about five weeks, Little Mary gained enough weight and strength, and Mark was no longer in fear of her catching germs or infections from people. Diana was finally allowed into the nursery. The nurses showed Diana how to feed her daughter with the glass dropper, and she was to continue this method until Little Mary learned to suckle instinctively. Diana was so thrilled to be able to hold her and feed her after five long weeks of watching through a window for much of each day.

The first time she fed her daughter, John came into the hospital for his first visit of the day. He couldn't find Diana in her usual spot outside the nursery window. As he peered through the window, there was Diana inside, sitting on a chair, feeding Little Mary. John was so overwhelmed with the beauty of this scene that he hoped it stayed in his memory forever. He tapped lightly on the nursery window, and Diana looked up and saw him. She smiled a big smile and saw a tear fall down her Johnny's cheek. She was still so much in love with him that it seemed like there was never a time in their lives that she didn't love him.

After several more weeks of Little Mary living in the hospital, she was finally allowed to go home to the farm, where she would be cared for and loved by everyone there, including Jacob and Mina, who desperately wanted their own miracle.

Dora had continued to have a healthy pregnancy, and she delivered a beautiful baby boy just before Thanksgiving that same year. There were no complications, and everyone was so happy for both George and Dora. Jacob and Mina still waited. Meanwhile, the happy parents announced their son's name would proudly be George Jonathan McDonald Jr. Grandparents Jeffrey and Tina were out at the farm a lot more now. They were so glad to be living so close to their daughter and grandson; Dora would take her son to town often to see them too.

Now almost twenty years after his wedding day, Jacob was losing hope of ever having children. He wanted to carry on the Allen name. He wanted his parents' legacy to continue. He wanted the Kente cloth robe to be passed on. Many times when he was sleepless, he would take the robe out from its place in the drawer of treasures, where it had been for almost a few decades.

In this drawer of treasures was supposed to be keepsakes and mementos that they would collect over the years from their children. It only held the robe his mother made in Africa. He sometimes would silently weep, remembering the stories he heard about the struggles and torture both his mother and father experienced before finally arriving in Canada to safety and freedom.

He wept for his father, who was struck down with a disease that could not be diagnosed.

Remembering that the older Dr. Marsh said they could not find these symptoms in any white people, only Africans, he always feared that he would suffer the same fate as his father. He was lucky that his health was good all these years, but he was told that he could, even if he didn't suffer the symptoms, be carrying the disease and might pass it on to any child he may have.

Some nights Jacob thought that maybe God had this in mind when Mina suffered miscarriages and delivered stillborn babies. Maybe the disease that killed his father, Jed, was the reason they had not been able to have a live birth. Maybe God had it in his mind to not let a child of theirs suffer, like his father had—a child that they so desperately wanted. He thought about this frequently. Jacob and Mina loved each other dearly but had so much more love to give to a baby of their own. They loved *all* of the children on the farm, but to have one of their own would be a godsend!

Six times they were to be devastated in the twenty years since their beautiful wedding ceremony held beside the cemetery where his parents rested. Thinking back to his wedding day, although he knew they were watching from heaven, he wanted to be near them in proximity. It had meant so much to him for the wedding to be there, and Mina understood and agreed to the location. Jacob would spend so much time at their graves through his life, talking to his parents.

Mina and Jacob talked often about the time when she was only eight years old, Jacob taking her hand, pulling her off the swing, and running to the family cemetery. He laid on his stomach and pulled her down beside him. He looked to her, still holding her hand, and started to speak to his parents. He said, "Mama, Papa, I knows y'all knows her 'cause you'se always watchin' from heaven, but I wants ya ta knows sometin'. Dis be Mina, and I'se gonna marry her someday. I'se know y'all likes her likes I does. We's gonna make grandbabies fer ya. I'se gonna make ya proud, I promise."

Mina looked at Jacob, smiled, kissed him on the cheek, jumped up and ran back to the swings, got on one, and started to go back and forth, not having much of a thought, except to swing back and forth in the summer breeze on that swing that Jacob's daddy had hung on that big tree years before. Jacob looked over at her and smiled. He turned back to his parents' grave and said, "I knows you'se listnin'. I'se gonna be happy wit' her. Don't y'all worry 'bout me." He jumped up and ran to push Mina on the swing again.

The birthing records for parents Jacob and Mina Allen were for the most part very tragic events! The first time Mina was pregnant was a wonderfully happy time for all. Doctors Ian and Mark Marsh confirmed it for her. Both doctors were to see her through her different pregnancies and disappointments over the years.

Their first time, everyone was elated with their news. There was going to be another blessed event on the farm once again. Dora and George's baby was going to be about one year old by the time this baby would be born. Jacob hoped they would have a close relationship between their children, like it was between George and himself. Mina continued doing the work on the farm that she always did. Her mother told her it would pass the time but to stop if she felt any pain.

There was no pain, but Mina hadn't told her or anyone that she was bleeding. She thought this was normal. She never asked. One morning Jacob was not feeling well. He had a cold but was still able to work. He slept in a little this particular morning. Mina was up before him. As he started to get dressed, he noticed blood on their sheets. He didn't even take time to dress properly. He pulled up his pants and ran out to the chicken coop, where Mina was, and asked her how long she'd been bleeding.

Mina told him, "Don't you worry now, Jacob. It be okay. I'se sure I'se okay. If you'se worried, we'll ask Mama." Jacob took the chicken feed bag from her and hung it up and took Mina to Diana's house. Beulah would be at work there this time of day, getting the breakfast and baking started for the day. They came through the summer kitchen door, and Beulah turned and saw that Jacob had a worried look on his face.

"What's wrong wit' you? What's wrong, Jacob?" Beulah asked. Mina wasn't sure what the problem was. By this time, Diana had come downstairs dressed to go to school. She asked if everyone was okay. She also saw the worried look on Jacob's face.

She asked, "What's wrong, son? Jacob, is it the baby?"

Jacob said to both mothers, "Mina, she's bleedin'. She says she been bleedin' a few days. We need da doc, don't we?"

Beulah looked worried as Diana said, "Take her into town, Jacob. Tell the doctor everything, and, Mina, you be sure to tell Ian or Mark how long and how bad you've been bleeding and how you've been feeling." Jacob hooked up a carriage and took her quickly into Chatham to doctors Ian and Mark Marsh's office. Ian was in. After the examination, he told them, "There is no baby. There hasn't been for a while. I'm so sorry." Mina didn't understand.

"Did da bleedin' kill it?" she asked through tears.

Dr. Marsh told her, "Well, Mina, I'm sorry, but the bleeding was the baby coming out early. I'm sorry. It came out a few days ago, by my estimation. I'm really very sorry, folks. But you should be able to become pregnant again. You're young, and I'm sure that you and Jacob will have many babies over the years." They were crushed but determined to try again.

In another year, Mina was pregnant again. She and Jacob were a little nervous but prayed.

She was careful not to wear herself out, and if there was a spot of blood, she would tell Jacob and Dr. Marsh.

After five months, all had gone well. They seemed to be over the rough part. They were so happy. They were sure God wouldn't take this one. One morning, Mina woke up with pain. Greater pain than she had ever known. Labor had begun. It was too early. Jacob rang the emergency bell on the porch and then yelled across the yard, "John, he'p, Diana, Beulah, he'p!" John came first. He saw Mina was in pain and mounted a horse. He rode into town to get Ian or Mark. Meanwhile the mothers came to Mina's aid. It was too late. When they put their ears to her abdomen, there were no sounds, no heartbeat. Even without the doctor, they both knew it was to be stillborn.

When Dr. Marsh arrived at the farm, he saw the looks on the women's faces. He knew the truth. He made it official, listening for a heartbeat. His stethoscope didn't lie. There was none. She was still having labor pains, and after another ten minutes, Mina delivered a stillborn child. It was a boy. He was met with many tears.

Jacob buried his son in the family cemetery, close to his parents. Mina did not attend. Jacob buried him with only Diana, John, Beulah, and Frank in attendance. Mina was too distraught to be there. She was sure it was her fault and that she'd never be a mother. What was wrong with her?

Why was God punishing her? What had she done? Was this her fate? All she could do was pray and hope she would be a mother someday.

Once again, it was George Sr. and Dora's turn. Dora and her husband were ecstatic. Nine years after his birth, Dora would give George Jr. a baby sister. She had a problem-free pregnancy, but delivery was a little difficult. The little girl's position was wrong in the womb. She was feet first.

Tina, Diana, and George Sr. waited at the hospital for the arrival. They had left George Jr. at the farm. After a couple of hours, a nurse came to let them know what was going on and tried to reassure them. George looked to his mother, and Diana patted his hand. He also took Tina's hand too.

With a tear in his eye, he said, "I'd like to pray, Mom … uh … Moms." He changed his wording with a look of fear but also of happiness, knowing he was going to be a father again. George, Tina, and Diana, holding hands, recited The Lord Prayer. As they finished, grandfathers Johnny and Jeffrey came into the waiting room. Everyone was glad to see them, and George Sr. was happy to have such a loving family who cared so much about him and his family.

John said, "Don't worry about Georgie, son. He's fine and doesn't know what's happening, just that his mother's fine. I thought it was best not to tell him any more than that." Right then George went to his dad and gave him a hug.

Shortly after that, Mark came out and told the anxious father and grandparents that Dora had given birth to a beautiful, healthy baby girl, and they were both doing fine. George and Dora had chosen the name Ann. There was happiness on the farm again.

It was more than four years before Mina was able to make love again. She had become so depressed. Jacob was patient. He never knew about his father's patience for his mother to be ready, but it was clear—he was his father's son. He loved his wife and she was worth waiting for. While he waited for Mina to be ready, he was always helping out with children on the farm, but mostly George's kids, who were growing like weeds. He always had time for them.

As Jacob would play with George Jr., he thought to himself how lucky George was to have a son to call Junior and a daughter too. He prayed that he would have a son, even if they named him something else other than Jacob; it was the last name, Allen, that was most important. And he thought how lucky George Jr. was to have his sister, even if they were several years apart in age.

Jacob would have loved brothers and sisters, but it was never to be. But when he stopped to think sometimes, he did have a brother—George Sr. Jacob loved George's children, George Jr. and Ann, like they were his own. Although he also loved George's parents, Diana and John, he wished his parents were still with him. But at times, only in his house, he had a feeling he was being watched. There was something peculiar in his parents' house. He felt a presence at times but shrugged it off and never said anything to anybody, except Mina. She felt it once in a while too. She didn't know what to make of it either, so they kept it between themselves. Clearly, there was a strong presence in the Allen house.

When Mina was ready to make love to Jacob again, she became pregnant right away. There should have been joy. Not this time.

There was fear again. They wanted this baby so bad. She could not imagine God taking three children from them while others around them conceived and had healthy babies. It was only three months this time before the blood came. She lost their third child. Jacob and she mourned another loss.

They closed themselves up for some time to share their grief and pray. Mina could not bring herself to go to church for a while, so Jacob stayed home on Sundays too. Reverend Collins understood. They didn't even golf with the family on Sundays. Jacob was looking after his father's gardens, which he held so dear, but he was not working in the potato fields for John. John and Diana understood too and paid him full wages anyway. The two kept to themselves for a few months.

When fall harvest arrived though, Jacob started working again in the fields. He knew John needed all his workers. Mina helped out at Diana and John's place again with meals for the workers and looking after the children. Beulah was happy to have her daughter around once again. She missed her. So did Diana. They missed her laughter and smiles and helping out with the little ones.

Diana often thought if Canada would get into the 1880s and hire black women, Mina would make an excellent elementary schoolteacher; she loved children so. Mina loved school and learning. She always wanted to learn more, and she had a desire to be a teacher herself someday! Diana frowned a bit. She looked up and whispered, "Lord, why does this have to be? Jacob and Mina deserve one of their own. Please, they need your help." She hoped he was listening.

Within the next eleven years there were two more miscarriages. One day, the younger Dr. Marsh, Mark, who was now completely taking over his dad's practice since his full retirement, smiled at her. He said, "Mina, it's happened." She was over three months along this time and excited, but then it was overshadowed by fear once again. He said, "This time, you won't work at all! Your pregnancy will be very special and carefully looked after, just as my father told me that Jacob's mother Mary's pregnancy was. It was as critical as yours is now. Now that being said, I want you to remember Jacob was born healthy and is in the outer office waiting for you!" She smiled at him. That was the most encouraging thing she could ever hear at that moment.

Jacob was very nervously waiting in the outer office. Mark went out to tell him to carefully get her back to the farm and to lay her down and pamper her for the next six months. He said he'd check on her every week, unless he heard she needed him sooner than that. He told them both, "Day or night! I'll be there."

They didn't speak all the way back to the farm. They thought they might jinx it. They just kept smiling at each other. And they prayed! When they pulled the carriage up in front of their house, Beulah ran out to check on them. Jacob grinned and nodded his head. Beulah started to jump up and down but was told by Jacob she could not hug her daughter until she settled down. Mina laughed. Jacob helped her carefully down from the carriage and asked her where she wanted to rest. She asked to rest at Diana's house so she could be with her mother. She was a little afraid to be alone. She wanted someone near her.

Everyone was happy with that since they were just as concerned for her. When supper was ready, the whole table was full for the first time in a long time. There were now fourteen people at the dining room table. Diana and John looked to each other and smiled. They remembered their friends being around this same table for their first planting over thirty years earlier. They could still remember the Lavalles bringing the eight chairs as a gift, matching the six they bought from them. They were both very happy. It was a blessed day on the farm again! Their Jacob might be a father this time.

During the dinner, John asked his grandson, George Jr., "Well, lad, when are you going to be getting married? You know around here we marry young and stay married forever. Is there any lassie you've been thinking about lately?"

George Jr. blushed. "Oh, Grandpa, there's time enough for marriage. I want to go to university and start a career first. I'm going to be a doctor." Everyone stopped talking and looked around the table. He was the first one who ever thought of doing anything other than farming or, for that matter, moving off the family farm.

George Sr. cleared his throat and said, "What's the matter with farming, son?"

John spoke up for George Jr. and turned to George Sr., "George, your mother and I made a promise over thirty years ago in Scotland that our children and all of our grandchildren would have as much education as they wanted and follow their destino." He looked to Diana and she smiled.

John continued, "For those of you who don't know or don't remember the stories, *destino* is the Spanish word for 'destiny.' That was the ship's name which brought Berko and Afua, our Jed and Mary, across the Atlantic from Africa. It was that same ship that brought Grandma and I from Scotland! I wanted to be a doctor and your mother, a teacher. She studied when we came to Canada, and I think she is the best teacher in all these parts, if not all of Canada! She loves her job, and I think that you have to love your job to be truly happy in life. Yes, I wanted to be a doctor, but, I say to all of you now, I am the happiest farmer in the whole country, maybe even the whole world, and I don't regret it for a moment."

As everyone listened, George Sr. spoke up. "Dad, why didn't you tell me you wanted to be a doctor?"

John replied, "I'll ask you the very same question that you asked your son a few minutes ago.

What's the matter with farming, son? A man has to follow the path that God set out before him. For me, that was farming, and to have children to carry on my name and to help them to be the best at whatever they choose to do in life. Tell me, son, did you want to be anything other than a farmer?"

George Sr. thought for a moment and spoke. "No, Dad, I always admired you for being a great farmer, and if I can be half the farmer you are, I'll be proud!"

John smiled and directed his words to his grandson. "Son, if you want to be a doctor, that's what you'll be . . . you just say the word, and your grandma and I are behind you 200 percent."

George Jr. smiled at his grandfather with a tear in his eye. Knowing that he had his grandfather's support meant the world to him. George Jr. then looked to his father, who had a loving fatherly smile and a very large lump in his throat. Dora had listened to the conversation as the others did, and she was touched with the relationship between her son, her husband, and her father-in-law. It was a very beautiful moment she'd never forget. It truly warmed the heart of all who were listening that night. Dora hoped that Jacob and Mina would experience this feeling of love and sincerity someday with their own children.

That was settled over dinner. George McDonald Jr. was going to be a doctor someday. He wanted to go all the way and become a general surgeon. He didn't want to specialize. He felt he could do the most good and help many more people being a general surgeon. When it was time, his high school would be helping with his application to Canada's finest university and medical school, McGill University in Montreal, Quebec. He wanted the best education, and the family happily supported him. He understood that moving to Quebec meant that he had to learn more French.

Ever since grade one, when George and the other students were taught French in Diana's school one hour each week by Mademoiselle Marcin, he loved it—and her! During his eight years at Chatham Public School 101, Mademoiselle Marcin got married and she became Madame D'Orner. George was devastated because he had the biggest crush on her through those years!

George learned more French in high school and wanted to learn even more. Madame D'Orner still taught French in the area, and so Diana would hire her for private lessons at the farm. She would come to the farm twice a week to teach. George's parents would pay for the lessons to prepare him for his move to Montreal. Anyone on the farm, who was interested to learn more, was welcome to join in with the lessons. Windsor and Chatham had a lot of immigrating French people. It was to everyone's advantage to take the lessons.

Although McGill University taught classes in English, George would be moving to Montreal, so he wanted to be able to speak French as fluently as possible to keep up with everyone.

After the excitement of learning about Mina's pregnancy and a wonderful supper, everyone retired to their own houses for the evening. John pulled Diana onto his lap as she was passing by him. She put her arms around his neck, and she kissed him tenderly. She asked, "Darlin', you remember how bad of a time Mary had keeping Jacob inside her, don't ye?" John nodded his head.

They looked at each other with worry. All they could do was wait and pray.

Diana kissed him again, harder this time. Suddenly, John picked up Diana, who was still sitting on his lap, and carried his wife to bed. As John opened her dress and let it fall to the floor, he was impressed, as always, with her beautiful body. Even after three pregnancies and two live births, he loved it, and he loved her. She pulled his suspenders down and unbuttoned his shirt and pulled it off him. They were both getting very excited. John let his trousers fall to the floor as Diana lay on the bed. He kissed her body. As he kissed her tummy and drew circles with his finger around her navel, she giggled. He kissed her abdomen and kept moving upward. His mouth found her breast and her hard nipple. She started to get more excited and quietly moaned. She pulled him on top of her, and he made love to his bonnie lass that night. It had been some time.

Their crazy, busy lives had taken over, and they seemed to have forgotten to smell the roses along the way. It was just as passionate as on their honeymoon. The romance and tenderness was still there. After lying in each other's arms for a time, Diana started to giggle as she picked up her pillow and it came down, right on the top of John's head. He grinned and grabbed his own pillow and the war was on. As both pillows burst and the feathers flew, they looked at each other and laughed. They talked about the first pillow fight they had in that room, about how she had to go to Michael and Eileen's farm to get enough feathers for restuffing both pillows. This time, they had all the feathers they would need; she'd been collecting them for years, just on the chance that a pillow fight might happen again.

Just as the first fight, she left everything as it was and would worry about cleaning it up the next day. Tonight was for them and their love for each other. After the laughter stopped, John put his arms around his wife, kissed her passionately, and he made love to her again. It had been a long time since they made love twice in one night. Afterward, they had the best sleep they'd had in years.

Mina made it to over four months this time, a stillborn daughter, not even one pound. They were more distraught now than ever. Dr. Marsh suggested they stop hoping, and he felt that maybe he should perform a hysterectomy on Mina. She has been having profuse bleeding during her monthly cycles in the last two years, and it was terribly irregular. She even bled during her pregnancies at times. She was too young for menopause. He also thought maybe her uterus may be the problem, and she would not carry a baby to full term, ever. He just didn't know what was wrong and thought she might have a deformed uterus, stopping her from having children, or perhaps a disease he couldn't diagnose or possibly a cervical problem. He told them that the hysterectomy would certainly fix the bleeding problem, but there would be no children. Jacob and Mina wanted some time to think about it. They went home to consider it.

In a few days they went into town to see Mark to give him their decision. He had one patient ahead of them. It was Jenny and Adam White's daughter, Priscilla. She was seven months pregnant. Jacob and Mina were happy for her. She frequented the McDonald farm with her parents as she was growing up and was still welcome, with her new husband, after she wed. Her pregnancy was going so well. She was able to help at the family store, look after her own house, and keep up with the daily baking and cooking, even golf at the farm with everyone else on Sundays after church.

The Sunday golfing after church became a great tradition on the McDonald farm. By now, John had widened the driving range and added a couple of holes and another putting green. This meant that more people could play or practice at one time since the family was getting so big and they all learned to play at an early age. Johnny had cut down a couple of sets of clubs to a size that the children could handle properly.

John was in the process of designing a special hole. Actually it was two holes in one. The family and friends were delighted with the additions and changes he'd made over the years.

Everyone helped him out when they could with the landscaping. Technology had changed for the better over the years, thankfully. Not only with farming equipment, but with lawn care too.

There were now lawn mowers that you could use to cut the grass. It made cutting so much easier. All they had to keep the lawns trimmed in the past were scythes. It took great skill to keep the lawns trimmed to an even length.

Where flat areas were needed, there were heavy rollers. They were pulled by horses, but in the last half of the century, they were replaced by steamrollers. They wished they lived in a climate where they could play year-round. Winters in Chatham were snowy, windy, and cold. Clearly not golfing weather.

John had stayed awake for two nights, designing the challenging double hole. The first one was a double dogleg, 515 yards, par 5. The second would be 150 yards, par 3. If he could pull it off, it would be a better hole than any course around Southern Ontario. He would start the hole at the back of the main property on the north side of the road. Play would continue on the south field. He thought he had a stroke of genius, no pun intended, grinning as he drew his design.

The tee off would be from the back of the property, near where their house was. The first drive would be facing south. First you would have to drive the ball between two rows of trees. The opening in the trees would be only thirty feet. The trees on both sides of the opening were forty- five foot majestic blue spruce trees.

The drive would also have to be strong enough to fly over a two-lane dirt road separating the north and south fields. You might have to wait for the occasional horse and buggy or wagon to pass by. Beyond the road, there was also a water hazard. Just on the other side of the road on the south field, there was a drainage ditch that was five feet across and one and a half feet deep. It ran the whole length of the field, with the exception of an access road on the east end of the property that was used to get the animals and wagons and machinery onto that field. There was a footbridge so players could just walk straight across the drainage ditch without having to walk all the way to the access road.

On the first hole, the par 5, after your ball landed successfully on the south side, there would be a dogleg right, and then there was a dogleg left and onto the green. After completing that hole, there was another one but with a shared green with the previous hole. After finishing the first hole, you then had to walk back about 150 yards north to tee off again. This was the par 3 hole.

The other thing that John thought of was, since there were so many people of different ages, the men's tee off would start 150 yards before the tree line. The women's tee off would be at one hundred yards, and the junior tee off, at fifty yards. He felt this was fair. He was excited about his new hole. He didn't divulge all the secrets of his new double hole. He only told to those who were helping him with the landscaping.

As he thought about the struggle he had of removing all the large rocks and trees out of his field about thirty years earlier, he could have kicked his backside. He wanted them back! They would make great hazards. He had now planned to replace a few of his smaller trees and rocks to make the hole much more challenging. He also thought about adding a sand trap or two.

He let George and Jacob know what he was doing because he needed their help. With the really heavy work of the rocks and trees, he asked a few employees to help too without letting them all in on his completed design.

After it was finished, everyone was thrilled. John was the first one to try the hole, of course. Then it was Diana's turn. John asked Diana, "Would you like to bet with me, like St. Andrews, darlin'?"

She grinned from ear to ear and said, "Later, m'love, after I practice, you scamp." John parred the first hole, and Diana got a double bogey . . . she clearly had to brush up on her playing.

They both bogeyed the par 3 hole. This new hole was enthusiastically played and always would be.

As Jacob and Mina sat in the doctor's waiting room this day, Priscilla was talking to them about the farm and golfing, children, and such. Mina couldn't help it; she started to cry. She was jealous. God help her, she felt horrible, but she was jealous.

The doctor called Priscilla in. After a few minutes she came back out and apologized to Mina for going on so. Mina thanked her and said, "No harm done, chile." They hugged, and as Priscilla left, Mina and Jacob went into the office. They told Mark they wanted to keep trying and didn't want the surgery.

He was glad in a way. He still wanted a child for them too since he enjoyed fatherhood himself. Several years earlier, Dr. Mark and his wife had their own family of three—three girls! They had the first set of triplets in Chatham's history. They were famous! He always thought there was nothing better than being a parent. Even though he didn't have a lot of time to devote to his daughters due to his busy practice, the time he spent with them was quality time! He made every second count and made sure they each knew how special they were to him.

Mina was in her early thirties now, and her tiny body couldn't take much more, let alone her spirit. Mark had a plan. He told them that as soon as they know she is pregnant, she would be admitted to the hospital for the entire duration. They all agreed.

It was another three years before they conceived this time. They didn't even get time to go back to the farm to pack anything after the appointment. Mark took Mina to the hospital right away. She was admitted for the next seven months. It was now 1896. Was this their lucky year? They could only pray and wait.

Mina never lacked visitors. Everyone around the farm came to see her. Her parents were frequent visitors. Beulah would come as often as she could. Jacob was there every day, and Ann was often there too. Diana was there every day after school. She was still teaching in the same school. She had been there for a few decades but still did not want to retire. She loved it and the children so much.

Diana really loved Mina. She'd known her from birth, and she was married to her Jacob. She wanted so much for him to keep his family name going. Jed and Mary deserved that.

After the fifth month, they were hopeful again. Mark told her this is a great sign. She was doing well. She was doing a lot of knitting too. In the few months she was in her "jail," as she called it, the only activity she could do was knit and read. Mina read everything Diana brought her. She read the Bible a few times, and she even read the dictionary!

AND SHE KNIT! Everyone on the farm and almost all of Chatham now would have a pair of socks, a pair of mittens, and a scarf if they wanted it! Everyone was getting a chuckle out of it, but as long as they kept bringing her some wool and she had the patience—and Lord knows she had the time—she just kept knitting until she was into her seventh month.

It was about 2:00 a.m., and she awoke to a pain. She could feel the baby moving slightly, but the pain was more than that. The nurse came to see what was wrong, and she was concerned since it was only her seventh month. She sent a message to Dr. Marsh, who lived close by. He came quickly. He was concerned . . . she was two months early!

After assessing the situation, he had a worried look to his brow and said, "This is it, Mina. This baby wants out now. There is nothing we can do but pray and deliver. I'll send word to the farm for Jacob to come now."

A tear rolled down her face, and he patted her cheek. "We've been really careful Mina. I think we should think positive and let it happen." Her water broke. Mark didn't even want to move her onto the delivery room table. He told the nurse it was going to be delivered right there in her bed.

Mark checked the heartbeat. It was there and it was strong. He smiled and said, "Mina, it sounds good and strong. I'm really hopeful this time, and I think it will be here very soon. He was still listening to the heartbeat as he was talking to her. He paused, and then he listened more carefully, and he held his hand up to quiet her. He kept listening and he smiled again. "Mina, I don't believe it! I can hear two heartbeats now! It sounds like there are two babies in there. You're having twins!" She was shocked. They both laughed. She was excited and couldn't wait to tell Jacob.

When he looked at Mina's abdomen, he could almost see the tiny ones moving around, and it looked like they were fighting for their position to get out. Her labor pains were getting stronger and more frequent.

Mina heard a clamoring in the hall. As Jacob arrived, he sleepily ran down the hall and bumped into a cart that had basins on it. He knocked them over and they all broke. He was upset, but the nurses told him, "Don't worry, Mr. Allen. Your wife needs you, just get in there." They were smiling as they told him. As he entered the room, he could see that she was in hard labor, and Mark was still listening with his stethoscope. Mina smiled at Jacob.

Mina said, "Jacob, come quick before da next pain. Mark, let him listen." Mark had let Mina listen to the heartbeats, and she was so thrilled to hear them. Jacob put the stethoscope on and was listening. He could hear the beats but was surprised to hear so much going on in there. Mina continued, "Jacob, dat's our chil'run you'se listenin' to. We'se havin' two babies." And just as his father before him, he passed out from shock. Things were starting to happen faster now. Mark just let a nurse help revive Jacob, as he was needed more by Mina right now. Mark could see the crown of one of the babies now. The heartbeats were still strong. He knew they would be very small, a couple of pounds, he prayed, at least. That would give them a fighting chance at surviving, God willing.

Jacob had now come to and was by his wife's side. He had no intention of leaving, and Mark understood and approved of his presence. They were excited; this was it. They were finally having a live birth. In a few minutes, they were going to be parents of two babies. Mina let out a scream, and she pushed. The head came out, and another push would bring the shoulders through.

With the head sticking out, the shoulders seemed like they were stuck. Something held them back. Dr. Marsh became worried but tried not to show it on his face. He knew this was the most important thing in the world for Mina and Jacob, and he wanted these babies to be all right. Since the baby was so small he was able to place his hand slightly inside Mina and help.

He could not feel anything that might be hindering the advancement of the birth. He was puzzled but kept trying to feel for some constriction. The head was out, and it had to have its airway cleared. He ordered his nurse to assist. She was able to clear it enough for the first breath. Mark still couldn't feel anything wrong, at first.

He gave a slight tug. The rest of the baby would not budge. He had to do a caesarean section right away. Mina was now starting to bleed profusely. She was bleeding around the baby, half protruding from her body. The nurse gave Mina chloroform to put her to sleep and handed the doctor the scalpel. He now had two more nurses with him, and one took Jacob to the waiting room.

He didn't want to go, but Mark insisted . . . and then he made his incision.

When Mark was able to see what was happening in the womb, he started to tear up. The first baby was still alive, thank God, and the reason he was not advancing was because his umbilical cord was wrapped around the neck of the other baby. She was now dead.

Through his tears, he cut the cord and released the live one so he could finish passing through the birth canal. He handed Jacob and Mina's baby boy to the nurse, and she quickly took over looking after him. He was still breathing. It was labored, but Mark had to make sure this baby lived! The nurse then spoke up. "Dr. Marsh, we've lost the mother!" Mina had died of shock and from loss of blood, compounded by the difficult births.

Jacob was in the waiting room with Diana, John, Frank, and Beulah now. They had followed along behind him when he left the farm. After the delivery was over, Dr. Mark came out of the delivery room. He looked at Jacob. It was going to be bad enough telling him, but now Mina's parents were here too. He took Jacob's hand and said, "You have a very tiny little boy that you have to stay strong for, Jacob. You all need to keep strong for him. He will have to live here at the hospital until he gains weight. He is only two pounds and six ounces. I don't want him to leave the hospital until he is close to four and a half or even five pounds. That may take a couple of months." Diana and John looked at each other, remembering Mark's dad telling them that Little Mary had to stay in the hospital for a few of months too because she was so premature.

Jacob's smile disappeared. Suddenly, he realized that Mark told him he had a son, not *they*, and where was the other twin? He asked and looked to Mark for answers.

Mark started, "Son, the other baby didn't make it. It was a little girl. She weighed about the same as the boy does. And there's more. I'm sorry, Jacob, Beulah, Frank, but Mina is gone too. She started to bleed really bad, and we couldn't stop it. I'm so sorry, Jacob, but Mina lost blood faster than we could start to replenish it. Mina went into shock . . . and . . . she died."

Everyone gathered around Jacob, and they all held each other. They were shocked. Beulah and Frank were devastated; they lost their daughter. They were all shocked. Jacob wiped his nose and said, "Dr. Marsh, I'd like to see my wife, my son, and my daughter, please."

"Jacob, no, you should only go see your son," Mark replied.

Jacob turned to him and said more firmly, "Dr. Marsh, I want to see them all!" Mark reluctantly asked Jacob to come with him. He took him into the room Mina was in. The nurses had her cleaned by now, as well as the baby girl. They had a sheet pulled over their bodies. Dr. Marsh told them, "Pull the sheet back so Mr. Allen can see his wife and daughter." They did. He saw the face of his beautiful wife, now lifeless, and tucked into the crook of her arm was a very tiny baby girl. He would never forget this sight! He asked Mark, "Can I take them back to the farm right away?" Mark told him he could. They were officially declared dead. He could take them both home to be buried.

Jacob decided to let the other four come in and see her one last time, if they wanted to, because he would not have an open coffin at the farm. They all came in. Beulah first, and then Frank, and then Diana and John. They saw the peaceful look on Mina's face and the baby. They cried as they tried to make sense of it all.

The doctor told Jacob and the others that the boy was in the nursery and would be looked after very carefully by everyone in the department. "This baby will live, Jacob. We will do everything in our power, and God willing, your boy will live to be a fine strong man! With all the family you have at the farm, your son will have a happy, normal, healthy life!" He didn't want to explain the entire scenario that transpired in the delivery room to the others. He wasn't sure any of them could handle it at all. If they didn't ask, there was no need to describe it.

He took everyone to the nursery. They all looked through the glass. The nurses were in a huddle around one special small crib. In it was the tiny Allen boy. Mark tapped on the glass and the nurses turned to look. He went through the door and asked if the baby could be shown to his father and grandparents yet. One nurse brought him over to the glass and held him up for everyone, but only for a few minutes. He had to get back to the warming crib. He was so tiny. Tears of grief turned to tears of joy. Jacob smiled at his son. Mark came out and told him he would not be able to hold him until he was bigger. He was disappointed but understood.

Diana walked up behind Jacob and put her arms around him. She softly spoke, "Son, remember how small Little Mary was? How scared we were?"

Jacob looked at Diana and nodded his head. "I remember like it was yesterday."

Diana said, "Remember, my sweet, she weighed less than your son does, and she is a beautiful, happy, healthy girl now."

Jacob smiled back at Diana and whispered in her ear, "Thanks, Mom!" He leaned over and kissed her on the cheek.

As they all stood staring at their new little gift from God, Jacob smiled. He now knew that God had given them two babies for a reason. Their daughter was to stay for eternity with Mina, and he and his parents would raise their son.

He and Mina were afraid to pick a first name for a girl or a boy too soon. They did decide that the middle name would be Jedediah or Mary, to honor his parents. He decided on his son's first name by himself. He felt that Joseph was a good name. After all, it was the name of Jesus's father.

He knew Mina would agree with him. He turned to Beulah, Frank, Diana, and John and said, "Grandmas and Grandpas, I wants y'all to meet Joseph Jedediah Allen, my son!"

Chapter 21

Baby Joseph Comes Home

ITWAS CHRISTMAS EVE 1896 when Jacob brought his son, Joseph, home. He asked Beulah to come to the hospital with him that Saturday morning. She just thought he wanted her to go for a visit, but what he really wanted her to do was hold the baby while he drove back to the farm. The doctor was happy that he could discharge his tiniest patient at such a wonderful time of year.

When Jacob and Mark told her that Joseph was going home, Beulah jumped and hugged Dr. Marsh and gave Jacob the biggest hug and kiss ever. She had never been so happy in her life. She was the first one to hold baby Joseph, other than his daddy, his nurses, and Mark. He asked Mina's mother to be the first one to hold him. He knew it would be so special to her since her daughter passed just over two months earlier. Diana would not be upset or jealous that he chose to do it this way, he knew that.

As they arrived back at the farm, no one paid any attention. Everyone just thought they were coming back from a morning visit with the baby. Jacob pulled the carriage in front of Diana's house because that was the center of life on the farm.

As Beulah walked into Diana's kitchen, holding baby Joseph in her arms, Diana looked at her and dropped her coffee cup on the floor and broke it. She started to cry, "Oh my Lord, he's home! Our baby is finally home! Praise Jesus, he's home!" She kept crying while she went to Beulah to get a better look at him. Little Mary was in the kitchen,

Cora was there, Tina, Dora, her daughter, Ann, and also some of the farmhands' kids. Diana and the kids were all making Christmas cards and decorations. All were excited that Santa would come this night. They got a little loud, and that woke Joseph up right away, and he cried.

He still had a weak cry, but the doctor said his lungs had grown. Jacob told them, "Don't y'all worry, I'se heard him cry loud, you just wait till he's good 'n' mad!" Everyone laughed.

Beulah reluctantly handed Joseph over to Diana. She was still in tears; she couldn't believe he was actually home. Her tears were very mixed on this wonderful morning. She cried for happiness at his homecoming, for Jacob finally having a child of his own to love, but there were sad tears too. Sadness because Jed and Mary could not be here to see their grandson and for the twin girl that didn't make it but, most of all, for baby Joseph's mama, Mina. Those were the saddest tears of all.

Beulah and Diana had talked to Jacob in earlier weeks while they were awaiting Joseph's arrival home, and they both thought that Jacob and Joseph should stay in one of their houses for a few months or take turns from one house to the other. They were excited at the thought. It was just so they could be there to help him out, being that Jacob was alone now. They thought Jacob might not be able to handle the night feedings and changes by himself.

By the time the grandmas had settled down, the men heard Joseph was home, and they all came in the house to see him and wonder at his size. He was a true miracle. Jacob was not looking forward to what he had to tell Beulah and Diana now.

Jacob decided to go ahead and have his talk, even with everyone around, and he was worried he would upset the grandmas. But since he'd been rehearsing it so long, he thought he'd better do it now, while he still had his nerve. He started, "Now you grandmas are gonna be a big part of Joseph's life. As a matter of fact, ya'lls gonna be in his life, everyone that lives here. But I'se gonna take my son and live in my own house. I'se just hopes y'all understand. I made a promise ta Mina in heaven. I'se Joseph's daddy, and I'se the one who be raisin' him the most. I'se know y'all wants ta help, and y'all can. I love everyone here on the farm, and I'se gonna raise my son ta love y'all too. He's gonna have all you folks and kids 'round him. We's all gonna protect him and love him, but he's my son. I'se gotta bring him up in his home.

"Y'all knows I love ya and I love everything y'all has done for me and Mina all the times we thought we was gonna have them other babies. We loved all of ya for your help, but it be my responsibility to raise my son now. I hope ya'll can understand."

There was a sudden silence in the house. Not even the children spoke. Beulah and Diana had some tears, but they tried to hold them back. John came and put his arm around Diana, and he turned to Jacob and said, "Of course we understand, son. Just know we're right here if you need us, and Frank and Beulah are just as close. Don't ever be afraid to ask for help. We all need it sometime.

Sometimes the Lord helps, but that's also why he made grandparents." Everyone laughed, and the tension was broken.

While still holding Joseph, Diana and John, gave Jacob a hug and handed him his son.

Diana kissed Jacob on the cheek and said, "You've made Mina proud, son, and your mama and papa too. We all know you'll be the best daddy you can be." Jacob let a tear roll down his own cheek this time.

Beulah came over to Jacob and wiped his tear with the apron she was still wearing from the morning baking before she went to the hospital, and she kissed her grandson on the forehead. She said, "Yeah, my baby girl would be so proud of ya. We misses her so much, but she be watchin' ya from heaven 'n' she be proud of ya, son!"

Through the day, everyone on the farm spent time with Jacob and Joseph. Everyone got to watch the tiny baby eat from a strange bottle. It was the funniest-looking thing to see. It was a glass bottle that looked like a banana. One end had an opening to pour liquid in. The other end had a type of nipple that slightly resembled a mother's breast nipple.

Joseph was fed Liebig's Soluble Food for Babies. This was a special food for babies who couldn't be fed by breast milk for some reason or another. It was very popular with hospitals, doctors, and parents all over the world. It helped to add weight to babies faster than regular cow's milk. This formula was developed in Germany a few years after Little Mary was born. She didn't reap the benefits of it, unfortunately. It took her longer to gain weight than Joseph.

While baby Joseph was in the hospital, the nurses used these types of bottles with the formula, and Jacob was given bottles and formula to bring home with his son too. It helped Joseph gain weight in the first few months, and his stomach tolerated the mixture well. That was a blessing.

Being bottle-fed was great because anyone could do it. When Jacob was out working on the farm all day, whoever was caring for Joseph would be able to feed him.

John went over to Jacob's house to get the cradle that Diana gave Mary for him so many years earlier. Both cradles that Diana and John had found that first night in the attic of their house had been used for all the babies on the farm. Frank refinished it without Jacob knowing as a surprise. Diana thought he did a beautiful job, so she asked him if he would refinish the other one exactly the same. This was even before anyone knew they may need it for Mina's twins, which, sadly, was not to be.

Jacob and Joseph stayed in Diana's house till late that Christmas Eve, talking and celebrating Joseph's arrival. After a wonderful supper, before long, it was time to get all the children into bed, or Santa Claus would not come.

Everyone said good night to Jacob as he wrapped up Joseph to take him to his house. Frank and Beulah walked the cradle back to his house for him and placed it in his bedroom, right beside his bed. Jacob wanted Joseph close to him.

John and Frank had gone over to Jacob's house earlier in the day to start a fire going for him and took turns tending it through the day till Jacob got there. It was so warm and cozy when he arrived home with his son. He smiled as he walked in.

As he laid Joseph in the cradle beside his bed, he sat beside it, rocking him back and forth, just as he did every night in the hospital after he had been allowed into the nursery. Joseph looked like he was looking at something, but Jacob knew babies did not recognize things at this age. But still, the baby was staring at something behind Jacob. He had that feeling again that he had before, that there was a presence in the house. That feeling that someone was watching. But he was never sure . . . until this very special Christmas Eve.

He turned around to see what Joseph was staring at. There, on the wall, was an outline of a woman, just floating against the wall. He stood up and walked to the wall. This shadow was Mina! He was sure it was her. He could just make out vague facial features, and he knew she was smiling.

She was holding their daughter in the crook of her arm, just the way he last saw her in the hospital after they died. Jacob turned again to look at his son.

Joseph looked like he was still staring in that direction. Jacob turned back to look at the wall Again, and surrounding Mina were Mary and Jed, Jacob's mother and father. They had their arms around Mina and their baby girl. Jacob shook his head, rubbed his eyes and looked up at the shadows. There were a few gusts of wind outside, and as he heard it, he could almost swear that he heard the words, "Jacob, we're always here for you. We'll love you and Joseph forever." He turned back to look at his son in the cradle, and he was sound asleep. He looked back at the wall, and all he saw was the wall. The feeling he and Mina had over the years must have been his parents visiting him and watching over them. Now Mina and their daughter had joined them to watch over him and baby Joseph!

He lay in bed and thought about Mina and their daughter. This would've been the twins' first Christmas. He looked at his son, asleep, and thought about the vision. He wasn't sure whether to share it with anyone or not. As he was slowly drifting off, he thought to himself that he wanted to talk to someone about this, but who?

He remembered when he was growing up a story that John and Diana had told about someone they knew in Scotland called Old Sam. He remembered that Sam thought he saw a dead Earl Beardie, Alexander Lindsay, the 4th Earl of Crawford. The story has been retold for three centuries. He was visiting Glamis Castle, near Diana's family farm. As the story went, while drinking heavily, he wanted to play cards, but his host wouldn't because it was the Sabbath. While very drunk, the earl said he'd play with the devil himself. A knock came to the door, and an unknown visitor came and played cards with the earl. The earl lost and the devil took his soul.

The apparition scared Sam so bad that his hair turned white overnight, and he was never able to go into the McGee barn ever again. Jacob thought, after recalling Diana's story, she would be the one who would understand. He did need to talk to someone about this, he decided. He was a little unnerved in one way, but at the same time, he was comforted by their visit. He would wait a bit though; tomorrow was Christmas Day.

When Dr. Marsh told Jacob a week or so before Christmas Day that he could take Joseph home very soon, Jacob grinned from ear to ear and started planning something but never told the family. He wanted it to be a Christmas surprise, but he went to see Reverend Collins.

There was much hustle and bustle on the farm on Christmas morning. It was Sunday, so this was like every other Sunday. Everyone got up and had breakfast, and they all went to town to attend church services. The church had expanded in size over the decades, and everyone teased that it was to accommodate the McDonald farm clan! The family took it lightheartedly when teased. They saw it as a compliment that they were thought of by so many people in their community.

Diana and John had contributed much money for expansions to the church, as well as the hospital and Diana's schoolhouse. They were happy and proud to be able to do this for their community since their farm was so financially successful!

As Reverend Collins spoke about the Christmas miracle of Jesus's birth, everyone rejoiced with him in song and in prayer. When his sermon was over, he welcomed baby Joseph Allen home. Everyone in the church was so happy to finally see him. They had all prayed so hard for him.

Reverend Collins asked everyone to stay for a few minutes after the service and asked Jacob if he would bring Joseph to the altar. He did. As he turned around to face the congregation, the reverend asked George and Dora McDonald to join him at the altar. They were puzzled but did what they were instructed to do and met Jacob at the altar.

Reverend Collins said, "Jacob asked me about a week ago if I would mind a christening on Christmas Day. I told him I thought that would be a very appropriate day for it. So, folks, can you please stand and, with the help of his godparents, George and Dora McDonald, we will baptize this little miracle from God."

Everyone was so surprised that Jacob arranged the baptism without letting anyone know.

After the reverend said, "I baptize thee, Joseph Jedediah Allen, in the name of the Father, the Son, and the Holy Spirit. Amen," while George and Dora held him, he welcomed this little lamb into the congregation. Although it was unusual to applaud in a church, there was a cheerful welcoming of baby Joseph from the crowd. He was always to be thought of as their own Christmas miracle.

Olde McDonald's Potato Farm was the most profitable farm in Southern Ontario during the first decade of the new century. They had reason to be happy. Their own farm community had grown to include many valued employees, and John and Diana took it upon themselves to build a few more houses on their properties to accommodate workers and their families. As always, they welcomed black families as well as white. There was also an Asian family.

In 1901, Canada mourned the passing of Queen Victoria, like the rest of the world. Her successor was her son, King Edward VII. At this time, Diana included the royal family in her history lessons. She always managed to incorporate the current news of the day in her lessons. She wanted her students to be well-read and knowledgeable of the happenings around them. It was not just local news; she tried to include world events too.

Little Mary married her high school sweetheart, Patrick McNeely. His family moved from Ireland in 1880. They decided on Canada, and the Chatham area, to live. Patrick's father and mother originally moved to Windsor to start a textile plant. There was so much need for various textiles, so they would never be out of work.

They never wanted to live right in Windsor but had to be close to their factory for some time. After Patrick was born, they decided to live partway between Chatham and Windsor. He ended up going to the Chatham High School after public school. That's where Little Mary and Patrick met and fell in love.

Their parents let them get married, and Patrick was happy to join the farm family. Everyone liked him right off. Their family would grow by two within the next few years. Their son Emmett was born in 1903, and Richard was born in 1904. There was excitement and children running around the farm that first decade. It was a joyous time.

Henry Ford manufactured the first motor car, or horseless carriage, as it was first called. It was the newest technology and everyone was thrilled. John saw one in Chatham, and while in Windsor on business with George one day, he immediately went to a dealer to buy one. It was said that you could have this car in any color you like as long as it was black! John was so excited he couldn't wait to get it home to show Diana. He was going to be the first farmer in the Chatham area to own a Model T. When he was finished doing his business and George was done with his business in Windsor, he purchased the Ford. John got George to drive the wagon back to the farm, and he would proudly drive the new car home. John was sure he would be back at the farm long before George, but he didn't take one thing into consideration. John did not know how to drive this horseless carriage. Something he overlooked when the race to get back home was on.

The dealer whom John bought the car from said, "I've got a boy here that can give you the basic lessons, Mr. McDonald." John looked at his feet. The dealer said, "Now don't be embarrassed, McDonald. Most people get a lesson right away, and you'll pick it up quickly. What do you say? Shall I send Ralph out for a bit to show you how it's done?" John was a little flushed, but he nodded. He'd appreciate the lesson.

It took only about a half hour or so for John to learn, and he was very good at it. He drove around Windsor for a while with Ralph and then drove him back to his work and headed down the road to Chatham. He drove cautiously and slowly home. Needless to say, George did beat him back to the farm but did not spoil his dad's surprise. Everyone was waiting, not sure what John was up to or how he was coming home.

When John pulled up to the house, everyone came running. Diana was a little nervous. She had seen these automobiles once or twice in town. Dr. Marsh had one now. It was much faster than horses, and it made sense for a doctor to own one, but a farmer? What was Johnny thinking?

Everyone admired it, and they all wanted to go for rides. John said, "Now I can't take you all out, and if I do, I'll run out of gas for sure. I'll have to get into town to fill the tank again." Chatham had the only filling station for miles around. He continued, "You'll all get turns. You'll just have to be patient!"

On the trip back to the farm, George was thinking that he wanted to buy a motor car too.

As a matter of fact, he thought John would start a trend on the farm. Most families would want to buy one. Although John paid them well, not everyone could afford them. George and Jacob could and Frank and Gerald too. They had been saving money for a long time. Within a couple of months, many of the families went to church on Sunday in their automobiles. The horses tied outside the church were unsure about these noise machines but got used to them. The congregation admired the parking lot after church one day. The McDonalds, the Allens, and the others were proud to show off their new automobiles.

The first decade also brought more property purchases and more potatoes and other crops; and they were starting to breed more Clydesdales, Shetlands, and Angus cows to sell. The younger generation felt they could handle the crops and the animals. George and Jacob were confident they could manage both businesses, and John agreed. Over the past few decades they only bred for local farmers. There was a lot of money in breeding and selling all over the province and maybe even all over Canada. Diana was happy there were more animals around. She missed that part of farming. Her family in Scotland still bred and were very successful.

Whatever they were doing on the farm over the years, they always had time to improve on the driving ranges, build another hole, and keep the putting greens as neat as could be. All were happy with life . . . that is, until the year 1912 came rolling around.

The whole farm was abuzz with excitement. Diana received a letter from her sister Penelope. They were finally coming to Canada for a visit. Everyone was so excited. They were finally going to meet some of Diana and John's family.

Johnny's brothers, Jason and Philip, married Diana's sisters Carol and Penelope in a double Scottish wedding ceremony a year after Diana and John left for Canada. They were sad they couldn't be together, but travel time was too long, and Diana and John could not be away from their new potato farm that long to attend the wedding. Everyone understood.

John's brother Arthur married Elsa, the shy, quiet Cupar librarian, a few years after his brothers married. They were a good match. Arthur was the quiet type too. Their other brother Charles remained a bachelor and enjoyed the company of his male friends. The family knew it and kept it a closely guarded secret.

Diana and John were aunt and uncle to a great many nieces and nephews, even some great-nieces and great-nephews in Scotland. They all received a good education growing up. Diana's sister, Carol, was their schoolteacher. Like Diana, Carol loved teaching.

There was the McDonald potato farm, on which Jason, Carol, and Charles lived. Then there was the McGee Clydesdale, Shetland pony, and Angus beef breeding farm, on which Penelope and Philip and Arthur and Elsa lived. Both families worked at both farms. Everyone learned the business of both farms so they could work wherever they were needed most. This included children. They also employed farmhands. They did not live on either farm, like the farm in Chatham. They all went back and forth each day from their homes.

The trip from Scotland to Canada was in April. Penelope and Philip were going. So were Arthur and Elsa. Jason, Carol, and Charles would stay home to run the family farms this time and maybe would travel to Canada in another year. Charles moved over to the breeding farm to take charge in their absence. He enjoyed the change. There were many hands around to help at both farms. It was spring, and there were births in the barns too. He was quite busy. Due to the colder temperature, plowing and planting was a little later in Scotland than in Canada.

Everything was all arranged and the trip paid for. They were getting excited. They were well- to-do folks by the day's standards and could afford first-class passage on most ships. After consideration, they all decided they would rather take second-class passage on the new White Star Line's RMS *Titanic* on her maiden voyage.

They would travel from Fife to Port Patrick, Scotland, and then they would make their way to Queenstown, Ireland, and stay overnight at a hotel near the docks. They would be right there to board on time Friday, the twelfth. The entire voyage was to be from Wednesday, April 10, to Wednesday of the next week. It would take them into New York, and then they would take another train to Chatham, Ontario. It was planned that their maximum travel time would be about nine days, unlike Diana and Johnny's trip, which took sixty-seven days decades before.

The ship left Southampton, England, before noon that Wednesday morning after a slight problem with another ship in port, breaking loose of its moorings and being swept toward the great ship in the suction. As so many people saw the near collision, some felt there was something ominous now. Fear changed back to excitement quickly as Captain Smith masterfully avoided the collision. There were great cheers again.

She sailed seventy miles, overnight to Cherbourg, France, to pick up their next passengers. Loading the new passengers and their belongings only took about one and a half hours. The port was not accessible to *Titanic* due to the enormity of the ship. She had to anchor in deeper waters, offshore, and have tenders bring the passengers and their luggage to the ship. When all were loaded, the floating palace turned toward Queenstown, Ireland, to pick up their remaining passengers.

The *Titanic* would reach Queenstown the next morning and would again anchor a couple of miles offshore due to the problem of not being able to fit her in their port too. There were White Star tenders here too to bring the passengers to the ship. The McDonald couples went out to the grand ship on the tender *Ireland*. When the tender pulled up to the side of the ship, all were in awe of her sheer size.

After everyone boarded, they set sail. They were expected to be in New York sometime Wednesday, April 17. On Friday they settled into shipboard life as they explored the ship and made friends everywhere.

On Saturday, Diana's sister went to the Marconi Room and paid to have a wireless telegraph sent. Penelope thought she would be funny and addressed the cable to Pete, from Sam, their father's nicknames for them. It read, "Pete: Loving the trip, wish you could see the majesty of this grand ship, having fun. See you in Chatham sometime Wednesday. Lots of love can't wait to see you, Sam."

Adam was kind enough to bring the telegram to Diana when he was coming to the farm to give John a hand with some farm equipment. Diana was so excited to receive it. She just kept reading it over and over again to anyone who listened. John was excited to be seeing two of his brothers. They all were getting on in years, and maybe life would not afford them another opportunity.

The McDonald couples had met some very nice people on the ship when they were exploring. They met some steerage passengers who were moving to America. They knew that steerage passengers were not to mingle with the other classes and were to stay in their part of the ship. The four, however, were welcomed below to join them. On the Saturday night, instead of going to one of the fancier, extravagant parties, they were invited by their new steerage friends to go and join their party.

Both couples agreed. They were welcomed warmly and were more at ease with these folks than they were with the second—and first-class snobbery. They played cards, sang, and danced through the evening and had a wonderful time.

By the time Sunday, April 14, came along, they had been on board the floating palace two whole days. There were no regrets about taking second-class passage on this magnificent ship. It was a wonderful experience traveling on this maiden voyage of the grandest ship afloat. There were church services on board, which most people attended, and the McDonalds were no different.

It was turning out to be a beautiful but chilly day. They were supposed to be in New York by Wednesday morning but heard a rumor that Captain Smith had ordered the last few boilers lit for more power. This would speed up the ship and maybe would bring them in to New York by Tuesday. If this were the case, the couples would get a hotel room and wait until Wednesday to travel to Chatham.

After supper on Sunday night, the two couples decided they would play bridge for the evening. After playing for two hours, the couples said their good nights to each other and retired to their staterooms at about 10:30 p.m. They all were having such a good time on board; they didn't want it to end. They started off to sleep, not knowing what was in store for them that night.

It was flat, calm water on the ocean that Sunday night. *Unfortunately,* there wasn't even a ripple to be seen. At 11:40 p.m. the lookout, Fredrick Fleet, rang the ship's bell three times. He picked up the phone and was asked by the bridge, "What did you see?"

Fredrick shouted into the phone, "Iceberg, right ahead." First Officer Murdoch was on the bridge, and he ordered the ship, "Hard astarboard, stop. Full speed astern," closing the watertight doors at the same time.

It felt like an hour before the men in the crow's nest and on the bridge actually saw and felt the ship making a slight turn to the left. All on the bridge and the crow's nest thought they had dodged this bullet.

Sadly, they did not. Captain Smith came to the bridge to find out what happened and asked the designer of the ship, Thomas Andrews, and the carpenter to sound the ship. Andrews came back to the captain to make his report. This unsinkable behemoth was going to do just that—sink!

The McDonalds were woken up by their steward and were asked to put warm clothes and life jackets on and go up on deck. When they heard what was wrong and that the women and children were being loaded into the lifeboats, they thought of their friends down below. Jason and Philip told Penelope and Elsa they were going to go downstairs and get their friends to come up.

They told Penelope and Elsa to get into a lifeboat, and they'd find them later and that there was nothing to worry about. The ladies didn't want to be separated from their husbands, so both wives went with them below deck to look for their friends.

Once they got down to steerage, they got lost in the crowd. There was panic down there.

The wives got separated from their husbands, and there was much time spent trying to find each other. When the rest of steerage was allowed to go up on deck, it was too late. The lifeboats were all away. It was here that the McDonald brothers found their wives finally. It was every man for himself as Captain Smith gave his last order. The *Titanic* sank at 2:20 a.m. on Monday, April 15, 1912, taking Philip, Penelope, Arthur, and Elsa McDonald with it.

Diana and John woke up to the news early Monday morning. Diana had to get to the school, but when all of the children came, she planned to dismiss them and get into town to get more news. She was met at the school by Tina, who had also heard the news and anticipated her help may be needed at the school to relieve Diana. She offered to take the students for the next couple of days, until Diana could find out about their family members.

Diana was grateful to Tina, who was always there for her in emergencies. John stayed with Diana. They drove into town to the newspaper office to wait for news. The whole world was waking up to the horrifying news; fifteen hundred men, women, and children died when the unsinkable *Titanic* went to the bottom of the sea. The survivor names were slowly coming into newspaper offices around the globe from the sole rescue ship, *Carpathia*. There were 705 survivors. When the names were sent, there were no McDonalds on this survivor list. Diana wept with John. She still had Penelope's telegram from Saturday in her pocket. She kept taking it out and reading it and crying.

In the weeks following, people were told to go to Halifax, Nova Scotia, where they were taking dead bodies for identification. Diana and John went. They were able to identify Johnny's two brothers and Penelope. They had never seen Elsa before, so she was never identified. Her kin all lived in Scotland and could not come to Halifax. Diana felt this was tragic, but there was no way they could know what body was hers or if it was even in Halifax. She was likely buried in the *Titanic* cemetery in Halifax in a nameless grave or lost at sea.

Diana wired her family in Scotland, and there were lots of tears on both sides of the Atlantic.

Diana thought their brothers and sister would want to go home to be buried. She and Johnny made arrangements to have their bodies cremated and the ashes sent back to Scotland, back to their home, to be interred in the Cupar church kirkyard, the church where they all were baptized, wed, and their own parents were buried. Diana was beside herself. She never got to see her sister, and Johnny, his two brothers.

Johnny and Diana were distraught. All the family in Chatham and in Scotland took it hard. After the ashes arrived in Scotland, Diana and John got a telegram that they received them and their internments would be the next day.

Life on the farm was sad for everyone for some time. The plowing and planting of the potatoes were being done. It was that time of year once again. George and Jacob were keeping all the work on schedule. They were not going to let the business suffer while John and Diana were preoccupied with the tragedy. They worked hard to keep things going smoothly. John and Diana were over seventy years old by this time. John was showing it so much since he lost his brothers. Diana was aging gracefully, even with the tragedy of losing her sister.

One day, while John was in the barn, he was not thinking of what he was doing. He was smoking his pipe and not paying attention; he tossed his match down without blowing it out. The dry straw caught fire, and within minutes there was a blaze, and he couldn't get out. By the time the Chatham fire brigade got there, Johnny McDonald was dead of smoke inhalation, and his body was badly burned.

Dr. Marsh found out where the fire was, and he followed the firemen to the McDonald farm. He saw Diana, and the doctor asked her if anyone was inside. She looked up at him with tears and said, "My Johnny, Mark, my Johnny."

Mark hugged her, knowing if John was in there, he wasn't coming out alive. He said, "He's in the Lord's hands now, Diana." He hesitated for a moment and continued. "You know I have to stay to pronounce him dead when they bring him out. I think you should go in the house and take the ladies and children with you. It will be a terrible sight, and I'm sure you don't want to remember him this way, my dear friend."

Diana nodded her head. She went around and told everyone to go inside until Mark said it was okay to come out again. She never told them why. She asked Jacob if he would go into town to see if Adam had a coffin she could buy right away. Jacob didn't want to leave, but he quickly got in his car and raced to town.

When he got to Adam's, he was in tears. Adam rushed to him and asked, "What's wrong, Jacob?"

"We needs us a coffin, Adam. Johnny died in the barn. It's burnin' ta da ground. Diana asked me to come to you." Adam was in shock.

Adam White sadly said, "Yeah, I got one for him. Let's load it on my wagon. We'll go over and tell Jeff and Tina about it before we head out to the farm."

Tina and Jeff were in shock too. They couldn't believe their best friend was dead. They went to the farm to see what they could do, if anything. As they drove to the farm, they noticed that Eileen was there. She saw the fire, and she and Toby got there as quickly as they could. Michael had passed away the year before, so she had Toby and his family living with her. They were running the chicken farm still. Dr. Marsh insisted Tina go inside to be with Diana.

The men were still outside helping the firemen put the fire out, and the women and children were all inside, like Mark asked. Jeff and Adam were now helping too. Diana sat in her rocking chair, staring into space. George and Jacob were in the house with her; Little Mary too. Her children surrounded her and were speechless too. They preferred to stay with their mom right now.

Outside, the men were able to get Johnny's body out. It was burned beyond recognition. They knew it was him; he was the only the one missing. They recognized what was left of his clothing. It was him.

Mark asked the men, "Adam, Jeff, can you get a few guys to help get the coffin over here. I want him put in right away, and I want it nailed shut right away. I don't want anyone to see him this way, especially Diana." They agreed.

Mark asked the farmhands to nail the coffin shut; and he, Jeff, and Adam went into the house to see how Diana was. She was calm, but when she found out they were sealing the coffin, she jumped up and demanded that they stop. Mark just thought she did not want to let go yet.

Little Mary said to the doctor, "Dr. Marsh, she needs to put half of her marriage kerchief in with him." They explained the tradition, so Mark went out to tell the guys to open it up for a few moments. George went up to his parents' bedroom and retrieved the kerchief and brought it to his mom. She took the scissors out of her sewing basket and cut it in half.

She said to Dr. Marsh, "I'd appreciate it if you would place this in the coffin on his chest, please, Mark. I can't bear to see him, and if I can't, I don't want anyone else to see him either." Mark nodded and took the half of the marriage kerchief and placed it on John's chest, over his heart, and the coffin was sealed again for the last time.

She now had to plan her Johnny's funeral. She asked someone, she didn't remember who, to go into town and bring back Reverend Collins. She wanted him buried the next day. She wanted to hold a wake for him that evening. Several of the people from the farm went to spread the word and invite people to join them at the farm in saying good-bye to John McDonald. His wake and funeral were very well attended. Diana was pleased that she had taken a page out of Jed's book, and had a grand celebration of John's life.

He was buried in the family cemetery the next day. Over the years, John and Diana had replaced the old wooden monuments they placed for their loved ones with granite ones. They were so beautiful and were admired by everyone. Johnny McDonald's would be a truly magnificent, fitting monument honoring him. Diana would see to it! They had kept careful records of who were buried, their dates, and where they were buried. They knew they would eventually have to clear some more land someday to accommodate the McDonald and Allen families as they grew from generation to generation. The farm family patriarch was now resting in peace, nearby where Diana could still see him every day.

By the time fall came around that year, Jacob's son, Joseph, had fallen in love. Marteen Hunt was the first lady doctor to ever work in the Chatham area. She was also black; she studied in Toronto and was top of her class. She wanted to set up a practice in Southern Ontario. She hoped she would be accepted. People had funny notions about professional women. She was confident that her color would not be a hindrance, especially in Canada. Dr. Mark Marsh was getting on in years, and he recruited her to share his office and practice. She was delighted. She accepted right away and moved to Chatham.

Mark owned his own house, and the flat above the office was empty. He let Marteen move into it. He told her there were lots of black folks around who may feel more comfortable with her, but she didn't want the white folks to stay away from her. Mark said, "I don't think you'll have that problem here. Folks will see you for what you are—a very good doctor. I'm sure of it." She was relieved. He continued with his advice. He asked her if she had any savings. She said she had. He told her, "You probably will need to buy a car. We do a lot of house calls here, and you'll need to get around. Can you afford one?"

Marteen said, "I've been looking into that, it's funny you mentioned it. I thought I should buy one right away. I know that the Ford is popular, but I've looked into another company. As a matter of fact, it is right here in Chatham—the Gray-Dort Motor Company. I've looked at their Model 4 roadster. I can afford it, but I had a problem."

Mark said, "Yes, they are a good company and a decent car, but you'll never convince me that it could even come close to Henry Ford's machine, my dear. Now what was the problem that you came across?"

She said, "The dealer has refused to sell me one. I told him I'm a doctor, and I need a car, and I like theirs. I don't know if it's the fact I'm a lady doctor or black. What do you think?" Mark was nodding his head.

He said, "I know them there. They are a little on the, shall we say, the light side." She understood. He had a solution. He continued, "How about, if that is the car you really want, you let me buy it, and I'll sell it right over to you?"

She thought for a moment and said, "But they know I'll be working with you. I think they'll know it is for me." He had to agree.

He said, "Don't you worry, you'll have the car you want inside of a week, I promise you that!" Marteen was so happy. She felt so blessed to know someone who cared about her so much. After all, she had just moved here a few days earlier, and she would soon find out that there was a large farm outside of town, and there were a bunch of people she'd never forget. She found them to be the kindest, most down-to-earth, friendliest people she would ever meet in her lifetime.

The first time Marteen met Joseph Allen, she was just as smitten as he was. She had the most beautiful eyes Joseph had ever seen, and she thought he had the sweetest smile. From that day, they were in love.

When Joseph proposed to her, he was only sixteen years old but mature beyond his age. Marteen was over twenty. There was a bit of a scandal about it, but it didn't bother the McDonalds or the Allens. The couple dealt with the rumors, and by the end of that year, the two were married.

The wedding of Joseph and Dr. Marteen Hunt was a lovely one. As most weddings in the Family, this one was held at the farm. The family celebration barn, which was used for so many occasions and came to be known over the decades as McDonald Hall, would once again have its interior painted and made ready for another wedding.

While plans were being made, she became busier, and people got to know her, driving around in her Gray-Dort Model 4 roadster. Adam White was the one who Dr. Mark got to purchase it for her. She still couldn't believe she had moved to a place that was so friendly and caring, with the exception of a rare few. She was so happy that life brought her to this town. She had many blessings, unlike her parents and grandparents who were slaves.

Diana asked Jacob if he thought Marteen might like to wear the Kente robe for her wedding. Jacob thought it was a good idea. So one day, when he was working with Joseph, he asked, "Son, do ya tink Marteen would like ta wear the robe your grandmother made for the wedding? She's welcome to use it. After all, it be yours when I pass on."

Joseph smiled at his dad. He thought this was a wonderful idea too. The next time Marteen came to the farm, he told her about the robe and she tried it on. Diana had to make a couple of minor adjustments to it, but it looked beautiful on her. Joseph was very proud that she wanted to wear it; Jacob and Diana too. She came to learn that the woman who made it, Joseph's grandmother, was a tortured slave too.

They were going to build another house, but Joseph's father decided that he would move into Diana's house, and Joseph and Marteen could move into Jed and Mary's house. Diana was pleased. Her house was a little lonely, even with Ann, Little Mary, and her family living with her. It was going to be nice to have Jacob home again.

He was a bit sad to be leaving his ghosts behind. His parents, Mina, and his daughter visited him at times over the years. He was wondering if they would leave that house and follow him to Diana's or if they would stay there for the next generation to see. He also considered that there was the possibility they might leave forever. It was time for him to move on and let Joseph have the house—lock, stock, ghosts, and all.

Marty, or Dr. Marty, as she was known around the area now, didn't mind moving to the farm. She loved and was honored to be welcomed by the big family community she was now a part of.

─────────── *Chapter 22* ───────────

The First War Years, 1913–1918

A FTER THE HUMAN LOSSES THAT the McDonald farm suffered the year before, things were rough for a time. The patriarch, Johnny McDonald, tragically died in the barn fire. There was the further pain of losing Diana's sister and John's two brothers and a sister-in-law in the sinking of the *Titanic*. It was a lot for Diana and the family to bear. But there was more to come.

On March 21, 1913, there was a storm. The temperature had been unseasonably warm. So much so that the plowing was started early. As the winds blew in that day, there were gusts of over 100 mph. Everyone who was around at the time was very nervous, remembering the devastation the tornado at the end of the 1850s left. The "big one" where the town lost their beloved friends and merchants, Rene and Emilie Lavalle.

Fortunately, this time it wasn't a twister, just high winds and lots of thunder, lightning, and rain. The damage, for the most part, at the farm were several trees being uprooted and the frame of a new building on their property being blown down. Other neighbors lost some barns—animals were injured and a few were killed—and a few houses had trees in their attics. There was no loss of life, thank the Lord! Everyone pulled together to help each other rebuild once again.

Diana thought she would throw a good ol' barn dance one Saturday night, later in the spring, in McDonald Hall. It was a chance for all friends, family, and neighbors to get together and say thanks to each other for saving and rebuilding their community. The party was well attended; it went on so long that most people didn't get much sleep before church. They all had a good time that night though.

Diana still relied on God and her Bible to get her through her days and nights. Nineteen thirteen was her final year in teaching. She had been teaching at the schoolhouse down the road from her farm for about fifty years, give or take. She was teaching beyond customary retirement age. She was seventy-three years old, and she wanted to retire from teaching to spend her days taking over as much of running the farm, in her Johnny's memory. She had her boys, George and Jacob, to help her; and all the families around her were a great support for her too.

From 1914 to 1918, time stood still for some. There was a war in Europe. Those years were a lifetime to those who lost their loved ones. Canada, being under British rule, had to participate in this Great War. Men were needed overseas. Many fine boys from Chatham and Windsor joined in and were part of the 620,000 Canadians that were shipped across the Atlantic to a war that wasn't theirs. On the McDonald farm, there were a few boys from the families who lived there that were sent.

Although they left proudly to serve their king as part of the British forces, they were never to return. In the Allen family, the only one that was within the appropriate age group was Joseph Allen. Canada was not sending black troops at that time. He remained on the farm.

In the McDonald family, Diana had to let her grandson George Jr. go. His skills as a fine surgeon were needed desperately. Diana was upset at the thought of losing him to Europe and his possible death. His mother and father were equally concerned, but he had to go. They were in desperate need of qualified surgeons, and he was one of the best. Diana thought back to George's talk at dinner one night, years earlier. He and his grandfather and father talked about him becoming a surgeon. Maybe God would spare him, as they now all thought, the day he left for his posting in France.

When George attended McGill University, he followed his dream! Just like his late grandfather, Johnny, told him to do that night at supper. He proved to be highly intelligent and it showed. He quickly graduated top of his class. He was Dr. George McDonald. The next couple of years, he continued to study more to become a highly skilled general surgeon just before the turn of the century. Everyone was so proud of him. Fortunately his grandpa had been around to see it all happen before he died. That meant a lot to George Jr.

After Dr. McDonald became a surgeon, he was offered jobs all across Quebec and Ontario by hospitals wanting to bring him on to their staff. There were two offers he found quite amusing. They both arrived in the mail the same day. He was offered a position on the surgical staff of Royal Victoria Hospital in Montreal, Quebec, and Royal Victoria Hospital in Barrie, Ontario. Although the Barrie hospital was very small, both were prestigious invitations. They both needed a surgeon to join their staff. He was honored. There were other offers too. They had come from London, Ontario; Quebec City; Toronto General; and a couple of smaller town hospitals as well. But right at the moment, he needed a break before making up his mind. He wrote to all the hospitals with their offers to say thank you and told them he would decide within a month.

When Diana heard this, she was shocked. How could he study so hard, so long, only to take a month to decide where he would practice. She telephoned him in Montreal and grandmotherly tore a strip off him. She'd never been so disappointed. He took her wrath, and then she handed the telephone to his grandfather. John said to him, "Have fun, boy. Don't mind grandma now. You know what she's like! Join us within the month if you can!" With that he hung up the phone, and Diana remembered this conversation and didn't speak to John for two days. Georgie's dad, George Sr., was on John's side, and so was Dora, to be honest. They agreed that he'd worked so hard; he could use a break to decide the course of his life.

George Jr.'s sister, Ann, was working on getting into the medical profession. She was studying at Guelph University, in Ontario. Being on a farm all her life, she loved animals. Ann was on her way to becoming a veterinarian. She was at the top of her class, as George had been in his! Everyone was so proud of her also.

George really did know what he wanted to do with himself for that monthlong break. Some friends took him out a few times in the past several years. They ended up in brothels while he went home to study. He was so busy becoming a doctor he forgot he was still a virgin. That was his real reason for time off. He wanted to partake of as much female flesh as he could handle.

Not always staying in Montreal, he traveled around to other cities too. He even went into Toronto but didn't let the family know he was there. They would not approve of his drunken nights of carousing with prostitutes. He had finally found out what he was missing. His chums told him about their sexual escapades during school. He had lied to his friends, telling them about his prowess during school. In fact, his stories sounded so good he had to go out and experience them when school was all finished.

When it was time to straighten up, he disentangled himself from the lifestyle he'd been keeping and went home to Chatham. He didn't tell anyone he was coming. It was a surprise for all.

George and Dora saw him first. His mom and dad were so elated to see him. Little Mary and her family were there too. She was thrilled to see her nephew. They always laughed about her being his aunt, but the truth was, they were born a couple of months apart. Ann was away at school, so she missed seeing him. Jacob saw a vehicle in the yard and was curious. He came to see who it was. He and George Jr. stood for a moment, looking at each other. They didn't realize how much they missed each other.

They hugged and held each other for a moment. George was happy to see Jacob and Joseph too. George was amazed at how much the two-pound baby had grown while he was away at university and medical school in Montreal.

George had arrived early in the morning, when everyone was waking up, and he really was glad to be home. It was summer, and that meant a very busy time on the farm. George said he'd help out any way he could but wanted to take the clubs out and hit a few on the driving range and see what he could do on the par 5 / par 3 hole. He missed golfing while away at school. He had little personal time over the past several years and was sure he was quite rusty!

When his grandma saw him, she just glared at him. He ran up to her and picked her up off the floor, swung her around, and kissed her on the cheek. She couldn't help herself; Diana started to smile and laugh. She told George she missed him. He told them he could only stay a week or so because he had to report to his new job in two weeks. Everyone held their breath. Which hospital did he choose? He put his grandmother back on the ground, put his arms around his parents, and said, "You know, folks, it really isn't that long of a drive from Chatham to Toronto for visits!" There was a cheer; they hoped he would stay in Ontario but were even happier that he was going to be that close to home. Dora and Diana cried tears of joy. His grandpa had a lump in his throat this time. John was so proud of his grandson.

When everyone found out Georgie was home, they were all glad to see him. Beulah and Cora always felt close to him too since he was born. He wasn't considered just one of the kids on the farm; he was the first, the eldest of all the children, with so many parents to love him.

George Jr. pitched in with farm chores every day while he was visiting. He enjoyed the change of activities. His grandpa said with a teasing grin, "I didn't realize that becoming a surgeon would put weight on, m'boy."

George blushed. "All right, Grandpa, we just don't have the time to eat properly while studying, and there certainly is no time for exercise or, unfortunately, golf!"

George Sr. smiled too as he spoke to his son. "I think some time here and we can trim some of the excess weight off."

George Jr. blushed again. "Dad, really, I'm healthy. I'm only about fifteen pounds heavier than I should be. I'll lose it when I can eat properly and can get some exercise." His mind went in the direction of women again. That's the exercise he was wanting.

They made time to golf most of the afternoons George was home. He did need practice. On the par 5 hole, the first day, he embarrassingly got a double bogey, the same score his grandmother had the first time she tried the hole. They all chuckled and teased that he should have tried it from the women's tee or even the junior tee. By the time he left, he was one under par, and pleased with himself, on the hole.

As he left on the Friday, they all watched as he drove away and headed for Toronto General Hospital and his new career. He had to go to Toronto a few days early to see about a place to live before Monday. If nothing was available, maybe he could use a hotel or residence for a short time. He just wanted to get settled and ready for work. But after a few years of being a successful surgeon at Toronto General, he was now called upon to go to war. He knew what for but hoped he was too old! Sometimes he wished he wasn't so skilled. He knew surgeons were desperately needed, even at his age. It seemed like only a moment from the time he was notified until he arrived in France, where many battles were to be fought. His grandma was scared for the first time in her life. Her firstborn grandchild was going to war.

He was stationed in Le Treport, France. It was a town that was about twenty miles northeast of Dieppe, a town that would become well-known in another war. There were several hospitals around Le Treport that were started up over the course of the war. He was stationed in Le Treport, at No. 3 General Hospital; it had begun operation in November 1914. When George was commissioned, he not only held the rank of major in the British forces but was also appointed chief of staff at this new hospital.

There was just one commanding officer who presided over all the military staff in the town. He would make his rounds of the hospitals weekly, and there were also scheduled meetings each week, which included all the chiefs of staff from all the hospitals.

Before he got there, George knew his surgeries would have to be done faster than he was used to, and he had to try to save as many lives as he could. He would find that a hospital in a battle zone was going to be constantly busy, and he would not get sleep or food on a regular basis. He also had to always be aware of his own health and the health of his staff, making sure to avoid dysentery and other diseases circulating among the troops. George was closing many wounds and had a lot of chest surgeries coming in. It seemed to be the most common spot on the body to get damaged. There were too many amputations to keep count of. After nearby battles, there were always mountains of limbs outside the hospital doors, waiting to be buried when there was time.

Sometimes, he thought the worst things he saw were the men who were gassed. Some of them, he thought, might have been better if they'd died in their trench. Nineteen fourteen started with the French developing tear gas grenades. By 1915 the Germans developed the chlorine gas bomb, but the worst would be in 1917, when the war saw mustard gas!

First, you would see the soldier's skin blister, and it would turn to a mustard color. Next came eye damage, which would end with sticky eyes and blindness. All the while, vomiting persisted.

Mustard gas caused internal and external bleeding and always found its way to the bronchial tubes to strip the mucous membrane off. After that, the pain was extreme, and most of the time the soldier was strapped down until he died within four or five weeks. This, George found the most unpleasant part of his medical military career and would never forget as long as he lived.

Canada in 1914 had a drought, and the economy was in poor shape for most. Especially for the wheat farmers. The potatoes remained a strong, healthy crop for the McDonald farm. They improved on the irrigation scheme that Jed Allen created in 1859 by utilizing the Thames River, which flowed through their property. Diana worried about a potato famine possibly happening. John had always kept up on this and taught the boys and hands how to deal with the crops so they would be healthy. Jacob and George assured her the crops were healthy. She would tell them about the famines in Europe and the British Isles. John had mentioned it on many occasions too. The boys listened and learned well.

In 1915 there were fifty thousand Canadians who were put out of their jobs. The railway business across Canada practically went under due a to huge debt. Worldwide, many countries were in debt due to the cost of the war. Canada's government had to recover from their debt load. They sold Victory Bonds, which generated almost two billion dollars. Many were bought by Diana and her family and their farm community.

Important news at the time included that in 1917. Robert Borden, Canada's prime minister, implemented another way for his government to pay for the war. There was the income war tax. Businesses and individuals had to report all income, which the government taxed, and when they collected it, the government could possibly start to recover.

Not only was the war on in Europe; 1917 also saw the Russian Revolution. Czar Nicholas II was forced into abdication, and he and his family were virtually kidnapped and held in an undisclosed location. The leader of the Bolsheviks, Vladimir Lenin, ordered the family executed in 1918.

In 1918 the world also watched in fear as Spain had an outbreak of a terrible strain of flu. It was first seen in the United States—soldiers going home took it with them. But the most serious outbreak started in Spain. There it got its name. It was quickly spread across Europe and Russia, and when more boys were shipped home, they would carry it through all the reaches of North America.

Olde McDonald's Potato Farm still showed a profit through the war years. Not as great as peace time brought them, but they certainly were still making money. George and Jacob were the ones to thank for this. They had learned so much from John. Diana was pleased with the way things were going. In 1917 the boys asked Diana to consider a purchase. Henry Ford and his son Edsel made a business move. They formed a company called Fordson. This company mass-produced the first farm tractor, the Fordson Model F.

There were shortages in manpower in the agriculture sector due to the men and boys going to war. Henry Ford capitalized on this by manufacturing a lightweight, frameless tractor. It ran by a vaporizer-fed engine, and there were four metal wheels. It could replace many workers, and they could keep up with the plowing, planting, and harvesting while being short on manpower. Diana agreed to it very quickly. After she and the boys went over the books, they were certain they had enough money to comfortably purchase two tractors. They turned out to be a godsend for them.

It could pull plows and discs and replace mules, horses, and ponies; and you could run it all day without it getting tired. It only needed to be refueled once in a while. It came with its problems, they were to discover. In the cold weather, it was a hard engine to start. The oil congealed on the cylinder walls and clutch. It had to be cranked by hand to fire it up. The other thing that happened sometimes, if you weren't careful and did not handle it properly, was that it would rear up and roll over. The McDonalds were to discover this about three months after the tractors were purchased.

One of the hired hands wanted to try the tractor for himself. He did it without permission and took it into the field without letting anyone know. About a half hour after he was supposed to be in for lunch, Jacob felt there was something wrong. Mickey, a hired hand, did not come in for lunch. Jacob and George went to the field. As they looked toward the field, they saw the tractor had upended, but they couldn't see Mickey. They ran toward the tractor and spotted Mickey crushed underneath the weight of it. His legs and chest were crushed. He was just barely alive when they found him. As George yelled for people to come and help, Mickey took a final breath. He couldn't have been saved.

Diana was horrified. Mickey was a sweet boy who lived in Chatham with his mother. His father ran off when he was born, and his mother was crippled. He was her source of income. Diana told George and Jacob that she was going to compensate Mickey's mom. The three of them went to town with the body of her son. They made sure she had everything she needed, and Diana helped her make funeral arrangements. Mickey's mother was so devoted to her son she lost the will to live and died three months later. Diana saw to her funeral too.

The end of the war finally came when nations signed the armistice agreement on November 11, 1918, at 11:00 a.m. Everyone was going home—all except for Dr. George McDonald. He sent word to his family not to expect him home too soon. After almost four years of extremely exhausting surgery in unbearable conditions, he told them he was going out to tour a bit and see where these battles were fought and maybe try and figure out why all these soldiers had to die.

What was it all about? He didn't know if he would ever have an answer.

He thought back to when he had visited France only a couple of years earlier on a furlough. He started not to feel. He was almost mechanical. Surgery came so easily he could do it in his sleep. It reminded him of Henry Ford's assembly line.

He was awarded the 1914–1915 Star by his commanding officer. It was also known as Mons Star, a British and Commonwealth medal given to officers who showed leadership and bravery and who were in active duty during those years and gave their services.

Major McDonald proved to be a great leader within his hospital and was well-known around the town. He commanded with assurance and strength, even when it felt like the war was about to walk right through the hospital doors and everyone gunned down. In the face of adversity, he kept his staff and patients calm and continued to perform exemplary surgeries. His staff remembers the time he operated for forty-nine hours straight, only taking ten minutes after every fourth or fifth surgery, to eat or drink and clear his mind.

By near the end of the war, he was notified that his efforts were even more appreciated. He was going to be the recipient of the highest honor, The Victoria Cross, which was first introduced by Queen Victoria to reward acts of valor in the Crimean War. After that war ended, followed by many years of peace, the next war began, and her Victoria Cross would carry over to this war and all others that would follow.

According to the monarchy, it is awarded for most conspicuous bravery or some daring or preeminent act of valor or self-sacrifice or extreme devotion to duty in the presence of the enemy. Major Dr. George McDonald Jr. qualified. George was invited to Buckingham Palace within a couple of weeks for a ceremony, in which King George V personally presented it to him.

When he left the hospital after the armistice, he wandered off, in search of feeling and women. He didn't care who they were or where. He bought women in every country he traveled through. In Le Treport, there were the town prostitutes. Whenever he could get a few hours off, he would be in someone's bed but was able to keep it a secret. Nurses and all women who were married were off limits. This was one of George's rules from the day he graduated. Don't take a married woman to bed or women you work with—only sleep with single, divorced, or widowed women!

He saw colleagues and friends fall into these traps with married women and women they work with, and it always somehow did end up in a trap. Besides, this was also the way to ruin a career. When he started working, George was always careful to keep his private life just that. No one knew about his sexual hunger. He never imagined himself ever marrying. It would ruin his way of life.

He found the best, most sexually free, and uninhibited women in France. They were all more than willing to fulfill his every fantasy. He could not face going home yet. He would be returning to his job at Toronto General. He was already certain of this. The family wanted him home, but he needed time for travel first. He told them that he likely would not be home for Christmas but had a surprise for his grandmother.

After leaving England, where he was accepting his medal, he was going to Scotland. Diana was so thrilled when he told her he was going to Scotland to meet the rest of the family. She couldn't believe it. Her grandson was going to her and Johnny's childhood homes. She was more excited than he was, she thought. George McDonald Jr. was going to be with the McDonalds and the McGees in Scotland for Christmas of 1918. Diana somehow felt a little jealous. She wanted to be there.

About a week before Christmas, George arrived in Edinburgh and was met at the train station by Jason and Carol. Carol picked him out of the crowd. He was a McDonald through and through on the surface. She threw her arms around him before she confirmed it was him. But she knew! They drove to Cupar and had a very large gathering waiting for him at the house. Both families were there, and all were so excited. Even George was. He was glad to be meeting his grandparents' family.

The next day was Sunday. Carol asked if he would go to church with them. He said, "Of course, I'd love to go with the family." They wanted to show him where everyone was baptized, married, and buried, as well as both farms. He really was in for a big day. He smiled. Carol said that she was sorry it was winter. She would have loved to take him to St. Andrews. There he would see where their parents had their honeymoon and the famous golf game. He thought about the family at home and knew Diana would be missing him, but being here, he felt like he was home. It was a warm feeling. Yes, he thought to himself, I *feel* again. He was happy. But there was more in what he felt. He didn't need to have sex. That gave him a sense of peace within himself, and it felt great.

At church on Sunday, he caught a glimpse of the most beautiful girl he had ever seen. She sat so straight and erect, sure of herself, paying close attention to the vicar; and he couldn't take his eyes off her. He was near her and heard her beautiful singing voice. He had never felt like this, ever. He wanted to meet her. He had to. It wasn't lust; he actually thought it was love at first sight. He never believed in that before, but it was real.

At the end of the service, the vicar welcomed George. He gave a brief history of the family, including those in Canada. Carol gave him the details. George was a little embarrassed, but it was harmless. He just kept thinking about the beautiful girl. When they left the church, he asked Carol who she was. Carol took him by the hand and caught up to this girl. She turned to the girl, they said hello, and they hugged. George thought, *Good, Carol knows her.*

His great-aunt Carol said, "George, I'd like you to meet Ms. Eleanor Ryan. She took over the school when I retired. She's the teacher at the Cupar school." George kissed her hand and bowed his head to her. He was used to doing this after living in France for four years. He was chivalrous, and she was impressed.

George said, "I'm very happy to meet you, Ms. Eleanor Ryan. As, you already heard in church, I am Carol's nephew, George." She smiled and gave him a slight curtsey. She was quite the young lady. Carol asked her to join them for the day. She said she'd be delighted. George was very happy. They also had another guest for the day. It was Old Sam. He was still alive! And he still lived in the caretaker's flat at St. Andrews. George was delighted to be meeting him since he had heard about him when he was growing up. Sam was equally as excited to hear about Diana and Johnny's life in Canada.

George was more thrilled than he ever thought he'd be to be in Scotland. His life was changing. He felt great! Through the day, there were laughter and stories. They told George about Diana and Johnny when they were growing up. George laughed so much. He was having the time of his life. Eleanor stayed through the day, and she seemed smitten with the doctor. It was his turn to tell stories. He went through the family and the farming, what Canada was like, and where he worked. Everyone had such a great time.

As evening came to a close, Eleanor looked at the time and said that she had to go. George offered to drive her home, if he could use his uncle's car. They let him use the car, and he helped Eleanor put her coat on. She said her good nights to everyone. When they opened the door to the house, it was snowing. It was a few days until Christmas, and this was the first snowfall. It seemed magical. George took her by the arm and escorted her to the car. She gave directions, and he started to drive. He saw she was shaking. He told her she could slide over and sit closer. It might help.

But he meant it very innocently. She did, and he let her hold his arm. She only lived a mile away, and when they got to her house, he asked if he could walk her to her door.

Eleanor said, "I would be grateful if you would. I hate going into a dark house alone."

He took her key from her and unlatched her door. He said he'd make her a fire. She was glad. That was one of the things she was nervous about. She lost her family in a house fire and still wasn't comfortable when she had to light a stove or fireplace. She told George the story, which still haunted her.

She was living away at the University of Edinburgh at the time. She was studying to be a teacher. Her mother, father, sister, and brother all died in a fire, which started on the kitchen stove. It was a grease fire. As she relayed her story to George, she teared up. He put his arms around her and held her until she stopped crying. It was a tender gesture, which he wouldn't take advantage of. This girl meant something to him. When she stopped crying, she looked at him and thanked him. He took her chin in his hand, turned her face, and kissed her on the cheek. Then he took her hand and kissed it, asking if she'd be all right. She told him she'd be fine, and with that, he said he had to leave and hoped he could see her the next day. She nodded, smiled, and said, "Good night, Dr. McDonald."

He turned, tipped his hat, and said, "Good evening, Ms. Eleanor Ryan." When he returned to the farm, most were in bed, but Carol stayed up. She smiled as he came through the door. He apologized for the delay because they had continued talking, and she told him about her family. He asked his aunt, "Carol, how old is she?"

Carol smiled again and said, "She's twenty-one and never been kissed. She's had her teaching career on her mind since the death of her family. She hasn't ever been courted by anyone, that I'm aware of. There have been many who have tried though." George frowned a little. Carol continued, "Oh, I recognize that look. I know you're eleven years older than her, and I don't think there is anything wrong with a relationship even if a couple has a twenty-year age difference, or even more. It is the love they have for each other that counts. I can tell she really likes you, and I don't blame her one bit! You're a McDonald!" Carol turned to him, kissed him on the cheek, and said, "Now, darlin' Georgie, you get some shut-eye. Tomorrow will be here shortly . . . and, oh, by the way,

Eleanor is celebrating Christmas here. Good night, lad." George smiled and gave his aunt a big hug before she went upstairs.

He drifted off to sleep thinking of the most beautiful girl—woman—he'd ever met. George arose with the men and worked with them. It was mostly barn work; there was no fieldwork at this time of year. The animals needed tending to, and he was glad to help. His uncle asked him if he liked Eleanor. George smiled, and that said it all. He questioned his uncle about the age difference. His uncle simply replied, "What age difference?"

The next day, Carol took George to St. Andrews to visit Old Sam. They couldn't golf, but he was shown around by Sam. He showed George the flat that his grandparents stayed in for their honeymoon and the historical book that showed the game and score of his grandparents' golf game. There was mention of a bet, but the winning details were not included. He was so happy to be shown around by Old Sam. He couldn't wait to tell his grandmother.

As Christmas Day arrived, George went over to get Eleanor before church services. They had been joined at the hip since she told him about her family. He never took advantage of her once. He never even tried to kiss her on the lips. He felt it was inappropriate and he should wait until they knew each other better. She thought he was quite the gentleman. He was back and forth between the farms and her house since she was on Christmas holiday from school. Everyone was pleased about the relationship. By near the end of the next week, George had asked her to marry him.

Eleanor was surprised and happy. He gave her a beautiful diamond ring. She looked a little sad. George wanted to know what was bothering her. Eleanor said, "George, I love you, and I want to marry you, but I still want my career."

He asked if she would like to teach in Toronto. She could have any of a number of teaching positions there. She smiled as she thought about that. She grinned and said, "Yes, George, I'll marry you and move to Canada with you." He smiled and went to kiss her on the cheek. She stopped him by placing his chin in her hand; she turned his head and kissed him on the lips. It was their first real kiss, and George was truly in love.

They told the family right away. All were happy, but when to do it? George would like to have gotten married in Canada with his family around him. He knew his bride would like to be married in Scotland, and he agreed. It was an unconventionally short engagement, and although they tried to include most of their traditions, time didn't allow for some because of the date they picked.

They wanted to be married on January 1, 1919, the first day of the New Year. In three days! Eleanor would still be off work then.

The family telegraphed Canada. Georgie received his grandmother and parents' blessing along with congratulations from the whole family with some sadness that they couldn't be together, but they were thrilled to know she was coming to live in Canada. Diana was impressed her grandson had fallen in love with a Scottish teacher!

Chapter 23

1919

J
ANUARY 1, 1919, WAS THE wedding day of Dr. George McDonald Jr. and Ms. Eleanor Ryan. It took place in the Cupar church, with many friends and family in attendance, followed by a big reception at the McDonalds' newly expanded house, since it was the largest now and could accommodate all the guests. Carol was a little disappointed that Grandma's wedding dress was in Canada. It was not a problem though. Eleanor had her own mother's wedding dress; it was in storage elsewhere and was not destroyed in the family's fire. The one thing they did have that they could use was the McDonald tartan. It was a hand-spun and woven wool kilt, and George was proud to wear it—cold . . . but proud. His aunt Carol made a traditional marriage kerchief for them.

They would live in Eleanor's house for now, which was provided by the community for the schoolteacher. Arrangements were made that she would remain teaching for a month, and then she would be leaving to move to Canada. That gave time to find a new teacher for the Cupar school.

After the wedding and reception, they drove to the house, where George picked up his bride and carried her across the threshold. As he let her down, he kissed her passionately. She was excited.

It excited George too, but she was different from the others. He loved his wife and wanted to be gentle with her. She admitted that she had never even let a man see her without clothes on. He would be the first, and likely the last, she told him.

He carried her up the stairs, and when he got to the top, he embarrassingly laughed and said, "Darlin', what room do I take you into?" She giggled and pointed to her room. He had never been upstairs at her house before. He took her in and put her down again. He could see that she was really nervous. She didn't know what to expect or do. She never thought about it until this moment, but she needed help to get out of her wedding dress. She never said anything and neither did George. He very gently turned her around and started unbuttoning the row of thirty silk-covered buttons on the back of her wedding dress. She was happy he did this because she was too embarrassed to ask. He seemed to anticipate what she wanted and needed.

Her dress fell to the floor, and he told her, if she felt more comfortable, to go to the water closet to change into her nightclothes. She smiled at his tenderness and hung up her dress and went to change. He undressed and he got into bed. After a bit, he called to her and said, "Is everything okay in there, El?" He'd started calling her that and she liked it. She told him she would be out in a moment. He continued, "Would you feel better if I put out the lamp?"

She thought it was so sweet of him to care that much about her nervousness. She opened the door and said, "No, I'll be fine, but thank you." As she came out of the water closet in a beautiful, long silky night dress, George smiled. He thought she was so beautiful. He pulled the covers open for her and she got into bed. He turned the lamp off and took her in his arms.

He was very gentle and slow with Eleanor. She was still a virgin, and he knew he might hurt her, and if it didn't happen on their wedding night, he would be patient and wait until she was ready to try again. He was able to bring her to climax quickly, but he could not get inside her. Her hymen was strong. He stopped and told her, "We'll try again tomorrow, love. I don't want to hurt you." She let a tear roll down her cheek, and he thought he really hurt her, but the tear was because she thought she disappointed him.

George took her face in his hands and said, "El, I am not disappointed. We'll try again when you're ready, there's no rush. Remember we're together until death do us part." He held her to him. They both slept well without having intercourse on their wedding night.

When morning came, El went to school, and George went to the farm to help out. Everyone was busy, but the men nudged him in jest to see if he would divulge anything about his wedding night and his young bride. George was a gentleman and told no tales. He smiled frequently, and they all acknowledged. They didn't need to know the truth.

Carol asked him if Eleanor was all right this morning, and George told her that she was fine.

She smiled at him, knowing he would have been a gentleman to her. Carol told everyone the latest news at breakfast. The terror of the Spanish flu now had been reported in Canada. George grew very concerned. Before he left the hospital in France, he had the flu go through the wards, and several soldiers died, but for some reason, he seemed almost immune to it. He kept working while some nurses and one doctor died of it too.

He was worried for his family in Chatham. It would likely be only a couple of weeks before it hit Ontario with a vengeance. He mentioned to Carol and Jason that he thought he should head home to help out. He felt he was needed. He knew Dr. Marty was there now, but he thought she could really use his help. Besides, he'd been dealing with it in Europe and could be very valuable.

He wondered how his bride would take it. When he picked her up at school that afternoon, he gave her the grim news that his medical experience was needed in Canada right away. She fully understood, but said she'd have to stay behind to wait for another teacher to replace her. She would join him later.

George was able to book passage on the first ship out the next day. He was on a troop ship. They were still transporting soldiers home. He worried that the flu could be on the ship. He hoped not. It would be a horrible tragedy. It could be a death ship he was embarking on.

That night before leaving Scotland, he told his bride, "El, maybe you should wait a couple of months to join me. I don't want you getting sick too." She would take his advice. They were sad that they were going to be separated a few days after their wedding, but it had to be. That night as they retired, Eleanor wanted to try again.

This time, she came to him and took his hand and led him upstairs to bed. She whispered in his ear that she wanted him. He smiled. They were both excited, and he thought of how much he wanted her. As he tried again to get inside her, it was painful. He stopped. She started to cry. He lay beside her and held her. She rolled over so her back was to him. All she could feel was shame and embarrassment.

George was much stronger than he looked. He sort of half picked her up and rolled her over at the same time and held her close. He said, "El, I don't want you to be upset over this." She looked at him and said, "George, what am I doing wrong? I want to be a good wife, but I don't know what's wrong with me."

George smiled at her and told her, "You will always be a great wife in my eyes. No one could ever say different. Not even you." He brushed her hair back off her face and gently wiped her tears away with his kisses.

She smiled again at him and said, "I love you, George. Please remember that always. I'm going to miss you so much after you leave tomorrow." She kissed him passionately. They both were aroused again and tried once more. George could not hold back; he ejaculated, but he still could not penetrate her.

He told her, "Don't worry so much, love. We have a lifetime to practice." She burst out laughing. He joined her and they fell asleep.

They had not really consummated their marriage yet, but there would be time for that when she comes to join him in Canada. He told her she might have to stay in Scotland for two or three months until it was safe. She'd stay until he sent for her.

She went to see him off in the morning, and even George had tears. He loved her so! She stayed on the dock until she could no longer see his ship on the horizon.

There were a couple of soldiers on the ship with the flu, but George was quick to realize it and isolated them for the whole trip. They were very lucky; they survived under his care.

George arrived at the farm just after the flu hit. He was met with hesitance because he might be carrying the flu. Diana was so glad to see him, but she had to tell him that his parents were resting in their house. They both had the flu. Dr. Marteen had diagnosed it and secluded them right away.

George said to his grandma, "Where's Marty? Is she here or in town?"

Diana told him, "She's so overworked, Georgie. She needs help, or I'm afraid she's going to get the flu too. Lad, Chatham hospital is full, Windsor hospital is full, and they are now using schoolhouses as makeshift hospitals. All school, church services, and public gatherings are cancelled everywhere due to the high risk of infection. There are some people that just aren't getting it, and they are looking after the sick. I feel fine, so I'm looking after your mom and dad. Jacob is running the farm with Joseph, Patrick, Emmett, Richard, and the hired hands. I'm glad it's the end of winter. I know if it were warmer, it would spread faster."

His sister, Ann, was currently home. She had been away at Guelph University, in Ontario. She was still studying to be a veterinarian and still top of her class, just like her big brother was the top of his class while he was studying to be a surgeon. She was home to help with the sickness.

Diana said, "Ann is fine, and Mary and her family are fine. They've moved to one of the vacant houses. They come to see me and help keep the farm running. Mary and Ann are helping at the schoolhouse as sort of nurses, when they can. One of them usually goes on rounds with Marty. She seems to be resistant too, I guess." Diana could stand it no more; she took her grandson in her arms and hugged him. She kissed him on the cheek and said, "Welcome home, boy. I've missed you. I can't wait to meet your beautiful bride! You'll have to tell us all about her later, love. Carol says she's a wonderful lady, and you are perfect together. I can't wait."

"Grandma, I may have to let her stay in Scotland for a couple of months. I don't want to bring her here and have her get sick and die. The flu has already passed there, and she was fine.

Grandma, I gotta go check Mom and Dad. I'll be back." He blew her a kiss on the way out the door.

George walked the short distance to his parents' house. The door was unlocked, like all the houses on the farm. He took his medical bag everywhere, and home was no different. This time, he needed it. He went upstairs to his parents' bedroom. He knocked on the door gently, as not to startle them. He heard a groan. He poked his head around the door, and he saw both his parents in their bed. Dora looked at him and smiled. She managed to get the energy to elbow George Sr. and said, "Now I know we're dead, dear . . . I'm seeing things. Look over at the door."

George tried to elbow her back, which made George Jr. smile. Those were his parents, just the way everyone loved them. His dad looked at him and said, "Yep, hon, I think we're dead!" George Jr. came in the room with a happy smile, and their faces brightened up. He heard a door open downstairs. It was Diana. She said, "It's just me, love. I've got some tea. Maybe they can get some down." George went downstairs to help her bring it up.

He came in the room, followed by Diana. His parents had struggled to get themselves into sitting positions in the bed. Dora had tears in her eyes. She said, "Don't come near us, Georgie. We're sick, darlin'."

He said, "I know, Ma, that's why I'm here. I worked with this flu in France. I never got it and I seem to be immune to it." She sighed with relief, and so did his dad. He brought the tea over but insisted on hearing their chests first. They both had pneumonia. It was unmistakable. He asked Diana, "Did they have the chills, fever, sore muscles and throat?" They both started coughing and he said, "That was the next question." He knew it didn't look good for them They were in the last stages. There was no medicine that could help. They took a little morphine for the pain, but it certainly wasn't a cure.

He and Diana heard the door open downstairs. It was Jacob. He called to Diana, "You here, Ma?"

Diana yelled down, "I'm here, son. What's wrong?"

Jacob ran up the stairs, and before he got to George and Dora's room, he started, "It's my boy. Joseph has it . . ." As he came in, he saw George and smiled.

George said, "Hi, Jacob. There's time for proper hellos later. Where's Joe?"

Jacob said, "He's downstairs."

George said, "Good, we have to contain the flu to only one area, and sorry, Mom and Dad, your house is the family hospital for now." He went downstairs and shook hands with Jacob on the way. Jacob responded with a loving pat on the back at the same time and followed him down the stairs. George found Joseph on the couch in the living room.

Joseph smiled at George and said, "Hey, Georgie. When'd you get here?" He was wrapped in a wool blanket and was shaking from chills.

He said, "Just a half hour ago. You just hush now, and let me listen to your chest." As he listened, Jacob watched George's face carefully. George looked troubled. When he was done listening, he said, "Your lungs are just starting to get fluid in there. Are you coughing with your fever and chills?" Joe nodded his head and tried to tell him but started coughing.

When he stopped coughing, he said, "It's just been a couple of days."

George said, "Joey, your wife is a doctor. Did you tell her how you were feeling?"

Joseph tried to take a breath to talk, and he started coughing again. When it settled down again, he uttered, "She had 'nough to deal with. I didn't want to bother her."

George gave him a look. "Joe, she's here to help with everybody. She has to be told." He turned to Jacob and said, "Are you feeling okay, Jacob?" He nodded that he was. George continued, "Jacob, we have to get him into a bed. Let's move him upstairs."

Both men carried Joseph upstairs. He had no energy left to make it on his own. Jacob started to get him in a bed in one of the spare rooms. Diana was still in with George and Dora. When they brought Joseph upstairs, Diana helped get him into bed and covered up. As she was busy tucking him in, she kept thinking to herself how fortunate they were to have given every house on the farm indoor plumbing several years earlier. Every house had a toilet, so you didn't have to go outside to use an outhouse anymore. It was a blessing, especially now with sickness about.

Diana gave Joseph some tea. He managed to get it into him, and he said he'd try to keep it down. Diana, Jacob, and George left the house after all three dozed off. As they left George and Dora's house, Marteen was driving in the yard. She got out of her car and saw George Jr. She was never so happy to see someone in her life. She got out of the car and ran to hug him. He looked at her with as much compassion as he could and said, "Hi, Marty, I'm here to help, but first, Joseph is in my parents' house. Marty, your husband has the flu."

Marteen fainted. Jacob and George picked her up and carried her into Diana's house. It was the closest. George listened to her chest. It sounded normal. They were relieved. George noticed that she had put on some weight since he saw her, and he had a notion. He placed his stethoscope over her lower abdomen. He heard a very fast, tiny heartbeat. Dr. Marteen was pregnant. When he told Jacob and Diana, they were both elated, but then they realized, she was at high risk and shouldn't continue working while the flu was still spreading. She came to and wondered what happened to her.

George asked, "Well, lady, how long have you known you were pregnant, and does Joseph know?"

She looked at him and said, "I've known for about a month. I'm about three months or more. Joseph doesn't know. Now, George, are you sure Joe has the flu?"

George nodded his head, and she saw the look in his eyes. He said, "He's just got the beginning stages. He's strong, I think he'll be okay. You know, you shouldn't work anymore. I'll take over for you."

As Marteen got up and started to go see her husband, she said, "I can't let you handle Everything. We'll both work. With a lighter workload, I'll be okay." Diana was happy. A new baby was on the way for the family. George helped Marty over to his parents' house so she could see Joe.

Diana went to her kitchen, where Beulah and Cora were busy preparing a large celebratory supper for Georgie's homecoming. They only saw George Jr. briefly when he arrived and were glad to see him home again. Diana's dining room table was going to be full again. George was welcomed by everyone that evening, and he had forgotten how great it felt to be home with family again.

George spent the evening telling everyone about his wife and how happy he was. He also told the stories from Scotland, especially mentioning Old Sam and that he fondly remembered Johnny and Diana and their honeymoon golf game. Diana was thrilled. He told them all, since the flu was on the farm, he decided it should be a couple of months more before he brings Eleanor over here. Diana was really disappointed about it but understood. Marteen was happy to hear this in a way. It was a wise decision.

Everyone wanted George to regale them with some stories from the war. They also wanted to see his Victoria Cross medal and to know what King George V was like in person. Marty excused herself from the table and told them she was going to set herself up in the living room in George's parents' place. She wanted to be closer to her husband. Georgie and Diana said that she'd better tell Joe about the baby, that it might make him fight harder to stay alive. She agreed. If he was awake and could comprehend what she was saying, she would tell him right away.

Joseph and Marteen had talked many times over the past seven years of their marriage about having a baby. Joseph had told her about the disease that his grandfather died of. She was very upset. She had to tell him it sounded like her father died of the same disease. She had told his family about it too, and there was concern. That was the reason she became a doctor. She wanted to study it, and hopefully she would know if she was a carrier or, now, if Joseph or Jacob were carriers. It did mean that they could pass on the genes, and their children and or grandchildren could have the disease or die from it. Although there was still no cure for it in 1904, in preliminary studies it was discovered that patients who were suffering from the same symptoms as her dad and Joseph's grandfather had red blood cells that were not the proper round shape. They were in the shape of a well-known farm implement—a sickle. This constricted their proper flow and caused the unusual symptoms. She was always trying to learn as much as she could about this terrible disease.

Years earlier, while she was studying to become a doctor, she not only kept up with current medical news in Canada but the world as well. She also studied old news and periodicals on subjects she was most interested in. Marty found a study from 1902 about a new device not yet marketed called an IUD, or intrauterine device. This device was inserted in the uterus and vagina so a woman could not get pregnant. She was interested in the study and wanted to see if there were updated reports on this birth control device.

In 1909 there was another study out of Germany that used a device that seemed to be a little more effective and comfortable to women. This device was inserted into and remained in the uterus only. It needed to be replaced every ten years. Although the device was not marketed at that time, she sought to get one for herself.

After her father died of the terrible disease, she wanted to find a doctor who had them and knew how to insert them. She found one in Toronto. She made her decision based on not wanting to pass on the disease. She knew if she wanted a child, she could have it taken out.

She never told Joseph about her birth control device; she thought it better. She wanted to work for some time before she was ready to stop working for a while to raise a child. When she felt she and Joe were ready, she would secretly go to the same doctor who inserted the device to take it out so she could become pregnant. No one had to know the truth. Marty was hopeful that there might be a cure around the corner for the disease her father and Jed had died of, but she also knew it could take many decades to find the answer.

Dr. Marty was very busy the first few years that she and Joseph were married. They hoped she wouldn't get pregnant right away, but if it happened they would deal with it. She wanted more time for doctoring and have a baby later. She went along with him in discussions of children but still never told him about the birth control. She would be the one who ultimately decided. And no one would ever know. They decided 1919 would be the year to have a baby.

One day she told Joseph she was going to a couple of meetings in Toronto for two days. She would be staying overnight. He never thought twice about it. She actually went so that she could see the same doctor who put the IUD in. He removed it with no problems, and she went home the next afternoon.

Unfortunately, the timing of becoming pregnant was bad, due to the flu epidemic. She had to help all her patients get over the Spanish flu and now protect herself and the baby from it. Her patients all loved her and would be thrilled to find out she and Joseph were going to have a baby.

Dr. Marsh had been right in the beginning—people would take to her, even if she was a woman. She treated most of the blacks in the area and in Chatham. Needless to say, she was the doctor for the McDonalds and Allens and all the workers on the farm. She was kept busy with so many patients now. Mark went into semiretirement in the beginning, until everyone got to know her.

His wife and two of their triplets were happy to see him finally able to take time for himself and retire when she was fully established. Two of their triplets were now on their own, and he and his wife were quite proud of them. The girls had admired Marteen so much that they went to Toronto University. One studied law, and the other wanted to be a professor. But there was sadness in the family too. Their other triplet, sadly, died while still in school. She drowned while swimming in the Thames River, near their house.

When George went over to his parents' house in the morning, Marty was just coming out. She told him, "George, Joseph is a bit worse today. Can you give me your opinion? Your parents are even worse than that. I was just coming to get you. They want to see you. George . . . it's grim." George kissed her on the cheek and headed for the stairs.

He turned quickly and said, "Joe, does he know about the baby?"

She smiled and replied, "He's so happy. Now you get up those stairs to your mom and dad." As George came into the room, he could see what Marty saw. Their breathing was getting seriously labored, and he knew these signs so well. He gave his mother a hug and asked if she needed anything. She whispered in his ear, "I'd like a cup of tea, if it's okay." He smiled and nodded that she could. He came around the bed to give his father a hug next. He was so much worse than his wife. George Sr. couldn't find the strength to lift himself up.

George Jr. put his arms around his father and said, "Dad, I want you to know how much I love you, and Annie does too. You've been the best father anyone could ever want!" George Sr. managed to give his son a little smile. He understood.

He coughed a bit and reached his hand out to Dora. He found hers and gave it a squeeze. He said, "Love you," took one last breath, and died in his son's arms. George laid him back down as a tear rolled down his face.

George heard the door open downstairs and someone running up the stairs. Ann burst through the door, and she saw her father dead. She knelt down beside the bed and cried out, "No, Georgie, do something." Marty had gone to give Ann the sad news.

George put his arm around his sister and said, "He's gone, Ann." She cried and then looked at their mother. She went around her side of the bed and hugged her. Dora was in shock and knew her beloved George was dead but heard what he said before he died. It made her smile.

George told his sister and mom, "We're going to have to bury him today." Ann nodded her head, and she and Dora cried. George started to cry too. He knew their mother was next. He couldn't stop it. It was probably only a matter of a couple of hours or a day . . . maybe two.

He got up and said, "Ma, we'll have to move him right away. I'll call Adam and arrange a coffin." He told them he'd be back in a minute. On his way to use the phone, he went to check on Joseph, and he agreed with Marty—Joseph was a bit worse than the day before, but he was ecstatic that he was going to be a father. Georgie never said anything to him about George Sr. George went downstairs just when Diana and Little Mary were coming in with tea and toast. He met them at the door and took the tray from her and said, "Grandma, Dad just passed away." She was in shock; Mary too. She loved her brother so much. George sat Diana down quickly before she fell. He continued sadly, "Mom won't be long." Diana started to cry. Her beloved son was gone.

Diana and Mary went upstairs to see Dora. Ann let go of her mom and held her grandmother; neither spoke. Diana saw her daughter-in-law slipping away too. While George was out of the room, he called Jeff and Tina and gave them the news. He called Adam, and he had a coffin the size they needed. George returned to the room and told Diana and his sister, "I called Tina and Jeff to let them know Dora was worse, and Adam's bringing a coffin out as soon as he can get it loaded."

As soon as the farmhands could dig the hole in the cemetery, they buried George Sr. near his dad, John. Everyone was aware that Dora would likely go soon too. She was not well enough to go outside, but they managed to get her in a chair so she could watch the burial through a window. After they got Dora back in bed, she asked for Diana, Little Mary, George, Ann, Jeff, and Tina. She wanted to talk to them before there was no time. She knew she was dying.

The six gathered around her bed while she was still weeping for her George. She wanted to say good-bye to each of them. She knew Mary, Diana, Ann, and Georgie could come close to her, but her parents, Tina and Jeff, couldn't. George told them they would have to stay by the door. They couldn't even hug their own daughter because there was a chance that they would contract the flu. Dora said good-bye to each of them and then lay back on the bed. She was exhausted. Tina was beside herself. She was losing her daughter. Jeff held his wife while she wept. Dora's breathing started getting shallow now, and they heard the distinct rumbling and rasping sound with each breath.

George had to leave to check on Joseph. He was sleeping, but he had a smile on his face still. George imagined that he was thinking about being a father. George stood and watched and prayed for Joseph to live and see his child. Joseph stirred a bit and opened an eye. He saw George standing there and asked if everything was all right.

George said, "Don't you worry, you just concentrate on keeping strong. So you're going to be a papa." Joseph smiled and nodded his head. He had a bit more energy and was able to sit up. He said, "George, I know something has happened. What is it?"

George told him that his father died, and they'd buried him in the morning, and his mom would be gone soon too. Joseph put out his hand for George to take, and he did. They shook hands and Joseph just held it for a bit. Suddenly there was a yell from the other bedroom.

Ann cried out, "Georgie, hurry." Dora's breathing was worse. He walked in the room and looked at his mother. She died just as he came into the room. George told them that she would have to be buried right away too. Everyone expected that, but now George and Dora were together forever and weren't suffering anymore.

The farmhands got busy digging a hole right beside George Sr. George called Adam, and he had already loaded another coffin and was ready to bring it out when they needed it. Unfortunately, it was needed right away.

Dr. Marty had been out on rounds all morning and afternoon. She didn't worry about Joseph or the others. She knew George was there to look after them. She didn't know about the two deaths. She stopped by the store to pick up a few supplies. Jenny told her that George and Dora were both gone. She was shocked and dropped what she was carrying, and she ran out the door and got in her car. She was upset about George and Dora, but this also meant she may lose her husband too.

She arrived at the farm and went into George and Dora's house. She was met by George Jr. and Ann. They told her Joseph was fine so far, but they had to go to Diana's house to be with her and Dora's parents. She hugged them both and said she'd be there after she saw to Joe. As she ran up the stairs, Joseph was sleeping. She was still wearing her stethoscope and very quietly put it over his chest. He was still the same as when she heard it in the morning. She saw a tray with an empty cup and plate. He obviously had something to eat and drink. She was glad but not sure whether it stayed in or not!.

George, Ann, and Little Mary walked into Diana's. Jacob had joined them and was equally devastated by the deaths of his beloved brother and sister-in-law. Tina, Jeff, Diana, and Mary's children were now all in the dining room with them. They were trying to be brave, but it was hard. Losing both George and Dora the same day was too incredible to believe. Gerald came in and told them the burial hole was ready. Adam had brought another coffin out, and they were ready to bury Dora right beside George. Everyone who could went outside again for the second burial.

When they all came inside after it was over, no one spoke. They didn't feel like eating supper. They just sat and tried to accept it. Diana was grieving the loss of her son; and Jeff and Tina, the death of their daughter. All at once, Diana cried out, "Lord, how could you do this?" She started to sob uncontrollably and asked loudly again, "Lord, why, how the *hell* could you take them both? *Why?*" Everyone just kept silent. George and Ann came to Diana and held her as she cried for her son . . . their parents. Mary started to cry again for her brother and sister-in-law; Jeff and Tina joined in for their daughter. This was a most tragic day.

George said, "Grandma, they say the Lord works in mysterious ways. You know that better than anyone. It was their time. They're not in pain and they're with God. Sometimes God doesn't make sense, but we have to be strong and carry on."

Diana looked at her grandson and said, "Well, maybe you can make sense of it, but I can't. He took my husband, he took my son, he took my daughter-in-law, my dearest friends, Jed and Mary, he took Mina and Joseph's twin sister. How much more do I have to bear, Georgie?"

Diana went upstairs to bed. No one bothered her as George said, "Grandma needs to be alone right now." As Jeff and Tina left, all anyone could say was good night.

Morning came, and Diana was upset that she was still alive. In about sixty years, the night before was the only night she never opened her Bible. She had slight pangs of guilt, but she was still mad at God. She started the day like always. It was as if the day before had never happened. She greeted everyone, as usual, and George told them to play along until he could observe what state she was in. Mary and her family were there to check on Diana; Ann too. They agreed with George.

After Marty came in the house to say that Joe was the same, it seemed like that was what Diana needed to hear. She was happy that he was stable. Marteen came to Diana and put her arms around her, and she just held her for a moment. Diana was glad to see her. She looked at Marty and affectionately rubbed her tummy. She was happy. There would be a baby on the farm this year. This was going to sidetrack Diana's grief.

Joe was feeling a little better, or that's what he told his wife. He didn't want to upset her. She knew better. He wasn't fooling her. His chest was slowly getting worse. She sat with him as much as she could. In her mind, she knew it was grim. Outwardly, to Joe, she showed optimism. He couldn't really believe he was dying yet; he was going to be a daddy. He kept thinking he was young and strong; he could make it through for his wife and baby. He was sure he was going to survive.

About ten days after George Sr. and Dora died, Dr. Marteen Allen's husband, Joseph, was dead. He lasted the longest, lingering with the dreaded Spanish flu, which by now had killed millions worldwide! Everyone was certain; it was knowing he was going to be a daddy that made him hang on. Unfortunately, he couldn't hang on any longer. Their child would be born in a few months with no father. Marty had to carry on for her child's sake now. Jacob was so devastated at the loss of his only child. He was now without his son. How could he go on?

George said to him, "Jacob, you know how sick he was!"

Jacob said, "What kind of God goes through a farmstead and kills the bess? My Joseph didn't know his mama or his twin sister and grandparents. Georgie, do you think dey's together?" A lone tear fell down Jacob's cheek as he spoke.

George put his arm around Jacob's shoulder and said, "Jacob, my dear friend, I have always thought of you as my second dad. I'm sure God has them all together. I'm sure of it. They're together watching over this farm and this family, who love each other very much." Jacob knew Georgie was right.

Joseph was buried with his mother, grandparents, and his twin sister. Marteen managed to get through the burial, and that night was her first experience alone with the spirits on the wall in her bedroom. This time, there was an addition. Her Joseph was there with his family. She smiled, knowing he was with his mother and twin sister now. Marty still visited a few patients the next day.

George was visiting most of her patients and the few left at the schoolhouse hospital. But the flu wasn't done yet at the McDonalds'.

With the Spanish flu running rampant everywhere, it was hard for doctors, nurses, and undertakers to keep up with the burials. While the bodies were still infectious, the preparation for burials were adhered to. The normal practice for burial was to wash the body thoroughly. There were volunteers who assisted the undertaker in this task. There were a few people on the farm, other than the few of the McDonald clan, who seemed to be resistant to this killer flu.

Since they were not getting the flu, Gerald and Cora volunteered for this job of washing and dressing the bodies for burials, with Ann's supervision. But it seemed like they were not resistant after all. When washing the deceased, they were told to do it as quickly as possible so they could be buried before anyone is contaminated. The virus caught up to them both. Cora and Gerald were dead within the next eight days. Diana saw to it that they were buried in the same cemetery as Rolly was.

The next loss was more devastating. Ann died. Diana and George Jr. took it very hard. Her beloved granddaughter, his kid sister, was gone now too. She didn't seem to have the symptoms, or she hid them well. She wanted so desperately to hide her illness. She knew her grandmother might not survive the news. She was the next and final victim of the Spanish flu in her family. She was interred in the family cemetery, near her parents, Dora and George Sr. While George was home, he told Marty he was going to pitch in and help her with her patient load. She had to look after herself and her baby; she was a widow now. He said that he was not going to go back to Toronto yet. She needed his help more than ever now. He would do whatever he could to make sure she was not going to get run down or possibly lose her baby. It was another month before the flu finally left the area, after claiming eighteen more lives in Chatham.

By March, Dr. Marty was seven months along in her pregnancy. Still mourning the loss of her husband, Joseph, she continued to work. George was helping with rounds. School and church services were back to normal, and everyone was starting to get ready for the spring plowing and planting. George and Marteen agreed that it was safe to bring Eleanor over from Scotland now.

A new teacher had arrived within the previous few weeks, and Eleanor got her acquainted with the school, the children, Cupar, and her new house. Eleanor was excited to be joining her husband. She missed him terribly, just as he missed and longed for her Carol booked passage for Eleanor on a ship, and she was off to a new life and a new country. Eleanor could hardly contain herself. When the ship docked in Halifax, she was relieved. There had been a bad storm at sea, but the experienced captain managed to keep his ship afloat, with no loss of life. There was a large group of people with seasickness though, and they all were glad to set foot on land again.

Eleanor took a train to Chatham. It took a couple of days, but she was almost there. Her mind drifted back to her wedding night. She hoped she would be able to consummate the marriage; she wanted so much to be able to please her husband. She smiled to herself, thinking about meeting so many new people, and she was related to all of them. She couldn't wait to meet Diana. George talked a lot about his grandmother. She was caught up on the flu news. She was aware that George Sr., Dora, Ann, and Joseph, as well as Cora and Gerald, had all died; and there would likely be a somber mood about the farm.

When she got off the train in Chatham, George was right there to meet her. She jumped into his arms, and they kissed with such longing and tenderness. They held each other for a moment.

Finally, George said, "El, it's so good to have you home with me. Are you sure you're ready for this?" He smiled at her with a devilish look to him. She was more nervous now than ever. He giggled a bit and said, "Don't worry, dear, I'm teasing. They're all so excited to be finally meeting you. Grandma is probably still pacing the floor, like when I left to come and get you."

They got in the car, and Eleanor sat close to George, remembering the first time he drove her home as she sat close to him again. She felt warm. As they pulled into the driveway, she was amazed at how large the farm was. George told her, "Sweetie, this is nothing. We own everything you see around you, both sides of the road, and down to the Thames River." She smiled at the mention of the Thames and was in awe. She never expected the farm to be so large.

Diana, Little Mary, and Beulah all came out to the car to meet her. Diana came to her and hugged her tightly. The other ladies took their turn welcoming her. Eleanor felt loved already. Diana said to her, "Eleanor, we're so happy to have you here and, mostly, to have you be part of our family. I hope you had a good trip?" El was a little overwhelmed but kept her wits about her.

She said, "Well, we had a bad storm at sea, but we survived it." As Diana put her arm around Eleanor's shoulders, they became quick friends, and Eleanor felt like part of the family already. El looked to her husband, and he smiled and knew she fit in. Everyone was introduced to Eleanor, who told them to call her El. She was the newest McDonald and she was so happy.

After supper, George told her, "Well, love, we do have a house. It was mine and Ann's. Now it's mine . . . ours. You and I are going to live there for now, I hope that's okay?"

She nodded and asked, "When do you have to go to Toronto General?" George wasn't sure when to tell everyone, but it *had* to come out now. "Love, I'm sorry, but we're not going there yet. Marty is only a couple of months away from having her baby, and she needs me to fill in for her and care for her patients. After she has the baby and wants to go back to work, I'll feel better about leaving. I hope you understand, dear." Diana was elated. She couldn't have better news. Everyone seemed pleased with the news too.

She turned to her husband and replied, "My darling husband, wherever you are, that's where I'll be too. I'm just so happy to be with you. I'll be by your side always." With that, George leaned over and gave her a kiss. Eleanor was going to fit in right away! Everyone loved her and was glad George had met and married her. They seemed so happy together.

When they retired to their new house that first night, George picked up his bride again to carry her across the threshold. Eleanor giggled and asked, "George, do you plan to carry me across every threshold we ever own?"

He laughed and said, "Of course I do, Mrs. McDonald. We're home for now." As he carried her up the stairs, he continued, "Did I happen to mention lately that I love you?" El blushed and smiled a tender smile at George. She had missed him so much.

They got to the bedroom, and George laid her on the bed. They still had their clothes on. He looked at her, and he gently laid on top of her, kissing her with such passionate force they both couldn't wait. It was very quick, and Eleanor wasn't quite sure how they managed it, but all of a sudden, they were both out of their clothes, and he was inside her with no trouble, and it felt good. As they each climaxed, they were both quite winded and very satisfied. George looked at his wife, and she looked so beautiful. Somehow, he thought, she was even more beautiful than she was even ten minutes before. Her smile said so much for her. She was happy and always would be as long as she was Mrs. George McDonald Jr.

For the next couple of months, George was off each day to Dr. Marty's office and her house calls while she stayed home and only worked part-time. Then it came time; she was due any day. Marty and El spent some time together. El felt she could talk to her. Eleanor was not feeling well but didn't want to bother George. He would just worry. She talked to Marteen. El told her what she was feeling, and Marty smiled.

She said after examining her, "Girl, you're gonna have a baby! I could tell by looking at you!" Eleanor was shocked. She was pregnant. Marteen did some calculations and figured her due date to be sometime in January of the next year.

Marteen laughed as she had a thought. "El, this is great. I'm having my baby now, and yours is due in the new year, 1920—how about we start planning their wedding now!" She was laughing all the time she said it, and then El started to laugh too. It was nice to see Marteen laughing. She had so much to be concerned with—a new baby, no husband, and wanting to work still. Eleanor admired her strength and courage to carry on.

Marteen and Eleanor went to Diana's, and they saw George driving in the driveway. They hoped nothing was wrong. George honked his horn and waved at them. He got out of the car and said, "I was just on rounds nearby, and I thought I'd stop by to see my beautiful wife and my patient. I don't know if you realize this, Marty, but if that baby gets much bigger, we might need to do a caesarean on you!" She hit him on the arm and told him she wasn't that big.

Eleanor winked at Marteen and said to her husband, "George, you're terrible. Are you going to be that mean to me when I get bigger too?"

George's jaw dropped and he was speechless. He just looked at El, and she nodded her head, and so did Marty. He said, "You're serious? We're going to have a baby?" Eleanor nodded her head again, and George put his arms around her hugged her. Then he started to whoop and holler in the yard. He was happier than he'd ever been in his life. As the girls laughed at him, Diana quickly came outside to see what was wrong.

George went to his grandmother, picked her up and swung her around, and said, "Grandma, we're having a baby!" At first Diana thought he meant Marteen was in labor, but then she looked at Eleanor. She smiled, and, as Diana has always done at these announcements, she cried. She was so happy and went and hugged Eleanor. Diana was so thrilled. She wanted to start telling everyone. It was a happy time on the farm again. One baby about to be born and one on the way! Diana was so excited. There would be a family celebration that night.

Jacob had kept to himself lately. Since his son died, all he'd been doing was farmwork. He was getting ready to hand most of the work over to some of the younger McDonalds. Little Mary was more acquainted with the farm than her nephew, George Jr., who was now considered the McDonald patriarch. Mary's husband, Patrick McNeely, had worked on the farm ever since they married out of high school. Their children Richard, fifteen, and Emmett, sixteen, were at the age where they were mature young men and valuable workers also learning the business. They would likely be running things one day too.

While George was there, he helped build another house. Mary's boys were growing up and would eventually need independence and privacy someday, when they marry. George helped on the farm when he could, but Mary had the mind for business. Diana watched over her daughter through the years and was impressed. There were enough farmhands that they could get the work done on time. There were plenty of McDonalds on the farm. There were no more Allens, except Marty and her baby. Diana hoped there would be more generations, for Jed and Mary's sake

Over the years, the farmhands had decided to live off the farm. There was nothing wrong with living there, but since their families were going in different directions, most moved to Chatham and commuted. They were personal decisions, which Diana took no offense to. The McDonalds looked after their workers while they lived on the farm, as well as off the farm. She decided that the farm residences would only house family now, with the exception of Beulah and Frank, who eventually moved in with Diana and Jacob.

Jacob missed his son, Joe, a lot. Lord willing, he was going to be a grandpa shortly and was excited about it, but he was hurting. He spent time fussing over Marty, making sure she was all right and she had everything she needed. He asked Diana if it would be okay if he refinished one of the cradles for his grandchild. She thought back again, like she always did, when a baby was born on the farm. She thought about the cradle and its identical mate, which had rocked so many babies on that farm since she and Johnny found them on the first night they moved there. Diana smiled and told Jacob, "Of course you can, son. But I'd really like it if you would refinish the other one to match. Jacob, we'll never know when we might need two at the same time." She gave him a curious smile.

Jacob said, "Ma, what's that look for? Do you know something I don't?"

Diana assured him, "Son, Georgie said there was only one baby in her, but some future generation may surprise us. Besides, Georgie and El will need it next year!"

Jacob smiled at Diana. He hugged her and thanked her for being his mother most of his life. He loved her so much. Jacob worked on the cradles and both rocking horses in the evenings, after he knew Marty would be tucked away in her own house.

Marty made dinner for just the two of them once or twice a week. She spent her time still seeing a few favorite patients, but mostly she was at Diana's or Eleanor's place for company. The evenings he spent with Marty, Jacob could sit for hours with her, talking about Joseph and Mina and what he remembered about his mother and father. Marty was interested in hearing as much as she could about her husband's family.

One evening, while Jacob was with her for supper and she was standing, washing the dishes while Jacob dried them, her water broke.

Her labor was starting. Jacob had her lay down. He said, "Are you deliverin' here, or do I get you to the hospital?"

Marty laughed, "Well, Pop, since my doctor is here, I don't think we'll need to go to the hospital. I don't anticipate any problems, and I'd like to have it here." He laughed. He forgot that George was her doctor. He covered her up with a blanket and said he'd be right back. He didn't ring the bell; it really wasn't an emergency. There was time to get to George's place.

He went over to George and El's house to get George. He knocked on the door, he opened it slightly, and called out, "George, you here, boy?" George came to the door and asked if it was time.

Jacob continued, "Her water broke."

George said to his wife, "Hun, go get Grandma. I want her and you to help. Marty wants to have the baby here, instead of the hospital. Or if Grandma can't, see if Beulah can."

He rushed over to Marty's house. Jacob and he went into the room. She was in the middle of a contraction. He took a look and saw she was progressing fast. Diana, Jacob, and Beulah came back with Eleanor. Marteen burst out laughing. She said, "I guess this is my entourage, my audience."

Everyone burst out laughing with her. She didn't mind them being there. They were all concerned. They wanted so bad for Jacob to have a grandchild and for her to be a mother. Marteen wanted Eleanor to watch and learn. El was frightened, but George thought it was a good idea for her to be there too. She'd never witnessed a birth before. She was nervous, but she sat right beside her husband and was ready to help however she could. The women went into the kitchen and told him to call if he needed them. He thanked them as they left the room. She wanted Jacob to stay. He wanted to too.

The contractions were getting quicker and harder. Eleanor was getting a little scared now. Marty told her, "Don't worry, girl. You'll do fine when it's your turn . . ." She yelled again. After a couple of hours, the head was ready to come out, and El watched with wide eyes. George told her to get a blanket or towel ready. His scissors had been sterilized by Diana and ready for the umbilical cord.

Marty gave a big push and the head came out. Another one and the shoulders came, and out slipped a beautiful baby boy. Eleanor was a champion helper, and George was proud of her. He was of Marteen too. She was so thrilled. It was a boy. He would carry on the Allen name. She let Jacob hold him first. He cried as he held his grandson. The women heard the cry and came running. They let out a cheer because it was a boy. The Allen name would live on in Joseph Jacob Allen Jr.

Chapter 24

1920s

JOSEPH JR. HAD A GREAT start in life. He had his mama and his grandpa and all the family on the farm to love him. He was also the new kid around, and all the family and farmhands came to see him and congratulate Marteen and Jacob. When word got around to neighbors and friends, they were sure to visit him too. He was healthy and beautiful. But the family wondered about the illness that took his paternal great-grandfather and his maternal grandfather in the prime of their lives. Would he carry the gene only, or would he possibly have the disease? Time would tell.

Diana loved him too. She was like a great-grandma to him. Marteen asked if she and Beulah would care for him when she returned to work. Diana and Beulah were excited and very happy to have a little one in their kitchen again. Diana wished those who have passed on could see him. He was such an angel.

Times were changing. Instead of so many house calls, there were more patients coming in to the office in Chatham. George would still visit those who could not get to town to see him. Many new patients came to the area, and they kept him very busy. George really loved being home and working in an office, but he was hoping Marty was coming back soon. He was also the only surgeon for miles, outside of Windsor.

George was working alone while Dr. Marty stayed home with Joseph for a few weeks. He was tending to every kind of infirmity, no matter how minor or serious. When she decided to go back to work, he cut back at the office a bit because there were people who needed surgeries. That, after all, was his specialty. While he was living at the farm, he held rights to operate in the Chatham hospital, and since Marteen went back to work, he decided that he would branch out and seek rights to operate in the Windsor hospital too. He was in his element. He was performing surgeries again.

Eleanor was getting bigger by the day and getting anxious. One evening she asked her husband, "When are we going to move to Toronto, love?"

George turned to his wife and said, "El, I need to talk to you about that." He took a breath and started, "Honey, I know you had your heart set on getting a teaching job in Toronto, but, sweetheart, I'm needed here. Toronto has more than enough surgeons to take care of people. Here, I'm the main surgeon in the Chatham hospital and hope to be soon in the Windsor hospital, and I love being home again. El, would you mind if we stayed and lived here? You never know when there might be a local teaching job opening up. It does happen once in a while. Please tell me what you think?"

Eleanor walked up to her husband, put her arms around him, and pressed her body as close to him as she could manage without squashing the baby. He laughed at her as he waited for her answer. She looked lovingly into his eyes and said, "I told you once before, wherever you are, that's where I'll be too. I'm just so happy to be with you. I'll be by your side always. I love you. I would be very happy to live here on the farm. I know you love it here, and I've been so happy here too."

George smiled at his wife and said, "El, I love you. Grandma is going to be so happy. I'll call Toronto in the morning and let them know. I'll have to drive up there and pick up some belongings I have in storage there and bring them home. Maybe I can take you and show you some of the city. It's wonderful. I think you'd like it. Darlin', you've made me so happy. Let's go next weekend." With that, he kissed her and they went to bed. George was very happy with his life, thanks to his beautiful wife.

As 1919 closed out the year, the farm had the largest productivity and income in five years. Things were on the upswing again. Diana was proud of the job that Jacob, Mary, Patrick, Emmett, and Richard were doing. George helped when he could, but the office and surgeries kept him very busy too.

Marteen left Joseph with Diana and Beulah during the day, when she was working. They loved looking after him. Eleanor was there most of the time when George was at work. She got a lot of knowledge and practice while she was with baby Joseph. Like everyone else, she loved him too.

January proved to be very cold and snowy in Southern Ontario. The McDonalds had always been self-sufficient on their farm. There was little need to go to town; they had, or could make, almost everything they needed. In winter, the only things they had to tend to were the animals and the repair of farm equipment, vehicles, and structural damages to buildings, if any. The men would always keep busy. Most farmhands were laid off in the winter. They all went out and got winter jobs elsewhere, but come the springtime, when it came time for plowing and planting for another season, they would all return to the McDonald farm. Diana was pleased to see them all come back, year after year. They all liked returning and working for Mrs. McDonald.

January 13, 1920, started out to be a normal, cold wintry day. El was sleeping so beautifully and peacefully that George did not want to wake her. He got ready to go to work and sneaked out the door. He went to Diana's, hoping to get a good breakfast. As he entered the house, he could smell bacon and fresh biscuits.

As he walked into the kitchen, he put his arm around Diana's shoulders and kissed her on the cheek, saying "Good morning, Grandma." He next turned to Beulah and kissed her on the cheek too while stealing a piece of bacon off the platter.

Beulah looked at him and said, "Georgie, you know you don't has to bribe me wit' kisses to git breakfast. But you wait now till the others get here."

He said, "Beulah, I'm shocked that you think it's a bribe. You know I love you! Always have, always will." Diana slapped his hand as he was about to snitch another piece. He pulled back his hand quickly with another piece of bacon and gave his grandma another kiss.

Jacob ran into the kitchen and saw George there. "Georgie, there be a lot of screamin' from your house, boy."

George started back to his house quickly. Diana and Jacob were right behind him. He burst through his door and ran upstairs. There, on the bed, was his wife, perspiring profusely and rolling in pain, screaming when it became unbearable. She saw George and was a little calmer. As George knelt beside the bed, he took a look under El's night gown and saw that her water had broken, and she was in full labor. George was shocked—the baby was trying to come out breech. Jacob immediately thought it's Mina all over again. He immediately thought it would be a difficult birth, that El might not live through it. It terrified him, and he silently began to pray for her and the baby! He also knew he was a breech baby that was delivered naturally. Diana told him about his birth, but luckily, his mother, Mary, survived it.

George said to Diana, "Grandma, go get Marty, fast. I need her help now." Diana ran over to the Allen house. Marty was just about to go to Diana's to drop off baby Joseph for the day and go to work.

She saw Diana and asked, "What is it? Eleanor?" Diana nodded her head. Marty handed Joseph Jr. to Diana and rushed past her, out the door, to go to George's house. As she ran upstairs and into the bedroom, she looked at him and he said, "Marty, it's breech. I have to operate . . . I have to get her to the hospital *now*! I want you to come with me and do the chloroform for me, please."

Marteen had learned anesthesia techniques and had done a few anesthetic procedures for George's surgeries in Chatham and was good at it. He liked having her in the operating room. They were a good team. George quickly wrapped and picked up his wife, and he carried her downstairs to their car, and he sped to the Chatham hospital. As he drove, El screamed with each pain in the backseat, in Marty's arms.

When they arrived at the hospital, George got his wife into the operating room right away. Fortunately, the baby hadn't advanced. Marty quickly put El to sleep. As soon as she was under, George made his incision, and within minutes, he was pulling out his beautiful baby daughter.

Diana, Jacob, and Mary were in the waiting room now. They had followed George to the hospital right away. When George finally emerged from the operating room and found them, he said, "Grandma, it's a girl! And El is just fine. We got her here in time to do a section, and we had no problems. Marty is looking after her right now." They were so excited it was a girl and relieved everything was all right.

It wasn't long before El woke up in a room and saw George holding their daughter. Diana, Jacob, and Mary were smiling. Jacob was so worried about the breech delivery he stayed close by. He was so relieved that Eleanor survived but sadly thought back to his poor Mina, who didn't. His tears were mixed.

George sat on the bed beside his wife and said with the biggest smile on his face, "Hi, Mama. I guess you want to meet our beautiful daughter, huh?" They both had tears of joy as he placed her in Eleanor's arms. They were a happy family.

Eleanor said, "I love you, Papa. I guess she was a little trouble?"

He nodded his head and kissed her. "You have nothing to worry about, Mama. You're fine, and so is she!" He let a tear fall. He loved his wife and new baby daughter. It was the most wonderful feeling he'd ever had.

Marteen came in the room and said, "Congratulations, you two. George, why don't you take the day off? I can cover the office. I'm sure Eleanor would love to have you here today."

George said, "Marty, you can't handle all the patients today."

She said, "George, you have been more help to me than you can ever know. I want to do this for you. Please, let me take the office today. Your wife and your daughter need you."

George was not going to win the argument, but he said, "Okay, I won't go to the office today, but I'll have no arguments—I'll do the five house calls we have today!" Eleanor and Marty were happy with that arrangement.

Marty looked at the time. She had to get going to the office. When she was leaving, she told George, "She looks good, George. Baby too." She now looked at both of them and said, "You're going to be great parents. Take care, and if there is anything you need, just call and let me know." They both thanked her with a hug. George walked out with her. They talked a bit, and then George went back into the room to his wife and daughter. He was happier than he'd ever been, and nothing else in the world mattered!

He asked his wife, "El, don't you think we should give her a name? I mean, I'm quite happy calling her Beautiful, but I'm sure you have something else in mind."

While Diana, Jacob, and Mary were still in the room, Eleanor spoke up and said, "Well, Papa, what do you think of Elizabeth Diana McDonald?"

All in the room fell silent and smiled. George sat on the bed again and said, "Honey, that is the most perfect name." He kissed his wife and daughter again.

As Diana was crying, she went around and sat on the other side of the bed and said to Eleanor, "El, you've made me a very happy woman today. I am honored that you want to use my name, but what about your family names?"

Eleanor took Diana's hand with her free hand and affectionately held it to her cheek and kissed it and told her, "My mother's name was Beth, short for Elizabeth." She was hoping this would not offend Diana to have her name second. Diana hugged her and said it was a beautiful name. She was happy and proud to be remembered in this beautiful little girl.

In 1922, there was another storm. This one was in the winter. On March 30, in the Windsor area, right up to a little bit north of Toronto, there was a freezing rainstorm. Winds gusted again, about 100 mph. There was loss of power, and everyone had to rely on stoves, fireplaces, and lots of wood to keep warm and for meals. Everyone on the farm stayed in Diana's house. That way they could keep each other warm, and they would know where each of them were. The boys were able to get to the barns to the animals, but it took a long time trying to get back and forth across the barnyard. Patrick, Emmett, and Richard told Jacob they would take care of things by themselves, but Jacob wouldn't hear of it. This farm was his responsibility too, and he always managed to do his chores every day, come rain, snow, ice, or shine!

A couple of months after this storm, the family found out that George and Eleanor were going to be parents again. Everyone was happy. It would be near Christmas. They were so excited. El loved her husband more than ever. They had a beautiful daughter who played with Joseph all the time, and now they were going to expand their family. She had asked George if he wanted a boy or girl. He said, "Either, as long as he's healthy."

El giggled, "As long as *he's* healthy, huh?" She smiled at him and whispered, "I'll do the best I can for you, Papa." She kissed him and he just sat there. He was concerned about something, but Eleanor could not get him to talk about what was bothering him.

He thought to himself, *How could I tell my pregnant wife I need more sex?* He was starting to get the old feelings again. He started looking at women more now. He seemed to be doing more surgeries in Windsor lately. It made for long days and kept him away from home longer, but Eleanor never minded. She believed he was doing the work he loved, and she was happy for him.

After the terrible ice storm in March that year, there was some good medical news, in a way. Marteen and George heard that a doctor, Vernon Mason, had penned the affliction that Jed and Marty's father died of and gave it a name. This disease was officially named sickle-cell disease.

It was discovered that it was indeed hereditary. It was classified as a genetic disorder. It was described as abnormal hemoglobin, and it was discovered that in these patients, some of their red blood cells stick together by their proteins. The cell in turn gets a rigid center, thus giving it the shape of a sickle. These cells get stuck in blood vessels, depriving the tissues of oxygen. It causes painful attacks and likely shortens the patients' life.

This disorder can cause strokes and organ damage. Up to that point, in medicine, the only ones who had the disease were those of African heritage. There are many symptoms, but not every patient would have all the symptoms. They include fatigue; pain; anemia; swelling of the joints; blood blocking the spleen and/or liver; chest pain (sometimes by pneumonia); fever; shortness of breath; swollen, hardened spleen; spleen not working properly; dead tissues in the kidneys; and priapism of the penis, an erection that lasts more than three or four hours, which can be very painful.

Now it had been confirmed that Jed Allen and Marteen's dad had many of these symptoms, and they actually died of sickle-cell disease. Most patients rarely reach the age of forty. When it came to Marty and Joseph, they were both very likely carriers of the disease, passing on the genes to their child, Joseph Jr. In this case, there was a 50 percent chance that their child would have the disease. Joseph Sr. didn't live very long or suffer, other than the occasional chest pain that he never told Marty about, but he had never been really diagnosed with sickle cell. Marty and George tested Joseph Jr., and it was positive. He had sickle-cell disease, and there was no telling how long he would live or how healthy or painful his life would be.

Although the disease was named and would now be recognizable by studying the patient's blood, sadly, there was no cure for it. All that could be done for the patient was to keep them comfortable from pain with morphine. When fever was present, the normal treatment was given— cold-water immersion or sponge bath to bring the temperature down.

As everyone was now aware what the disease was, there was still little anyone could do about it. Joseph Jr. could suffer from bouts of different symptoms, and they could only pray that the disease wouldn't carry on too frequently in the generations to come.

It was almost three years after Elizabeth was born before George started to get an itch that he tried hard not to give in to. He wanted his family, especially with another baby about to be born soon. He tried to get these thoughts out of his head. While he was daydreaming about the sex- filled days in France, he would remember the orgies. They were not mixed; he was the only male. One time he had bought five prostitutes at one time.

Right then, he got a call from his grandma in the office. It was Christmas Eve. She told him to come home, that his child was on the way. He grinned from ear to ear and told Diana, "Grandma, do you think she has long enough so that you can drive her to the hospital for me?"

Diana said, "Is there something wrong, Georgie? Is she okay?"

George cut in, "Grandma, does she have enough time to get there? Please tell me."

Diana said, "Yes, Georgie, the baby won't be here for a bit. We'll get her there. Does she know she's to go?"

George said, "Yes, grandma, she knows. Thanks. I'll meet you there." Diana hung up the phone but was concerned. This babe would not be farm-born either. She turned around and saw Eleanor standing in her kitchen with a travel case in her hand and a large smile. Diana was certain something was up, but what was it? Diana drove Eleanor to the hospital, and George was there to meet her. Beulah and Mary stayed home with Elizabeth.

George kissed his wife on the cheek, asking if she was all right. Eleanor smiled at him. She was so in love with him. He had a bed prepared for her. As she was getting on the bed, she had a rather large contraction and let everyone know. George had a delivery room on standby. Diana was happy to be there. She was in her glory . . . she was going to be a great-grandma again!

Eleanor's water had broken at home, and she was in labor for hours in the hospital. As she got closer to the time, they got her into the delivery room. Diana looked at the clock and said, "Georgie, it's Christmas Day!"

George smiled at his grandmother and said, "I think our presents will be here shortly, Grandma!" Diana smiled and waited . . . and waited and dozed off for a second, and then it hit her! George said "Christmas presents." Plural! Was it twins? She couldn't wait!

At 3:30 a.m., Christmas Day 1922, George brought out his two sons to meet their great- grandma. Diana really cried this time. Two boys to keep the McDonald name going.

George let Diana hold one. "Grandma, they are very beautiful, healthy, fine boys. One is 4 pounds 10 ounces and the other is 4 pounds 3 ounces."

George wanted to stay overnight at the hospital with El and the boys, but Eleanor insisted that since it was Christmas Day, Daddy should be home for Elizabeth to tell her about the new brothers Santa brought them. So with a smile and a wink, George drove out of sight, a very proud and happy dad again!

Diana had left earlier because she knew that everyone was going to be up and would want breakfast and presents soon. Diana cried all the way home. As she got back to the farm, she slipped into the house to get a couple of hours of sleep, she hoped.

George knew Elizabeth was at Diana's house too, so he crept into her house and quickly fell asleep on the couch with a very content smile. But it was not long before Elizabeth was downstairs and she climbed up on her daddy's tummy and asked where Mama was. He hugged her and kissed her and said, "Honey, Mama went to the hospital. Santa found her there and he brought her a special present, and he also gave the same present to me and to you, but you'll have to wait before I tell you, until everyone is here for breakfast."

Elizabeth would not have to wait long. She played while she waited. Within an hour, the whole family was gathered at Diana's house, and George said he had an announcement. He cleared his throat and said, "Ladies and gentlemen, I want . . ."

All of a sudden, his daughter said, pointing to her and Joseph, "Daddy, what about us?"

He looked at her and smiled and started again. "Ladies and gentlemen, children, and Ms.

Elizabeth Diana McDonald, I would like to give you all an important announcement. At 3:30 a.m. this glorious Christmas Day, my beautiful wife Eleanor gave birth to twin sons!"

No one knew there were going to be two babies. Not even Marteen. All cheered and were so happy. It really was a wonderful day. Diana said, "What better start to life than being born the same day Jesus was." Diana, Caroline, the newly hired housekeeper and part-time cook, and Mary made breakfast, and then the gifts were handed out. They went to church, and they made the announcement in church that morning. The congregation was overjoyed with this news and congratulated George and the family.

After church service was over, the family all went to the hospital. George took everyone to the window of the nursery. It was easy to see which ones were theirs. Their boys were the only babies in the nursery this Christmas Day. The nurses brought the babies closer to the glass and let the family have a good look.

Meanwhile George and Elizabeth slipped away to Eleanor's room to see her. Liz was so excited. She threw her arms around her mommy's neck and hugged her. George got Eleanor into a wheelchair. He wheeled her down to the nursery with their daughter on her lap. Everyone was happy to see her looking so well. There was a beautiful glow, not only to her, but George too.

Marteen noticed it but never said anything. She was feeling a little jealous. She wished her husband, Joe Sr., was still around so they could have had more children. She envied the happy couple but never let it show.

The babies were able to go home within a couple of weeks. The family was happy to have babies around again. The boys were named Abraham (Abe) Lincoln McDonald and Simon Peter McDonald.

By 1925, Joseph Jr. and Elizabeth (Liz was being used most of the time when addressing her.) were six years old, and El had become the new teacher at the Chatham Public School 101. She was happy to be teaching again.

Although Joe and Liz were only a few months apart in age, the regulations of the school board was that they have to go by the age of the child before December 31 of that year. Joseph could start school one year before Liz could. She was so upset. She wanted to be with him. He was her best friend. It was hard for her to understand, but she would have to get used to it, and she could start school the next September. The twins would stay with Diana and Beulah during the day while El and George both worked. They loved watching the cute little boys. They were best friends, just like Liz and Joseph were. Diana was so happy looking after Abe and Simon, and it seemed she didn't have a worry in the world, until one summer day in 1925.

That warm summer day, Jacob was driving into town, and he was run off the road by a driver who had been drinking. The road he drove on was along the Thames River. His car flipped into the river, upside down. He was conscious and trying desperately to get out of his car, which was filling up with water. He tried and tried but ran out of time and oxygen. Jacob Marcus Allen was dead at the age of 65.

The local police went to the farm and talked to Diana. "We're sorry, ma'am, but we have to tell you that one of your nigg—black boys was killed a while ago." Diana was appalled at the way they told her, and it took a moment to sink in.

She sternly said to the officer, "Could you please rephrase that and tell me again. I don't think I understood you!"

The young policeman cleared his throat after being admonished and said, "I'm sorry, ma'am, but we believe that one of your farmhands has died in a car accident. His license says his name is Jacob Allen. Do you know him?"

Diana couldn't believe it. Her other boy was dead. Jacob was gone now. She asked how and where he died. The officer told her and said his body was at the hospital. She thanked the officers and asked them to leave.

The telephone rang. She knew who it was. She picked up the phone and said, weeping, "Georgie, I know. The police just left." All she heard from the other end was breathing and crying.

George was able to mutter, "Grandma, he's gone. I loved him so much. Grandma, are you okay?" All he heard now was his grandmother softly weeping. He said, "I was here when they brought in his bod—um . . . brought . . . him . . . in. Grandma, I'm coming home, but I'm going to make arrangements to bring him home. I know you want to bury him there. I'll be there as soon as I can."

Diana hung up the phone. Little Mary was beside her. She didn't know what was going on yet. She asked Diana, "Mom, what is it? What's wrong?"

Diana took her daughter into her arms and, through her tears, said, "Jacob's gone, Mary. My Jacob is gone, my little boy. He died in a car accident. Some ass ran him off the road, into the river. He drowned in the car." She was crying harder now. Mary joined her. They couldn't believe it. He would never walk through the door again.

Mary sent Joseph Jr., Liz, and the twins to play until they had to tell them. It was better they weren't underfoot while trying to deal with things. The older ones went into the yard, and Liz got on the swing that Joseph's great-grandfather, Jed, had put up for Jacob when he was just a little boy. Liz sat on it, and Joseph wanted to push her. The two of them always loved the swings. They liked to play in the yard with toys too. The twins loved to play on the rocking horses that were a matched set. Just like Liz and Joe, Abe and Simon did everything together too.

Jacob had loved all of the children that came along at the farm. He refinished the cradles and horses the day after the twins were born, and recently he just bought two new bicycles for Liz and Joe and tricycles for the twins. They were almost getting too big for the rocking horses. They were learning how to ride. Jacob was trying to teach them all to ride. He loved all four kids very much.

Soon, George drove in the driveway, followed by Marty. They made arrangements with the undertaker to transport the body back to the farm for burial. He happily obliged. He wasn't too fond of darkies being laid out in his parlor.

Some of the newer people who moved into the area were not exactly like what regular folks were like. These new residents moved here with prejudices. This farming community wasn't used to this behavior. For the last century, black and white lived together with very little problems. First it was the police officer and now the undertaker.

Diana wanted a wake, just like Jacob's daddy, Jed, had. Diana asked Patrick, Richard, and Emmett if they could get the inside of the hall painted. She told them to use as many hired hands as they could so they could to get it done in one day. It was done.

Word went out to everyone, and his wake and funeral were attended by almost as many people as those who came to pay respects to his father and his mother, Mary. Diana was pleased with the turnout. Everyone talked about him fondly—the funny stories and also the sad parts of his life. Diana didn't like the sad parts, but George told her, "Grandma, to understand the man he was and the love he had for people, the sad must be included. He would want people to know it all. You know that." Diana did agree after a while.

Once again, farm life went back to normal, as it always had after their tragedies. Beulah died in 1926 from a heart attack, and Frank passed away a year later from pneumonia. Diana had spoken to them in earlier years and told them that she would take care of their arrangements. She paid for their funerals and burials, like she had done for Rolly, Gerald, and Cora. They were all buried in the same cemetery just outside of town.

Marteen, El, George, Mary, Patrick, and their boys carried on through the few years Jacob had been gone. They missed him, but Diana's heart seemed broken. In a way, she felt like she was alone. Even with all those around her, she felt alone. She was getting on in years, and she trusted in God again. She now took to reading her Bible during the daytime too.

George and Marteen still had their office in Chatham, and their practice was thriving. George was doing surgeries at both hospitals regularly. Eleanor was teaching for a new school year, and they were now building larger schools and separating children into grades. There would now be eight teachers at each school to teach grades one through eight. She was happy. She chose to devote her time with the little ones. She loved to teach the grade one students.

Joseph and Liz were in grades four and three by this time. They both liked school. They would always do homework together, still play together, and sit together at church. Now they were given some responsibilities around the farm. There were chores they could do.

They loved doing them and always did them together. They were best friends, and it would always remain that way.

Joseph missed his mother. She was very busy in the office. Liz and her brothers missed their father too. George didn't do as much office work lately. He concentrated on surgeries most now.

He was chief of staff at the Chatham hospital, and he was doing surgeries one day a week in the Windsor hospital, where he also had an office. Liz saw her mom all the time since she worked at the school. Joseph, once in a while, would think of his grandpa. It had only been a few years since Jacob died in the river. Although Joseph was young when he died, he still remembered him. He would always remain in his heart.

At night, Marteen, Joseph, George, Eleanor, Liz, and the twins would usually eat supper at Diana's house with her. Mary and Patrick and their boys would usually eat at their house.

Diana had hired a housekeeper and part-time cook before Beulah passed on. She was getting too old to take care of everyone on the farm and make lunch for the large amount of farmhands.

She tried but could not manage alone. The new housekeeper would live in. She would have one of the empty bedrooms in Diana's house. Diana interviewed a few women before she found the one for her.

Her name was Caroline. She was a young woman of twenty-five, born and raised on a cotton plantation in Alabama and had only been in Canada for three years. She was black and recently widowed. She liked to work in kitchens, which she was very experienced at. She loved cooking, baking, and cleaning. She also loved children of any age, but sadly she would never be able to have any of her own. She was the type of woman who could singlehandedly run the business of looking after many children at one time. She had so much love to give.

By fall of 1929, things were changing. The economy was changing in the USA and Canada too. Diana was concerned about the farm, and so were Mary and Patrick. There had been rumors of a recession in the States. Were they true? They wondered, wondered and watched what was happening with banks, stocks, and the overall economy of Canada.

On October 10, 1929, Diana didn't come downstairs to help with breakfast. Caroline thought she'd let her sleep in. She could handle the breakfast herself. When Eleanor and the twins came in, she looked around and said, "Where's Grandma?"

Caroline shrugged her shoulders and said, "Sleepin' in, I 'spect. She tole me today be a special day for her and da farm. She say dat dis very day she an' her Johnny and da Allens, Jed and Mary, was all married, yess'um, dis very day. She sure dis be da first day da Good Lord decided dat dese people was meant to be tagedder! It be dere . . . uh . . . she, uh . . . calls it dere *destino*! Dere relationship started dat day dey was married, a tousand miles 'part. Even afor dey met, here on dis very farm. Can ya'll imagine dat? I tinks she said near 'bout seventy years ago. I ask her what her Johnny would like for supper. She say a nice roast pork, he loved it so. So dat's what I'se makin' fer her."

George and Liz came in the house. George said, "Where's Grandma?" Eleanor shrugged, and he ran to the stairs and went up. As he entered his grandmother's room, he could feel it. There, on her bed, Diana lay dead. Sometime through the night, George figured she must have suffered a heart attack. He went to her and kissed her on the cheek and held her hand. She was eighty-nine years old. Just then, Eleanor came in the room, and she knew too. Liz had followed her to her great-great-grandmother's room. Diana, the grand matriarch of the McDonald farm, had died on her wedding anniversary. George asked Eleanor to pass him the telephone so he could call his aunt Mary's house. She did, and he asked Mary to come over. Mary asked, "Is it Mom?"

George said, "Yeah, Aunt Mary, she's gone." Mary hung up the phone and ran across the compound to her mom's house. George went downstairs and told Caroline and met Mary at the door. He told her, "She must have had a heart attack in her sleep. There was likely no pain." He hugged her and took her up to see her mother. She looked so peaceful. Mary didn't even cry yet.

She just looked at her for a moment and smiled at her. Patrick and her boys were now standing in the bedroom too.

The door downstairs opened again, and Marty came in with Joseph. She asked Caroline, "Where is everyone this morning?"

Caroline sniffed and wiped her eyes and said, "She gone, Doc. Ms. Diana be dead. Everyone be upstairs wit' her."

Marteen ran up the stairs, Joseph running behind her. Everyone turned to her. She tried not to cry, but she couldn't help it. George got to his feet and held Marteen in one arm while he held his wife in the other. She sobbed for a few moments, and then she pulled herself together.

She asked, "George, what do you think it was? A heart attack?"

"I expect so, love. She was in good health. The postmortem will tell us," he replied and then went on, "We have to plan a grand funeral, Mary—a grand funeral for a grand lady!"

There was silence for a moment. Caroline had come upstairs then and asked if she could come in the room. Patrick took her hand and led her in to see Diana. She had been shedding tears in the kitchen and wanted to be with the family. They had no objections; she was like family too, and welcome.

Just then, Eleanor started to recite the 23rd Psalm. Everyone knew it was Diana's favorite.

Just like her favorite hymn was "Amazing Grace." They would be sure to have this sung at her funeral. After El finished the psalm, with everyone still standing around her bed, she led them in the Lord's Prayer, and everyone joined in. After another silent moment, with many tears, everyone started leaving her bedroom.

George would take a couple of days off work. His aunt Mary asked him to so he could help take care of his grandma's business and arrangements with her.

Time was getting on, and the farmhands started showing up for work. Mary and Patrick went out to greet them. It was a beautiful sunny autumn morning, and they were in the thick of the potato harvest. Work had to go on. They were all told about Diana and were quite sad. They didn't feel much like working after that news, but for Diana's sake, they did the hardest day's work ever on the farm. They wanted to show their respect for this dear lady, whom they all cared for and revered.

After Johnny passed away seventeen years earlier, when she took over, they respected Diana as a good businesswoman and a great boss, just as John had been. They all knew that Mary and Patrick were in charge, but Diana, Mrs. McDonald, was a very kind, fair, generous employer. She had the final say on all business matters on the farm.

The workers started talking immediately and decided that they would collect money from all the farmhands to purchase a large flower arrangement for the funeral parlor and for the McDonalds' house. Priscilla, Adam and Jenny White's daughter, who was now running Lavalle's General Store full-time, would see to it for them. George and Mary were touched. Diana had even outlived her dear friends, Jeff, Christina, and Adam White, whom she had met that very first day she and her Johnny arrived in Chatham in the 1850s.

A wire was sent to the farm in Scotland. They informed them all that Diana passed away.

Over the last several years, family news was passed on to Diana too. Things were unhappy and grief filled at times in Scotland too. John's last remaining brother, Charles, had lingered in and out of a sickness that the doctors were having a hard time diagnosing. He seemed to be constantly sick. He would suffer weaknesses, colds that wouldn't clear up, swollen glands, fevers, and chills. These were the most common symptoms in the beginning.

After a time, it got worse. Charles was constantly sick with a cold that turned into pneumonia, which he recuperated from the first few times. He was strong then. Every time he got a cold after that, the pneumonia surfaced again. Each time, it was more serious than the last. He started to lose weight. Eventually, he was no longer the strong man he used to be, and it was more than just aging. Something told his doctors it was turning into something more serious. As he got sicker and sicker, he was spending more time in his bed at home. Then he had to go to the hospital, and these visits got longer every time too.

The doctors were at a loss as to what it was. It seemed like he was catching every virus or bacteria going around. Even the simplest bugs turned into a major problem for him. His immune system was breaking down fast. He had no resistance for anything.

In Chatham, they were informed about Charles's death. Everyone was saddened, but the doctors were more bothered because they could not tell them why Charles had died. His death certificate would read pneumonia, but there was more the doctors couldn't or wouldn't say.

After Charles had died, there were several other people dying in the area of what seemed to be the same symptoms. It was odd to the doctors that all the others were only men. And they all had one thing in common. They were all very close, personal friends of Charles McDonald.

Diana McDonald was given the most lavish funeral. It was held in the mortuary in town, and after it concluded, there was a very long, slow procession with her coffin to the farm for burial in the family cemetery. George and Mary decided that one of her beloved Clydesdales and a Shetland right behind it would pull the original wagon that they purchased when they landed in Canada and brought them to the farm near Chatham. They still had it and used it at times. The workers were given the day off with pay to attend the funeral.

Diana's daughter, Little Mary, took her place as the McDonald matriarch. Even though her name was her husband's, it was still to be. Caroline asked Mary if she could hire some help for her. There was to be a large reception in McDonald Hall, and she needed help preparing and serving food to all the guests. Mary told her to hire as many girls as she would need to help her. George paid for everything and spared no expense. People came from miles around to pay respect and reminisce about Diana and her Johnny. Mary was sure to see that Diana's half of the marriage kerchief was laid in the coffin with her. They were happy to know that she and Johnny would be reunited in their afterlife according to Scottish tradition. It brought them all comfort.

From that day forward, George and his aunt Mary declared a paid holiday on the farm.

October 10, the day Diana died, would be the farm's own personal holiday. It would memorialize the reason they lived there. It was the wedding anniversary of Diana and Johnny McDonald and also Jed and Mary Allen. It was the *true* beginning of Olde McDonald's Potato Farm.

A few days later, Diana's lawyer came to the farm to read Diana's will. He asked for George and Mary, Eleanor, Caroline, and Marteen to attend. He didn't need the youngest family members to be in attendance. They would get their share, as Diana prescribed, in her will. She would not forget anyone.

By the time she died, the farm had grown to a few thousand acres. The only thing Diana did not own was the Allen house. It was legally deeded to Jed and Mary a year or so after they came to live and work on the farm. Then it became Jacob's and then Joseph Sr.'s. Now it was his wife's, Marteen's. She was the legal Allen heir. She would be passing it on to her son, Joseph Jr. She did not know what Diana could be leaving her. There was nothing she wanted or needed. She was happy in her house and garden.

While they were gathered, the lawyer read, and there were no real surprises. The McDonald farm would be divided equally between Diana's daughter, Mary, and her grandson, George, with the exception of 320 acres, the original west field, where Johnny had built the house for Jed and Mary Allen.

This property would now belong to Marteen. Marty had no idea Diana would do this, and she was stunned. The others weren't. They smiled and told her that she could do with it what she wanted. If she wanted, they would divide the land so that her property was separate from the farm, or she could stay part of the farm, and they would pay her for the use of her land, do the work for her, and share the crop's income with her.

She asked if she could take time to think about what she wanted to do with it. Everyone told her to take her time. The other thing that Marteen would get was the Kente cloth robe that Afua, Mary, made in Africa and had survived many years. Jacob had given it back to Diana after Marteen wore it for her wedding to Joseph. He knew she would look after it and pass it on when she felt it was time. Eleanor was to receive the McGee tartan sash. Diana knew George approved.

The stipulation was that they had to be passed down from generation to generation, along with their history. They promised they would. Diana's daughter, Little Mary, received Diana's grandmother's wedding gown, boots, hat, and every bridal piece she had. It also had a stipulation.

Mary was to pass it on to the eldest female of each generation but also was to let whoever in the family who gets married to have the use of it, if they wished. It was suggested by Diana that she might want to leave it to Eleanor or her daughter, Elizabeth, since Mary only had boys. She would eventually do this without hesitation. Her sons agreed that it should go to Eleanor and then Elizabeth.

There was a lot of money. Diana was sharp when it came to learning the business from Johnny. They had a great deal of money. No one realized before, but Johnny had amassed well over a million and a half dollars, and he had invested wisely. After he died, Diana took over, and she was just as wise as her husband. She kept investing and making more, and the farm was making out better than anyone ever realized.

Caroline was given a lump sum of $10,000 for her dedication and hoped she would stay on with the family. Everyone agreed and hoped she would stay on too. She would. She was also to receive $3,000 per year if she remained in their employ.

Along with the will, there was an unopened package. It was addressed to the lawyer, with instructions not to open it until after her death and at her will reading. The lawyer opened the package. Inside was the most beautiful, frilly, embroidered, hand-laced apron. Mary thought it was so beautiful; Caroline and El too. The lawyer started to read the letter.

"This letter is now being read to those in attendance of the reading of my will. Since my Johnny and I have both passed on, this is the way we wanted to answer that one question that people have asked over the decades. What was the bet between my Johnny and I on our honeymoon golf game at St. Andrews, Scotland? Here is the answer!

"If I won, Johnny was to wear my most delicate, pretty apron all day and night, no matter if company came or what he was doing. To John this would be torture to his manhood. He would have to do this for one month, and he could not explain to anyone what was going on.

"If John won the bet I had to go out every day and clean all of the manure out of each stall for one month. This was my most hated job of all on the farm.

"Enclosed is the apron that Johnny McDonald wore for the entire month, and I never moved one shovelful of shit!"

They all laughed. They finally knew the secret and were all happy to finally know the rest of the story about Johnny and Diana McDonald. The lawyer was the only other person who knew the result of that bet that was made so many decades ago. But he was entrusted not to reveal her secret until she passed on. He kept his word. It was a few days before everyone got over the laughter of knowing the secret. The apron was to remain in the McDonald house, hanging in the kitchen!

It was only nineteen days after Diana's death that the world came crashing down, so to speak. In the Unites States, it was known as Black Tuesday. The stock market crashed, and their Federal Reserve's reduction in the money supply made their recession turn into a depression. The collapse of their market very quickly had Canada following suit.

Canada relied on its wheat and other crops. When their prices fell over 50 percent, they suffered because of their international trading with so many other countries. The one thing that Canada had over the United States was it had a more stable banking system. There were nine thousand small US banks that collapsed.

Since Canadian exports fell, there were reduced work weeks, and in turn, many people were being laid off, and all were in search of jobs. The pay for most of those who still held onto their jobs was not affected. But the hours in their work week were shortened.

The McDonalds would still make money from their potatoes, vegetables, fruits, and their Angus beef and provide a great service and kindness through the Depression of the 1930s.

---————— *Chapter 25* —————---

1930s

T HE WORLD WAS STILL REELING from Black Tuesday and the Depression, which carried on a lot longer than anyone expected. By 1933, in Canada alone, 30 percent of the workforce was out of work, and one-fifth of the population needed financial aid from the government.

For the ten years of the Depression, the McDonalds would help their community as best they could. George Jr. and Mary kept as many farmhands as they felt they could, although they did drop many of their workers to part-time. They would work half days, every other day. This was primarily so they could help others.

They felt it was their Christian duty to help their fellow man, and they had a plan to do so. They started a program that would allow local people to come one half day every second week to work. When people heard about this, they flocked to the farm. Mary had to start turning some away. There just wasn't enough work for everyone. She and George decided that they would take more people, but the frequency at which they came back was decided by how many people they helped.

The first shift would start at 7:00 a.m. until noon, and the second shift would start working at 1:00 p.m. to 6:00 p.m. Both shifts were given lunch together from noon to 1:00 p.m. if they wanted to stay for it. They always would.

These occasional workers would receive thirty cents for their work, and they would receive food for their families for one week. The stipulation was that they should still be searching for other work. And Mary would ask them each time they came where they had applied for work.

Little Mary, who still maintained the nickname bestowed upon her after her tiny weight when she was born, kept good records of who they helped and how frequently they came and how much food was given to them and the size of the family they had to feed. They would do their best to help these local families. The McDonalds started their program in the spring of 1930 and carried on through to the end of the Depression.

The McDonalds had an overwhelming amount of vegetables in all the root cellars on the farm, as well as the massive cold house they built to keep the crops preserved over winter. They knew they were okay, but they still had to sell to make money for the farm and share it with the government.

The McDonalds slaughtered an Angus cow or two a few times a year and provided small amounts of ground beef when they could. Each worker would receive potatoes and other vegetables, along with fruit when in season too. They tried their best to help families cope with the Depression.

During these ten years, the potato crops were still quite successful. This was in large contrast to the Canadian prairie farmers and their wheat crops. There was serious drought for a few years, and their crops were very poor. So were the farmers and their communities. Canada relied so much on their wheat crops for world trade and was one of Canada's main sources of income. It was not only Canada that suffered but also other countries. They didn't have the wheat to sustain the populations of their countries.

This commodity was in dire straits. The crops failed from 1933 to 1937. The railroad was bankrupt, and Canada could not keep up with everything. On Olde McDonald's Potato Farm, they were affected very little by the drought. They remained successful because of Jed Allen and the irrigation plan he had been taught in Africa. They could utilize the Thames River, and their crops flourished year after year. This proved to be a saving grace.

The McDonalds had fairly successful crops each year. Even during a hot summer drought one year in Ontario, they still made money.

There were also government contracts to help out in other provinces with their potatoes.

George and Patrick wanted to make a business acquisition. They talked to Mary about it, and she agreed. Down the road about a mile was a brand-new golf course not even a year old. It had nine holes completed, but there was enough land around to expand it to eighteen holes. The owners put a lot of money into it, but when the crash came, they lost all their money and abandoned the course. The McDonalds certainly had enough money to buy it. The three excitedly agreed to it.

They sought out the owners and made a low offer. They happily took it. So Olde McDonald's Potato Farm had bought a new business, which, of course, would be called Olde McDonald's Golf Course.

The family was so excited. Around the dining room table, one night, it was decided that on the farm, they would only keep one putting green, one driving range, and the challenging double hole designed by Johnny McDonald. The rest of the golf areas on the farm would be turned back into workable crop land. They would also start to develop the land on the course to make more holes. It was going to be eighteen holes, whenever they could get it landscaped. The first thing they wanted to do was duplicate Johnny McDonald's double hole while expanding. They decided that the family-favorite hole was going to be number thirteen!

Even with the Depression on, there were still people who could afford to golf. After they got the existing nine holes ready to play, the course was open every day, except Sundays, during the season. They felt they could maybe model their course after St. Andrews in Scotland in some ways.

They even had the idea to duplicate a few of St. Andrews's challenging holes and maybe some of the bunkers too. Diana and Johnny had described every detail of St. Andrews to the whole family.

Richard was left in charge of the course, and he could hire the staff he needed to run it, including a couple of caddies.

As the years of the Depression went on, George and Marteen's office was never empty. There were so many people sick and needing medical attention that they worked every day but Sundays. They only made house calls when it was absolutely necessary. They didn't have the time.

Their children were growing fast. Elizabeth and Joseph were going through their awkward teenage years while Abe and Simon had started school already. They went to the same school all the kids went to, and Eleanor still taught grade one. During the Depression, the grades six, seven, and eight were sparsely attended. Most families needed these children to go out and work to help support their families. Eleanor thought it was such a shame that they had to sacrifice their education.

In the summer of 1933, when Liz was only thirteen years old, one of the occasional men the McDonalds were helping out took a shine to the girl. She was developing into a lovely young lady. Joe worked out in the field, and Liz took the pails of drinking water out twice every day. Joe always tried to stay near her and linger, but either Patrick or Emmett would tell him with a grin, because they knew where his mind was, to get back to work. He reluctantly would. The two kids would always see each other later at supper.

The worker that liked Liz slipped away one day without being noticed by anyone, he thought. He followed her, and he hid in one of the empty grain bins in the barn while she went into the house. He didn't know when his opportunity would come, but he was lucky. She came out of the house and went right in the barn and into his trap.

As she came in the door, he jumped out and grabbed her with one arm, and he put his other hand over her mouth to muffle her screams. He pushed her down on to the barn floor and was sitting on her, still with his hand over her mouth. Out of his back pocket, he pulled a rag. He stuffed it in her mouth.

The man started ripping her blouse off; she was not wearing a bra. She still was small in the breast department, but her mother assured her she would grow more. She hoped her mother was right. But it didn't matter to her attacker!

The man overpowered her more and ripped down her work trousers. She tried desperately to struggle and keep them on and get away, or at least she tried to injure him. She could not. He was too strong. She now lay there almost naked, and his pants were unzipped. His penis was very large and hard. She was afraid. He tried to enter her, but she was still struggling with every bit of energy she could muster.

He tried to get into her, but she was a virgin; it would take a couple of attempts.

All of a sudden, the entire weight of his body came falling down on top of Liz. At first she wasn't sure what was happening. Then it became clear. She saw a pitchfork in the back of the man and Joseph standing right there beside them, still holding the handle. The man was dead. Joe had killed him. They would find out later that as Joseph grabbed the pitchfork from inside the barn door, he saw what was happening, and he lunged forward and brought the force of his stab and the whole fork almost right through him.

After they realized what Joe had done, the kids were both in shock. They heard some quick steps running toward them. All of a sudden, Emmett came into the barn and saw what transpired. Joe and Emmett removed the worker's body off Liz. Emmett grabbed a horse blanket to put over Liz. He said, "Come, you two, let's go in the house, and you have to tell us everything that happened." Liz, still very shaken up, and Joe, who was still in a bit of a daze, went to the McDonald house with him. George had just dropped by on his way to a house call and saw the kids come in.

He and Eleanor were horrified at the condition of their daughter.

Both kids told them about the near rape and Joe killing the man with a pitchfork and then about Emmett coming in just a few seconds too late to stop Joe. They had to call the police, but there were extenuating circumstances with the scenario that went on in the barn. There could be serious trouble for Joe when police arrived. He was black. To save Joe, Emmett had a plan. And it had to be agreed upon quickly so they could call police in as soon as possible.

Everyone sat around the dining room table after El helped Liz change into fresh clothes but kept the torn ones as proof. When they returned to the dining room, George was enraged that someone touched his little girl in this way. So was Joe. As the five sat around the table, Emmett told them about his plan.

Emmett started to tell his plan quickly. "Now we know killing is a crime, whose punishment is death most times. The worker is black. Joseph is black. The bigoted police officer that works in this area won't care that the victim is black and dead, but Joe, being black, killing anyone, means his own death no matter who it was, what color he was, or how old Joseph is. We tell the police about the near rape of Elizabeth, and I'm sorry, honey, you'll have to go along with the plan . . . as a matter of fact, it falls mostly on your shoulders, kids.

"We tell them I came in and killed the man with the pitchfork, trying to save Liz. Joe can't even say he was in or anywhere near the barn. In all likelihood, being white, killing a black rapist, I won't even see jail time. Do you all agree?"

George and Eleanor looked at Emmett. George said, "Emmett, are you sure you want to do this?"

Emmett said, "It's the only way to save Joe's life. But there's more. Not one of us in this room can tell my parents or my brother I'm not guilty. We have to make my family believe I did it We can't even mention Joe. If anyone saw him leave the field, he was going to the outhouse and has no knowledge of anything in the barn!" George knew he was right. So did Eleanor.

Just then Marty came in the house. She looked at the faces of them all. She wasn't sure what told her to go home, but something told her she was needed. Marty quickly said, "What's going on here? What's happened?" She walked over and put her hand on her son's shoulder. She knew something happened with him. She felt it. "What is it? Someone tell me now!"

When she found out her son murdered a man, she wept. She knew it would be a death sentence for him. Emmett put his arm around Dr. Marty's shoulder and said, "Don't fret, Doc. I did it!" Emmett explained his plan and swore her to secrecy too.

She looked at Emmett and she felt such a feeling she'd never had before. She couldn't believe someone would save her son's life like this. She held Emmett. Then Eleanor went to Liz and asked her if she could follow the plan. Liz said she could. George remained with Marty, tenderly comforting her.

Joe looked at her and he said, "I'm so sorry, Mama. I couldn't let that man get away with hurting my Lizzy. I had to save her! I guess that makes me like my Great-Grandpa Jed. He killed a man trying to rape his Mary. He had to save her, just like I had to save Liz." The adults looked at each other shocked but had to agree. Jed was never arrested for it, and if they follow Emmett's plan, Joe would not be arrested either.

Both George and Marty held Joe, knowing he would have to be strong; Liz too. Joe said he could follow the plan, and his mom breathed a sigh of relief. Eleanor held Liz, trying to comfort her after her attack. Liz stayed strong and brave.

George did the postmortem because there was no pathologist in the area. He sometimes had to double up on this duty. He didn't mind; he was glad to put more skills to use and learn more from the human body.

He found that both of the man's lungs and heart were pierced. Joseph had no idea exactly where he was aiming; he just took the fork and hit the man with it. George discovered that the hit was just below both the left and right scapula, somehow missing the ribs and spine. He died instantly.

Elizabeth McDonald was the strongest one during the interrogation and the trial. Emmett was arrested that day, but within an hour, he was home, back working in the field. After the trial Emmett was acquitted and hailed a hero for saving Elizabeth from being raped and possibly murdered by the black transient. It was always to remain that—only six people on Earth knew what really happened in the McDonalds' barn that hot summer day.

Joe and Liz would complete grade eight and high school just like all of the kids raised on the farm. Diana and Johnny made good their promise that all the kids on the farm would go as far as they could with their education.

As well as school, the kids all had their own jobs to do. There was so much to do on the ever-expanding farm. Even golfing had to take a backseat sometimes. The families would tend to the putting green and their driving range at the farm and sometimes go down the road to play at their course when there was time. The only holes they maintained on the farm now was the double par 5 / par 3 holes. There was a new generation of golfers in the families, and they would be taught well and enjoy the game. The golf course was slowly being landscaped into eighteen holes during the decade.

George and Marteen seemed to be at the office all the time. El thought Marty was working too hard and did not make enough time for herself. She should be getting out to meet people and date. After all, her son was growing up fast. He did not need her as much as he did when he was younger. He was a very independent boy. He wanted to talk to her or George about a few things. His chest was sore at times. He wasn't overexerting himself, and there was no explanation—just chest pain and shortness of breath. The other thing he wanted to talk to George about was most embarrassing. For that he wanted to talk to George alone. He just couldn't talk to his mom.

Joseph had recently been getting erections that would last longer than they should. He wouldn't dare tell his mom about this. It would be too embarrassing for him. When he told George one night, George became upset. Joe thought he did something wrong. When George reassured him he hadn't, he told Joe to let him know how long these symptoms had been happening.

Joe told him his chest would become sore once in a while over the previous two years. The erections had been happening about once every ten weeks for about a year. George told him that he had to tell his mother. Joe was worried what his mom would say.

George said, "Joe, you've done nothing wrong, son, but this could be serious. You don't have to be there when I tell her if you prefer." Joseph was relieved! He saw a very concerned look on George's face.

Joe asked, "George, am I really sick?"

George replied, "Son, don't worry. Let me talk to your mom, and we'll see what we come up with. Please, Joe, don't worry, okay?" Joe nodded his head. He thanked George for his time and gave him a hug, which he hadn't done in years, and went off to his house. Just a little while later his mom got home, and Joe was hungry. They went over to Diana's house, where Caroline was still making the best meals and much of the family gathered to eat! Everyone loved her cooking.

Little Mary's family had grown during the Depression years too. Her boys both got married and now had their own children. She hired her own housekeeper to work for them. She didn't live on the farm, but she came early in the morning and stayed until after supper. Mary and her family had their meals together at her house until the boys' wives took over at their own houses. The rest of the times were spent working together to keep the farm successful, as well as their golf course just down the road.

The next day at the office, George talked to Marteen about Joe. She sat down in his office chair and started to weep. The writing seemed to be on the wall. Joseph Sr. and Marty were obviously carriers and passed the genes on to Joseph Jr. Not only the genes, but he also had the disease. Joseph Jr. had sickle-cell disease. How long did he have to live? Marty's father was only thirty-six when he died, and Jed Allen died at twenty-three years old. She wept. George put his arms around her to console her. She lifted her head and stared at him.

She stood up and said, "George, my boy is going to die. I thought we escaped the disease.

George, why my son? Why? Is God punishing us for what we've done?"

George looked at her and replied, "Marty, you know as well as I do the symptoms could surface at any time. He was tested. We knew, hon. I guess it had to happen sometime. I'm sorry. I wish we could spare him the pain he'll go through. I hope he has time to marry and have children. I would love to see him grow old. I hope science can find an answer in time to control this disease or cure it. Sweetie, you be strong for him. And no more asking if God is punishing us. We can't help it that we've been in love. When I hold you or hug you or even a peck on the cheek, you send electricity through my body. I ache for you. I want to tear your clothes off and make love to you. Even now, I want you."

As he held Marteen, he kissed her like they did that first time eleven years earlier. There was such passion and such intensity. He now did the same thing he did the first time they made love. He locked the office door and cleared the desk off. He sat her on the desk and continued to kiss her. He couldn't wait to get inside her. She was feeling the same then and now. She wanted him. As he quickly pushed her skirt up, he pulled off her underpants. Within seconds, he was inside her, and she was experiencing an intense climax. Seconds later, George climaxed too.

Marty remembered the first time they did it. When they finished, she sat on the edge of his desk and put her arms around his neck and said, "George, El can't find out about this. I don't want to hurt her."

George agreed, "No, love, I don't want to hurt her either, but I want you and need you! As odd as this might sound, Marty, I *do* love my wife very much and my children." She tenderly kissed him and assured him that she knew and understood. She'd had no expectations about their relationship over the years, and she would always be there whenever he wanted her.

For eleven years they'd made love as much as they could. It was at least three or four times a week, mostly in the office. There were times when they could steal a few hours and run to a small flat George kept in Windsor just for that reason. Eleanor had no idea that George kept an apartment in Windsor. Only Marty knew. She thought of it as theirs.

After Joe Sr. died, Marty didn't really think she would pursue relationships with men, but she wanted to be safe. She went back to the doctor in Toronto to place another IUD in. She did not want to get pregnant, unless she never married again. George knew she had it and was glad.

With having Marty a few times a week and occasionally his wife, George still wasn't satisfied though. The prostitutes in Windsor and sometimes in Detroit, just across the river, serviced him as frequently as he needed and had time for. Marty wasn't aware of this; she thought she was the only other one.

Marteen had to give her son the news she'd dreaded for years. That evening, after supper, she explained sickle-cell disease to him and that he had it from birth. She explained that he had inherited it and that she never said anything until now because she was waiting until symptoms arose, if they ever were going to. She told him that she prayed they never would. She apologized for not telling him before, but she wanted to spare him any worry. There was nothing anyone could do about it. They held each other and cried.

Joseph asked with a lump in his throat, "Mom, is it okay to be scared? I don't want to die. Can't you help me?"

As tears rolled down her cheeks, she helplessly put her arms around her son and said, "Oh, my beautiful son, I wish it were different. I wish you could never feel pain. I love you so much I wish that alone was enough to make this disease go away, but it can't. I'm so sorry, my darling boy." She stroked his hair as she held him to her. She wiped a tear from his eye and continued, "We have to remember, you could still have many happy, full years. You've only had a few symptoms so far.

It's possible they may not be severe or frequent. We just don't know if and when they will surface. We have to be positive, son. You must make up your mind that you're going to have a good life . . . don't lose hope, darling!"

Joseph wiped more tears away, and he said to his mother, "Mom, you know I love to play hockey and golf. Do I have to quit?"

Marty said, "I know you do, dear, and there is no reason that you should quit, unless you have too much shortness of breath or chest pain again . . . or any of the other symptoms. In that case, you have to stop and rest. As I told you, the blood flow to your organs has a hard time moving through the veins and arteries because your blood cells are not shaped a normal round shape. Your blood cells are in the shape of a sickle . . . you know, what they used in the fields for years to cut the hay and other crops? Your blood has a harder time getting to where it's going, and that causes the pain, and when it's in your chest, your lungs, that causes the shortness of breath.

"Honey, you don't have to quit hockey altogether or anything else you do in daily life. You just keep doing everything you normally do, unless you have the symptoms. There is no reason to change your life or routine right now." He felt a little better and gave his mom a forced smile of relief. She couldn't help it; she smiled too through her own tears.

Joe said, "I wish Dad or Grandpa was here." His mom looked at him and said, "I do too, sweetie. I miss them too. Joe, I know you're having what's called priapism of the penis. That is when an erection doesn't go down for hours. I'm sorry, baby, but that's one of the symptoms of the disease too. There is no cure for that either, dear . . . I'm sorry."

Joe told his mother, "Mom . . . you know . . . well . . ." He kind of gave a chuckle and continued, "I'm sure everyone knows how I feel about Liz. I love her. I want to marry her someday. Do you think I have enough time to finish school, start my career, and get married? I'd like to be a dad too. Do you think I have time?"

All of a sudden, her Joseph seemed to grow up right before her eyes. She was a little surprised and disappointed. She seemed to have been too busy to notice he was growing up. All she could say to answer his question was, "Oh, honey, only God knows that. We have to trust in him now. But if I were you, I'd go ahead and plan my life and carry on, just like you always wanted, okay?" All she could do was hold him.

Joe kissed his mother and sat in his favorite recliner. After crying and praying, he found sleep. Much like her son, Marty cried and prayed and fell asleep on the sofa. As he drifted off, he decided that he did not want to tell Liz about the sickle-cell disease just yet.

Joseph was lucky. During high school, he hardly had any severe symptoms at all. He was a firm believer in prayer. This was mostly due to Liz. She was the best influence on him, and she helped him through everything he asked of her. They knew they were truly in love when he was in grade ten and she was in grade nine and decided they wanted to be together forever. It was after the near rape of Elizabeth. They were inseparable still. Their parents knew and approved. The kids still did everything together—their chores, their homework, skating in the winter, and golfing in the summer. They would be together most of every day, unless they were in classes.

In the winter, Liz skated around on the Thames while enthusiastically watching her Joseph and some boys play hockey as much as they could. He loved it and he was a natural at it. He had great potential as a professional player, if they only accepted black players! Liz wished that there was no prejudice, but at least they lived in Ontario, where it was nothing compared to the way it was across the border, in the United States.

Joseph was a strong boy, capable of heavy tasks, just like all the males in both families. His disease did not rear its ugly head too often. He was very fortunate. Whenever he had chest pain or shortness of breath, he would take a rest. As soon as he felt up to it, he would continue. He'd paid close attention to what his mother taught him about his disease and coped with it very well. He even participated in high school sports. His favorite sport, of course, was hockey. He got winded and had to sit out at times, but he loved it and wanted to do it anyway. His mother said that if he was happy and could accept what might happen, he had her blessing.

He also had her blessing to go to university. Most blacks in the United States could barely get to high school. Their schools were segregated. There were white schools and fewer black schools. His plan was always to become a structural engineer . . . he wanted to build bridges. Liz wanted to be a teacher. She learned about the many women in her family being teachers, and she decided that was what she wanted to do too. She loved children.

In 1937, Queen's University in Kingston, Ontario, accepted Joe with an unprecedented scholarship while Liz was finishing her last year of high school in Chatham. Joseph was the first black student accepted at the university. He was highly intelligent, and it showed in his studies and excellent grades in high school. That, and his legendary hockey skills. He was well-known around Chatham, Windsor, London, and Toronto. He played every year for the Chatham Harvesters as a teenager. The sports department of Queen's University had scouted him for a couple of seasons, and the coach went to the dean and the board of directors and requested that they offer the boy a hockey scholarship. As long as he remained in good standing in his program and played hockey for them, the university would pay his tuition and rent.

It was also the first time Liz and Joe were to be *really* separated. They knew the time would come that they would be apart, but Liz was going to apply to Queen's the next year to become a teacher. They would be separated that first year by many miles.

Queen's University was established in the city of Kingston, Ontario, in 1841 by the Royal Charter of Queen Victoria. It was twenty-six years before Canadian Confederation. They were the first Canadian University in the united Province of Canada that gave degrees to and admitted women.

This university was modeled after the University of Edinburgh. George was happy because of the Scottish connection. He knew his grandma, Diana, would be pleased. This university was meant for the McDonalds and McGees. George was pleased about Joe being admitted and receiving the first black hockey scholarship ever. George always kept an eye out on the team sports when he went to McGill University.

There had been a great rivalry between Queen's and McGill, where he had gone years before. He was interested in seeing if Joe was up to the challenge. The university knew about Joe's health but still wanted him. They needed him to beat McGill! The Queen's-McGill rivalry was the second longest rivalry in Canada's history. It was second to the rivalry of Queen's and the Royal Military College.

The Queen's-McGill rivalry went back to February 2, 1895. Queen's won over McGill, 6–5. In Kingston, Queen's referred to it as the Kill McGill game. After that, the games against McGill were always called that. Queen's hockey team was The Tricolors. All of Queen's teams were called that. Their school colors were red, gold, and blue, hence the tricolors. Their rally cry was always, "Oil Thigh," which was their fight song. It was sung in Gaelic, another Scottish connection.

During Joe's first year at Queen's, he could only come home on holidays. Although Thanksgiving was around the beginning of the varsity hockey season, the boys were all able to go home that weekend. Joe would only be able to go home for Thanksgiving, Christmas, and Easter. Liz was heartbroken. She started to think that maybe he would find someone at the university. Would he fall in love with someone else? She was afraid to ask him. She wasn't sure she could handle the answer.

When Joe went off to university, he took a part of the farm with him. Although his dorm room was furnished with a bed, desk, chair, and dresser, he found a way to take his favorite recliner with him. It just fit in the dorm room. He was happy. Joseph named his recliner Old Reliable—just like Diana and Johnny's first rooster. This was his thinking chair. It got him through many challenges in his life.

Marteen and Liz were always telling him he should get rid of the ratty old thing, but he wouldn't hear of it. What they didn't know was Old Reliable also took him home whenever he was lonesome. The chair held many memories of his childhood, and it would bring a smile to him, when he needed it most.

In midfall, right from his first year of university, he was a major star on the varsity hockey team. He was to be assistant captain for 1937, '38, '39, and '40. After that, several years of varsity sports were to be interrupted by another war.

The university thought maybe they should not make Joe captain due to his color, although he really deserved it. What might the other universities think? They named a white player, Wayne O'Shea, who was to become Joe's good friend, the team captain for those four years. He was pleased with this arrangement; it was a great responsibility, and he wanted to concentrate on studies, not just hockey.

Joe was star material from day one, according to the coach. This was the primary reason that he didn't come home often; he had so many games to play for the season. Their practices kept him just as busy as his studies. The coach and the team knew about his medical condition, and he was free to rest if he had to. He loved playing. The university placed great faith in their new star. He was nervous about it sometimes but handled it well.

In November of that first year, Eleanor and George let Liz travel to Kingston by bus so she could visit Joe and get to know the university, since she was planning to be studying there the next year. She hoped to be accepted into the teaching program. It would take an eight-hour bus trip just to be with him. It was a surprise for Joe, and she was so excited.

When she got to Kingston, she was on her own, until she found him. Liz's mom made sure she had enough money for travel around the city, as well as money for meals and a good hotel room. The hotel was walking distance from the bus station. She got settled into her hotel in the late afternoon on that Friday. She could hardly contain her excitement. She had a copy of Joe's practice schedule, as well as his game schedule. If she could not find him on campus or in the dorm he lived in, she was sure she could find him at the arena.

Chapter 26

University Years

I N KINGSTON, AT QUEEN'S UNIVERSITY, Liz checked with the housemother at Joe's dorm.

Helena was a lovely woman who had a firm hand with the boys when it came to the rules and curfews. When Liz introduced herself to Helena, she said, "Hello, ma'am, my name is Liz, Elizabeth—"

Helena said, "No, wait, let me guess . . . you are Liz McDonald from Chatham, and you're here to visit your beau, Joe Allen, right?"

Liz was wide-eyed and asked, "How did you know that?" Helena replied, "Honey, everyone in this dorm knows about you and how much that boy loves you!" Liz was so touched and a little embarrassed. Helena checked Joe's schedule to see where he should be in the afternoon. She told Liz, "Well, dear, he is done with classes for the day and should be at the arena for practice. There is a game tonight and tomorrow night too. They don't normally have back-to-back games, but this weekend is different. They are playing McGill in two games. There was a storm previously in Quebec, and they had to cancel a game. It was decided they would play the regular game this weekend, and they scheduled the cancelled one this weekend too. And I'll tell you, girl, this is some weekend you picked to come and surprise your honey."

Liz was pleasantly surprised by her meeting and thanked Helena for the information as she gave her directions to the arena. The arena was just off campus and within walking distance of the dorm. She thanked her new friend again and told her she would see her again over the weekend. Liz felt really good about meeting Helena. She was so nice. Liz thought of her as sort of a white version of Beulah. She expected that Joe thought so too.

After Liz had left, Helena thought to herself, *I never expected her to be white! I never would have guessed.* It didn't matter to her, but she was very surprised.

Within five minutes, Liz found the arena. There was lots of noise on the ice as she entered the building. They were having a good practice. Liz slipped into the bleachers and just watched. She would not bring attention to herself; she wanted to see if Joe would notice her.

Joe was playing well, but Liz worried about his chest and his breathing. He, Marty, and Liz's dad explained the sickle-cell disease to her just before he went away to the university. She accepted it and would always support Joe, and whatever God had in mind for them, they'd go through it together.

As she watched him, she stared off into space for a moment. She was thinking about spending time alone with him over the weekend. All of a sudden, her concentration was broken. Right in front of her was Joseph with the biggest, most beautiful smile she'd ever seen.

He said, "Excuse me, ma'am, am I interrupting a daydream?" She jumped up and threw her arms around his neck and kissed him. He kissed her back. All of a sudden the noise stopped from the rink. The players were all standing still and staring at the couple.

Suddenly, in unison, the whole team yelled out, "Hi, Liz!" She turned and giggled and gave them all a big smile and waved at them. She went back to kissing Joseph.

The coach said, "Okay, guys, now that we've all said hi to Liz, can we please get on with our practice? Joe, get back to practice. You can see your gal later!" Joe kissed her again, gave her a big smile, and told her they'd be done in an hour.

The coach allowed her to stay for practice as long as Joe concentrated on the game and not her. She sat quietly and watched. She was so impressed with his performance. He'd improved, even though she never thought that was possible. To her, he was the best hockey player in the whole world! She remembered how he loved to skate on the Thames at the farm. He loved it just as much as she loved golf.

As Liz sat in the arena, she remembered that every year the Thames would freeze over near their place and toward Chatham, and the boys from around would always play hockey after chores.

Many of Joe's friends from school would come out and play in the evenings until it became too dark. They also played on Saturdays and Sundays if they could get away with it. Some parents disapproved of sports on Sundays—it was the Lord's Day and a day of rest.

Eventually the boys' skills were known in town, and people came out to watch. Parents and town officials decided to form a town team and play other town teams. They formed a team, known as the Chatham Harvesters, which would live on for a very long time. Everyone in and around the farm knew how to skate. Just like everyone knew how to golf. Each generation would pass down the love of sports to the next. They always had so much fun.

Liz's thoughts were interrupted by the loud horn, signaling the end of practice. Joe came to the bleachers and kissed her again. He was so happy she was there. He told her that unfortunately, he would not see her much; there were rules from the university and the coach. She was disappointed but so happy to be in his arms. The coach called to him to get to the change room, and he kissed Liz quick and told her to stay there. Within twenty minutes he was back to her, and the coach told him that he could go have supper with her, but he had to be back at the arena at 6:00 p.m. sharp, no exceptions or excuses.

As they were leaving the arena, Liz was so thankful to the coach that when they saw him as they were leaving, she ran up to him and gave him a big kiss on the cheek. He was so surprised that he said to Joe, "You look after her, son. You were right! She's a pistol!" The coach smiled at them as they left and followed the team to the university dining hall.

When they left, Liz burst out, "I love you, Joe. I've missed you so much. Are you surprised?"

He said, "Surprise doesn't even come close, love. I'm so happy you're here. It is such an important weekend for the team, for Queen's, and now I have your love and support from the stands. I'm so thrilled! I know you're disappointed there won't be much time you can see me, but my heart is always with you." They kissed, and he continued, "You have to come and meet Helena at my dorm." She told Joe they were already acquainted. He looked more surprised.

Liz told him, "She's really sweet. I like her. My dad picked this weekend to let me come for a visit because of the Kill McGill games. He wanted me to be here for you and a little bit for him too. I think he was jealous a bit that I was coming. Dad, Mom, and your mom arranged it all.

When Joe was away from the team that afternoon, they gossiped a little about him. It never occurred to the team that Liz was a white girl, and they would be classified as a multiracial couple. It was quite unheard of in most parts of Canada and never in the United States. Some of the team never gave it a second thought, but a few needed time to get used to it.

Joe took Liz off campus a couple of blocks away to a place where the boys always took their dates to eat. They had good food and reasonable prices. They had a great dinner, although Joe rushed through it. He wanted to go to the hotel Liz checked into and make sure it was good enough for her. He was impressed. It was beautiful.

As Joe kissed her in her room, he suddenly quit. She was taken aback and said, "What's wrong, Joe?"

"Nothing," he said. "It's getting on to time I have to report back." His real reason was that he was getting excited. He couldn't risk getting an erection without it going away for several hours. It would be too painful to skate. He just couldn't tell her the reason. It was embarrassing.

As Joe and Liz were leaving the hotel, her father, Marteen, and Eleanor were getting out of a taxi. They both were shocked. George said to his daughter, "Honey, it's not that we don't trust you two or you being so far from home—"

Eleanor cut in, "Hon, you know your father. He just couldn't stay away this weekend, the Kill McGill games and all. He would not be happy until we all came. I hope you don't mind, dear."

Liz had tears in her eyes as she reached up and hugged her father and then her mother and said, "I'm happy you're here to see his games. I didn't know if I could remember all the plays and goals to tell Daddy anyway." They all laughed.

Meanwhile Marty went to her son and put her arms around him and said, "Hi, honey. How are you? Is everything going okay? This is a big weekend for you. I love you, darlin'. Do you mind your old mama being here to cheer you on?" She kissed him, and he told her that he was so happy to see her and Liz's parents. It meant a lot to him that they would come so far to see these important games.

Joe checked the time and said he had to get to the arena. He only had fifteen minutes to report to the coach. As he hugged everyone, he told them to be there by 7:00 p.m. to get the best seats. He kissed Liz and whispered, "I love you!" She smiled and he was gone to get ready for the first game of the weekend.

George, El, and Marty had time to check into the two rooms George had booked for them, one for him and his wife and one for Marty. They had rooms on the same floor as Liz. She wasn't surprised her dad managed this! They also had time to eat supper . . . while Liz impatiently waited for them.

The twins stayed home for the weekend. Caroline was delighted to stay with them. She didn't mind. She loved Abe and Simon being around her. Caroline would also mind Mary's grandchildren while the adults were all out working too. The more, the merrier, she always thought. She really missed not being able to be a mother herself, but she was happy! By this time, Caroline had a staff of two girls. Edwina was twenty and Jane, twenty-two. They were two black girls from her church. They lived together, off the farm, and traveled back and forth every day.

Mary, Patrick, and their families stayed home to look after the businesses but sent their love and best wishes to Joe for his games. Joe was very overwhelmed by all the love and support from his family.

The harvest was going well, and they were just wrapping the season up for another successful year. Potato prices were up again, and toward the end of the 1930s, the McDonald farm was still a great moneymaker. The golf course was thriving through its seasons too.

In Kingston, Friday night's game started poorly for Queen's. McGill came out fighting for their goals. Their attitude was strong: "Queen's is good . . . McGill is better!" There were many people from Quebec who also came to see the game. McGill definitely had their cheering section.

Queen's had Liz! She was their personal cheering section. The whole team heard her and were inspired. By the end of the first period, the score was McGill, 2; Queen's, 1. Joe scored the goal for Queen's.

She continued her cheering, and people around her were getting a kick out of her enthusiasm. When she wasn't yelling, she was telling people around her that her boyfriend was number twenty-four and pointed out his mom to them. He seemed to be everyone's favorite, but many around her weren't sure that they understood. Was she saying the black boy was her boyfriend? But she's white . . . Her mother started to feel it. It was in their stares at them and at Marty too.

Eleanor felt uncomfortable, as did Marty. They had very rarely come up against bigotry and were surprised it was here. They were still in Ontario. George was not upset; he just sat back and watched his daughter have the time of her life and watched Joe. He didn't dare tell her he hoped McGill would win.

Some people, out of ignorance, left the seats around the McDonald party, but most stayed and forgot their thoughts and got back to the game. Liz yelled through the second period, which ended with McGill at 4; Queen's, 4. By now, Joe scored once and assisted on two goals. George thought he was going to have to restrain his daughter before she had a heart attack.

Period three started bad for Queen's. The battle call from Queen's came out, along with the chanting, "Kill McGill," constantly . . . started by Liz. McGill scored a goal in the first five minutes.

Queen's would just have to work harder.

Marty and Eleanor were on their feet. They were yelling "Kill McGill" with the crowd.

George was very amused that his wife got into the spirit and was just like their daughter. He smiled.

He was having a great time with El and Liz. He never glanced at Marty once. Halfway through the third period, Joe scored again. The whole arena was on their feet now. Another nine minutes went by with no goals.

With one minute to end the game, the score was still McGill, 5; Queen's, 5. They had to break the tie. Liz started yelling, "Queen's twenty-four, go Joe!" Joe's mom joined her. Next was El, and then George started to yell with them, and it went through the arena. There was nine seconds to go in the game, and Joe took a chance at the centerline and gave the best slap shot he'd ever made.

The puck slid right in, under the goalie's knees. Queen's won over McGill, 6–5. There were roaring and cheering from all around. The team picked him up and delivered him to Liz, right over the boards. She jumped into his arms and kissed him, and he set her down and hugged his mom. He whispered in her ear, "Mama, don't worry, I feel fine, no pain." He looked at her and saw calm come to her face. He knew she would worry. He hopped over the boards, and the coach told him to join the congratulatory line and victory skate, since he was the star of the game, while McGill left the ice. Everyone cheered as number twenty-four skated by and waved to them. Everyone was excited; there was another game the next day. Would it be as exciting?

After the game, Liz, El, George, and Marty went back to the hotel; and Joe had permission from the coach to go to see them when he was changed. There would not be a really big celebration for the team this victorious Friday night. The coach wanted them fit for practice early Saturday morning. Joe also had permission from Helena to return an hour after curfew. He did not tell his mates he got special treatment, but if they knew, it was only because his family was there to see him. His mom and his girlfriend's family came all the way from Chatham to see him. The team would understand; most were his fellow dormers too. Helena had her hands full with many of the team in her dorm but loved them all. She also attended every game!

Joe came to the hotel and went to his mom's room. Everyone was waiting there for him. Liz got to him first. She jumped in his arms again and hugged him. He set her down and went to his mom again. He hugged her with a tear in his eye. He held her by her shoulders and said, "Mom, I can't believe you're here. I still can't believe you're here. Oh, Mom, I love you." He pulled her close in a hug and wept on her shoulder a little.

"I love you too, dear. Where else would I be on my son's most important weekend of hockey? I can't wait for tomorrow night. I want to see if Liz makes it through the whole game without passing out," she said with a laugh as she held her son.

Everyone laughed but Liz was quiet. When asked what was wrong, she spoke, and she sounded like she had an army of frogs in her throat from all her yelling. She was losing her voice. Everyone was laughing harder; she joined them. They had a good time together, getting caught up on farm news and university news. Their parents had an appointment to meet Helena on Saturday.

This made Joe a little nervous. Not that he thought Helena would say something about him, but he didn't want his mom saying anything embarrassing about him.

It was time for him to leave and go back to the dorm. Marty wanted to go with him to walk him back. He wanted Liz to go too. George would not hear of the two ladies walking back to the hotel unescorted, so he went along with them. Eleanor was tiring out and whispered in George's ear that this could be their honeymoon since they never really had one. He was excited by this. George took his wife in his arms and kissed her passionately. He had taken several moments to hold El on this trip so far. It felt so good to both of them. He kissed her more than usual, and they seemed to have a spark in their eyes for each other that hadn't been there for a long time. Liz saw it . . . she was happy. Marty saw it . . . she was sad.

Saturday morning came early. Liz had set an alarm clock for 8:00 a.m. She told her parents she wanted to see some of the practice, which was starting then. Her parents were going to stay in their room for a couple more hours. She knocked on Marty's door and told her, "I'm going to have breakfast and go to practice. Did you want to come with me? Mom and Dad are staying in bed for a couple more hours." Liz smiled as she said it.

Marty said, "All right, love, just let me finish getting dressed, and we're off."

Marty and Liz went to the restaurant at the hotel for a breakfast that was badly in need of Caroline's touch. Afterward, they walked to the arena and slid into the seats to watch the practice. They were there for over half an hour before Joe noticed and waved at them. He concentrated on the practice, and the coach was happy with the morning the boys put in. Joe had most of the afternoon hours off. They had to let McGill have practice time too. They were allowed to have the rink almost the entire afternoon. The Queen's team had to meet at the campus dining hall with the coach at 4:30 p.m. sharp that afternoon to start prepping for the game.

Joe, Marty, and Liz went back to the hotel and met up with George and El, who looked like a couple in love! They had shared the most intimate night since the beginning years of their marriage. They made love several times, and George was satisfied and happy to have his wife in his arms. He really loved his El and always would. He was starting to think about the mistakes he'd made over the years and how, if she knew about his secret life, it would hurt her so much. Liz was so happy to see them like this.

They all had lunch together, and then Joe showed them all around the campus. They took their parents back to the dorm, where they were invited to take tea with Helena. The kids excused themselves to have some time alone, which no one minded. They went back to the hotel.

They went to Liz's room and took their coats off. Joe held Liz for what seemed like an hour.

She was so happy. She was starting to feel a little excited too. They never really spoke before about their virginity and if they would wait until they were married. They rarely spoke of sex since Liz's near rape over four years earlier. She stood for a moment and looked at Joe. She wanted him.

Although he wanted her, he knew he couldn't let it happen that day. He could not risk the priapism, or the long-lasting erection, he occasionally suffered.

Joe said, "Honey, I know we haven't seen each other alone much, but I need a nap, love. Do you mind?" She smiled at him and led him to the bed and lifted the covers and let him lie down. She tucked him in, and as he was about to drift off, he asked her to wake him up at three thirty. She sat quietly in the room, watching him and worked on her homework, which she brought with her. She did quite a bit on the bus, but there was more reading she had to do for English class.

At about three fifteen, there was a knock on her door. It did not wake Joe up. Liz tiptoed to the door and opened it. Their parents were back. She motioned for them to come in but to be quiet; he had fifteen minutes more to sleep. She told them as soon as they got back to the room he went for his nap, and it was obvious she was hard into her studies. By this time, she was now working on senior biology. Their parents trusted their kids, and no one felt anything inappropriate went on. Joe rolled over and woke up. He was startled to see their parents there.

Marty said, "Well, sleepyhead, how was your nap?" He looked at the clock and saw it was time for him to get up.

He yawned, stretched, and said it was a great nap and that he was feeling good for the game that night. He looked at Liz with her books and said, "As soon as you leave tomorrow, that's what I have to do.

Homework! Liz, thanks for letting me sleep. I know you hadn't planned on being left alone so much, but I really had to have this nap."

She closed her books and went to him and hugged him. "You know I'd do anything for you, sweetie!" She kissed him. Marty watched them and was proud of her son and wished his father was there to see him. She knew he'd be so proud too. She also knew if Jacob had been alive, he never would have missed his grandson's big weekend!

George patted him on the back fatherly and said, "I'm so proud of you too, son. We all are.

And just wait until we get back to Chatham and tell all of them about your success. Everyone who knew we were coming sent their love and best wishes, especially the lads you played hockey with at home. They're proud as well, son." Joe couldn't help it. He hugged Liz's dad, and Eleanor hugged him too. He knew he was loved.

He had to leave to meet the team. The family had a wonderful dinner and told Liz that their tea with Helena was nice, and they really liked her too. They learned that Joe had a bit of a hard time at first, with him being the only black person on the campus. He was a little ostracized, until students learned that he was going to be the star of the hockey team. That was enough to take the color right out of the equation.

First his fellow dormers and his teammates got to know him, and then classmates welcomed him, and there were even young ladies in some of the circles he was in who also called him their friend. He was accepted by about the fourth week of school.

As everyone piled into the arena, Liz and her family were already there. They knew they had to go early for good seats. People from the night before remembered Liz and wanted to be near her. She was fun, and they wanted to get to know her and cheer with her. The seats filled up around them, and some people introduced themselves. Liz discovered that there were several of the teammates' girlfriends there. They sought out to be by the crazy girl, as they called her, and cheer with her. It became a great feeling in the stands Saturday night. People were talking to Marty, telling her she must be so proud of her son, and she was quite happy to talk about him to the people around her. As the game started, Liz had already recruited the other girlfriends and some of the other fans around her.

As the puck dropped, it was Joe at center ice again, not the captain. He was not nervous. He concentrated only on the game, nothing or no one else. He had to. He couldn't let his team down.

Joe quickly took control of the puck and skated left. He got as far as the blue line and shot. It went in. Joe had scored the first goal of the night within the first twenty seconds of the game. The cheers were deafening. Marty was right up beside Liz, cheering and screaming. They faced off Again, and McGill took over. They scored. The puck would elude both nets for the rest of the period.

When the second period began, Joe sat on the bench. He knew where his family was and looked over at them and gave them a thumbs-up. That meant he was fine. Marty was relieved. She and Liz figured he was going to be playing most of the third period and was resting up for it. He was pacing himself. McGill scored two goals within a couple of minutes about ten minutes into the period. Queen's coach sent Joe in before they could get any further. As he played a good game in the second, no one else scored on either team. During the second period, the cheering was not as loud until Joe went on the ice. Then with no scoring, things got quiet again, until the third period began.

Third period started as Joe went to center ice. The crowd was up on their feet again. Could he pull it off again? This time it took eight seconds to get to the net and shoot it in. The arena was gripped with excitement now. Number twenty-four was on the ice, and giving McGill hell! Liz and the girls started the battle cry, which they had taught her, and cheered their number twenty-four! Five minutes later, Wayne, the captain, scored a goal assisted by Joe. The cheering got louder.

By the middle of the third period, the score was 3–3. Joe was on the ice now until the end of the game. McGill snuck in on the Queen's goalie and scored again. There were resounding boos from the crowd. McGill was back in the game with eight minutes to go. Queen's got the puck, and they scored a goal within minutes. This one was by another teammate of Joe's. It was now 4–4 and only a few minutes of play left.

They were down to the last two minutes and the "Kill McGill" cry went up, loud and clear! Everyone was on their feet, stomping and cheering. They were thankful that this was a new arena with concrete-based seating. Wooden seats would have never taken their cheers this night! McGill scored again! It was do or die now.

Joe was behind McGill's net, and the other teammates were sending the puck back and forth for a couple of shots; the goalie kept his eye on the puck. He was good. All at once a teammate shot the puck just to the outside of the net; Joe came out from behind it and shot it into the net. There were only thirty seconds to go. You couldn't hear anything then if you wanted to. Joe had broken the tie. Their hero was on the ice and hard at work. At nineteen seconds to play, Joe gained control again as the puck was dropped, and he scored one more time. It was now Queen's, 6; McGill, 4. As play stopped, there were only fifteen seconds left. The puck was dropped and McGill got control. They could not get it to the net in time before the horn went.

As the congratulatory handshake line formed, Joe was first instead of Wayne, the team's captain—Wayne insisted! McGill was not very friendly toward him, but their coach congratulated Joe and asked if he'd consider changing schools!

Joe laughed and said, "I don't think so, sir. I kinda think they like me around here!" The coach laughed, gave Joe a friendly pat on the back, and told him he's sure he'd see him again later in the season and congratulated him on two great games. The victory skate around gave way to more cheering as McGill filed out of the arena again, defeated—the second time in two days.

As he went to find his family, Joe could not see them after he changed. He finally saw Eleanor and asked where everyone was. Eleanor said, "I'm sorry, dear, but Liz overdid the cheering. She was jumping so much that she landed wrong. Her dad and your mom both agreed that she likely has compound fractures . . . oh, here comes your mom."

Marty came to Joe and kissed, hugged, and congratulated him. "Did El tell you? Liz has a badly broken ankle, son." Joe was shocked, but all three of them burst out laughing. They could not help it. Liz was so enthusiastic she couldn't sit down. She had to jump.

Her mom said, "Don't either of you tell her I laughed." As Joe and Marty laughed still, they nodded. It would be their secret.

The arena had an ambulance pick up Liz, and George went with her to the hospital. The fluoroscope showed as he expected—a serious compound fracture on her right ankle. The surgeon said she needed a plate, pins, and screws to try and put the ankle back together. George told the doctors who he was, and they were more than happy to have him in the operating room, if he wanted. He did . . . he was relieved they invited him into the operating room. He wanted to be with his little girl right now. Liz was not afraid . . . she was still in a state of euphoria. She was talking to everyone about the game. Right into the operating room she was describing how great the game was and her boyfriend too.

George suited up for the operating room and said, "Will someone please shut my daughter up so we can fix that ankle?" Everyone laughed. They couldn't help it. When George came out of the operating room over two hours later, Joe, Marty, and Eleanor were waiting for him.

He said, "Surgery went fine, but she may have a permanent limp. Time will tell. They took Liz to a room and said she'd be there overnight, at least." Then George asked the surgeon, "Can I take her home on the train tomorrow?" He introduced Marty to the surgeon in charge and suggested, "With a doctor and her father a surgeon at home, do you think it would be okay?" He told him it shouldn't be a problem if she was up to it. She was still asleep and would be the whole night. They all gave her a kiss on the forehead before leaving.

They took a taxi and went to the dorm. George went in with Joe to explain to Helena the circumstances why he was late. Joe hugged George and thanked him for being in the operating room, watching over *their* Liz.

Helena broke it up and told him, "Now you scoot, Joe, and get to bed!" She smiled at him.

George got in the taxi, and the three of them went back to the hotel. Eleanor and George continued on with their honeymoon. Marty went to bed alone and sad. She wished she were Eleanor right then. But she was happy to be visiting her son. She'd missed him so much.

Joe knocked on his mom's door in the morning. She was up and packed. She said, "Why don't you and I go have a nice breakfast alone?"

Joe looked a little funny. "But, Mom, shouldn't we wait for George and Eleanor?"

Marty said, "No, dear. Just let them sleep. I'm sure they're worried about Liz. Let them rest a bit more before we have to go home." There was a little sadness in his mom.

Joe held her hand and said, "Mom, you okay?"

She let a tear fall and said, "I'm just so happy to see you and spend time with you, son. I miss you." She could never let her son know how jealous she was of Eleanor and George probably making love or sleeping in each other's arms at that moment.

He accepted her answer, not giving it a second thought, and thought that she was telling him the truth. They went for breakfast. As they were finishing, El and George walked into the dining room hand in hand, just like young lovers.

Joe and his mom stayed and had more coffee while George and Eleanor had breakfast. When they were finished, they all went over to the hospital together. There were lots of commotion down the hall. It was coming from Liz's room. Liz was awake and telling everyone about her boyfriend's goals in the weekend games.

Her parents and Marty heard and started laughing. Joe just nodded his head, saying, "That's my sweetie!" They all went in the room; she was sitting up, holding court with the doctors, patients, and nurses.

Her dad laughed more when they went in. He said, "Tell me, ladies and gentlemen, would you like me to take this maniacal young lady off your hands today? I'm sure your ears are getting sore."

The surgeon greeted George with a handshake and said, "Well, Doctor, you certainly can see your daughter is not suffering too badly. You have my blessing to take her home with you today." Liz got dressed with her mom's help. She was still gabbing a mile a minute!

She thanked the doctors and nurses and said good-bye to everyone around. Her dad helped her hobble out on crutches to the taxi. Everyone went back to the hotel. They gathered everything, checked out of the hotel, and went to the train station. As they left for Chatham that day, Liz cried; she was already missing Joe.

After their train left, Joe headed back to his dorm and hit the books. He had to stay on top with his grades, or he would lose his scholarship. His hockey was second to his education. But he managed both.

During his time playing hockey for Queen's, he truly was the star, but they did not win the championship once in the time he was there. That first season, McGill eventually won the championship. After 1940, there would be no playing of any varsity sports due to another war.

Chapter 27

Another World War
and a Wedding

T O BECOME A STRUCTURAL ENGINEER, Joseph had a lot to learn. He wanted to specialize in bridges. He didn't realize all the knowledge and science it would take just to build a strong, safe bridge and keep it aesthetically pleasing to the public. There were so many factors to consider.

He would learn about man's earliest bridges, rope bridges. It was estimated that they were built by Incas around the 1500s, or maybe even earlier. The 1800s would see wooden bridges, and the 1900s would start to see truss and wrought iron. The six types of bridges Joe would study were beam, cantilever, arch, suspensions, cable-stayed, truss bridges, and wrought iron. Of course his favorite bridge of all was the Windsor-Detroit Ambassador Bridge. Coming in at a very close second was the Golden Gate suspension bridge across San Francisco Bay.

Joe had always been so fascinated by the sheer length of the Golden Gate Bridge. Never had a human built something this long over such a large body of water. It was a triumph to man's dreams, skill, and ingenuity.

He learned engineers must take into account many factors in bridge building. It depends what corner of the earth you build in. There is gravity, snow, rain, wind, seismic activity, temperature, and so many more minute details of construction. He would learn them all in his program. For the duration of his time at Queen's, he was able to get in the same dorm each year with his teammates. Their dorm eventually became known as the Team Dorm around the campus. Helena was still their housemother all of those years too.

In 1938, Liz joined Joe at Queen's. He started his second year while Liz was starting her first. She was able to get into a dorm three buildings away from Joe. Her housemother was a lovely lady called Bernice. She was older but had raised five boys and four girls. After they all left home, she missed being needed. She knew Helena, and she was the one who recommended her for the job. She was so happy to be needed by all these girls at a university. Everyone got along with Bernice.

Liz had visited Joe a few times during his first year. She learned her way around and was introduced to so many new people. By the time she arrived after Labor Day of 1938 for her first day of classes, Liz felt like she already belonged there, and she had so many friends. Most were from the hockey team, their girlfriends, the coach, and some of the faculty knew her too.

Joe was happy to have her so close by now. He could see her in the evenings and shared lunchtimes a couple of days a week. Much of the time, evenings were spent doing homework or cuddling and planning their lives while in Joe's old reliable recliner. Liz had to admit the chair was good for some things. She thought that it wasn't so bad after all.

During the autumn and winter, he was working hard at hockey practices and games.

Wherever the team went, Liz went too, unless she had lots of homework. She was the leader of the cheering squad. It wasn't an official school-organized squad. It was made up of the girlfriends of the players. Of course, Liz was the leader. There was never any doubt about that.

Even after she shattered her ankle while cheering at Joseph's second game the weekend their parents were there, she still did her jumps and cheers. Everyone loved to watch her and listen to her. She was so much fun to be with, and everyone accepted Joe and her as a couple. Sometime during the second hockey season, the coach gave her the nickname Leapin' Liz. The name stuck!

Her dad was not surprised and neither was Marty that Liz would end up with a limp. She was told by her doctor the day after the surgery it was quite possible that she would have a permanent limp. When she was told, she said, "If that's God's will, then so be it. I am ready to accept it."

She had a few months of intense physical therapy, but even with the plate, screws, and pins to help the healing process, she still would have a limp for the rest of her life. But her cheering went on, regardless. So did skating, golfing, and anything else she chose to do.

Liz was so thrilled to be starting her education to become a teacher. Queen's had one of the best teaching programs in Ontario. She would never consider going anywhere else. She studied hard to get accepted by Queen's. She wanted to be with her Joseph. She already spent a year without him on the farm, and she missed him. One year was one year too much.

Liz had to earn a bachelor of arts degree in education. She would also have to go through exams to get her certification in any country, province, or state she chose to teach in. Like most of her family of teachers, she chose to become a primary teacher. She loved small children. She *a*lways wanted to work with children in kindergarten or grades one, two, or three. The potential of these young minds fascinated her, and she was excited to become a big part of their young lives and education. When Liz visited Joe in his first year, she had also become acquainted with the Queen's University Radio Station. She was so excited about this and wanted to be part of it. It had a great history to it.

It had the longest history of radio in the world, except for the originating company, Marconi. The first wireless telegraphy at Queen's campus was in 1902. This radio station was used in World War I. The first play-by-play broadcast of a Queen's-McGill football game was on October 7, 1922. They started to broadcast all the sports games, including hockey games. The best sports games, of Course, were games between Queen's and McGill—the Kill McGill games.

Liz was asked to be part of this club. Her enthusiasm was unstoppable. She was always recruiting people to be in-studio talent for concerts, and she also was helpful in getting people to give donations to keep the radio station going. She was instrumental in approaching both levels of government to help fund the station too. After listening to this high-spirited girl, they felt they had to help. She was quite the little workforce.

At one point, she became an on-the-spot commentator (called Leapin' Liz) for the period breaks in the hockey games. Everyone loved to hear her play up the Queen's team, especially their star, number twenty-four! She would cheer during the periods, and then she would race to the broadcast area so she could do her broadcast.

During 1938 and 1939, the McGill Hockey Team would be the champions again. Their streak ended in 1940. As hard as Joe and his team worked, they would elude the championship this year too. But so would McGill. It was Toronto University that came out in first place that year. After the 1940 season win by Toronto University, interuniversity varsity sports were put on hold due to another war. Liz remained on the air at every hockey game, until their sports were temporarily cancelled.

Queen's had an agreement with Joseph that as long as he played hockey for them, they would pay for his tuition; but with the war and hockey being cancelled, he would have to pay for his last couple of years of university, which was no problem for his mom. He was very fortunate.

On September 1, 1939, Adolf Hitler, chancellor of Germany and head of the Nazi regime, declared war on Poland, and World War II began. It was again the war to end all wars and a couple of years longer than its predecessor, World War I. Canada would fight for their king once again. They would fight for King George VI and his queen, Queen Elizabeth.

Britain and France pledged to help Poland. After that, Britain knew they were in danger of being invaded. On September 3, 1939, both countries declared war on Germany. Canada was the oldest Dominion in the Commonwealth; therefore, on September 10 1939, King George VI announced that Canada had declared war on Germany in a bid to assist Britain. Canada would defend the United Kingdom once again.

After Poland fell, there was what was called the Phony War. There was not much action between October 1939 and April 1940. Then, Germany had invaded Denmark and Norway. The war was on again. On May 10, Germany then invaded countries Holland, Luxembourg,

France, and Belgium. Fortunately, the phony war gave England and Canada time to build their defenses.

France was not as strong as Britain. They surrendered to Germany on June 22, 1940. They didn't have sufficient forces to save themselves and fell completely under German rule until the end of the war.

Italy had joined forces with Germany, causing Canada to declare war on them in June 1940 and after Japan invaded Pearl Harbor in the United States on December 7, 1941 Canada also declared war on Japan that December.

With so much of the world waging war on Germany, it fell in April of 1945, when Hitler and his wife, Eva Braun, committed suicide. The defeat of Japan and the end of World War II came about in August 1945, with the USA dropping an atomic bomb on the cities of Hiroshima and Nagasaki.

During the war, there were more than one million Canadians who fought. Of those, there were forty-five thousand who died and fifty-five thousand wounded. Dr. George McDonald would elude serving in this one. Even with his skills, he was much too old to serve. Many boys from the area went to war, but Joseph was exempt due to his sickle-cell disease. Marty was happy in a way, and Liz was too.

Marteen was not called upon. She was a middle-aged black woman. Liz could not enlist; she wouldn't pass the physical with the plate and screws in her ankle, and with the limp she had, basic training would likely be too much for her.

There were men and boys on the farm who enlisted, and others went off to jobs in car and munitions factories in Windsor and Detroit. Olde McDonald's Potato Farm would still function normally. Again, the farm had government contracts to sell and ship potatoes overseas to help feed troops and continue to make money to assist in the war effort and to help Canada to pay for their part in it. Like always, the McDonalds were happy to participate in any way they could.

The contracts between the government and the McDonalds ensured that their boys remained on the farm, assisting with the farm, and only if they wished to enlist, would they take these boys off the farm. The McDonalds needed the workforce on the farm to fulfill the contracts.

By the end of spring, 1943 Joseph graduated a full structural engineer. His first job started just after he graduated. He was hired by a company that the Ontario government had a contract with. They were building bigger and better roads around the Toronto area because traffic was becoming a big problem. He would be on the engineering team that would build overpasses and bridges in the Toronto area.

His mom bought him a new Ford car (the family favorite) to commute. He really did need one where he was going to be working. He would also take an apartment in the city and come home to the farm on weekends. While Liz was still at Queen's, he would drive to Kingston to see her whenever he could. When Marteen bought Joseph a car after graduation, George and Eleanor bought one for Liz too. It was a Ford as well. She would be commuting too from Kingston to Toronto and to the farm, and it would take less time than buses and trains. For that next year, until Liz graduated, they were separated for short periods, but nothing had changed. They were still deeply in love.

Joe and Liz would meet at the farm for the Christmas holidays of 1944, which was going to be a special one. Joseph Allen had plans for Elizabeth McDonald! Joe's Christmas holidays started on December 24. Or so Liz thought. Joe had actually gotten off work a few days earlier due to mild temperatures and lots of rain—too much to be working outside on overpasses. He had gotten off work on December 22 that Christmas. She didn't know he was home a couple of days earlier than her. He didn't tell her. He wanted time to finish getting her present together and talk to the family.

Since Joe wasn't going to be at the farm until the twenty-fourth, Liz decided to stay in Kingston and come home the same day. She had several class projects on the go and wanted to take advantage of the time and the university and city libraries to complete them. They were due when she got back to classes after Christmas.

Christmas morning of 1944 started just like all Christmases started at the farm. The family awoke, and all would gather at the McDonald house. There would be George, El, Liz, her twin brothers Abe and Simon, as well as Marteen and Joe. On Christmas mornings, Little Mary and all her family would join them for breakfast too. Caroline, Edwina, and Jane put on a great morning feast, and then they all went to church.

After coming back to the farm, there were presents everywhere to be opened. Young and old were all unwrapping gifts, and there was wrapping paper falling to the floor, but no one cared.

Liz was sitting with Joe on the couch. Liz told Joe he would have to guess what his gift was before she would let him unwrap it. She brought it in the living room, and Joe cracked up laughing. She bought him his favorite brand of hockey stick, and she wrapped it . . . like a hockey stick. She kissed him on the nose as she gave it to him. He was thrilled with it. It was a really good quality, expensive professional stick. Most serious players like to use these sticks. He was very happy with his gift. He loved it. They shared a long kiss.

Everyone noticed that nothing had changed over the years. They were still in love. Up until then their parents were wondering when they might get married, and Liz would keep saying, "Oh one of these days, whenever Joe asks me." As of late, she would pause and continue, "I'd marry him in a minute!" Although she said it often enough, she wondered herself if it would really happen. She wondered if he had lost his love for her. She kept her doubts to herself.

Joe slid her present over to her. It was a huge, very heavy box. As she opened up her gift, she was so excited. She couldn't imagine what was so heavy. To her surprise, Joe had given her a brand-new set of encyclopedias, the new *Webster's Dictionary*, a large beautiful world globe, and the newest, up-to-date world atlas.

He said, "Hon, I thought since you are going to be a teacher, these might come in handy for you." He smiled and looked so proud of himself. As they sipped some hot cider, they held hands. Liz was a little miffed. While everyone admired the books, she thought it actually had been an insensitive gift of very little use to her but didn't say it. She had already told him that every classroom was supplied these items, and she saw no real need to have them at home.

As they sat a little longer on the couch, Liz asked Joe, "Sweetie, would you like to go skating and try out your new stick?"

Joe said, "No, I really don't feel like it right now, maybe later. Actually, the river is too dangerous right now. I don't think it is completely frozen. I think I'll just sit around the house and listen to the radio, maybe have a nap, or maybe I'll go for a drive. I'll talk to you later. I'm going home to see if Mom wants me for anything. See ya later, hon." He then patted Liz on the head, kissed her cheek lightly, and left the house.

She was surprised by his comment and very disappointed, but she knew they had another few days to spend at the farm together before they had to head off to school and work again. She supposed that he had maybe had some time set aside for just the two of them before they had to go their separate ways once again. At least she hoped he did!

It had been a warm, dreary, rainy Christmas morning. The more time went by, the more Liz started to get more upset by the way Joe had treated her. She wanted to go over and tell him, but she decided she was going to be mature about things and just let him do as he wanted.

After lunch, the sun came out and it warmed up. Liz still hadn't seen Joe or heard from him. She decided that she was going over to his place to give him a piece of her mind about his behavior. When she looked up, Joe was standing in the doorway. He came into the house carrying two sets of golf clubs, one with a giant red bow on it.

He said, "Does anyone know of a beautiful lady around here that would like to go to our driving range to try out her new Christmas present?" Liz jumped off the couch and ran to Joe. She threw her arms around his neck and kissed him so hard she almost knocked him off his feet. He set her golf bag down, and in one arm, he picked her up off the floor and said, "Merry Christmas, darling. I love you."

He kissed her again and then set his clubs down too. He had both arms around her now, and she felt so loved. She knew from this moment she would love him and no one else the rest of her life. She always said that he was her *destino* . . . just as she was and always would be his.

Liz said, "Are you serious about going out? Isn't it too wet to practice?"

Joe said, "Don't tell me my own little cheering squad, Leapin' Liz, is afraid of a little rain and some puddles!"

She picked up her bag, and they went out to the family driving range. They practiced their drives for a while and then moved onto the putting green. They could not go to their golf course down the road. It was closed for the winter. The two of them laughed and had fun. It was very wet and a little cold, but the sun came out for a while. Several of the family members came outside to watch the two having fun.

After practicing their drives and putts, it was time to head to the double hole to see how good they were. It was a disaster. Both of them were out of practice, and Liz blamed the wet fairway. As they horsed around and walked back toward their parents and brothers, who had come to watch them, Liz trailed behind a little. She wasn't used to the weight of the clubs and bag and all the puddles she was dodging.

Joe took her clubs and gave them to Simon to carry. He picked Liz up and carried her across the puddles, much like the story of Johnny carrying Diana over the puddles on their honeymoon on St. Andrews Golf Course.

As he came over to their parents, he put Liz down. More of the families were now there to watch too. Joe turned to her, got down on one knee, puddles and all, and said, "Elizabeth Diana McDonald, will you marry me?" He had asked her just as Johnny had asked Diana on the golf course in Scotland, with their families watching.

While still on his knee, she sat down on the knee that was up. She put her arms around his neck and kissed him so tenderly. She said, "Joseph, I will marry you. I love you more than anything, and yes, I'll be your wife forever." She kissed him again as the family cheered. She looked deep into his eyes, and she knew what she'd always known—he truly was her *destino*, as she was his.

Their *destino* had no wood or any sails or a captain to guide them through life's sometimes troublesome waters, like their great-grandparents did in the beginning. But like Johnny and Diana, they would love each other through anything life had to throw at them. Just like Jed and Mary did too.

Both mothers were in tears, and even George was a little choked up. His baby girl was going to be a married lady. Liz's brothers were happy for them. When Aunt Mary saw the ring, she threw her arms around Liz. She was so thrilled for her and Joe. Since she never had a daughter of her own, she often felt of Liz as partly hers too. She had always thought of her as more than a niece.

They all headed to Mary's house, since it was the closest, and sat around her table, having coffee and a great chat. Although traditional Christmas dinner was turkey, like the one Mary was keeping her eye on for her clan, Caroline was at the McDonald house, cooking a few large chickens for the Allen and McDonalds, which they preferred.

After everyone had their fill of Christmas dinner, the families met back at the McDonald house, and they all had dessert together and lots of talk, far into the night. There was so much to celebrate this year. Everyone would remember Christmas Day of 1944 for a very long time.

Joe finally told Liz that he had been at the farm for a couple of days before her and that he had asked George and Eleanor's permission for her hand in marriage. He had even gotten approval from her brothers and Aunt Mary. He also told her that their parents, her brothers, and Aunt Mary knew about the gift of the books, the clubs, his nonchalant treatment toward her, and when he was going to propose so they could be there. Joe was so proper and romantic. She couldn't have been more touched and impressed by him. With family about, they began planning their wedding.

Liz would graduate in the spring of 1945, and Joe wanted to give her any kind of wedding she wanted . . . before or after graduation, whenever or wherever she wanted. But he had some ideas of his own that he wanted to share.

Joe had a special request, which he kept to himself until now. He hoped no one thought it was stupid. He asked everyone to hear him out about this idea he had. Liz and their parents obliged, as did Mary and Patrick and all their relatives. They listened as he started to speak. "I know the family history, and I respect it. I know the story about the little girl, Afua Kakira, making the Kente cloth robe and the occasional use of it in weddings in our family."

Liz thought he was going to suggest that she wear it for their wedding and started to say, "Honey—"

He put his hand up to her lips to stop her from talking. When she did, he continued.

"Ashanti Kente robes were traditionally made by and worn by men, but I know over the years women started wearing them too. So my question is, does anyone object if I follow Ashanti tradition and wear the robe myself? It may be a little short, but I don't mind, and there is enough material that I know it will go around me with no problem . . . and I thought maybe Liz could wear her Scottish great-great-great-grandmother's wedding dress that Aunt Mary has and the McGee family tartan sash.

"And honey, do you think you could repeat the Scottish wedding vows that Diana made to Johnny, and I will recite the same Twi vows which Berko said to Afua? We have a copy of them from a letter which was in some of the old correspondence between Mary and Laura Brookes from Jamaica. The other thing that I would like to do, if it's okay with you, is I'd like to jump the broom just before we kiss. Does this all seem like a dumb idea?"

Liz and their parents were stunned. They didn't know what to say. Liz had no idea that he had put so much thought into it. She knelt before Joseph and took his hands in hers. She kissed the back of both of his hands and held them up to her cheeks as a tear rolled down each one and fell on his hands.

She said, "I love you so much. Sweetheart, I wouldn't change one detail. That will be the perfect wedding. How about we get married on the farm holiday, October 10?"

Joe smiled and said, "Of course, I was hoping you'd say that." He kissed his bride-to-be.

Eleanor and George had a warm feeling; Marty too. They were so touched that Elizabeth and Joseph would want to carry on both family traditions and common threads. Mary and Patrick were just as happy and very impressed with Joseph. The family spirits would be just as happy with the arrangements of the upcoming celebration and the fact that Joe and Liz didn't want to forget where they came from!

Mary got a little teary. In a way, she was jealous. Although her sons were already married and had families, she had always wanted a daughter so that she could have helped plan a wedding with her. She was more than happy to give the dress to Liz to wear. She would be the one to own it after she wore it for her wedding since she was the eldest girl in this generation. Liz was so happy. She went to her aunt Mary and hugged her.

Mary was so happy for the couple but still was envious of Liz's mom and Marty being the mothers of the bride and groom. Mary said, "Ladies, and I mean *only* the ladies! Please follow me back to my house." Mary led them up to her bedroom. In the back of her closet, she pulled out the old family wedding dress. Marty and Liz were stunned at its beauty.

As she held it up to Liz, Aunt Mary said, "You are going to be a beautiful bride, my dear." Liz always knew that the dress was there but never actually saw it before. She'd always wanted to wait and see it before she got married. She wanted it to be a surprise for herself. It was so beautiful. Mary said, "My great-grandmother wore this herself. Then my grandmother, then my mother, Diana, wore it for her wedding in Scotland. I was the first to wear it in Canada, and Dora wore it too. Now it's your turn, Liz. You are the fifth generation of McGee women to wear this wedding gown. We cannot count Dora as McGee, of course . . . bless her heart. Do you want to try it on?"

Liz said, "Oh yes, I'd love to." It was a good fit. It just needed a slight alteration. The ladies went to the kitchen. The men were there, drinking Patrick's bottle of Scotch whiskey and celebrating. They all continued to discuss the wedding plans. As Liz thought for a moment, she said, "I'd like it to be here at the farm by the family cemetery, where Jacob and Mina married . . . that way everyone in the family will be there. Jed, Mary, Jacob, Mina, Joe Sr., Diana, Johnny, Dora, George Sr., even the babies. I'd like to have our reception in McDonald Hall, if that's okay with you, darling." Joe smiled and quickly agreed. There were smiles all around. She knew everyone wanted the same thing.

In May of 1945, Liz graduated, and there was a job opening at Chatham Public School 101 for teaching grade one. She was accepted and would start in September of that year.

As October 10 came closer, they both began to get nervous. They wanted the perfect wedding day. They checked the *Farmer's Almanac*, and it advised that it was a favorable time in October for weather. That was good enough for Liz! If the almanac said it was going to be nice, it was going to be nice!

Liz started teaching grade one after Labor Day that year, and she loved it. She now understood how fulfilling it was. She was another generation of McDonald teachers, and she was happy. While she was at school, it gave her less time to worry about wedding details, and she didn't have a lot of time to miss Joseph. He was coming home every weekend now. They spent their weekends discussing wedding plans and their future. They also talked about having children.

They talked at Joe's place and sometimes at the McDonald house. George and El decided, after Liz had started at the university, that she could move into Johnny and Diana's house, where Caroline still lived. It would give her a little more privacy for doing her homework when she came for visits and a little more independence but she also enjoyed sharing the house with Caroline.

Many evenings at the farm, the two of them would also sit on the family swings, planning their wedding day, their lives, and their future together. Sometimes they would sit on the swings for hours, just like when they were kids! These were the times they both cherished the most, up until now!

Their talks usually came around to children. Liz wanted a house full of them. Joseph also wanted children, but he was concerned about the sickle-cell disease. The more the doctors and scientists studied it, the more it looked like there was a fifty-fifty chance he would pass on the disease or at least the trait to children he might father. He and Liz would discuss this many times and learn everything they could. Even though his symptoms were not as regular as his two grandfathers, he still had some. His flare-ups were not as strong as theirs were yet.

It was decided by Liz and Joe that they would have children. If God chose to pass on the disease or if they were to become carriers of the disease themselves, so be it. They would be prepared and would love any and all children that God would bless them with.

The morning of Liz's wedding, her mother helped her get into the family wedding gown and the McGee tartan sash. She had her mother shorten the dress a bit. She was the same size as the gown everywhere else, but with her limp, she wanted it hemmed a bit higher so she would not trip on it or rip it. El thought that was a good idea too and took care of it for her. Liz had tried on the boots, and they fit too. She was surprised and pleased. They were a bit big, but that gave room for the larger foot.

Her lame ankle, with its plate and screws, made her ankle and foot about a half size larger than the other one. Buying shoes was annoying to her. She had to buy two pairs all the time. She would buy her normal size for the normal-sized foot and another pair a half size larger for the other one.

Liz chose her aunt Mary to be her matron of honor, and although it was a little unorthodox for a groom to select a female, Joe asked his mother to stand up for him. Marteen was so touched. She was so happy to be included in the ceremony. Joe chose the twins, Abe and Simon, to hold the broom he and Liz would jump over.

They were thrilled to be a part of the African tradition. It would be something they'd always remember. Abe was taller than Simon, so they rehearsed with Liz a few times so she wouldn't trip and fall over the broom. She did very well, and the boys knew how high she could jump and would make sure not to hold the broom any higher. Eleanor made Liz a marriage kerchief. She copied the one that George's aunt Carol made for their wedding, with slight variations. The couple were delighted to have it. It held such significant meaning, and they wanted to keep some of the Scottish traditions going, as well as the African ones. Their parents couldn't be happier. Liz obviously respected and honored where she came from, as did Joseph.

As George walked Liz down the aisle by the family cemetery, Marteen was standing in front with the minister and her son. Joseph was a very nervous groom. Marty watched as this very beautiful young woman she had known all her life was about to become her daughter-in-law. She made a lovely bride, and Marteen watched with a tear in her eye. She also saw Eleanor was crying, and George's chin was quivering. George couldn't believe he was this emotional. He loved his daughter so much.

As he slowly walked with his daughter, he started to think about all the mistakes he'd made in his life. The women, and there were so many. Then he thought of the best parts. Eleanor, Liz, Abe, and Simon. He regretted not seeing his terrible mistakes sooner. A tear fell down his cheek, and Liz saw. She knew he loved her. But she didn't know what the second tear was for. She disregarded it as an emotional father losing his baby girl. He really didn't want to think about his horrible problems now, just his daughter.

As they reached the minister, Joseph, wearing his Kente robe proudly, smiled at his lovely bride with her dad. George took her hand and Joseph's hand and joined them and then kissed his daughter and stepped back to stand with his wife and put his arm around her. Everyone was so happy that wonderful day.

George listened as the vows were made and then watched them jump the broom. He looked at Marty; she was so happy but yet so sad. Was she thinking the same thing as George? What had they done again? What had he done to her? This time there were much bigger consequences. There was a disease now.

After the beautiful wedding ceremony, the reception was a combination African and Scottish all-nighter. Unlike Diana and Johnny not knowing the house down the road was bought for them, Liz and Joseph knew there was a house on the farm for them, but Joseph was going to move into the McDonald house with Liz after the wedding until the Allen house became his someday . . . although they hoped that would be many years down the road, and Joe's mom would be around a long time.

The reception was held at the newly painted and decorated McDonald Hall. The song that the bride and groom danced to was a favorite of Liz and Joe's. It was released that same year on July 3 by Perry Como. They chose "Till the End of Time."

Everyone applauded as they watched the happy couple dance. You couldn't notice Liz's limp. She glided along the dance floor in Joe's arms so gracefully. The crowd enjoyed watching them while hoping the best for their future.

George had a surprise for the wedding couple. He arranged for a beautiful room in the most expensive hotel in Windsor for their wedding night. He also arranged a chauffeur and a fancy car to take them there. They would also be picked up again in the morning to return them to the farm.

There was no time for a honeymoon, but the fact that they had their own house, so to speak, made up for it. After the reception, they were picked up and driven to Windsor as the party went on into the night.

At the hotel, Joe picked up his bride and carried her over the threshold of the bridal suite.

Once inside, Joe put her down and they kissed. Over the past several years, they never gave into their passions. They decided that they wanted to wait until their wedding night, which they did. They were very happy with their decision.

As Joe helped Liz out of the family wedding gown, he was amazed by her beautiful body. She was slender yet muscular, delicate but strong. She had beautiful breasts, and he took time to caress and tease her. She loved it.

When he stood before her naked, she was so shocked by the size of his penis. They'd never given in, even during their teenage years, to look at each other or cross the line sexually.

His erection was large. She was concerned there might be a problem since she was a virgin. He promised her he would be gentle and take time and that he would never hurt her. He assured her if it didn't happen that night, he would wait for her until she was ready. As he lay on the bed beside her, she admired his strong naked chest. He had worked on the farm without his shirt on most of his life, like most of the farmworkers in the summer, but somehow tonight, it looked so different. There was such a masculine sexiness to it, which she'd never noticed before.

She placed her hands on his chest and slowly ran her long fingernails through the hair. Joe was very excited by this. He was so turned on; he didn't know if he could wait much longer!

As he slowly touched her curly mound, she moaned. It was such a shock to her, but she immediately began to have a most intense orgasm. While she was continuing to have multiple orgasms, he moved on top of her and so quickly slid inside her. It was a slight struggle to get past her hymen, but her complete wetness made it easy for them. Joe quickly ejaculated inside her, and they experienced the most wonderful first time they could have ever imagined.

The love they shared and the love they made that night was beyond all of their expectations. They would always be this close for life, however long or short it would be, together.

Chapter 28

Farewell to the Farm and a Tragedy

T HE BEGINNING OF THEIR MARRIAGE was a little hard to get used to. Joe was still working in Toronto during the week, and Liz was teaching in Chatham. They only saw each other on weekends.

Joe's and Liz's jobs were Monday to Friday. Joe had very little overtime in the winter, and Liz was glad. Joe would be home by 8:00 p.m. on Friday nights and would have to leave the farm every Monday by 4:00 a.m. Joe thought to himself one Sunday night, when he said good-bye to everyone before going back to Toronto, that George was looking unwell, and he seemed worse each week when he came home. He mentioned it to Liz, and she agreed. She would talk to her mom the next day to see if there was something up with her dad's health.

George had been having problems for several weeks. He was having pain urinating, thick pus discharges, and testicle and prostate problems, causing pain in his scrotum. George suspected the worst, and he was right. He had all the symptoms of gonorrhea. And there was a bigger problem. He had fallen off the fidelity wagon at the office and made love to Marty again. She became infected too. The worst though was yet to come.

Just after Liz and Joe got married, Eleanor asked George about a urinary infection she thought she had. He said, "Oh, hun, it's probably nothing. If you still have it in a few days, I'll bring home an antibiotic for you." He became very nervous. Would his secrets come out? Would his world come crashing down around him? He still loved his wife, but could she ever forgive him?

El started to wonder. She thought maybe she had a woman's problem he didn't want to discuss . . . or could it be the change? The next day, she went to Marty after she got home from work and asked her about it. She thought Marty would be more receptive and understanding since she was a female doctor. It made her a little more comfortable about these types of issues. Besides, Marteen was her best friend too.

Marty said, "You know, I have the same symptoms. I wonder if there is something going around." They both giggled.

Eleanor said, "Then there must be something really going around because George is not well in that same department either. But he has it bad." Marty stopped laughing. She hung her head and lowered her eyes like El had never seen before.

Suddenly Eleanor's demeanor changed. Something was wrong. She felt it! She said, "What is it, Marty? Are we sick? If George and I have some disease down there, how could you get it too?" El had always been shy talking about her sexuality and health problems in that department, as she referred to it.

Marty could not raise her head. El thought for a moment, and a horrible thought came to her mind. She continued, "Marty, is this a venereal disease? If George and I are having the same symptoms, why are you having them too? You haven't dated anyone since your husband died. How could you have the same thing we do?" Eleanor felt sick to her stomach and was starting to tear up . . . she knew the answer. She looked at Marty again and stood up. Marty still could not raise her eyes to meet El's.

El said, "How could you? You slept with my husband. How long has this been going on?" She couldn't help it. She screamed out, "Marty?" Eleanor had never yelled in anger before. It just wasn't in her. She slapped her hand hard on the table and yelled again, "Marty, how long?"

Marty still could not lift her head to look at Eleanor. She quietly, in almost a whisper, said, "I don't know, El." She was trying to spare her.

Eleanor demanded, "How long, Marty?"

Marty jumped a little. She never heard her angry like this. She didn't want to answer but still, in a quiet voice, said, "About a dozen years, I guess." She still did not raise her head.

Eleanor cried out, "Twelve years! How could you? You are my best friend! I've considered you my sister! I've loved you since I've known you! Our children are married. How could you ever do this to me?" Eleanor had never felt so betrayed in her life. She was devastated.

Eleanor was crying as she started to run toward the door. After she turned, Marty spoke a little louder this time. "I'm afraid it's worse than we think, El. George didn't get it from you . . . or me. There's obviously someone else." Eleanor's tears were flowing faster now as she ran out Marteen's door. She did not run back to her own house. She was much too upset to face anyone! She couldn't believe what she'd just heard about her husband, whom she loved more than anything in the world, and her best friend carrying on a sexual relationship right under her nose for twelve years!

She ran to a potato field and sat down. She pounded the ground, and she cried. She just couldn't believe what was happening. Her husband, whom she loved unconditionally, had a twelve- year affair with Marteen. She felt like such a fool for not knowing all these years.

Thinking about George now, she thought about the last thing Marty had said. There was someone else he was sleeping with besides them. Her heart was completely broken! She wanted to know who else he had slept with, how long, where, and when . . . but did she *really* want these details? She cried in the potato field for quite some time. No one really missed her. George thought she was at Marty's, and Marty thought she went back to her house to have it out with George.

El would not go back inside her house until she was done crying. She could not let her daughter or sons see her cry. Liz and the twins must never know that their father had an adulterous affair with Joe's mother. She could never put that thought in her children's minds. She could never tell them the truth, and she hoped George and Marty had the decency not to tell any of them the truth either.

After the wedding, things seemed to change around the farm. The business of the potato farm was still going well, and the golf course was very popular and busy in season. But there seemed to be personal problems. Liz could feel tension between her parents. They barely spoke to each other, and Eleanor barely mentioned Marty's name anymore. Marty had told everyone that she wanted to start making her own meals, and Eleanor had suggested that her 320 acres should be sectioned off from the farm so she could do what she liked with it. Liz knew something was wrong, but she couldn't imagine what it could be. When Joe came home one weekend, she mentioned the tension to him. He noticed it in his mother too. They thought they'd better keep away from it and let their parents work out whatever problems they had with each other.

As the weeks went on, George seemed to be getting sicker. He had constant infections, and Liz noticed his health failing. She then thought that whatever was going on had to be health related, and she felt she had a right to know. Maybe her dad had something and he's going to die. At that point, she decided to ask her mother what was going on.

After school the next day, Liz went to her mom and asked, "Mom, is Dad dying or really sick? Joe and I noticed that he doesn't look well. Is there something to be concerned about, Mom?"

El dreaded having to answer this, but she had to tell Liz something. "Well, dear, he isn't feeling well, but I don't think it's something you should worry about."

Liz knew she was lying. She said, "Mom, you're not telling me the truth. What's wrong with Dad? There's something wrong, now what is it? Don't I have the right to know if Dad is sick or dying? If you won't tell me, I'm going to Joe's mom. She'll tell me the truth."

As Liz turned to leave and see Marty, her mother said, "Don't go to her, dear. Please, don't go to her."

Liz looked at her mother, who was now starting to cry. Liz put her arms around her and just let her cry. After a few moments, Eleanor stopped, grabbed her handkerchief, and wiped her tears. She cleared her throat and said, "Honey, I didn't want to tell you this, but I guess I'll have to. I don't want you hearing this from *her* . . . Um . . . uh . . . well . . . your father and Marteen have been having an affair for most of yours and Joseph's lives. Practicing medicine wasn't the only thing they were doing in that office over the years!"

Liz was so shocked; she flopped into one of the kitchen chairs and started to cry too. This time her mother came to her and put her arms around her. They both cried together. Liz asked, "How did you find out?"

El told her, "Your father, Marteen, and I all have gonorrhea . . . it's a . . ."

Liz interrupted her mother and said, "Yeah, Mom, I know what it is. I know how it gets passed on, but where did it originate?"

Eleanor really hoped to avoid this part. She was sure that Liz would not ask, but she did. El told her reluctantly, "Honey, all his adult life, he has been paying for sex too. After it came out about him and Marteen, she and I had to ask where he got it from. His answer hurt me more than you can imagine.

"He told both of us that after he became a surgeon, he started paying prostitutes. Honey, I'm so sorry. He says he's been with hundreds of them over the years. They're mostly from Windsor and Detroit. He says he had an apartment in Windsor for many years." It was a lot for her to take in.

Liz asked, "What do I do about Joe's mom? Joe has to be told too."

Eleanor patted her daughter's hand and said, "Don't you think we should give his mother the opportunity to tell him first?"

Liz thought for a second and said, "I'm going to let her know that I know, and if she doesn't tell him, I will, when he comes home tomorrow." That was her decision, and there was nothing her mother could do about it.

That evening, when George came home from the office, Liz stopped him at the door. She said, "I know about you and Joe's mom!" George was shocked.

He said, "Honey, I know I can't change what I've done over the years, but you have to understand even when I was with her, I didn't love you or your mom or your brothers any less.

I've been here with you all as much as I could."

Liz raised her voice in anger. "Apparently not, Dad. You seemed to have had a lot of your time that could have been here, and instead, you were in some tramp's bed. Dad, Mom loved you so much every day of your lives together, and now because of this sick need you have . . . oh, Dad, I can't even look at you. You disgust me, and you make me sick!"

George's first impulse was to slap his daughter across the face, but he couldn't. She was right. He just looked at her. He was so sad he started to cry. Not only had he lost the love of his wife but also his daughter's.

The twins walked in just then. They heard raised voices but didn't hear what was said. Abraham asked, "Whoa, what's the yelling about in here?"

Liz said, "Ask our father. If you're lucky, maybe he'll tell you the truth . . . or I should say if you're unlucky!" Liz stormed out the door and walked over to Marteen's house. She didn't knock, but she burst through the door. Marty was sitting in her kitchen, holding a large glass of whiskey.

Joe and Liz suspected his mother was drinking for some time but never approached her about it. They thought it was just the prospect of losing her son to marriage. Joe could never find the alcohol in the house. She hid it well.

A few moments earlier, Marty had been on her way over to ask Liz something but stopped and turned around and went home. She heard the loud discussion and knew they were now found out by Liz. She knew Joe would be next to learn the truth. Could she face him with the truth? Now Liz was standing before her, and she had to listen to her. She swallowed down her glass of whiskey and prepared for her daughter-in-law's wrath!

Liz was furious with Marty! She said, "Marty, I know everything. How could you sleep with my father for twelve years and hurt my mother like that? She loved you like a sister!" She didn't give her a chance to answer before she continued. "Joe has to be told . . . Tomorrow, when he comes home! And if you don't have the guts to tell him, I can assure you, I will!" She stormed out of Marty's house and let the screen door slam behind her. Liz went back to her house and she called Joe. When he picked up the phone, she said, "Hi, honey, miss me?"

Joe was not only smiling to hear his wife's voice, but his voice was also smiling too. He said, "Of course I miss you, my love. I've missed you all week, and I can't wait to get home to you tomorrow night! Did you miss me?"

Liz put a smile on her face after she heard his voice and forgot about the disgrace in the family for a moment. She said, "Yes, I love you, Joe, more than you can ever know. What time do you think you'll be home tomorrow night?"

Joe replied, "Same as usual, I expect, by eight. Is something up?"

Liz tried to hold back the tears and said, "I just love you and want to see you, darlin'."

Joe said, "I'm sorry, honey. I'm really tired. I'd like to go to bed so I can maybe be done earlier tomorrow. Maybe I can get home sooner. But, honey, don't count on it . . . okay. It *might* happen. I want to be with my beautiful wife."

Liz smiled and said, "Okay, love. I'll see you tomorrow night. Drive home safely. I love you, sweetie!"

Joe responded, "I love you too, babe. Bye." With that, they both hung up the phone. Liz cried. She did not want to hurt Joe like she had just been hurt. She would have to see what tomorrow would bring.

Friday night came and Joe arrived home. Liz jumped in his arms and kissed him. She had tears, and he thought them happy tears for him. He was quick to learn that they weren't. They were hurt tears. Marty saw him drive into the yard, and within two or three minutes, they were walking through Marty's door. She was downing a large glass of whiskey.

His mom hugged him and said, "Hi, honey, I'd like to talk to you." Joe noticed that his mom and his wife could not make eye contact. He said, "Okay. The most beautiful ladies in my life can't agree on something. What is it?" Liz looked at Marty and said nothing.

Marty slurred her words a little from the booze and said, "Son, I have to tell you something."

Joe replied, "Ma, I just got home from not seeing my wife for almost a week. Can it wait until morning?"

Liz gave Marty a look like no other. It was with disgust, more than anything. Marty said, "No, son, it can't wait. Let's sit down. Liz, do you really want to be here?"

Liz said, "Oh yeah, I want to be by my husband's side. I love him more than anything in the world, and I never want him to hurt alone!"

Marteen started to talk to her son. "Joe, George and I have been having an affair for around twelve years or so. We never wanted anyone to know or to be hurt. We loved each other . . . or so I thought we did. Honey, it came out because Eleanor and I have gonorrhea. George gave it to us both. Liz, do you want to continue with the rest?"

She rested it on Liz's shoulders to further soil her father's reputation. Liz spoke up. "Dad has been paying for sex with prostitutes for years. He must have caught the gonorrhea from one of them. There is now a three-way infection at home. My mom and your mom have started on new antibiotics to clear it up. I don't know what dad is doing, and frankly, I don't care. Joe, I knew about it last night. But I wanted your mom to have the opportunity to tell you tonight, or I would have. I hope you don't hate me!"

Joe didn't know what to say at first. He looked to his mom, and then to his wife. He went to Liz and said, "Lizzy, I'm sorry you had to deal with this on your own yesterday, but you really could have told me, hun."

Liz started to cry. "Honey, I felt your mom should be given the chance to tell you first.

Please forgive me for lying on the phone last night, when I made you think there was nothing wrong."

Joe took Liz in his arms and said, "I love you, darling. I could never hate you, no matter what. I understand you giving Mom the opportunity, and I appreciate it, as I'm sure Mom does. Honey, we'll all get through this." He was calmer than expected as he held his wife. She wondered if he knew already and asked if he did.

He hugged his wife and said, "No, honey, I didn't know or suspect, but it will not come between us, ruin our love or our marriage!"

He looked to his mother with much disappointment and said, "My wife and I are going home. We haven't seen each other for days. Right now, she is more important to me than anything else in the world. Good night, Mother!" With that, they turned and went back to their house. He didn't hug his mother, and she hung her head in shame. As they walked to their house, Joe said, "I'm sorry you had to deal with this alone. You really could have told me on the phone, sweetie. I would have come home last night."

She said, "I know, but I wanted to give your mom a chance first. Are you mad at me?"

Joe said, "No, I'm mad at my mom and your dad. That's something they have to work out. I know it hurts, but it's up to them, Liz. I'm just so sorry for your mom. We have to make sure she knows that we love and support her, and we'll be there for her. She is the very innocent party in all this mess. She's the one who got hurt the most!

"We're just their kids, and we have our own lives. You are a McDonald, and I'm an Allen. We have the right to live here and be proud of our Scottish and African heritage. We're starting a new life together. We'll hold our heads up, and to hell with the gossip that may come our way. Can you accept what they've done?"

Liz stood facing her husband, her hand gently caressing his cheek, and said, "I love you, Mr. Allen. You're the best thing that ever happened to me. Yes, I guess I can accept it. What choice do we have? I'll never forget it or forgive Dad. He hurt my mom so bad. She's doesn't seem like herself anymore. I can see it in her face, Joe. She is more hurt than I've ever seen in my life. I never put much stock in the broken-heart theory, but I've seen it, Joe. Mom's heart is broken. I've seen it firsthand and I can't help fix it." As a tear went down her cheek, Liz said, "I feel so helpless." He tenderly held his wife while she softly cried.

Joe said with a devilish smile, "You know, darling, you're right about one thing. I *am* the best thing that ever happened to you!" With that, they cracked up laughing; they hugged, kissed, turned out their lights, forgot about the world, went to bed, and made love.

Saturday morning, Liz and Joe woke up to the great-great-great-great-great-ancestor of Old Reliable, the distant offspring of the rooster that woke up Johnny and Diana the first morning they were in their new farmhouse. Joe and Liz stayed alone in their house for the most part over the weekend. They decided they were not going to let family turmoil ruin their lives.

Joe went to see his mom, but she didn't talk about it. Instead, she made small talk and kept drinking straight whiskey. He tried to persuade her to stop, but she told him she was fine and she'd stop . . . after the bottle was empty.

El dropped by to see Liz frequently that weekend. She needed to be with her daughter. She didn't talk much. She just cried and held onto her daughter a lot. By Sunday, George hadn't seen his daughter in a couple of days. He went over to her house on Sunday after supper. He felt the need to explain himself.

Liz said, "I don't want to hear all the disgusting details, but I'm willing to listen now."

Liz and Joe listened while George started, "Honey, I want to tell you about what I've done. This need to have sex is a compulsive disease, which I've never learned to control. I know it's not an Excuse, but there are studies . . . psychological tests that prove it is a disease, a-a . . . sickness of sorts. It's an addiction . . . if you will. I'm sorry, honey, it's probably hard for you to understand, but I have to deal with it. Along with my need to have casual relations, I was always at risk to get a disease and pass it on. I infected your mom and Marteen. I caught gonorrhea from a pros . . . pros . . . a-a . . . partner. I don't know who . . . or where I got it from.

"Elizabeth, I know I've given you several reasons to hate me. I've hurt your mother in the worst way possible. I know I can't ask you to forgive my actions, because . . . well . . . that's just too much to ask. Honey, I need you to tell me you don't hate me. I just can't lose the love of my little girl too.

"When you were born, it was the second most wonderful day in my life. The first was the day I married your mom. You've always been your daddy's little girl. I love you, honey. Please believe me when I say there has never been a day that has gone by that I haven't loved your mom. I loved her from the first time I set my eyes on her in that church in Scotland after the war. She was . . . and still is so beautiful. She hasn't changed a bit."

Liz told her father, "I'll never forgive you for hurting Mom." She paused as she shed some more tears and then continued, "Daddy, I love you, but right now I don't like you and the way you've shattered lives around here . . . especially Mom's."

With that said, she kissed her dad on the cheek but pulled away when he wanted to hug her. She wanted to hurt him a little too. She was trying to make a point. She wanted him to know that he was not going to get off the hook. She wanted him to atone for his sins. It was a juvenile tactic, but she pulled away anyway.

George said with hesitation, not sure he wanted or was ready to hear the answer, "Liz, honey, tell me I won't lose your love . . . I need that. Please tell me?"

Liz felt a pang of guilt and gave her dad half a smile and said, "Daddy, I love you. I hate what you've done all your life, but you're still my dad." With that, she did hug her dad and gave him a kiss on his cheek. He had a sigh of relief and shed a tear, thanking his daughter for still loving him.

George turned to go and then turned around again and held his daughter one more time. He took her face in his hands. They both had tears now, and he said, "Good-bye, darlin'. Please . . . always remember you've been the apple of my eye since that cold winter day you were born twenty-six years ago. You've made me a very proud papa every day of your life, sweetie . . . your brothers too. I love them just as much. Please don't ever let them forget that either, honey."

He turned to Joe and said, "Son, and believe me, I've always thought of you as a son . . . I'm sorry. I know I was never much of a father figure to you, but . . . well . . . I know I've hurt you too. There's no way I can ever ask the two of you to understand or forgive me, but just know that I've loved you both since the day you were each born, and, Joseph, I'm the happiest father in the world that you married my beautiful daughter. You really are each other's *destino*! Hold on to each other forever . . . love each other. I know you'll have a happy life together. I love you both. Good night, kids." As he held his daughter, he put out his hand, and Joe took it to shake it, and he pulled him close and gave him a hug.

Joe said, "You were a great father, I always thought of you that way, and I always loved you too, Dad!"

George smiled happily, knowing he still had the love of his daughter and son-in-law. He said, "You take care driving back to Toronto tomorrow, son. Good-bye, you two. I love you both."

As he went back to his house, Liz and Joe felt a little uneasy about George's behavior. Liz said, "I guess the writing is on the wall. Mom has probably asked him to move out. I guess I can understand her, but maybe she'll let him to live in another house on the farm so he won't have to leave the property. I'll ask her in the morning to consider letting him stay." Joe agreed, and they went to bed.

As Joe was getting ready to go back to Toronto to work really early Monday morning, he heard what he thought was a gunshot. It was too close for comfort. He looked outside, but there was nothing amiss. He heard a scream. He ran toward it, and Liz sprang up in bed to follow him.

He ran toward George and El's house and through the door. There he saw George, lying on the kitchen floor, holding a revolver in what was left of his mouth and his head.

Joe heard the summer kitchen door slam. Joe turned and tried to catch Liz at the door before she saw her father dead on the floor. He didn't get to her in time. She saw her father and let out a scream; she couldn't help it. Her mother was just staring in shock, and the twins were now in the kitchen by their mother's side too. Liz was beside herself with grief!

Eleanor had to sit down. She was in agony over her husband taking his life. Marteen ran into the house just then. She'd also heard the shot ring out. Liz glared at her and said, "Get out of here, you whore!"

Marty turned and left, running toward her house in tears. Joe quickly looked at his wife but held is tongue. He understood and knew his wife was hurt and lashing out. Joe kind of took control since everyone was in shock. He quickly changed the subject and said to El, "Is he to be buried here, Mom?"

El said through her tears, "Yes, dear . . . in the family cemetery . . . by his parents."

Joe called the new county coroner to inform him so he could come and pronounce him dead and remove the body. When Joe got off the phone, he looked around. Suddenly, he took Eleanor by the arm and said, "C'mon, Mom, I'm taking you to the hub." He had forgotten that the twins were there too. He told them, "Abe, Simon, please come with your sister back to our place. I'll call Mary and Patrick from our house." But it was too late; they were already there. Joseph ushered everyone out the door. He was not letting anyone in to see the body anymore. It was a horrendous sight! He told everyone to go to the hub.

He had an ulterior motive. His eyes caught sight of something in the dining room. He saw an envelope. Joe picked up the note after he got everyone out of El's house and tucked it in his inside suit pocket. After everyone got into the McDonald house, trying to deal with their grief, he took Liz and El into the family office and shut the door. He gave El the note and said, "I found this, Mom. I thought you'd like to read it away from everyone else. Liz and I can leave, if you like."

El was slightly stunned but said, "No . . . I want you both here." She sat down in the chair and started to read what was George's suicide note . . .

The note read:

My beautiful Eleanor:

From the first day I saw you, I fell in love. I can't tell you what it meant to me that you accepted the invitation after church to come to my aunt's house for supper that Sunday night. I looked at your beauty, and I knew you were the woman I was going to marry.

I know you're probably thinking it's a lie, but it's not. We had many good years together, and I thank you and God for them. We have three beautiful children, whom I adore.

I know you can't understand why I did this. I could not let you go through the shame of trying to live an unhappy life with me . . . hating me. I couldn't do that. I really deserve your hatred and know I could never have your forgiveness, but I want you to know I've loved you every single day of our lives together. Please understand this was the only way to deal with the heartbreak I've put you through . . . the humiliation I've caused you and our children.

If you choose not to put the marriage kerchief in my coffin, I do understand. If you do, I'll be waiting for you, my one and only true love. I love you. Please tell Lizzy, my beautiful baby girl, and the boys I love them too, and this is the best way for you all to put this behind you and carry on with your lives. Just knowing I'm not around to make you all live with the shame . . . of my being your husband and their father is really the for the best.

I'm sure you'll all agree with me, in time. I've made peace with Elizabeth, and I hope I can make it up to you in heaven, my dear sweet, beautiful lassie. I'm so sorry, El. Please believe me when I tell you I've loved and will always love you more than anything in the world, m'darlin'. Until we meet again, my love . . . good-bye.

Your One and Only,
Georgie

She sat and stared silently for a few minutes, crying at the letter, and handed it to Liz and Joe to read and asked her to keep it to themselves for now and to leave her alone for a few minutes.

After a little solitude and thought, Eleanor decided she would place George's half of the marriage kerchief in his coffin.

It was going to be a difficult few days. Joe called Toronto and told them about a death in the family and that he was needed at home for burial and legal business. His boss gave his condolences to Joe, his wife, and family and told him to take the time off he needed.

There was an unusual feeling at the funeral. There was love, hate, contempt, and betrayal. All in all, everyone from the community attending the funeral loved him and were none the wiser as to what was really going on. The family preferred it that way.

Christmas of 1945 was an unhappier one than that of 1944, when Joe proposed to Liz.

Although the world was happier that the war was over, it was not the same at home on the farm.

George was gone, and El was taking high doses of antibiotics to clear her gonorrhea. She seemed to be winning the battle back to good health again. She was hardly speaking to Marty at all. Joe would see his mom when he came home on weekends while Liz avoided her most of the time.

She saw her own mom and brothers and her aunt, uncle, and cousins, etc., but would not see Marteen—unless she had to. She would get together with her for Christmas, if Joe insisted, but that was the extent of her obligation. Joe reminded his wife that it takes two people to have an affair.

Liz thought about it. She'd forgotten that her dad was just as responsible as Joe's mom was for the affair. Liz apologized and told him that she would start talking to her. She couldn't forgive her though. Joe thought that was at least a good start.

Everyone got together Christmas Day, like usual. Caroline and the girls still made breakfast, and everyone was together at the McDonald house and then went to church together, including Marty. When they returned home, they opened presents. It was a peaceful day. Liz did not want to ruin it. She hugged her mother-in-law and said, "Merry

Christmas, Mom." Marteen was touched and cried a little. Joe was very pleased.

Over the next few months, Liz was happy teaching and keeping busy at school, as well as at home on the farm. Joe was very busy working in Toronto and commuting to the farm on weekends. They were not really happy anymore at the farm. They talked about moving away, but Joe noticed his mom was looking sick and was drinking much more now. She was taking days off work and stopped caring and looking after herself.

Frankly, Joseph was worried. Each weekend when he came home, she looked worse. George was not there to give his opinion. He wanted to know what was going on. Joe asked Liz if she noticed anything about his mom.

Liz said, "Honey, I know she only went to work twice this week. But other than that, I'm not sure."

Joe was going to be finishing the job he was doing during late summer. His boss had a request come across his desk for highly skilled engineers to work in the United States—Mississippi, to be exact. He showed the papers to Joe, and when he read it, he became excited. He wanted to apply for the job but had to check with Liz first. His boss told him that he would get a glowing recommendation from him! Joe was thrilled!

When Joe got to his apartment that evening, he called Liz and excitedly told her about the job prospect in Mississippi. She was excited too. She said, "Hun, if you want to go for it, let's do it!"

When he arrived home that Friday night, he went to his mom's house and told her about it right away. Liz thought it was the right thing to do, to let him give her the news himself. She said, "Son, I'm so proud of you. I always have been, and your daddy and grandpa would have been so proud too." Joe hugged his mom.

He thought to himself that now might be the time to get some answers. He said, "Mom, you know I love you, but I can't say that I understand what you did or why . . . well . . . I guess why is because you were so lonely after dad died, but, Mom, why George?"

She looked at him with tears in her eyes. He patted her hand and said, "Never mind, Mom. You don't need to answer that." He changed the subject, saying, "You don't look well. Are you doing okay, or do I need to take you to see the doctor? I also think you should slow down your drinking, Mom."

Marty got up from the chair and kissed Joe and told him not to worry; she's just fine and promised she would slow down her drinking. She went into the living room, lay on the couch, and almost passed out. Joe guided her up the stairs and helped her to lie down on her bed. He pulled a knitted afghan over her, kissed her on the cheek, and whispered, "I love you, Mom." Then he left to go back to the hub.

When Joe was home that weekend he was armed with the information he needed to apply for the job in Mississippi, and he and Liz put together a rousing resume. He also had the written recommendation from his boss and other letters of reference. By the time he was going back to Toronto early Monday morning, Joe was ready to drop his envelope in the mailbox.

Joe was so excited to be able to post his information and application that he could not sleep much Sunday night. He just kept imagining moving to another country so he could do the job he loved so much!

He got up and started to get ready to leave Monday morning, but Liz came up behind him while he was buttoning his shirt. While standing behind Joe, she put her arms around his waist and grabbed each side of his shirt. She pulled his shirt open and turned him to face her. She was standing there with nothing on. She took his hands and put them on her breasts. She was softly starting to moan. She wanted him. She pushed his shirt off, and it fell to the floor. Liz took one of his hands and led him to the bed. She lay down on her back.

She really wanted him *now*! As he opened his trousers, she could see he was excited too.

He was hard and ready. As he slowly got on top of her, he kissed her breasts and upward toward her neck and her lips. She was getting so excited. She didn't want to wait. She grabbed him by the waist, and she pulled him on top of her, and he had no problem entering her. It was only moments before they both reached their incredible climaxes.

As they lay in each other's arms, Joe looked at the clock and said, "I'm sorry, my love, but I have to get on the road. It's a long drive. She let him get out of bed, and she went down to make breakfast. After Joe left, Liz had another coffee and waited for farm life to wake up and start a new day.

She got ready to go to school. But something told her not to go yet. She couldn't put her finger on it, but something on the farm was wrong. Instead of going to see her mom right away, she knocked on Marteen's door. There was no answer, and her car was right there. She knew that she should be home. She knocked louder. Still no answer. They still never locked their doors on the farm, so Liz walked in. It was eerily silent. She didn't feel right. Marty was nowhere downstairs. Liz climbed the stairs and went into Marty's bedroom.

Liz found Dr. Marty, lying on her bed . . . dead . . . right where Joe had put her the night before. It was still too early to try to get hold of Joe. He would still be on the road to Toronto. She couldn't reach him for another hour or so. There was nothing she could do. She went over to her mom's house and told her.

El said, "You'll have to call the coroner. Get hold of Joe and get him back here, and, Liz, she does deserve a spot here in the family cemetery. She's an Allen."

Liz lowered her eyes and said, "I know, Mom, but please put her with Joseph Sr., as far from Daddy as you can . . . please?"

Eleanor agreed. Liz went back to her house and kept trying to call Joe and finally got hold of him just when he got through the door.

Joe picked up the telephone and said, "Good morning, Joe Allen."

Liz said, "Honey, it's me. You have to come home."

Joe said, "What's wrong, love? I just left there. Don't tell me you miss me already." He blew kisses in the phone. Luckily his coworkers were not around to hear him.

Liz said, "Honey, I love you more than anything in the world, and I wish I didn't have to tell you this, but, honey . . . I went into your mom's house this morning and found her in her bed. Honey, your mom is dead."

There was silence for a moment. Joe said, "All right, hon. I'll get home as quick as I can. I love you . . . you okay?"

Liz said, "I love you too, dear. Yes, I'm fine . . . just worried about you. Please drive safely and get here when you can." As she hung up the phone, she thought to herself what a calm, strong man her Joe was under pressure. She truly loved and admired him and knew the grief he would be feeling on that long drive home.

Liz called the county coroner, and he said to he'd be out to the farm as quickly as he could and take her back to do a postmortem. Liz said,

"Her son, my husband, is a few hours away. I'm sure he wants to see her first. Can we make arrangements for after that?"

The coroner said, "I'm sorry, Mrs. Allen, it doesn't work that way. You called and reported a deceased person. I have to come and declare her dead and then remove the body to do the postmortem."

Liz felt backed into a wall but said, "Yes, sir, I'll see you when you get here."

Joe arrived home a few hours later to find his wife weeping uncontrollably. He put his arms around her. She kept saying how sorry she was to him. He wasn't sure what she meant. Liz said, "Joe, I called the coroner, and he had to take her before you got home, before you saw her. Honey, I can't tell you how sorry I am. Honey, please forgive me."

Joe said, "Liz, you did what you had to do. You're not at fault. Don't worry. I'll see her later. It's okay, love." They hugged.

Just then Eleanor came in and hugged Joe and told her how sorry she was that he lost his mother. He held her for a bit and he said, "Mom, I'm okay. We'll get through this. I love you, and I always have. You've always been my second mom, and that will never change. I'm just so sorry my mom hurt you. I wish I could change all that, take back what my mom did to you, and I wish George was here. I hope we can heal as a family."

Eleanor said, "Son, I love you and I never wanted or imagined things would ever be this way."

Joe hugged her harder and said, "I love you, Mom."

Dr. Marteen Allen was buried two days after her death in the McDonald-Allen Family Cemetery. She was buried beside her husband, Joseph Sr., who had been buried near Jacob, Mina, and their daughter. They were all alongside Jed and Mary . . . near Jed's famous potato coffin. The Allen part of the cemetery was smaller than the McDonald side but just as respected.

There was a community celebration in the hall so everyone could come and celebrate her life. Her many patients and much of the town attended. They all dearly loved Dr. Marty, and she was respected. Eleanor made sure that her celebration was just as grand as all the others had been. She wanted this for Joe . . . not her, the other woman!

It saddened her that he was now the last Allen. She so hoped that the name would live on in children that he and her daughter would have someday, and she prayed that maybe they would be around, in some capacity, to help run the family farm and golf course.

The next day, the result of the postmortem was delivered to the farm, to Joe. He was with Liz and Eleanor. He opened the envelope and read the results. As a tear fell down his cheek, he told the women, "My mother didn't take the antibiotics that you were taking, Mom. The cause of death was serious infection through her body, directly related to her gonorrhea. I guess by deliberately not taking her medication to cure the disease, she committed suicide too, Mom."

Joe started to tear up as he continued, "It says that she also had liver disease caused by excessive alcohol use. I guess she was trying to drink herself to death too. I hope she wasn't in too much pain . . ." Joe excused himself and left the room and cried. He took a walk to the freshly dug grave in the cemetery. He still had the postmortem results in his hand as he sat down beside his parents' graves. As the tears flowed, he said, "Oh, Mom, you could have saved yourself . . . why . . . why didn't you take the goddamn pills?" Joe sat beside her grave and wept for a while until his wife joined him.

Liz found him sitting beside Dr. Marty's grave . . . somehow she knew he'd be there. She sat down, put her arm around her husband's waist, and said, "You okay, baby?"

Joe smiled at her and said, "Yeah . . . I'm fine . . . Know what I wish?"

Liz tenderly rested her head on Joe's strong, masculine shoulder that was always there, ready for her whenever she needed it, and lovingly said, "What's that, darlin'?"

Joe looked at her and said, "I really wish I could have seen that big ol' potato coffin!" They looked at each other and burst out laughing together. Liz knew her Joe was going to be all right and would get through this.

It was a tough few months to swallow. So much tragedy had happened, but the family grew closer. Joe was on pins and needles, waiting for word from Mississippi on the job he'd applied for, and El had kept taking her medications and recovered from the gonorrhea.

If that wasn't enough, on June 17, 1946, a very destructive tornado made its way from Detroit up toward Windsor and surrounding counties, which included Olde McDonald's Potato Farm. Half of the crops were ruined, but it was early enough to maybe replant and have a late fall harvest.

In the surrounding counties, there were houses, trees, some barns blown away, and dead animals everywhere. There were seventeen human deaths in Ontario, and in Windsor alone, there were four hundred homes destroyed. There was looting in Windsor, and the police were busy trying to keep law and order within the city. In the country, where the farm was, it wasn't as bad.

The McDonalds, like always, assisted their neighbors where they could; and El and Liz organized a midsummer celebration—an old-fashioned barn dance. McDonald Hall was the place once again for a thank-you celebration, for the community to get together and thank everyone for their hard work in helping each other get back on their feet after the tornado.

By the end of school in June, Liz was pregnant. El couldn't be happier. She was excited she was finally going to be a grandma. But sadly, she remembered she would be the only grandparent of this child. She would have to have enough love to give this child from four grandparents . . . but she knew she up to the challenge. She couldn't wait!

But there was some other news. Even though he had not been personally interviewed, Joe's application, resume, and references were accepted. Joe and Liz would be moving to Philadelphia, Mississippi in the fall of that year.

Eleanor was heartbroken. She was now losing her best friend—her daughter. Even though she would still have lots of family on the farm to keep her company, she would miss Liz terribly!

There was another issue. The Allen house was now legally Joseph Allen Jr.'s. The same with the 320 acres Diana gave Marty. This would be the first time in almost a century that there was no Allen living on the potato farm. It was a little sad to think about. Was it an era gone by? Joe and Liz decided that while they lived in Mississippi, one of her brothers could use it.

The land was still going to be part of the potato farm, but the profits from their portion of the land would now be paid to Joe and Liz. It was quite a nice income they would receive from it each year. They planned to put it away for their children and their future.

Little Mary and Patrick were getting on in years, and her boys were taking over running the farm and golf course quite well. But now, the families that shared the farm for almost a century were separating. The Allens were moving off the farm. Liz, Eleanor, and Mary were very sad about it. But Liz tried to cheer them and said, "Don't worry . . . maybe Joe's and my children will come here someday to help run the farm! They'll be Allens!" El and Mary could only muster half a smile. Liz said, "Remember, we'll be back to visit lots, and if I get teaching, I'll have summers off, and I can come back then, and Joe can come on weekends!"

El's twins were both engaged, and they were to be married just before Liz and Joe left for Mississippi. It was a double ceremony, but the four decided to marry in their church, in town, and the reception would be held in McDonald Hall . . . their fiancées, Joan and Maria, preferred it, and the boys agreed. Liz offered the family wedding gown, but since there were two brides, they did not want to decide which bride would wear it. They each decided to get their own gowns. The family was not offended. Liz was sure it would be used by family again someday . . . maybe by a daughter of hers someday . . . or maybe a daughter-in-law.

As a gift to both couples, Liz and Joe gave the gift of privacy, much like decades before, when Johnny flipped a coin to see who would use the hired hands' house when Rolly moved back into Diana's house. Back then, it was between Cora and Gerald and Beulah and Frank.

On the day of the wedding, Joe flipped a coin, and Simon got to call it. He called heads, but it was tails. Abe and his bride, Joanie, would live in the Allen house with the understanding that when an Allen comes to live there the couple would have to move out. Everyone was thrilled with this gift and agreed. Simon and his bride, Maria, lived in the McDonald house—the hub—with Caroline. When Joe and Liz came home for visits, Abe and his wife would let them use the house, and they would also move over to the McDonald house while they were there.

Liz started learning all about where they would live. Philadelphia, Neshoba County, Mississippi. She started with Mississippi. December 10, 1817, it joined the Union as the twentieth state. Then after Abraham Lincoln became president in 1860, Mississippi feared he would end slavery and they seceded on January 9, 1861.

Mississippi whites believed in the use and dominance of black slaves. They didn't want to lose them. They would fight to keep things status quo. But by the end of the Civil War, the slaves had been freed by Abraham Lincoln. Mississippi had so many cotton plantations, and with it being a major export, they helped finance the state. When the slaves were freed, the cotton exports dropped because there was no free workforce anymore.

She learned that Mississippi had a warm, humid climate. They would have to get used to long summers and short mild winters. It was great for Liz and golfing but not so great for Joe and hockey. Southern Mississippi was at risk for hurricanes because it was on the Gulf of Mexico. They also experienced a lot of thunderstorms in that region.

The Mississippi Delta, also called the Black Belt region, is the wealthiest region to have property. Mississippi had the largest black population in the United States. Liz felt happy about that . . . Joe would be accepted right away.

Liz was so thrilled. She couldn't wait to tell Joe that there were a lot of blacks in Mississippi. He wouldn't feel so centered out now. And she would proudly be by his side as his wife and soon-to-be the mother of his child.

Their new life and home would be in the town of Philadelphia, in Neshoba County, Mississippi. It even sounded like a most peaceful, wonderful place to live. She knew they would happily be accepted and make a lot of friends. The hard part would be leaving the farm and family.

CPSIA information can be obtained
at www.ICGtesting.com
Printed in the USA
BVHW041914080422
633814BV00019B/179

9 781475 968842